WEENIE KLEEGAN

THE BROKEN PLACES

WEENIE KLEEGAN

THE BROKEN PLACES

For my great Friend (and sister)

HAMLIN TALLENT

Bea

From Ham

Braveship
BOOKS
Aura Libertatis Spirat

WEENIE KLEEGAN - THE BROKEN PLACES
Copyright © 2021 by Hamlin Tallent

Braveship Books
www.braveshipbooks.com
Aura Libertatis Spirat

Cover Artwork & Design by Rossitsa Atanassova

ISBN-13: 978-1-64062-134-3
Printed in the United States of America

I wish to thank my editor and champion, Dell Putman, whose unwavering support pushed me to continue with this novel after I lost my faith in it. She loved my story and convinced me to love it too.

I also want to thank my friend and old navy buddy, Chris Andersen, whose many wonderful conversations, unrelenting encouragement, and thoughtful advice guided me.

WEENIE

Today, I fly navy jets for a living, and when I look at the moon, it is always above the clouds, and therefore its brightness is conditional on me staying there. It mocks me and my upcoming task, going back through those clouds and into the inky darkness and onto the tiny, pitching, heaving, unforgiving deck of an aircraft carrier. So, my notion of the moon is of it laughing over my shoulder as I sink below its world and into the other, and it wasn't always that way.

I grew up looking at the moon with awe and wonder. It was a constant friend, but more so in the summertime, and I would hold out my hand to see if it were waning or waxing--the smooth curve in my left the former, and if in my right, the latter.

I lived on a farm near a small town in the Missouri Ozarks called Militia Springs, and the nights there were dark enough to see the moon and lots of stars too. I would lie by the alfalfa field and in summer smell the sweet tang of the new hay and in the fall sniff wood smoke and damp earth. The pond was on the other side of the barn, and it was home to the frogs. I could hear them and was comforted knowing I wasn't watching the moon alone. Frogs might be the best companions for deep thoughts in a moon-lit hayfield.

Militia Springs was a serene and peaceful community of hay fields, clear streams, milk cows, small businesses, and good people. I loved growing up there. We had a town square with all kinds of stores that made shopping easy because your mom or dad could park anywhere, and you could walk around until all your money was gone. We also had a Dairy Queen and a theater that closed in the summer because the drive-in opened. There was even a gas station that stayed open all night and sold every kind of soda you could imagine and a wide assortment of beef jerky. It was conveniently called the All-Night Station.

My parents named me Winfred after my two uncles, Windell and Fredrick, but everyone called me Weenie. I have a little sister, Molly, who is five years younger. My grandfather also lives with us, and we call him Grandpa Two Bears because when I was a little kid and heard my grandma call him by his name, Tobias, I misunderstood it and called him Grandpa Two Bears. Now, everybody calls him that. My grandma died when I was young.

My journey from Militia Springs to the navy was an unplanned path and more of a testament to the wonderful options we Americans have than the result of an executed agenda or the stirrings of ancient warrior blood. In fact, I had lived the mostly sedentary and unremarkable life of a good but nerdy student until I binge-watched navy movies one night and decided naval aviation was my calling. At the end of *Tora! Tora! Tora!* when the actor playing Admiral Yamamoto said, "I fear all we have done is to awaken a sleeping giant and fill him with a terrible resolve," I felt like I had been awakened too.

I entered the navy through Aviation Officer Candidate School, AOCS, which I had hoped was a little like church camp. I quickly discovered that the only commonality between church camp and AOCS was God, and he was a US Marine Corps Drill Instructor! Grandpa Two Bears had been a US Marine in World War Two, and he warned me about drill instructors. He said they were hand-selected because they looked sharp in uniform and didn't have a shred of humanity.

Despite my puniness and zero self-esteem, I performed well and felt myself grow and mature as a leader. That might seem impossible if you haven't ever been to a place like AOCS. Still, the magic of the military is that it offers so many opportunities to lead, yourself and others and always under pressure. It's not like sitting down in class with an instructor telling you to open your leadership book to page 236. Leadership isn't so much about learning from a text as it is about experiencing under duress, understanding in chaos, believing when in pain, enduring when you thought you would quit. I don't think there is such a thing as leadership without pressure, and if there is, it probably doesn't mean much. AOCS touts itself as The Pressure Cooker. Pretty funny unless you are in it.

I also met a girl while I was at AOCS. Her name was Jane, and I loved her. She died, but before she did, she gave me the gift of loving someone, loving someone with all of my heart, and although I didn't realize its value at the time, I sure did when it was gone.

I met some great guys in AOCS, and two of them were my roommates, Raoul Hungus and Charles Crosby. Raoul was gregarious, charismatic, sharp as a tack, and exuded confidence. Pretty much the opposite of me, except for being smart. Charles was a Black guy, so that set us apart right there. He was the only Black man in the class, and at first, I didn't know how to deal with him. I mean, I felt terrible about what we had done to Blacks and how we had treated them, but I didn't know what I was supposed to do about that. My Mom told me that I should respect them first, and armed with that advice, I developed a great relationship with Charles. He was also smart and charismatic and all, but he was more than that. He was a real leader. Charles later took the callsign of Cotton, which was either cool or not depending on how you looked at it. I thought it was cool.

Raoul and I had terrible eyesight, so after commissioning, the navy assigned us down the naval flight officer path to fly in tactical airplanes' rear seats. Cotton went to pilot training, and I kidded him about getting to sit in the front of the bus. He laughed, kind of.

Through some luck and God's grace, we all joined up again as members of the same F-4 Phantom squadron! The F-4 is a very neat airplane, and the three of us flew it in combat in Vietnam. Cotton and I were shot down over Vietnam, and I rescued him and got us out of there. He thanked me for that, but he didn't have to.

The navy has been a most wonderful but sometimes heart-breaking experience. It has taken me to the heights of personal growth but with the steep price of tragic loss. There is this new thing called Post Traumatic Stress Disorder, PTSD, that I have read about, and I think some of us might have it. If not today, then later. I think it might be the wages we must pay for the highs and lows. Especially the losses. So, when I look at the moon now, I sometimes wish for the moon from before. The one when I was a kid, lying on my back, listening to the frogs. The one that I watched until Mom called me in, instead of the one the ship calls me down from.

UNVERIFIABLE TRUTHS

So, now I am a naval aviator, stationed at Naval Air Station Miramar in San Diego, California. In my short time among my fellows, I have found them to be a fascinating lot. I suppose that sounds self-serving, given I am one, but I make that judgment as an observer because I am not exactly like them. While I do possess real gifts of intelligence, spatial awareness, courage to a degree, and an excellent ability to compartmentalize and focus on those things that are important, I differ from my cadre in that I do not think of myself as brilliant, handsome, and dashing. I do not have the ego most have, or at least I do not think so. As I said, I make my comments as an observer. I suppose what is most curious and disturbing about my squadron mates is the never-ending competition and the fact that the only questions that matter are: Which is better? What is better? Who is better?

I have observed that if a naval aviator can talk loudly and recite unverifiable truths, he usually wins the which is better/what is better battle. For instance, he could say, "the F-4's J-79 is the strongest jet engine built because the compressor blades can be cleaned by throwing a bushel of walnut hulls down the intake." Or he could say, "Steve McQueen's 390 GT Mustang in *Bullet* had over 700 hundred horsepower." Who knows the truth of those two statements? Who is going to challenge them? By the way, both are false.

There is one which is better contest that takes more than reciting numbers and facts, regardless of their veracity, and that is which plane is better. After all, numbers and facts don't account for personal greatness, and numbers and facts don't account for magic. So, numbers and facts can never decide which plane is better because the pilot must be brought into the discussion. There is a quote from Ernest Hemingway that underscores the drama behind the which plane question. That quote is, "A man has only one virginity to lose in fighters, and if that is a lovely plane, he loses it to,

4

there his heart will ever be." I couldn't believe Ernest Hemingway would write something like that, so I looked it up and, sure enough, he wrote it. That quote is a bit lofty for most of us, and I doubt if the word lovely is in any of my squadron mates' lexicon, but the fact is for most of us, the F-4 Phantom is the best. It is especially so for those of us who flew it over Indian Country and back.

When I first joined the Phantom community, we argued with the F-8 Crusader pilots about which plane was best, but as the Crusader phased out, so did the verbal battles that supported it. For a while, happy hour arguments over which and what were about sports teams, cars, the club dancers' titties, and the aircraft carrier that served the best auto-dog. Auto-dog is our term for the soft serve that flows from the ice cream machine. Chocolate is everyone's favorite.

Then along came the F-14 Tomcat.

The Tomcat and the Phantom are both fast and can reach Mach 2 speeds, over 1500 miles per hour, but the similarity ends there. The Tomcat is much more maneuverable, its radar can automatically track over 100 targets, and the aircrew can fire at six targets simultaneously using the new Phoenix missile! It represented a tremendous technological leap over our Phantoms, and that, of course, made us angry and jealous. The Tomcat pilots and back seat radar intercept officers, RIOs, didn't help any as they began populating the officer' club bar with their air of superiority, looking down their noses at those of us who still flew the Smoking Thunder hog.

There weren't many of them at first, and they stuck together in their MENSA clan-like way. If you got close enough, you could hear them speaking their strange, Tomcat language while throwing out terms like Zone Five Afterburner, Launch Acceptability Region, and Track-While-Scan. However, since all Tomcat pilots and RIOS for both east and west coasts trained at Miramar, the place started filling up fast.

One such Tomcat pilot was Jack Grant. I met Jack one Friday afternoon, and over the next weeks found that he had, in a relatively short life, gathered every undesirable trait a human can own. He was like a popcorn ball of shit kernels, a supernova of flaming assholes.

But before I knew anything about his assholeishness, I just thought he was a newly arrived fellow aviator in the officers' club. I noticed him at the edge of the crowd on a Friday afternoon in the WOXOF room. WOXOF is an acronym for the weather, and it means Overcast, Ceiling Obscured, Visibility Zero in Fog. It is a good description of the minds of those there. Jack was a handsome guy in a masculine Cary Grant kind of way, and he looked like the quintessential fighter pilot.

As I said, he was on the crowd's edge, and that drew me to him. I knew life at the side of the group, although I felt centered now. Whether on a flight, in the ready room, or here at the club, I felt right where I was now. So, I confidently sidled up to him and extended my hand.

"Weenie Kleegan."

He gave me an automatic grin, the one that is too quick and too wide to mean anything. It is the greeting people offer just in case you turn out to be important. He did reach out and accept my hand.

"Jack Grant."

"Buy you a beer?"

He frowned, and his eyes darted over my shoulder into the room. Once again, I got the feeling he was looking for someone more worthwhile, but then he glanced at me and smiled. His white teeth gleamed inside a mouth that housed the sincerity of a used car salesman.

"Sure."

I motioned to Ruthie, the bartender.

"So," I nodded at this name tag. "I see you're in the Tomcat RAG." RAG is a navy acronym for Replacement Air Group. It is a training organization that provides the fleet with new personnel.

"Yep," he grinned again, but this time it was more genuine. I might not be important, but the fact he was flying the Tomcat sure was.

"How is it?"

"It is one hell of a plane. A lot to learn, you know?"

"I bet it is. It sure looks neat coming into the break. Have you flown it yet?

"Sure. I am on a fast track. I did well in the training command and got Tomcats instead of just Phantoms."

I nodded and let the word "just" pass. The beer came, and we both took a sip.

"Maybe someday you can tell me about the Tomcat. And I can tell you about the Phantom."

He grinned, but as his eyes crinkled, he managed a curt nod that lifted his head. It was accompanied by a little snort of haughtiness. "Why would I want to know anything about the Phantom?"

I straightened as my face grew hot. "We just fought a war with it, for one." I stared back into Jack's grey eyes. "It has been in combat, actually been shot at, for two."

"If the Tomcat had been in Vietnam, we would have killed every MIG there."

"But it wasn't there. And you weren't either, were you?"

Jack squinted, and I saw his nostrils flare.

"Whatever." He smirked and turned to the bar.

For an embarrassing moment, I stood there, face hot and unsure of what to do until I turned and joined the comfortable embrace of my squadron mates. After my encounter with Jack, it felt good to be next to Arlo, Cotton, and Raoul as they drunkenly shouted encouragement to the stripper to show them her tits. Raoul screamed with a British accent, which I found to be oddly pleasing. I watched the stage for a bit, and the thin but busty girl finally took off her top, which appeared to satisfy whatever was missing.

I looked around, and Jack was gone.

That incident was enough for me to know Jack Grant was nobody I wanted to be around. But what he did to Missy Sanders the next week made me loathe him.

Missy was also a lieutenant junior grade, like me, and she was a pilot. She was attached to Fighter Squadron 126, the services squadron, and was one of the first female aviation officers at Miramar. I must admit right away that I am not keen on women coming into naval aviation. I mean, it's a man's game and my pals, and I strongly felt women had no place in any combat unit. They were not part of the warrior culture and never would be. However, the navy must have felt pressure to allow them in, so they assigned women to shore duty pilot jobs. There, they could live at the edges of our he-man universe but never enter it. Now an outsider might think it odd for macho men to not want to be around women, but outsiders don't know us. There is a place for women. It just isn't with us warriors.

Given my life's destiny of appearing insignificant and non-threatening, I was a natural person for Missy to gravitate to. That, and not many of the other guys would talk to her. By that, I mean people would say "hi" and stuff, but nobody wanted to be a chum with a girl. Not in the officers' club anyway. But I did talk with her, and she was a bubbly, fun person who was attractive, despite the flight suit.

"After a couple of beers, she's as good as anybody," Raoul once observed. Raoul could be like that. He could say terrible things but

then turn around and be the gentlest and most kind man I knew. I
discussed Raoul with my Grandpa Two Bears last Christmas, and he
grinned and asked me what I would say if Santa asked if Raoul was
naughty or nice. If I said, "naughty," Raoul wouldn't get anything
for Christmas. But, if I said "nice," I wouldn't get anything because
I lied to Santa. So, I smiled at Grandpa Two Bears and said, "He's
kind of okay. You know, good enough for an orange and some
underwear." Strange, Raoul became somewhat of a protector and
big brother to Missy, perhaps due to feeling bad about his remark.
Or, maybe, Santa had whispered to him.

Missy might have talked with me, but she had her eyes on
Lieutenant Nolen Roundtree, one of the F-14 cadre. Nolen was a
former F-4 Phantom pilot, was well respected across the fighter
community, and it was easy to see why Missy liked him. I could tell
by the way she glanced his way, nervously smiled when their eyes
met, and glowed whenever he was around. I am good at telling
when women I am with like other men.

My intense dislike for Jack Grant involved Missy, and it began
on a Friday afternoon when Raoul and I walked out of the Navy
Exchange. We saw him standing next to Missy's car. It is hard to
miss because it's a bright orange Volkswagen. Jack slid something
under her windshield wiper and then walked away. I frowned at
Raoul, and he shrugged, and we went to the squadron. Around 1630
in the afternoon, the skipper and XO called us into the ready room
and told us we had the choice to either go downtown to the
Christian Science Reading Room for two hours or follow them to
the officer's club. Not being big readers, especially on a Friday
afternoon, we had 100% attendance in the WOXOF room. Other
skippers must have offered the same choice to their ready rooms, or
maybe it was just drinking time because, in no time, the place was
packed. Raoul and I were standing at the bar, waiting for the
stripper to start when Missy ran up to us in a gleeful rush. She was
all dolled up in civilian clothes, and her fresh makeup and perfume
caused me to momentarily forget she was a naval officer.

"Have you seen Nolen?" She looked over my shoulder and
around the room. Then, she smiled.

"There he is!" She winked and handed me a slip of paper. "He
left this on my windshield."

I opened it and read, "Meet me at the club for a drink and
dinner, Nolen."

I thought of Jack Grant standing by her car.

"Wait." I held up my hand to stop her.

But she was off. I followed her with my eyes as I handed the note to Raoul. Nolen was at the end of the bar, talking to a group of F-14 bubbas, and Jack Grant was next to him. I saw Missy run to Nolen and tap him on the shoulder. He turned, and I could see Jack Grant's grin. It was pure evil. Nolen smiled at Missy and bent over to hear her. It was loud in the club, but I could see her say something into his ear. Nolen frowned and straightened. He looked around at his mates and then smiled at Missy and said something back. Everybody laughed, and Missy put her hand to her mouth and stepped back. She stood there a moment, then turned to run. I grabbed her as she brushed past me. Missy sobbed into my shoulder, and I said, "Come on, girl," and took her out the back door into the parking lot. I felt so badly for her.

Moments later, the door flung open, and Jack Grant stormed out with Raoul and the F-14 guys in trail. Jack turned around and held up his hands in a fighting pose.

"Jack, you look like you've done this before," said one of the guys.

"I was a boxer in college." Jack grinned over his shoulder.

"I wasn't," said Raoul, and he stepped forward, and his right fist snaked. He popped Jack right in the middle of his face. I mean, it was a killer blow, and Jack dropped like a rock. Raoul stepped back and looked around. Nolen stood in the open door, so Raoul nodded toward him.

"Got some of this for you too."

Nolen turned and ran back inside.

I walked Missy toward our car and then turned to see Jack sit up and put his hands to his nose. He moaned and writhed while his friends gathered around to help him up. Raoul and I put Missy into Raoul's car, and we took her to Alphonso's in La Jolla and had Mexican food. After a couple of margaritas, she seemed better, but I could see the hurt and the humiliation in her eyes. We had a third margarita, and I called a cab, and we all agreed that Jack Grant was a worthless piece of shit, and that Nolen Roundtree wasn't worthy of somebody like Missy Sanders.

That night when I prayed before bed, I asked Jesus to tell Santa that Raoul was pretty, darned nice.

GOTTA FIND A STATION

A week after Raoul slugged Jack Grant, my pilot, Arlo Grundeen, was scheduled for his last flight in the squadron. It was also his last flight in the navy, and when I heard that, my heart broke. I thought Arlo was always going to be there, maybe not in the same squadrons with me, but in the navy, and available to mentor me. It seems everything I knew about how to fight the airplane and how to handle myself on the ground came from him. I was hurt that he was leaving and hurt that he hadn't confided in me, so I went to his house. It was just north of the base, and as I drove, I reflected on the fact that Arlo and I had never discussed his plans. I had never imagined broaching the subject. Arlo was on a different level than me; he was a legend. It would be like asking, "Hey, God. What do you plan on doing after being God?"

Arlo lived with Wanda, and she led me through the house to the back deck. It was a holiday, Veterans Day, and since it fell on a Friday, we had a long weekend. I found Arlo drinking coffee and reading the *San Diego Tribune*. After pleasantries, I sat back in my lawn chair.

"So, they say you are leaving the navy?"

"That's right." Arlo nodded and took a deep breath. "That's right."

I frowned and looked down at my hands. Now that I was here with Arlo, I wasn't sure what I wanted to say.

"Why?" I looked up to see him shrug. "Why? I mean, you are so good at it...at everything."

Arlo smiled. "Thanks, Weenie."

"I mean it. You are the, you know, the ace of the base. Why would you leave?"

Arlo nodded, and his eyes drifted off me and up toward the sky. I followed them up there and saw a cloud. After a second, his gaze found me.

"Weenie, I love the navy. I do. But I have been on this train since kindergarten, and I want to get off."

"Train? What train? I don't get it." I frowned and leaned forward. "What are you talking about?" Arlo had a profound and thoughtful side to him that made him even more mysterious to me. He was a guy that could light a fart in the back of the ready room one moment, then say something so probing and thought-provoking the next that I was always in a bit of awe.

"Weenie, when I was five or six, my parents put me on the kindergarten train, and I rode that to grade school, then I rode the middle school train to the high school train."

"What do you mean, train?"

"The institutional train. The American public-school education train that we all ride—the train whereby the passengers all know the schedule and the plan. Certain outcomes are expected. Responsibilities of children, parents, the school are accepted. And, if anything confuses you, you can ask someone because all of us share the experience of the train."

I frowned and leaned back.

"Then, there is the college train, and, for guys like us, Weenie, the navy train." Arlo leaned forward and took another sip. He frowned and sat his cup down. "The navy train is the most restrictive, of course. But, here again, there is a common experience and clear expectations and responsibilities. The navy is a paternalistic train too, and its conductors tell us what to do, often what to think, even how to cut our hair and what to wear."

"You make growing up in America sound pretty restrictive."

"Oh, I didn't mean to do that." Arlo leaned back in his chair and smiled. "I mean, of course, we aren't a bunch of zombies on the train. We are witting and can make decisions." He shook his head and stared off into the yard.

The screen door squeaked, and Wanda walked out with a coffee pot. "Weenie, did you want some coffee? I'm sorry for not asking."

"No, I'm good." I shaded my eyes and smiled at her.

Wanda wore house shoes and padded across the wooden deck to Arlo. She filled his cup, and he patted her on the leg. "Thanks, Babe."

"Let me know if you change your mind." Wanda waved the coffee pot to me, smiled, and walked back into the house.

"I guess the train analogy has to do with me being at a decision point. A point where I can not only take total control of my life but also make an honest effort to savor it."

"Savor?" I frowned. I instantly understood the appropriateness of that word and what Arlo meant.

"When I graduated from college, I had reached a point of control. My parents were no longer the conductors of my journey; they were now supportive bystanders. They were willing to help, of course, but it was now time for me to decide what to do. So, I left the college train, and I stood at the station and looked around for the next train, and there were none there except for the masters' degree train. At that point, Weenie, I had this wonderful feeling of control. I was educated, I was a bachelor. I could have done anything I wanted, and it was a bit exhilarating, to be honest. But it was also surprisingly unsettling. Heck, I had been on a train all my life. I hesitated, and something pulled me, and I heard the whistle of the navy train. I wandered toward that sound, and the next thing I knew, I was on board. When I signed up for naval aviation, to be a pilot, I knew I was in for seven years after I got my wings." Arlo smiled at me. "So, I knew Uncle Sam had me for a good number of years." He sipped from the fresh cup and shrugged. "Weenie, it was all good. It felt natural and right, and I truly, truly have enjoyed every minute of this ride. But it is time for something else. As I said, it is time to savor the journey."

"You are almost half-way to retirement. Are you sure? What are you going to do?"

"Wanda and I have spent many a night around the kitchen table mulling this over. I guess when it comes down to it, I am a pilot. When I stand in front of the mirror and ask myself what I am, I am just a pilot."

"But you can be a pilot in the navy."

"Not quite the same, though." Arlo looked at me. "Is it?"

I frowned, and he laughed. "We are naval officers, Weenie, who just also happen to be naval aviators. You read your fitness reports. There is only one block on the whole thing that refers to aviation. All the rest of the report tells the tale of what kind of officer you are. And the longer you stay in and the more senior you get, the less flying you do. I want to fly more, Weenie, not less."

"Are you thinking about the airlines?"

"No. I said I wanted to fly more, Weenie. I didn't say I wanted to drive."

"I guess I don't get it."

"Nothing to get." Arlo took a long drink from his cup. He placed it on the table and smiled. "I visited my uncle down in Georgia a couple of weeks ago."

"I remember when you took leave."

"Yep, spent a couple of days with him, and do you know what he does?"

I shook my head.

"He owns a crop-dusting company. I flew one of his planes and had a ball! I am going to be a crop duster!"

I know my mouth fell open because I could feel the breeze against my teeth. "What?"

"Yep," grinned Arlo.

"Christ, after all the train stuff and the philosophy of life's control, I was thinking you were going to walk to Tibet or something. A crop duster?"

Arlo laughed at my confusion.

I shook my head. "That is more than strange, Arlo."

"Not if you are a pilot, Weenie."

I frowned again.

"There aren't that many of us. Not really. There are a lot of guys that fly airplanes. But not that many pilots."

I shook my head again and sighed. "Well, I am going to miss you, man."

Arlo smiled again. "So, we need to talk about what we will do for my final flight next week."

"When is it?"

"It's Monday, and ops tells me it will be a two versus two. Two of us against two Tomcats."

"Tomcats!"

"That's right, and the XO told me our wingman pilot is a Captain Jensen."

"A navy captain, an 0-6?"

"Yep. Captain Jensen is an old friend of the XO and supposedly is the real deal. He is a former F-8 pilot.

"Oh, yeah?"

"Yes, he was a squadron commander, then an airwing commander, and then commanded an aircraft carrier. A lot of talk about him being an admiral, so no pressure on us to perform." Arlo laughed and leaned back in his chair. "Well, maybe some pressure on YOU to perform. He won't have much an effect on me in Georgia."

I smiled at my friend.

"The XO is going to be in his back seat, so we need a plan to beat those Tomcats."

"Christ!"

"I can hold my own in the front, Weenie, and I'm sure the captain can too. But we need a way to get past those big-assed radars."

"Well, they aren't invincible. Of that, I am sure."

"Oh." Arlo narrowed his eyes and put his cup down. "Why do you say that?"

"You know, you can go to the trainer building and check out tapes to learn about the plane."

"You can?"

"Yep. I have been checking the tapes out for some time now. Just so I could get a leg up for when I transition to the Tomcat."

"Now you are scaring me," laughed Arlo.

"Hey, I know that eventually, we are all going to transition. All of us that stay in anyway. So, I thought, what the heck, check it out."

"What did you find?"

"It is very maneuverable and can fight at slower airspeeds than we can, but you already know that."

"I have heard that," said Arlo. "Go ahead."

"The radar has a huge scan volume and is automated to establish track files on airborne contacts. But it is a pulse doppler system, so it needs to see velocity to work effectively."

"Go ahead."

"The radar isn't mechanized for dogfighting. I talk with the F-14 RIOs a lot, and they tell me stuff. I think they feel sorry for us F-4 back seaters because of our aircraft limitations. They tell me maneuvering targets are hard for the radar to process, and it will generate a lot of false tracks."

"Really?" Arlo smiled and leaned forward. "Really?"

"Yep. We can fool it."

"Honey, time to get going." Wanda poked her head out of the door.

"Oops, sorry." Arlo stood, and I stood with him. "Got to go. Weenie come up with a plan. Something you can brief for our hop."

"Me? Brief the hop? I am the junior guy."

"I will brief the front seat stuff, the flight stuff. You need to brief the tactical stuff. And, Weenie, this is the last time I will ever fly a navy jet. Get me to the kill."

CINNAMON TOAST

I spent the afternoon developing a plan to defeat the Tomcats. I didn't want to let Arlo down, and I sure didn't want to screw up in front of the XO and Captain Jensen. I got into the details and even used some graph paper to plot out my idea. Fortunately, my roommates Cotton and Raoul were off somewhere so I could concentrate.

While Arlo was my mentor and hero, Cotton and Raoul Hungus were my best friends, and we rented a three-bedroom house on Foothill Boulevard in Pacific Beach. It was a cool place, nestled among old neighborhood homes near the corner where Foothill turns into Turquoise Street. Of course, we were all bachelors, and Raoul's description of the place was a "snake pit." To Raoul, the term "snake pit" meant a palace of great sexual conquest. To me, it was dirty dishes, empty beer cans, and an occasional whiff of perfume from some girl Raoul ensnared.

Our primary hunting grounds for such girls were the Miramar Officer's Club on Wednesday night and the Marine Corps Recruit Depot, or MCRD, Officer's Club on Fridays. Why officer's clubs amid the land of the fair? It was 1973, and the nation was snarled in the Vietnam War, many seeing it as an infamous and horrific result of the military-industrial complex gone awry. Civilians looked on military men with suspicion, if not open hostility, and since civilian men in America wore their hair down to their shoulders, we were easy to spot. So, as Raoul said, "We go to the officers' clubs because the women there don't hate us yet."

Raoul was an aggressive pick-up artist whose desires and primal, bright eyes centered upon looks and breast size. He told me once how he got the name Raoul, and I think he might have inherited some of his preferences and tendencies. It seems his father, James Hungus, from the southern Alabama Hungus clan, as Raoul described him, came home to find his new wife in the embrace of the pool boy, Raoul Benetiz. James dispatched the man with his quail gun, a gift from his father. Of course, he was cleared by the law due to self-defense. However, and surprising to everyone, James apparently felt deep remorse, and when a baby boy was born, he named him Raoul.

That is the story Raoul tells me, but I am not sure I believe a word of it.

At any rate, and for whatever reason, Raoul would always wind up at the end of a Wednesday or Friday night with a girl on his arm. She would have a gorgeous rack, and Raoul would wink at me and grin. "Eyes on your own paper, Kleegan," he would whisper as the bedroom door shut behind him.

That said, Raoul treated his guests with total respect, and I never heard him talk disparagingly about them. Even in the ready room corral of braggadocio, Raoul didn't brag or tell sexual prowess tales. Grandpa Two Bears once said to me that women could fall in love with bad men because they believed they could change them. So, they put up with their craziness. Grandpa said that men, on the other hand, want to keep women the same. They don't have to put up with anything.

Cotton was a smooth operator, and since he usually didn't drink, avoided the poor choices that alcohol often brings. In fact, he once told Raoul and me the most beautiful woman he ever met was in a bar in Boogie Street. The ship was on a port visit to Singapore and she had a wonderful English accent. Later, in the back seat of a taxi, she, awkwardly, turned out to be he.

"Were you pissed?" Raoul had asked.

"No," said Cotton. "But I was damned disappointed. If it would have worked out, I was ready to jump ship and learn how to play cricket."

I am the opposite of Raoul. It's not that I don't appreciate good looks and big breasts and all, but I have a timidity that stifles even my best intentions to approach women. Part of my problem is that I'm not that striking. At five feet eight and 145 pounds, I am a bit puny, and when I walk into a bar, the only thing people see is the open door. Raoul tried to comfort me by telling me I was tall if I had been born in England in the eighteenth century.

I have brownish-blond hair, and my beard is so thin I can't even grow sideburns. This was a time when everybody grew sideburns, and all I had were these blow aways that I made by combing my hair down along the side of my face. I also wore glasses, something I started as a fashion statement in high school because I thought they made me look like John Lennon, the Beatle. But the John Lennon look did not jive with being a naval air warrior, so I ditched the glasses when I went to Pensacola, only to find I needed a prescription! One night, while getting pleasantly drunk in the MCRD officers' club's backroom, a girl pulled my glasses off.

"You're cute!" She exclaimed before planting a wet, hops, and cigarette flavored kiss on my lips.

Unfortunately, she passed out shortly after our kiss, but my memory of her passion convinced me to lose the glasses. I started going out "without the bicycle on my face," as Raoul said, but I had to squint to see girls that weren't standing next to me. I would ask Raoul, "Hey, check out the girl in the corner by the jukebox." Raoul wore contacts and would flash his plastic enhanced laser eyes and report back with a "Go for it" or a "Keep looking."

I guess my real problem goes beyond being timid. My problem is Jane. I didn't even know I was looking for a girl until I fell for her, and in those few days that I knew her, she blessed and cursed me. She blessed me with the magic of love. Falling and then being in love were new feelings for me, and Jane blessed me with both. But she cursed me. She cursed me by dying, and now I am left with this full sponge and nowhere to wring it. All it takes is a whiff of gardenia or the sight of a corsage, and I twist my heart. Once I kissed a girl, and when I tasted her cherry lipstick, Jane's cherry lipstick, I freaked out. So, it's unfair to the girls I do meet. Maybe they, too, are seeking falling and being--the two most beautiful things in the world. I caution myself and hope I'm not just looking for the notion of being in love. Romantic movies fuel that kind of thing, and I think many people fall for the illusion of love, the Hollywood idea of falling in love. The most famous love stories in history are all about the falling part, not the rest, not the...being. The love of Romeo and Juliet, Helen and Paris, Marc Antony, and Cleopatra...all ended before they began. Of course, I am a guy, so there is no one on this planet I would dare talk to about this. Well, maybe Mom and Grandpa, and I know how pathetic that sounds.

I also developed quite a liking for bourbon. I worry about it some so I will go the occasional weekend without any booze to prove I'm not an alcoholic. I try not to take drinking too seriously. My fondness for the distillate is a far cry from my college days of near teetotalism and even the early navy days of only an occasional bout with the jug. My first cocktail, by that I mean some mixture with a real name instead of "purple stuff," was a Singapore Sling that I had as an Aviation Officer School candidate, and I drunk enough of those in one night to swear off gin. My next foray into the demon madness was with a hurricane, also while in Florida. I over imbibed in that tall glass of heaven too and promptly swore off rum. So, I went to beer for a while. I think my real introduction to hard liquor drinking was on the ship during the Vietnam cruises. There was an attitude of an inevitable fatality, the frailty of our lives that endorsed rule-breaking and wild behavior. After all, a cold glass of milk didn't hack it after a day of dodging missiles and bullets or going to the memorial service for those who failed in that. So, we drank even though drinking on naval vessels was strictly forbidden. I was introduced to vodka, and it was good because it didn't have to be mixed with anything. Or, if you preferred, it could be mixed with everything! I always mixed mine with bug juice, what we called Kool-Aid, on the ship.

Raoul introduced me to bourbon via that southern delight, the mint julep. It was sweet and therefore drinkable to me, and it's service in a chilled, silver glass added to the charm. However, mint juleps are hard to drink if you aren't watching a bunch of horses run around or aren't from the deep south, and whenever I ordered one without the mouth of Rhett Butler, the bartenders always looked at me like I was a poser. So, I evolved to bourbon and 7Up, maintaining the sweetness I had grown fond of. Raoul's demand that I "squat to pee" if I drunk that girly stuff caused me to leap into bourbon mixed with bourbon. So, now I find myself coming home from the officer's club on a Friday evening, after joyful hours of stripper's pasties and beer, ripping off the wax top of a Maker's Mark bottle. I drink it with ice and a splash of water to "open up the flavor," as Raoul says.

Raoul and Cotton are usually out somewhere, so I drink alone. I wake up sometime during the night and stumble off to my rack, and the next morning the bottle is half empty. That leaves the other half for Saturday night, so it works out well. I stop drinking on Sunday and don't drink during the workweek because I don't want to become an alcoholic. My habits with alcohol are pretty much my business, and I like it that way. I caution myself while drinking at the club because I have seen too many who don't and get a bad reputation. Believe me, as much as we all drank, if you had a bad reputation for drinking, you were doing some heavy hitting. Just the other day, Rip Daniels was in the back bar with his wife, Rose, and they were both pretty boogered up. We were talking about radar tactics when suddenly the topic changed to women's underwear. I swear I don't know how that happened. I mean, it's not a clear juxtaposition even if you think about it hard. So, Rip says, "I think Rose is wearing blue skivvies tonight."

Rose grins and belches and says, "Guess again, pal."

Rip grabs her by the waist and lifts her upside down! Rose is now bare-legs-up with her skirt down around her head, and she doesn't have any underwear on! I mean, it was beaver city, and I couldn't help but say, "Looks flesh-colored to me."

Rose screams, so Rip sets her down, and she takes her beer glass and slams it down on his hand. That is the kind of thing drinking too many leads too. Rip was off the flight schedule for three weeks until his hand healed. I have no idea how long he was off any other schedule he might have had with Rose.

I was resigned to a life alone when I came across a phone number, scribbled on an Ozark Airline napkin. I had put it in my dresser drawer in case I needed it. The number belonged to Cinnamon Tyler, the stewardess I had met on the plane trip home from Militia Springs the previous summer. I gathered some courage from the small jar where I keep mine and asked her to a party at our snake pit. A more intimate date would give us a better chance to know each other, but I wasn't ready for that. She seemed hesitant, but said," Yes."

The party was on Saturday night because, according to Raoul, that would give us all of Friday night to find dates.

Cotton already knew he was bringing Melody Clark, whom he met in Sunday school class. The first time Charles introduced us and mentioned where they met, I almost spit my beer on her! I thought the Sunday school thing was a joke. Well, it wasn't, and she gave me the stink eye for a while. However, I was able to get her into an animated discussion about my interpretation of Paul's first seven letters and the specific crisis each letter was supposed to address, and that got her on my good side. Or I bored her to death, and she was too tired to dislike me anymore.

Melody was a bit of a puzzle to me because I couldn't figure out how to treat her, I mean, more than just with respect. I guess part of the problem was I had never talked with a Black female before. Well, I spoke with Pearl when she introduced me to Jane, but that hardly counts. Cotton and Blackness was a new world for me, but at least he was a guy. I guess Melody was a puzzle because I didn't know how I should think about her. Or what to say. I mean, she was very foxy. But I felt uncomfortable with that. You see, if I told Cotton that I thought she was foxy, he might wonder what I meant by that.

"Thank you, Weenie. Do you mean like Thomas Jefferson thought Sally Hemmings was foxy?"

So foxy, sexy, hot, all those words that sell perfume and promises to men were out. She did look glamorous, but that is kind of an older person's word.

So, after I met her, and when I was alone in the kitchen with Cotton, I said, "Melody seems really cool, man."

He smiled, and we clicked beer bottles, so I guess that was okay.

I stayed home Friday night and worked on my plan to destroy the Tomcats, and it turned out that Raoul didn't find anyone. However, his legendary Rolodex turned up Blaze, an inamorata from his past. On Saturday night, he was whistling Dixie when he went out the door to pick her up. However, he reported finding Blaze living with her husband again, so he wisely decided to walk away from the drama. He showed up stag.

Bachelor parties center on a keg of beer, and as a nod to the Californians, we served Corona. I know Corona is Mexican but, what the hell, for some reason, we deemed it to be cooler than Budweiser. We also got some pizza, chips, salsa, and a small plate of vegetables with ranch dressing dip if any of the new-world chicks that lived next door showed up. They were from the marijuana and cat-pee crowd of my college days, but now sold surfboards and posters or T-shirts with stuff like Che or the peace symbol on them. According to Raoul, such chicks could be had, but you had to walk them off the…being a warmonger…thing. I remember asking Raoul if he ever smoked dope with the new-world chicks. I figured he did to get into their pants. But he "Never. I never smoke dope, Weenie. It dulls the man out of you."

That surprised me, given he was a child of the seventies. I mean, I even smoked dope one night. It was with my dad and before anyone knew what it was. I cast an eye at Raoul. "What do you mean?"

He frowned at me and cocked his head. He does that sometimes when he thinks my upbringing made me too insulated.

"Weenie, I am a champion. Of women, of championship wrestling, of things that need defending. I never smoke dope. I never want to surrender my option for violence."

He said that in a non-threatening way. Like he might have said, "I always take the Sunday paper. It supports my community." Like it was just a matter of fact and principle.

Anyway, I took great care choosing my wardrobe for the evening. Cinnamon was a flight stewardess, and they were really attuned to fashion. They traveled the world, saw all kinds of cool people, and had access to international magazines.

The problem is the stuff civilians wear goes with their long hair and sideburns and other facial hair. I mean, if you have a shirt collar the size of a slice of New York Pizza, you can lose an onion noggin like mine pretty quick in it. In fact, military guys in civilian clothes look like their heads are afterthoughts. The other day I walked into a Gap store, and I swear I heard somebody ask, "Did you forget something?" At any rate, in that Gap store, I bought a light blue leisure suit and a white turtleneck. The woman tried to sell me a gold medallion to go with it, but it reminded me too much of this white professor I had in college. He taught sociology 101 really wanted to be cool so he sat cross-legged on his table and said "wow man" to everything.

I felt spiffy when I picked up Cinnamon in the Triumph and was quite sure she would be impressed by my little sports car. Of course, I had the top down and thought cruising to the party would be so southern California. I never factored in her hair, though. The trip from her house to mine was a disaster. By the time we pulled into my driveway, she looked like a cross between Sasquatch and Dolly Parton. She was miffed, I could tell, and we never recovered from that ride. I mean, she is gorgeous, and I have to say I liked the reaction I got when I introduced her to my party guests. This was after she fixed her hair, of course. But we just didn't click, and it wasn't her fault. I wasn't fair to Cinnamon by asking her out because I still pined for Jane. I compared every girl to Jane, and they all came up short, and I think I showed that. People know when someone is into them or not, especially when they have their antennae up, and everybody on a first date has their antennae up! Cinnamon even asked me if anything was wrong a couple of times, and she probably wished she had stayed home and watched Jimmy Durante Presents the Lennon Sisters or anything more exciting than me. That is when Raoul came to the rescue in an odd sort of way.

We had an unstated rule that we didn't try to steal each other's dates. It's a rule most bachelor roommates have, at least those who plan on living together more than a weekend. But when Cinnamon excused herself to go to the bathroom, Raoul sidled up to me with a smile.

"I detect unresolved issues." Raoul was in the sweet, deep syrup of Rhett Butler's southern gentlemen voice by this time of the party. So, 'I detect unresolved issues,' had the sound…as Grandpa Two

Bears would say… of a shovel scraping molasses across gravel, then dripping it on a biscuit. Plus, he did have on the gold medallion.

"What are you talking about?"

"I see you and your beautiful woman have lost some…some… simpatico." Raoul's pained smile had just the right mixture of sadness and sincerity to be more welcome than offensive, and I knew he was up to something.

"Oh," I nodded. "Yeah, you are probably right."

"With your permission, I might try to enliven her evening. With your permission, of course." He bowed slightly.

"You mean, you are asking if it is okay to steal my date."

"I would not put it as indelicately as steal. I would say, acquire."

"Well, you have my blessing."

I purposely drifted to the corners of the house and left Raoul to his new mission. He took Cinnamon home, and I felt good about it.

TURKEY FOR DINNER

Monday morning, the XO invited Arlo and me to his office to meet Captain Jensen. It was thirty minutes before the brief and a chance to get to know each other before the flight.

Captain Jensen was about six feet tall and lean in his sage green flight suit. He had light brown hair and friendly blue eyes, and his handshake was firm. His call sign was Jaybird. He exuded an air of authority, but it seemed to be something he was willing to share, and I felt instantly comfortable. I think Arlo felt at ease too, especially when Captain Jensen told him that Arlo was going to lead the hop and not fly wing.

"Nobody flies wing on his last flight in the navy," the captain said.

I liked him even more after that.

We had some coffee and small talk, but my head was spinning. I didn't want to let the XO or Arlo down, and I sure didn't want to be a doofus in front of Captain Jensen. I also wasn't sure if my plan would work. I had tried to explain it to Raoul, but he was busy updating his Rolodex and said, "Just put them on the nose and go fast, Weenie, what the fuck?"

We adjourned and walked down the passageway to the ready room. There stood Nolen Roundtree, two RIOs I had seen in the officer's club bar, and Jack Grant! They were our Tomcat adversaries!

We shook hands all around and settled into ready room chairs. Arlo led us through the mechanics of getting out of Miramar and over the coast to the offshore training area. Nolen led the F-14 discussion and said they would like to have two engagements: the first being a scripted scenario and the second, free play. He wanted the Phantoms to fly toward the Tomcats side by side about a mile apart for the scripted scenario. This allowed the Tomcat RIOs to exercise the systems and fire simulated missiles as they progressed through the launch acceptability regions. The Phantoms were, for

23

the most part, targets for this scenario. However, the second engagement allowed free maneuver, but the only permitted kill was a behind-the-wing line sidewinder or guns for the Tomcats. The Phantom didn't have a gun, which Jack reminded us in the brief.

"If you had one, you would try to use it and just get killed sooner," he smirked.

The Tomcat folks didn't think much of us.

We then separated for our individual briefs, and I went to get fresh coffee. As I filled my cup, Jack Grant sidled up to me. His nose was still a little swollen from his round with Raoul, and I smiled.

"Take a good whiff of that captain's butt, Kleegan, because this is the last time, he's going to let a loser like you back there." Jack glared at me.

"There's creamer and sugar if you want it." I turned and went to my brief.

Captain Jensen, the XO, Arlo, and I settled into the ready room, and I walked to the chalkboard. "On the first run, we just do as they want and fly the profile. But we don't use any afterburner and save our gas for the second run." I pulled down the projector screen to which I had taped a large page of graph paper, turned around, and smiled. "But on the second run, we can outfox them. We just have to be careful."

I pointed to two triangles at one end of the graph paper and a single triangle at the other. "This is us," I said, pointing to the single triangle. "There is only one triangle because we are going to fly welded wing. We only give them one target to see." Heads nodded, so I continued. "Let's use 180 degrees as an example heading that we will fly. Of course, once out there, we will fly whatever heading gets us to them and proceed towards them at 25,000 feet and 300 knots."

"Why so slow?" The XO frowned, and I could see the beginnings of WTF on his face.

"Because at twenty miles," I pointed to the twenty-mile marker on the graph paper, "We will hit minimum afterburner and each turn ninety degrees off our inbound heading and descend to 5,000 feet." I pointed to the two, now separated, Phantom triangles each heading away from the other and ninety degrees from the original heading. "The reason to go down is to confuse the Tomcat radars further. Even pulse doppler has problems with the ground return. And, if we are smoking a little, the ground hides that too. The Phantom on the right will head 270 degrees, and the one on the left will be head 090 degrees. See how that works?" Everybody nodded, so I continued. "As we head downhill, we will hold that heading for thirty seconds. I suspect our speed will be approximately 500 knots, so we will have traveled three-and-one-half miles, and that puts us here." I pointed to the graph paper. "In the meantime, depending upon the Tomcat speed towards us, they will travel between three and five miles. That puts them here." I pointed to the paper. "We will turn back toward them in a six G turn, and due to the distances traveled by both them and us, we will turn forty degrees beyond our initial inbound heading. So, the Phantom on the right will turn past 180 to 140, and the Phantom on the left will turn to 220. Everybody with me?" Again, everybody nodded, and I could see Arlo beginning to grin. "The Tomcats will be high on our noses between five and seven miles. XO, we will need to be in ten-mile pulse to see them on our scopes." The XO was grinning too.

"Once the captain and Arlo get a tally, it turns into a visual fight, but, if the XO and I can find them and get a radar lock, I hope our first shot will be a radar-guided sparrow, followed by sidewinders."

"What happens if the Tomcats follow us with their radars?" asked Arlo.

"In that case, we will each meet them head-on, and depending upon what we see, either engage them or run for it."

"One or both of the Tomcats can track just one of us," said the XO. "In that case, one of us will meet them head-on, and the other should get a good beam or even tail-end shot."

"Yes, sir," I said. "Questions?"

Everybody turned in their chairs and looked at Captain Jensen. He had his head down, writing notes on his kneeboard. I gulped and crossed my fingers behind my back. Captain Jensen was a warrior, a real warrior. He might think all of this was a bunch of bullshit.

Captain Jensen wrote a few more notes, then raised his head. "I like it," he smiled.

I glanced at the XO and saw the relief in his eyes and on his lips. He knew me longer than anyone else, except Raoul and Cotton. He knew me from the days at Glynco when I was pretty screwed up. He also knew he was, in part, the guy who had changed the timid Win Kleegan to Weenie Kleegan, a man who could at least stand with his fellows. The XO's relieved smile, and I suppose his thoughts of me were both looking forward as well as historical.

"A word." Captain Jensen stopped me as I moved to leave the ready room.

"Certainly, sir." I followed him to the skipper's office. The skipper was on leave, somewhere, trout fishing. Nobody dared enter his empty office as it was hallowed ground, and I hesitated at the doorway. Captain Jensen turned and grinned at my discomfort. "Come on in, son," he said.

I stepped forward and sat in the chair in front of the skipper's desk. The only other time I had been in that room was when he had given me my fitness report. That report had been glowing, and I remembered feeling my face grow hot as I read the wonderful things he said about me. I had spent an hour with him that morning, and after it was over, I wanted to stay in the navy forever. He had ranked me number one out of the four ensigns. Later, that night when I went home, Raoul grumbled that he was number four. I told him I was number three.

"You are the same Kleegan that saved the kids in Honolulu?" Captain Jensen smiled and swiveled in the skipper's chair. It squeaked a little, and I remembered how much I had liked that during the fitness report brief because the sound made it seem like we weren't alone. It took the discomfort of intimacy out of the meeting, and that is always good when you are talking to your skipper.

"Yes, sir."

Captain Jensen nodded. "I am surprised how little I have heard about it. I mean, it was tremendously heroic. Don't you think?"

"I…I, well, sir, I think I did what every one of us would have done. Don't you think so?"

"I would hope. But, still, it is strange to hear so little about it. I mean, didn't the Tonight Show call you? That's what the XO told me."

"Yes, sir. At least somebody who said they were representing Mister Carson."

"And?"

"And I didn't feel it was right. The guy who shot me was sick; the kids were okay. It was the end of it."

"I see." Captain Jensen nodded and leaned back in the skipper's chair. My God, but it looked comfortable. A flicker went through me, a hope really, that one day I would sit in a chair like that.

"Sir?" I started to stand, figuring the Captain was through with me.

"Weenie, I applaud your desire to avoid the spotlight. It is refreshing, given so many want to find it." He picked up the skipper's red pen and twirled it in his fingers, and as he did, he stared at me. "But what if your conversation with Mister Carson emboldened some congressman to fund research on veteran's health issues more fully? The guy that shot you was sick, wasn't he? Would that have been worth going on the show?"

"I suppose so, sir."

Captain Jensen nodded and twirled the red pen. He seemed lost in thought for a moment, and I wasn't sure if I should leave or not. I had no idea how to act around a navy captain. I heard the best you could do was just not make them angry. I decided just to sit still and let it play out. The captain made a final twirl and looked at me with a smile. "It was a superb brief Weenie of a great plan. Let's hope we are good enough aviators to fly it for you." He nodded toward the door, and I stood.

"Yes, sir." I backed out of the room.

We manned up and taxied to the hold short area. The Tomcats rolled out of their parking spots and came down the taxiway like birds of prey. They were huge and menacing, and as they rolled past us, they swung their wings forward, and I wondered how in the hell we were going to beat them. They had the nickname of turkey because of the way they approached the ship with their big wingspan. But they didn't look like turkeys to me. They looked like sharks with wings.

Captain Jensen wanted to do a section take-off, so we took the runway side by side, and Arlo pushed the throttles to full power, cycled the controls, and looked at Captain Jensen. He nodded, and Arlo selected afterburner and, after a quick check of the instruments, looked at Captain Jensen again. He nodded; Arlo dropped his hand and released the brakes at the same time. Both Phantoms jumped forward, and the thrill of all that power moving together rippled through me. There is nothing like a section take-off in a Phantom, and every time I was a part of one, I thanked God for the opportunity. I called the airspeeds to Arlo, and at 140, I felt the nose lift off. Captain Jensen matched us perfectly, and in a second, we were airborne. Captain Jensen tucked in so close I could look inside his cockpit.

We flew to the coast and out to the warning area, then split apart to do our combat checks. After some communications checks with the Tomcats, we headed toward each other. As desired, we were in combat spread, level, and about one mile apart. Shortly after settling on our heading toward the Tomcats, we heard the Tomcat RIOs call "contact." We were still around sixty miles apart. As we traveled downrange, we listened to each Tomcat RIO call his "Fox three," which meant he shot his simulated Phoenix missile at us. Then, we heard the pilots call "Fox one" as they shot simulated Sparrow missiles at us. I found both Tomcat's using my pulse search mode, and they were side by side. Arlo and I were on the left side of our formation, so I locked the left Tomcat at thirty miles. Arlo called a tally at eight miles, and we watched the big jets approach us from the side. Moments later, each called a "Fox two," the kill shot with a Sidewinder.

"Closing to guns. That is a guns kill on the lead Tomcat." I heard Jack's snarking voice over the radio.

Arlo and I joined Captain Jensen and the XO at the northern end of the area, and after the Tomcat's called "fight's on," we headed south toward them. The captain and the XO joined tight on our side, and they were so close I thought we were overlapping our wings! At twenty miles, Arlo and I cut to the right, and our wingman went left, and we executed the plan. Thirty seconds later, I called "mark" on our squadron frequency, and Arlo planted a six G turn on the plane. I grunted as he turned toward the heading, and as Arlo lifted the nose, I prayed and inched the thumbwheel of my radar up. I almost cried with joy when I saw those two giant blobs at eight miles. I locked the closest one, and Arlo called," Tally two, they don't see us." I am sure I cried when I heard Captain Jensen call "Tally two. Fox one on the eastern Tomcat." He made the call on the fight standard frequency so the Tomcats could listen to it too. Arlo called "Fox one on the western Tomcat, followed by Fox two."

"Fox two," said the captain! We were both behind our Tomcats!

Arlo closed on his Tomcat, and I hoped it was Jack. The plane went nose high, and I heard Arlo grunting and the beginning of a laugh. He was in hot mic so I could listen to him, and he was talking to himself, and me.

"In burner. Keep going up there, pal. Keep going up there."

"170 knots," I said.

"Come on, baby, don't stall." Arlo was chuckling!

"140."

"Drop the flaps to half to hold up my nose. Hold it, baby. Hold it, baby."

The Tomcat was right in front of us. I could see both helmets in the canopy. I saw the Tomcat's nose shake.

"That's it, stall you turkey!" Arlo's scream was manic. I think he realized this was the last time he would ever do this.

The Tomcat slid in front of us, and I couldn't see anything but its wings on either side of the cockpit.

Christ, we were close!

I heard Arlo key the UHF. "If I had a gun in this thing, you would have a bullet in the back of your head." He screamed with joy as the Tomcat shuddered and fell off to the side.

"Little rudder, little rudder," coaxed Arlo as he whispered to his plane.

We instantly flipped down, and our nose arced wildly for a second before settling on the Tomcat.

"Fox two…again," said Arlo.

Nolen and the two RIOS came to the debrief and were genuinely impressed with how we had so wholly fooled them. We had a great discussion, and I loved to hear the RIOs talk about what they were doing in the back of their jets. One day I was going to be in the back seat of a Tomcat! It turned out that Jack was the pilot that we gunned, but something came up so he couldn't come to the debriefing.

I shook hands with Arlo, and he gripped my shoulder and said, "thanks for the kill Weenie. I will never forget it."

I wanted to hug him, and I wanted to tell him how much he meant to me. I wanted to tell him how much I would miss him and how much he had done for me. I wanted to tell him so much.

"Hey, man," I said. "Be careful."

A TASTE OF CHOCOLATE

Have you ever had a dream that occurred night after night? Not the same dream but bits and pieces that begin to hang together, and you can't make any sense of it? I have had such dreams lately. They don't scare me, so they aren't nightmares, but man, they do bother me. I think we all have dreams that concern us. I have the one where suddenly I realize I'm naked. The naked dream happens every so often, but it isn't a continuation of previous naked dreams. When I have the dream, I am always in a crowd, and I suddenly realize I don't have anything on! Weirdly, nobody seems to notice, but I rush around looking for something to cover up with until I wake up. I read that it means I am insecure or that I am dishonest with myself. In that regard, it makes some sort of goofy, dream sense.

But not this new dream. It doesn't make any sense. If the pharaoh had dreamed my dream and had summoned me to interpret it as he did with Joseph, I would have been put to the knife.

"Uhh, seven fat cows…seven thin cows, uhh, beats me, sir."

"Off with his head!"

When I do have the dream, it seems to build on itself. By that, I mean, the dream continues its story. Well, like most dreams, it isn't so much a story but a set of faces, instances, images, feelings that sometimes relate, and other times don't. And the weird part is that it is a dream about a puppy. No kidding! A puppy is the center of the most disturbing dream I have ever had.

I began to dream about this puppy the day after the crazy man in the park shot me. I later found that he was a down-on-his-luck, deranged Vietnam vet who somehow thought he would protect some children by shooting them. He was sick, and I understand he is still in a VA hospital. He hit me instead of the children, and I am lucky he had a .38 instead of a .45 or a rifle.

I am young in the dream. I know that because I can see myself and watch myself pet this cute little beagle with his big brown eyes and floppy ears. And I hear his glorious bugle voice! Velvet fur, the warmth of his small, pink tongue; I can feel it all. I can smell him. I can see him. These were the pieces of the dream at first. Unnerving because something seemed to be coming.

But I don't even remember having a beagle pup.

Then one dream day, we walk to the car. Are we going to church? Mom, Dad, and baby Molly get in the front. Grandpa Two Bears, and I crawl into the back. The engine starts, tires crunch on gravel...then this terrible cry!

We scramble out, the little dog pants to breathe. Did Dad run over him? His little paws dig into the gravel as he tries to come to us. His tongue lolls out, and his eyes hold a misery that makes me scream. Some nights I wake up to that scream, gripping the sheets and breathing hard.

Grandma and Mom and Molly cry too. I put my hands over my ears to stop it. Then, I am next to the dog, but Dad pushes me aside and leans over the dog and whispers, "It's gonna be okay, Toby, it's gonna be okay, Toby."

I have this terrible image of that little beagle's eyes. They look right into me, and he says, "I could have been a contender. I could have been somebody." And he says it just like Marlon Brando said it in On the Waterfront. He says it in Marlon Brando's voice. It sounds funny coming out of his dog's mouth, and I start to laugh, but I scream and wake up with wet eyes and this tremendous feeling of loss and guilt.

What loss? Guilty of what?

REESE

The first week of November, the airwing returned to sea, and it was good to get back on *Constellation*. She is the best carrier in the fleet, and it was going to be a short, fun, couple of weeks—a refresher before we started operations in earnest following the new year.

The telephone's sharp ring pierced our bunkroom's dark tranquility and brought me scrambling to my feet. Since my rack was closest to the phone, by rule, I had to answer it. I had not considered this until my roomies, Raoul, and Cotton, reminded me of it, the day after we moved in.

I clicked my desk light and grabbed the receiver on the third ring. "Ensign, I mean, Lieutenant Junior Grade Kleegan." Raoul, Cotton, and I had been promoted from ensign to lieutenant Junior grade two weeks prior, and I had not yet gotten used to it.

"Weenie, this is the skipper."

I automatically stood at attention.

"Yes, sir."

"The captain is going to take the ship to general quarters in a couple of minutes. You guys need to get up here ASAP."

"Sir?"

"Some of the Black sailors have mobbed up and are roaming the decks looking for guys to beat up. Everybody else's stateroom is up here on the 03 level. Weenie, they might be between you and the ready room, so be careful."

"Yes, sir."

"If you get stuck after we set Condition Zebra, tell whoever asks that your skipper gave you permission to break it."

"Yes, sir." I hung the phone on the receiver and spun around. Cotton and Raoul were awake and frowning.

"Get dressed for general quarters. We have to get to the ready room."

"What's going on?" Cotton hopped out of the top rack.

"Skipper says some sailors are roaming the decks, looking for trouble. The captain of the ship is going to take us to general quarters any minute.

"Wow!" Raoul slipped into his flight suit and bent to tie his boots.

"Guess it is even worse than we thought," said Cotton. He glanced at me but I dropped my eyes. I didn't want to give him a reason to shake his head or sigh...or explain. You see that afternoon the executive officer of the ship had briefed us in the ready room. His discussion centered on the many disturbances throughout the carrier during our at-sea training period. It was the first week in November, and we had just put to sea when many arguments and even fights had broken out among the crew, much of it due to resentment among Black sailors at how they perceived they were treated. According to the executive officer, there was some merit to their beef. The fact is the draft hit poor minority communities particularly hard since so few of them had college deferments. There was also some data suggesting white men got the bulk of draft board waivers and deferments. Many men joined the navy rather than risk being drafted into ground combat in the army, and a significant number had college educations. These men shouldered out lower test scoring minorities, so there were comparatively few Blacks in the navy, and those in often scored at the lower end of the scale. That resulted in Blacks having more menial and labor-intensive jobs. The bureau had also sent too many men to the ship, and Constellation had 250 more men than berthing allowed. There were all kinds of rumors swirling, and one of the worst was that all the Blacks were going to be court-martialed. I sat next to Cotton during the brief and I heard him swallow. I saw him fidget and squirm.

Cotton opened the door just as the general quarters' claxon sounded, and we soon heard the pounding of boots and shouts from the crew. We had five minutes to set Condition Zebra, which means the closure of all water-tight doors/hatches and other vents and exhausts. Once set, the crew is forbidden to break the condition until the ship grants permission.

Cotton led the way, and Raoul and I followed him up the ladder to the mess deck. Our new rank of lieutenant junior grade had enabled us to move out of the eight-man octagon to a four-person stateroom. However, it was located below the galley and a long trek to our ready room up on the 03 level.

Melee and chaos are not appropriate words to describe a ship transitioning to general quarters because there are rules to follow and follow very quickly. But as the three of us broke out onto the mess decks, we joined into a frantic mix of sailors as they donned gas masks, manned fire hoses, or just ran for their appropriate GQ stations. We edged through the crowds, and just as we entered the forward section of the mess decks, a glowering sailor stopped us.

"Where you think you goin'?" He tilted his head sideways and grinned. He had his dixie cup on the back of his head, and if it weren't the look of hate in his eyes and the huge butcher knife in his hand, I might have demanded he move aside. He slowly whacked the blade against his leg.

Cotton backed up a step, and Raoul and I moved to our left, looking for another exit. A group of sailors closed it off, and one grabbed the front of my flight suit and pulled me close.

"Reese?" I frowned. Reese was one of the yellow shirts that directed us on the flight deck, in fact he was the best. He was one of the very few we trusted to taxi us on the bow at night. You see, it's frightening dark up there, and after you land, that's where they take you to get you out of the way. The yellow shirts taxi you right next to the edge of the deck...inches away from slipping off into the water. If they screw up and taxi you a bit too far, the plane will slip into the sea. So, who are you going to trust? I mean, you eventually must park the damned plane to get out of it and get a cheeseburger. So, we all trusted Reese. He was the best! He was the king of the dark!

"Reese?"

Reese's eyes flickered, and he took a breath, and I knew he was a frustrated man, most likely for good reasons, but I didn't see a mutineer. I didn't see a man who would hurt a shipmate.

The sailor with the sideways dixie cup stomped across the room and pushed Reese aside. I noticed the name Maynard, stenciled on his shirt. He grabbed Cotton by the flight suit and pulled him close and glared at him, and I could see something different in his eyes.

He hated us.

"What's up, nigger?" His eyes were wide, make-believe wide, and he grinned again while he looked around.

WHACK! He hit his leg with the butcher knife.

"What's up, nigger?" Maynard looked back at Cotton. He panned the room, and the men cheered and waved their hands. Most of them had a knife or a wrench or some weapon.

"What we have here is one of us..." Maynard stepped back. "Well, what we have here used to be one of us. Now, he's an OFFICER! Why, yes, sir. Sorry to bother you, sir. Can I clean your airplane, sir?" Maynard flipped an exaggerated salute, and the crowd cheered.

"Ain't that so?" He looked at the name tag, "Cotton."

Maynard smiled and looked around at his crowd again. The sailors cheered, and many of them smacked weapons against their legs, bulkheads, or the deck. I gulped and looked at Raoul.

"Ain't that so?" Maynard slowly lowered his butcher knife until it rested against Cotton's nose. I thought he was going to kill him right there. I thought he was going to kill all of us right there.

"Maynard, DC Central wants to know if we have Zebra set." A sailor wearing headphones yelled over the crowd. "They want to know if all is normal."

Tell them Zebra is set at the time," Maynard looked at the clock on the galley wall, "2346 and all is normal."

"Roger." The sailor spoke into his handset.

"What's the point of this?" Reese stepped forward and held up his hands. "What do we get out of messing with these guys? That's not going to get us anywhere."

"Yeah, Reese is right," said a skinny sailor wearing a cook's cap. "What we need is to list our grievances. List them and give them to the captain."

"The captain don't give a rat's ass about our grievances!" Maynard whipped around and stuck the butcher knife in the scrawny sailor's face.

"He took the ship to general quarters," said Cotton. "He has to report that, doesn't he? It isn't a training drill."

Maynard cocked his head and scowled at Cotton. More importantly, he lowered the knife.

Cotton smiled. "A list of grievances could be part of that report."

Maynard frowned and leaned forward until he was nose-to-nose with Cotton. "We could tell the captain we have three hostages. Three of his precious pilots and we are going to kill them unless he makes things better for us."

"You could," said Cotton.

I watched a trickle of sweat make its way down Cotton's face, amazed at my friend's calm. I was about to crap in my pants.

"But if you do that, you commit felony kidnapping, and you communicate a threat." Cotton stepped back from Maynard and shook his head. "No need to do that. We are here at our own volition. Remember, we came to you."

Maynard frowned and stepped back. He looked unsure.

"I'd like to know how many of us there are," said Reese. "I mean, how many Blacks are there on Connie, and what are our ranks? I'm a second-class petty officer, and I'm the senior Black man in the whole V1 division."

"I think you are on to something," said Cotton. "Instead of telling the captain to make things better, let's find out what jobs Black men perform and their ranks." Cotton smiled at Maynard again, then scanned the crowd. Everyone looked at him. "What is our disciplinary rate compared to everybody else? What is our advancement rate compared to everybody else?" He emphasized the word *our*. "Reese, why don't you and I sit down with some of the others and come up with a list of the data we would like to see. The things you just mentioned and any other facts that would help."

"Sure." Reese looked relieved, and I felt the tension leave the room. Reese and Cotton grabbed two chairs and sat at a galley table. "Weenie, why don't you and Raoul get a list of grievances. You know, real things that have happened to this crew."

I nodded to Cotton. "Great idea." I was still nervous but felt better now that sure death was not upon us. I motioned to Raoul, and we took seats at a galley table. We were soon crowded by sailors, all with a story to tell.

"This is bullshit! This is fucking bullshit!"

I looked up to see Maynard standing on a table. He waved the butcher knife as he screamed.

"Don't you see, this is how they always manipulate us. We sit here like children, telling our stories, and nobody gives a shit! The problem isn't a list. The problem is NOBODY GIVES A SHIT!" He jumped off the table, stomped to Cotton, and raised the knife. Reese stepped in front of Cotton as Maynard swung the blade. It hit Reese's right arm, and he screamed as blood spurted all over his shirt. Maynard raised the knife again, and Reese reached toward him with his left arm. Maynard hit it too. A mob of sailors grabbed Maynard, and Raoul and I ran to where Reese lay. Cotton was already beside him. He looked at the sailor with the headphones, "Tell DC Central we need a medical team!" I could see the panic in his eyes. "Tell them NOW; we need them NOW!"

"Give me your belt." Raoul reached toward a sailor who whipped off his nylon belt, and Raoul wrapped it around Reese's right arm. The butcher knife had nearly severed the arm midway between the wrist and the elbow. By the time he tightened it, another belt appeared, and Raoul pulled it on Reese's left arm. It, too, was only held together by skin.

"Put his legs up; he is going into shock." I reached for a chair, but it was too high. A sailor scrambled to the floor, and we placed Reese's feet on his back. The sight of blood and the violence shocked all of us, and many of the mob cracked open the various hatches and disappeared. Nobody wanted to be part of this mess. I looked around, and Maynard was gone too.

Within minutes, the medical team appeared. They pushed Cotton, Raoul, and me aside, then transported Reese to the infirmary.

Cotton, Raoul, and I gave statements to the captain in charge of the marine detachment since he was the security head. We also had a long talk with the ship's executive officer and others. Cotton made an impassioned plea to take the lists we had developed and create a ship-wide document to seek truth and discover Black life's reality on Constellation. I think we would have been successful if it hadn't been for Maynard. His violent action became the center of all that had happened, and the legitimate reasons for the unrest faded. When we returned to port, security escorted Maynard to the brig in shackles, and the captain punished another twelve Black sailors at mast.

Two weeks after we returned from sea, I journeyed over to Balboa's naval hospital and checked in. I wasn't a patient this time; I was kind of a mentor, I guess. The navy had a program whereby wounded officers visited wounded enlisted men. It was a kind-hearted idea to connect those who were hurt, and I think it was also a way to allow officers like me to grow. The skipper asked me if I would participate in the program, and I told him I would. Besides, the sailor I wanted to visit was Petty Officer Reese.

He had stubs where his arms should have been. The angry, pink ends were the first thing I saw when I walked into his room.

I couldn't take my eyes off them. I had never seen an amputated limb, except in the movies and on television. Even then, the wounds were bound in gauze and bandages. I think gauze and bandages make it easier because they hide the point of loss and the reality that the loss entails. They hide the moment where a person's life changed forever.

When I pushed open the door to his room, Reese's eyes were closed, and he didn't stir, so I thought he was asleep. I stole a quick peek at the stubs, then found myself staring because I wanted to see an amputated limb. I wasn't fascinated or anything, but I always wondered what lay hidden under the bandages. I stared at the stubs, as a selfish feeling of gratitude swept me, gratitude that they weren't hanging off me. I shook my head as I exhaled, and then glanced up.

Reese was staring at me.

I drew a quick breath and blinked, but our eyes met in that instant, and I saw anger. I think it was anger at what had happened to him, but it was more than that. It was anger at what lay ahead, and anger that I so rudely invaded his privacy. But, layered in those angry eyes, I also saw fear and envy, and I suspected it was fear of living in a two-handed world with no arms, and envy for those of us who had them.

My face grew hot, and I stepped closer to apologize. I knew I was wrong to gape at Reese's wounds; for not first looking into his eyes. I mean, that's what you are supposed to do. When you meet someone, you are supposed to look them in the eyes; to make a connection and get permission. That is the way it is supposed to work. You don't just grab a guy's hand and shake it. You don't just bum rush a girl and put your arms on her shoulders, no matter how much you might want. So, the rule is you look into their eyes first.

"Hey, Reese." I grinned and felt like an idiot.

He straightened a bit, and his eyes softened, or maybe just lost their intensity due to fatigue.

"Hello, sir."

I scooted a chair close to him, but not too close and sat. There was another bed in the room, but it was empty, and the curtain meant to separate the two was bunched, giving a spacious air. I was surprised at how much I didn't like that much space. What I wanted was the rush of nurses and intrusion of others so it wouldn't be so…so intimate. I didn't want to be alone with him. I wanted to whisper and to apologize for the lack of privacy. That way, I would be forgiven for not staying exceptionally long and not saying anything magnificent and comforting. I had volunteered for this assignment, at the skipper's urging, but I wasn't sure what good I could do. I had seen the metal hooks that lay on a table across the room. I had no idea how to help him with those.

"How are they treating you?" As soon as I said those words, I knew how shallow they must sound to him. They were movie and television words, told by actors who knew each other better than I knew Reese, but who followed the script because that is what they were supposed to do. I smiled again but felt it hang lamely off my lips.

Reese frowned, and my smile sagged even more. He took a deep breath and shrugged, and that made the stubs jiggle, which made me look at them again. I gulped and wished I were better prepared. I wished I were wiser and that I had the power to bless and encourage. I wished I could say something profound and comforting. But, mostly, I wished I weren't there.

I had visited people in the hospital before; Jimmy Wilson, when he had his appendix removed, and Cotton, of course. But Jimmy and Cotton were on the way to recovery when I visited them, with no lousy memory other than their lime Jell-O's taste. I guess visiting my cousin, Grady Owen, was the worst. I saw him at Barnes Hospital in Springfield when I was eleven, and he was nine, and they found he had polio. I didn't fully understand what was happening to him, and I don't think he did either.

I suspected that Reese also had more to cure than the loss of his arms. There is the physical loss, for sure, and it is enormous, but there is also the loss of being full, of being complete. And there was probably a memory of some sort where he had looked at a disabled man and had said to himself, "Whew, what a poor bastard." And now that poor bastard was him. Reese was a little like me, I suppose. I had gotten shot in Hawaii by a sick man. I hadn't gotten my wounds from actual combat. Reese hadn't got hurt in combat either. He did not have the glory of his nation's enemy in his story.

"The docs say you will be using those things in a few days." I mustered up the courage to talk with him and nodded toward the hooks on the table. "Have you tried them yet?"

Reese looked at me for a long, uncomfortable moment, and in the space of that, I remembered Grandpa Two Bear's description of his battlefield friend, Kevin Stone, the loser of both legs at Guadalcanal. Grandpa told me, "I visited Kevin in the hospital, and when he looked at me, I could see he was past the shock of what lay in front of him; he was past the initial horror of it. Kevin was in the trough of miserable melancholy; a place where his mind wanted to wallow in the worst thoughts of what lay ahead. His mind wanted to wallow there so it wouldn't be surprised at how terrible things were going to be in his new world without legs."

"I tried them, sir." Reese lay back, deeper into the bed. He took a weary breath, and I saw his chest rise and fall. He flicked his eyes to me and gave me the look enlisted men give to junior officers. It was the thing in his eyes that said, I will listen to you because you are an officer, and I must. It was a look that I had learned to rise to and to challenge with my authority and wisdom. But now, as he lay before me, I didn't feel like I had much of either. Despite that, I had now been with Reese long enough to see him beyond his wounds. His afro was tight against his head where he had lain on it, but puffy where he had not, giving him a comical look which I found to be very bizarre, given the circumstances. He had that same washed-out, depleted look that all hospital patients have, the result of too many pokes and prods and lights flicked on in the middle of the night and the endless questioning from well-meant people who feel they must do their job despite what it does to you. I forced myself to rise to the occasion.

"There was a man in the town where I grew up. Mister Delmus was his name." I shifted in my chair, and it squeaked beneath me. "He had a missing arm and used one of those hooks." I felt a surge of gratitude that Mister Delmus had been in my life, lived in my town, and now gave me this segue. "He didn't seem to be bothered by it much."

Reese looked at me and sighed, but I couldn't read much into it, so I continued.

"He owned a hardware store," I didn't know what to say and looked at Reese for a gauge. "I dated his daughter once." I looked at him again and let my eyes fall to the floor to rest. I shook my head and glanced back at him. He stared at the wall.

We sat in silence for some moments, and I saw his eyebrows bunch as he looked out the window. I hoped they were gathering good thoughts but knew they probably weren't. After a while, Reese's eyes struggled with rapid blinks, and he rubbed them with his shoulders. He turned his head toward me, and I saw the wet prisms of his sorrow in the dark irises.

"Back on our last deployment, my twin girls sent me a photo every couple of weeks. I think my wife put them up to it."

Reese's eyes flickered again, and tears dropped off the lashes and made dark spots on his green, hospital gown. He smiled briefly, and then his face darkened as he stared at the wall over my shoulder.

"They used one of those instant cameras. The ones that spit out the photo right away. You know that camera?" His eyes found mine.

"I sure do."

Reese turned his head to the side again, toward the refuge of the window. There wasn't anything to see but a concrete wall, but I think it gave him something to look at besides me. I think we were both grateful for it.

"I used to get on them because the garbage can in the kitchen was always full." Reese's voice thickened, and I saw him look down at his sheets. His stubs quivered, and I think he wanted to clutch the sheets. It's what I would have done.

"None of them would take out the plastic bag and refill it."

He swallowed, and I heard his breath, and he swallowed again.

"I used to say, what are you going to do when I have to leave? Who is going to change the garbage bag then?" Reese blinked his eyes to fight the tears.

"On our last deployment, the one you were on, they sent me the first photo about a month into the cruise. We had just pulled into Singapore. It was of the garbage bag with just a little trash in the bottom."

Reese turned toward me and shook his head, "Better get home quick, Dad, was written on the margin."

I looked at the floor.

"They sent me one every month, and each time there was more and more garbage in the bag. 'Dad, you better get home' was hand-written on the margins."

Tears spilled down Reese's cheeks, and I rose to grab some tissue for him. But he rubbed his stubs against his face, and I stopped and squeaked back into the plastic chair.

"The last photo I got, the one just before we got to Hawaii on the way home, was of a full garbage can. There was trash falling out the top and all over the floor." Reese leaned his head back into his pillow as the tears streamed down his face.

"Dad, get home... NOW!"

I fought tears and used the tissue I had grabbed for Reese on my own eyes. I was grateful Reese was so embroiled in his grief that he wasn't looking at me. He sobbed and furiously wiped at his face with his shoulders.

"Dad, get home NOW!"

His head drooped forward, and he cried openly.

I looked at the floor and wished I weren't there, and Reese grew quiet again. I heard him wipe at his eyes with his stubs, and I didn't know what to do or how to help him. I felt like a fool, sitting there. Reese deserved better than me.

I chanced to look at him. He turned his head toward me and blinked through the tears. "How am I going to take out the garbage now, Mister Kleegan?"

I shook my head, looked back at the floor, and felt ashamed. My thinking had been how I wasn't prepared to deal with this. Reese was thinking about how in the hell he was going to go on. And his real question wasn't about the garbage can. He would learn to use the hooks and take care of any problem like that. What he wanted to know was if he was still a man. He wanted to see if he was still capable of being a husband and father. And, maybe most of all, he wanted to know how in hell he could explain what happened to him. How would he explain that a fellow Black sailor had done this to him while protecting a Black officer?

I stood and walked to his bed. I put my hand on his shoulder, careful to stay away from the raw end, and kneeled so we could look at each other. "Petty Officer Reese, what happened to you was terrible." I took a breath and shrugged. "No getting over that. But what we do know is that you have a wife and daughters, and they will need you to come back to them. That is what we do know."

Reese turned to me and frowned slightly. He coughed and looked like he wanted me to continue.

I felt better. I felt a surety that I was going to help Reese. "You will go back home, Reese. You will learn to use the devices on the table. You will use them to take out the garbage, drive a car, and hold your wife and children. You will be a man in every sense of the word."

Reese looked at me and frowned. I saw the disbelief in his eyes.

"You can do it, Reese. You aren't the first in this situation. I desperately tried to think of something to help him. There was a quote from Hemingway's *A Farewell to Arms* that played in my mind if I could only remember it.

Reese frowned but held me in his eyes, waiting.

"I, there is a quote from a book I read by Hemingway. It's about how the world breaks us. But...I. I can't remember it."

Reese swallowed and nodded, and I felt terrible that I couldn't help him, that Hemingway couldn't help him. He swallowed again and appeared deep in thought.

"Go home to your family, Reese. Everything will be all right. I promise." I stood to go.

"Are you married, sir?"

I stopped and faced Reese. "No."

"So, you don't have kids, then?"

"No."

"Do you know what it's like to change a diaper?"

I stared at him, completely lost.

"Do you know the feeling of fatherhood that sweeps over you and warms your heart when you are changing your little girl's diaper?"

I stared at him, now fixed on his face. I wanted to turn my eyes, but I couldn't take mine off his. I didn't deserve to. Reese was telling me something from the core, from his essence of being a father. I returned his stare with all the grace I could.

"Mister Kleegan, can you remember the feel of your dad's hand on your face?"

I nodded.

"Did it smell like tobacco Mister Kleegan? Or, maybe, Old Spice, or motor oil? Was his hand warm, Mister Kleegan?" Reese's voice was soft and ragged, and his red eyes were set on me. "And, did he say, 'Good boy, you're a good boy' when he touched your face Mister Kleegan?"

I looked at him and wiped my eyes with the back of my hand.

"Good boy," whispered Reese. He took a breath and stared once more at the wall. "I...I am the one that bakes the cake. You know, their birthday cakes." He turned back to me. "When I'm home, I bake their birthday cakes. They were born in April, so I bake a sheet cake and cut it into pieces that I shape into a rabbit's head. Rabbits are for the spring, you know. And I put white coconut on it like fur, and I put candy eyes, and..." Reese stopped, and his soft eyes hardened. He looked at me like I was an interloper to something sacred and something I did not deserve to hear. I stood and backed away.

"How would you know what faces me? How would you know what I feel, what it's going to be like to be a husband, and a father without any hands?"

I was surprised by his response to my outreach.

"I'm sorry, Reese. I didn't mean to insinuate everything will be easy."

"Mister Kleegan, I can't take out the garbage, I can't bake the cake. Mister Kleegan, I can't feel their faces when I touch them. If they even let me touch them with those things!" He glared at the hooks on the table, then looked at me. "Mister Kleegan, I can't even wipe my ass. How am I going to be a man?"

"I...I." I didn't know what to say or how to respond. I just looked at him, and he looked at me, then turned his head to the window. I stayed there a moment longer, then I left.

I walked to my car in a daze. I couldn't have been less helpful to Reese if I had tried. I started to drive back to Miramar but headed toward the bay and the 32nd Street Naval Station. I found the chapel and the library inside, and a young sailor helped me find *A Farewell to Arms*. I sat in a soft chair and thumbed through it; then I found what I was looking for. It was the quote I tried to remember for Reese. I held the book up for better light and read, "The world breaks everyone, and afterward many are strong at the broken places. But those that will not break it kills. It kills the very good and the very gentle and the very brave impartially. If you are none of these, you can be sure it will kill you too, but there will be no special hurry."

The sailor photocopied the quote for me, and I took it back to Balboa Naval Hospital. I put it in an envelope addressed to Petty Officer Reese and gave it to the nurse.

September is a beautiful month in Missouri, so I took leave and went home. Mom met me at the airport in Springfield. She was alone since Dad and Grandpa Two Bears had to do the milking, and Molly was not yet home from college. She was a freshman at Southwest Missouri State and would not be in until tomorrow morning. Mom and I chatted about the farm and Militia Springs until the conveyer brought my bag, then we hopped into the Fairlane.

"I'll drive," said Mom.

I smiled and settled into the seat. Time alone with my mom is a treat, and as I grow older, I realize I had taken her for granted most of my life. I am not sure I ever even missed her until I went into the navy. Now, my time with Mom is rare, and I do miss her. But rare as it is, my moments alone with Mom are always warm and pleasant, and despite our often months apart, there is no awkwardness. It is a bit like wearing Sunday shoes, comfortable yet still grand and special. Time with Mom is something I now savor and regard as precious.

It was chilly, early evening, and the moon was just coming up, translucent and flickering through the trees as it waited for the dark. I held up my left hand and saw it was a waning moon and soon to be heavy with its ever-dimming light and squinted to see it more clearly. I smiled at my old friend in the sky and felt a welcome melancholy. I used to look at the moon almost every night when I was young. I used to ponder it and use its fixation to let my mind wander to other mysteries. I glanced at Mom and smiled again. It is the kind of thinking that she always inspires in me, and it makes me want to talk about what is on my mind.

"Mom, did we have a dog when I was young? A beagle, maybe?"

I glanced at her face, lit in the green-glow reflection of the dashboard light. I could see her eyes bunch in a frown, but I couldn't read them.

"Yes," she looked at me, then back to the road. "We did have a puppy when you were six. Why do you ask?"

"I keep having a dream about this beagle. I think it gets run over by our car."

Mom frowned again but looked straight ahead. Her nod was barely perceptible. "Dad backed over it in the driveway." She glanced at me, "How do you remember that?"

"Wow." I shook my head. "Was his name Toby?"

"Yes!" Her eyes flicked to me and then back to the road. "But you were so young! I can't believe you remember."

"I can't either. And it's not like I am reviving old dreams or memories. I don't recall Toby. At least, not until recently and, I don't know why."

"It was a sad thing, an unfortunate thing, and maybe you blocked it out."

"Were we going to church or something? In the dream, it seems like we are all dressed up."

"We were going to the hospital to see Grandma Catherine."

"And the dog got out?"

Mom glanced at me and, once again, frowned. "The pup was Grandma's dog. Tobias had gotten it for her. But Grandma took a turn for the worse, and we had to put her in the hospital. We were going to visit, and the dog got out and under the wheels."

I nodded, and we drove in silence for a few miles. But I was troubled. The dream made me troubled.

"Mom, did I do something bad? In the dream, I am kneeling next to the dog, then, Dad shoves me away and holds the dog and tells him everything will be okay. I have this terrible feeling that I did something wrong." I shifted my weight so I could look directly at Mom. She gripped the wheel.

"Mom?"

She took a deep breath and sighed.

"Mom?"

"Grandma loved chocolate, and she had these little Hershey Kisses in a bowl on her dresser. You loved chocolate too, and whenever you went into her room, you always grabbed a piece. And you always tried to sneak chocolate to the pup."

Mom glanced at me, then reached out and touched my leg. "You were always a sweet and kind boy, Weenie. You wanted the pup to have something you liked. You wanted the pup to have a taste of chocolate too." She patted my leg. "Grandma would catch you and scold you and tell you never to give chocolate to a dog."

"But why do I have this feeling of doing something wrong? I think that is why I have this nightmare."

"On the day we went to visit Grandma, you played with the pup, and Dad told you to put it in his kennel. The cage was in Grandma and Grandpa's room, but I think you went in and grabbed a piece of chocolate instead. So, when we all went out, the pup managed to get out too."

"So, I am the reason it got killed?"

"You were a baby, Weenie. Nobody held you responsible." Mom put her hand back on my leg and softly patted it again.

"Wow," I whispered. "Wow."

"So, as Toby lay there, you took out your piece of chocolate and tried to give it to him. Your dad pushed you aside."

"Was he angry with me?"

"Yes, for a little while, he was."

"Why do you think I did that? Try to give Toby chocolate?"

"I think you wanted him to be able to taste it once in his life. I think you knew the pup was going away. Even at six years old, you knew something was happening, and you wanted the dog to experience a treasure."

I nodded and put my hand over my mom's. It was still on my leg, and I could feel her warmth.

"Then Toby died?"

"The dog was suffering pretty badly. Dad put his hands over its mouth and nose and held them there. The pup died then."

I shook my head, then took a deep breath.

"Jesus."

I stared into the darkness of my side window and put my head so close that I couldn't see my reflection. I didn't want to see me.

"You okay, honey?"

It was my turn to be silent. Even though I had been just a kid, it bothered me that I was responsible for a puppy getting killed. And, worse, I was responsible for having my dad, who just might be the kindest man on the planet, kill a puppy with his bare hands. Mom respected my silence, and we rode like that for some miles.

But why a dream about all that now?

I turned toward Mom. "I feel that somehow, this connects to Jane. I mean, I saw Jane, and Grandma, and...Toby, in heaven. You remember I told you about it. After I was shot and almost died. I remember Grandma called him Toby. She said, 'Toby's here.'" I shook my head. "I had forgotten that."

I stared out the window some more, hoping for answers in the dark but knowing they weren't there. I turned to Mom. "You do believe that I went to heaven, don't you?"

Mom cleared her throat and glanced at me. "I believe there is such a thing as a near-death experience. I certainly believe that you had one."

"Sometimes, I'm not sure if it happened after all. Maybe I dreamed it."

"I don't think so. I think something happened to you."

"But why me? A lot of people have a close call with death, and they don't see anything."

"Maybe you were supposed to see something. Maybe you were supposed to understand something for your future. Weenie, the mystery of our lives often lies on the other side of the page. In our book of life, we only get to read the part we are living. We never see the life we might have lived if we made other choices. But we want to. Those unread pages haunt us, and that makes us dissatisfied and jealous of other people's pages. We don't want to live life in our book. We want to live the best pages in everyone else's books too."

"But Mom, my trip to heaven didn't show me any of that. I just saw Grandma and Jane and the dog."

"Weenie, I think God was trying to show you his greatest gift."

"You mean, Jesus?" I was confused.

Mom smiled. "Jesus is a gift to Christians, for sure. Jesus is a great gift, but he is not God's greatest."

I frowned as Mom glanced at me. She smiled again. "Weenie, God's greatest gift to us, to all of us, regardless of what we believe or whom we believe in, is that we get to determine our heaven."

"What?"

"Heaven is a reward, son. A reward for living a good and caring life and the goodness of those lives is what drives heaven. It is a reward for living your own pages and making the most of them and not begrudging others' pages. I think your dream tells you that Toby holds no grudge, and Jane and Grandma wait for you. But the dream also suggests that their books may be incomplete."

"This is not what we were taught in Sunday School. Did you read this somewhere?"

"The Bible can be read in different ways, Weenie. You know that. We have discussed it often. Some read it literally, word for word." Mom glanced at me. "I read it that way, but I also see other things in those words."

"For instance?"

"For instance, in John, we read that those saved by God will have new bodies without sin. In Isaiah and Philippians, we read that those saved will build their own houses in heaven and plant and eat from their own vineyards. To me, that doesn't just mean the literal construction of a house or vineyard; it means we are given the ultimate gift of building our own heaven. As long as our heaven doesn't hurt anyone else's."

"Wow! You have a wild imagination, Mom!"

Mom chuckled as she glanced at me. "My greatest strength is my firm conviction that God, above all, is fair and practical. Now, I know that a white woman growing up and living in America might seem an imperfect messenger for that thought. A child in a slum in India might disagree. I know people live desolate and even hideous lives here on earth, but I believe the fairness is supplied in heaven. For me, anything less would not make any sense, and this world we live in, this life that we all have, has to make sense, or why would God go to the trouble in the first place?"

"Mom, I think the folks out at the monastery might not agree with you on this." I laughed, and so did Mom.

"Maybe not," she grinned. "I know that to many, heaven is hard to get into, and I think we have been taught that to convince us to treat each other better or follow the rules. But there is a hurt to that way of thinking too. The Jehovah's Witnesses believe only 144,000 faithful followers will get to heaven, for instance. That excludes virtually the entire human race. But exclusion is a human trait, Weenie, not God's. We often make things special by preventing others from getting something. I don't think that is the way God works. I think the least of God is better than the best of us. I don't think God knows or uses the words just and only."

Mom looked at me again, and we both looked at the road in front of us. There was no traffic, and it was clear.

"Weenie, I think God was trying to tell you that heaven will be what you want it to be. I think that is what Grandma was trying to tell you. When she said,' dogs can eat chocolate here,' that is what she was saying to you."

"So, I can make my own heaven?"

"As long as your heaven doesn't hurt somebody else."

"So, a Muslim who thinks he will get seventy-two virgins will have to find seventy-two virgins that think the same?" I laughed and glanced at Mom.

"Exactly!"

"But, why me, Mom? Why is God telling me this? What am I supposed to do with that information?"

"Maybe you are already doing it?"

"What?"

Mom glanced at me. "Weenie, you have a melancholy about you. You have always been a sensitive boy, but I detected a lingering sadness since you came home from the war. After you were shot and, in the hospital, and came home on leave last summer."

I looked out the front and watched the twin beams cut through the darkness of the night forest. There were no other lights in front of or behind us. We were alone in our little, dashboard-lit world, and I found myself desperately wanting to talk to Mom, but doubtful if it would do any good. How do you talk about the inability to get over someone you barely even knew, somebody who died before you even got to know her? How do you explain the word, hollow? Because it's a lot more than just empty. That said, I was not surprised that Mom had detected my melancholy. She was my mom, and despite the time we now spent apart, me gone to the navy, she still knew me. My sadness wasn't such a secret, though. Charles and even Raoul had noticed my quietness. Charles just kept away when he detected my mood and waited until I got over it. But Raoul was more direct with his hand on my shoulder, and his tender and well-meant, "What the fuck is wrong with you?"

I turned to look at Mom and took a deep breath.

"I can't get Jane out of my mind."

Mom nodded and looked ahead at the road. "There is a particular feeling of loss when people die young."

"Her dying young is part of it. But I don't know. I mean, I am sad she is going to miss so much. I know I am selfish about this because we are going to miss so much, Jane, and me together."

"Whom the gods' love dies young."

"What? What did you say?" I frowned and looked at Mom's face.

"Herodotus said that. I think the sentiment is that when we earn our way to heaven, we are taken there."

I nodded and returned my eyes to the dark road.

"You must read Wilder's *The Bridge at San Luis Rey* sometime."

"Will it help?"

"Maybe. It talks about that notion."

"But Mom, just because a person earns their ticket into heaven doesn't mean they aren't going to miss all the wonderful things of life. I think that is what bothers me about Jane. She is going to miss so much."

"And so, it is up to you, and others, when you see Jane again, to give her those rich experiences. She will have you to be part of her heaven, and you will be part of hers. So, the message is to live your life as wonderfully and carefully as you can so you can bring that experience to her and others there."

"Does that mean to be celibate, not to have any other relationships?"

"Of course not. It is heaven we are talking about, not the priesthood. Toby's message to you is to taste the chocolate, Weenie, experience a full and wonderful life while you are here. I think that is why you have the dream."

I looked at her a moment, then stared out the front windscreen.

"Maybe."

We drove for a while longer, and I thought of Reese. "There is this enlisted sailor that I visited in the naval hospital in San Diego."

"Oh?"

"The navy has a program whereby wounded officers visit wounded enlisted men, so they asked me to participate."

I stared at the road. "In some ways, I think the benefit is as much for us as it is for them. I mean, what can a young officer like me, someone without much life's experience, do or say to comfort anybody?"

"And you had an opportunity to visit with such a person?"

"Yes, and I didn't help him much. He is older and has a family, and he lost his arms."

"Oh, that's terrible."

"Yes, it is. It is terrible. His name is Reese, and he is alive, but in danger of, like you say, of missing out on many of the wonderful things in life."

"Perhaps you can help him adjust to his situation Weenie. Maybe you can help him find some goodness in his pages, a reason to stay interested in his book. God can't provide all the perspective by Himself." She looked across the car at me. "Maybe you are supposed to help him with that."

I nodded, and we drove on. It was fully dark, and we still had the road to ourselves. The moon, now low on the horizon, was our silent wingman.

"But, again, why me, Mom? What am I supposed to do with this…insight?"

"Maybe God is telling you that you need to move on, son. You need to move on and live your life and experience all the things it can offer you to share that with Jane when you get to heaven. Maybe the dream about Toby is telling you something like that."

"In what way?"

"Have you had a date since Jane died, or since you last saw her?"

"I have hung out with girls."

"But have you attempted a relationship? Have you tried to move on from Jane?"

"No. Well, there was this girl I met on the airplane, but it didn't work out."

"That's it?"

"Not unless you consider swapping spit behind the officer's club a relationship."

"Jesus, Weenie." Mom shook her head, but I could see a smile.

Mom and I made it home around seven and were surprised to see Dad and Grandpa Two Bears had somehow managed to cook supper without burning the house down. That said, how hard can it be to open cans of Campbell's soup?

CHASING MAMA'S HEART

I found the Thornton Wilder book Mom mentioned, *The Bridge at San Luis Rey*. It was in our upstairs library where she keeps all our books. I always pack a bottle of bourbon when I go home because Mom and Dad never drink, and we didn't even have beer in the fridge. Grandpa Two Bears doesn't drink either, which I think is a shame as I would like to get drunk with him and hear his stories. So, I poured myself a glass and began to read about Wilder's Bridge. I didn't get too far because while drinking enhances listening to music and watching sports and other fun experiences, it doesn't go well with reading. That was unfortunate because reading is the thing I like to do best. I did manage a few chapters before I lost the ability to focus on Wilder's incredible writing, but I pledged to finish it before going back to San Diego.

I also dreamed about Toby again. It was the worst dream yet. He was all mashed and bloody and crying as he dragged his broken hind legs.

"Dogs can eat chocolate here." Grandma Catherine's kind eyes sought me.

I reached for Toby, to give him a bite of Hershey's Kiss so that he could have one taste.

"I could have been a contender," he said.

I woke up.

Blinking away the memory of the dog, I took a shower and rummaged through the closet, where I found a pair of khaki slacks and a sweater. I felt just like Beaver Cleaver, but Missouri is chilly in early fall, and comfort trumps fears of nerdism.

I helped Dad and Grandpa Two Bears with the milking; then, we went into the breakfast kitchen.

I have heard that a tunnel is a reward for having a Harley Davidson motorcycle, the rich sound of the engine reverberating back into you. I don't know if that is so, but I know that the Midwest kitchen is the reward for being an American with the rich smells and memories reverberating back into you. Celery and onions simmered in butter, and the pungent, woodsy aroma of Mom's sage-flavored sausage whispered fond memories to me. The morning smell was just act one in the play, and I knew it would be followed by animated talks with a wooden spoon in Mom's hand, and the sound of Grandpa Two Bears trying to find some kind of ballgame.

Mom had made pancakes for breakfast, so I helped myself to a stack with Aunt Jemima syrup. Mom warmed the bottle in a pan of boiled water, so it flowed out as hot as the cakes they smothered. I was just about to put a wedge of goodness into my mouth when Molly walked in! We didn't expect her until noon, so everybody jumped up to hug her. I was last in line, and she grabbed me hard. I grinned and held her.

"Good to see you, kid."

Molly didn't answer. She just hugged me back.

I squeezed her tight, then let her go and returned to my pancakes. Molly fixed herself a plate and sat next to me but didn't eat. We talked a bit about how things were going in school as she traced her fork in the syrup.

Mom had a zillion things to do, and a couple of them got Dad headed to the grocery store. Molly drifted away to her room, so that gave me time to sit on the porch with Grandpa Two Bears. I expected him to take out his tobacco pouch and roll a cigarette, but he fished a pack of Lucky Strikes from his shirt pocket and plucked one out.

"What happened to the fixings bag?"

"My hands shake too much these days. I have to smoke the factory-made kind."

"What's the shaking? Anything wrong?"

"Not sure. It came on a couple of months ago. Old age, I suspect. It's not all bad, though; it helps me get the last few drops off when I pee." He winked, and I lit the cigarette with a kitchen match.

I settled onto the familiar comfort of the porch. It was a concrete slab covered with an overhang and supported by a white column at each end. The height of the porch allowed for comfortable sitting with your feet on the grass below.

"Your friend, Cotton, reminds me of a gent I met in the war."

We had talked about the navy and what I was doing the night before and during breakfast. I spoke about Cotton quite a bit. Of course, everybody knew about Cotton and me getting shot down.

"Oh, how so?"

"Well, he was Black for one." Grandpa Two Bears chuckled and took another puff.

"The Corps was segregated back then." Grandpa Two Bears grunted softly and squinted at our alfalfa field across the way. It was long past the growing season, and Dad's third cutting had reduced the area to brown stubble. He would plow it up again in the spring and then plant the seeds. Grandpa glanced at his cigarette, and I watched him roll it around in his fingers.

"But, once the fighting starts, well, things change. I met this gent on Guadalcanal. It was in '42, and the Japanese had pretty much had their way up 'til then. But your navy flyboys at the Coral Sea kept them out of Australia, and at Midway, you broke their momentum. Guadalcanal was our turn to move forward. Blacks were ammo haulers for the most part, but the fighting got so fierce that everybody started shooting."

"Were you an officer then?"

Grandpa Two Bears glanced at me and smiled. "No, I was a lance corporal. Didn't become an officer until Iwo Jima in '45."

He smiled again. "Guadalcanal was strange. We waded ashore without a shot fired. Then, after we started to take over the island, we found all kinds of Japs. When we started making our push, they hit us with fierce counter fire. They were trying to knock us back into the sea, I suppose."

Grandpa grunted and nodded to himself. "One particularly ferocious day, we got pinned down by mortar fire, and I jumped into a small crater and started to dig a fighting position. I heard a guy jump in beside me and hell; he was digging faster than I was. I looked over and saw he was a colored kid." Grandpa looked across the field again. "I didn't think much of it. A guy that digs that fast is your best friend, no matter what color he is. Anyway, we dug a good hole and waited for the charge from the Japs. We huddled back-to-back since we weren't sure where they would come from. Well, they never came, so the sergeant formed us up, and we started looking for them. The colored kid was in some unit in the back, but we kept him with us. His name was Conrad Washington, and he was from Selma, Alabama."

"I didn't know Blacks fought at Guadalcanal," I said. "I never saw any in the newsreels."

"Well, they were there. Blacks fought throughout the Pacific while I was there. As I said, they were mostly used to haul stuff until the fighting started. Anyway, I introduced myself and offered him one of my Camels. They came in our ration packs. I preferred

Luckies, but all I had was the little four-pack of Camels, so I gave him one and lit it for him. "Grandpa Two Bears shook his head and smiled. "Conrad took a deep drag, smiled at me, and said, 'Tastes a little better when a white man lights it.' I knew right then I liked him."

Grandpa and I laughed, and he took another puff.

"Conrad stayed with us when we moved forward, and he and I got to be friends. There's a lot of guys that didn't like colored folks for some reason, and they scowled at him and muttered mean things, but he was a good marine, so after a bit, they at least pretended to let him join in. I mean, it became workable for Conrad, I guess. You know," Grandpa looked at me, "Nobody is a racist if he can lie, Weenie."

I frowned and nodded, telling myself to think about that some more later.

"Anyway, as we sent patrols over the island, looking for the Japanese, they sniped at us with good effect. The man out in front, walking point, had a good chance of getting hit. We called walking point, Chasing Mama's Heart."

"Chasing Mama's Heart?"

"Yes. You see, if you got wounded, you received a Purple Heart medal. If you got killed, they sent the medal home to your mama. So, we called walking point Chasing Mama's Heart."

"Jesus!"

"You have to find humor wherever you can, Weenie. Anyway, every morning after breakfast, the platoon sergeant would form us up and give assignments. He would tell us who was walking point. He rotated it, so we all got an even chance. He would say, 'Hey Jones'...or... 'Hey, Roberts ... you're chasing today.' That meant you're walking point."

Grandpa Two Bears stopped, and he swallowed so loud, I looked at him. He took a final drag, stubbed the cigarette out on the concrete behind his legs, and straightened up. "Then, one day, I woke up and knew I was going to get it." Grandpa took a slow, deep breath and looked at me. "I knew that I was going to die that day." He shook his head and looked back at the field. A crow flew by, and I didn't feel the usual resentment I had for them. I just watched as it winged its way to aggravate somebody else and disappeared behind the trees.

"It is hard to describe what that feels like." Grandpa's voice was low, and it broke a little. He glanced at me, and he knew I heard the creak. I hoped it made him feel better about what he was going to say.

"To know you are going to die... not...that you might die. Hell, we all felt like we might die. But I mean the feeling that I was going to die." Grandpa looked at me. "Do you understand the difference?"

I shook my head and gripped the edges of the porch.

"Weenie, I'm telling you this because I think it is important for you to know. I think you can understand, and there are things young officers like you need to understand."

I nodded and wondered what had gotten Grandpa so emotional.

"I remember being gripped by a...an emptiness. It wasn't about feeling pain or anything like that. It was my sorrow about all the things I wasn't going to be able to do. I wouldn't see Catherine again, or your dad. He was just a little guy then. I wouldn't see Windell and Fredrick again. I wouldn't get to farm this land anymore." He looked across the field and didn't talk for a long time. I didn't speak either. It was time to listen. Finally, Grandpa took a breath and stabbed the ground with his toe.

"I didn't eat breakfast that day, and I'm always a good eater. I just sat on my gear and waited for the sergeant, and, soon enough, he yelled at us to gather 'round. I stood with the rest, and he looked at me and..." Grandpa paused and swallowed. "Sarge looked at me and said, 'Kleegan.' But then, Conrad stepped forward and said, 'Sarge, I want to volunteer to chase today. I'm feeling lucky.' The sergeant frowned and stepped back. I don't think he knew what to do for a second. He was one of the men who treated Conrad fair. He was a teacher from California by trade and a good and smart man. But he shrugged and said, 'Okay, you got it. You're chasing for Kleegan.'

Everybody started putting on their gear, and Conrad looked at me, and underneath the brim of his helmet, I saw his eyes, and I could see that he knew what I was thinking. He knew what tormented me." Grandpa looked at his hands, and I could see them tremble. Not shake, but tremble just a little, and I watched his hands as he reached for his cigarette pack again.

"He knew."

"How?" I whispered.

Grandpa just shook his head. "He just knew."

I looked back at the grass between my feet, and I heard Grandpa swallow hard again, and, other than that, it was quiet on the porch. I felt cold and shivered and put my hands together in my lap. But, despite the chill, I felt privileged that I was sitting here, hearing this.

Grandpa put the cigarette between his lips, and I scratched the match against the porch. The flame leaped out of the head, and a whiff of sulfur touched my nose. Grandpa took a drag and slowly let the smoke into the breeze, and I smiled at the smell.

"Conrad looked at me, and I knew that he knew about my premonition. And he knew that I knew, and at that instant, I could have taken my place back. I could have said, I should have said, 'Nope, Sarge, it's my turn.' But I didn't." Grandpa turned to me. "I know you agonize some over whether or not you should have tried to save your skipper back when you were shot down in Vietnam. Maybe that led you to do what you did with the man at the kid's school. Maybe that desire to prove yourself is what drove you to go after an armed man with nothing but a cup of coffee." Grandpa slowly nodded and took another drag. "You know?"

I nodded.

"About ten, somewhere around mid-morning, Conrad got shot. I was back in the middle, but I heard the sound. We all hugged the ground and looked around, waiting for more shots. But they didn't come, and Sarge got us back up, and we came upon Conrad. He had been hit in the throat and most likely died before he hit the ground. I remember looking at him, feeling sad. No, it was more than sad." Grandpa frowned and shook his head.

"It was… it was." Grandpa's lips quivered, and his Lucky shook a little. He took it out of his mouth and spat a bit of tobacco. "I felt rotten. I felt guilty that he had been killed in my place." Grandpa looked at me, "But, Weenie, the strongest feeling I had was none of that. The strongest feeling that I had was gratitude that it wasn't me." Grandpa Two Bears looked at me again and shook his head. "It was the first time I ever admitted to myself that I didn't want to die. Strange, before that morning, I hadn't thought of dying before. With the death and destruction, the killing and getting killed around me, I had never really thought about it."

I heard the screen door open and turned to see Molly. I started to stand, but she held out her hand. "Let Grandpa finish his story."

Grandpa Two Bears turned toward the door. "Hi, sweetie."

"Finish your story." Molly gave me the strangest look; then the door closed behind her.

Grandpa took another drag on his Lucky. I felt such a closeness to him and wanted to put my arm on his shoulder. But something held me back. Maybe I didn't want to acknowledge his vulnerability.

Maybe, just because I needed to hug him, it didn't mean he needed a hug from me. He looked at me, "The difference between people who have been in combat, real combat, and those who have not is the knowledge that after the glory, and after the talk and proclamations, and cheers, the only real emotion you have is just gratitude for being alive." We sat there on the porch for a while, as Grandpa smoked his cigarette.

"I went to look up Conrad's folks after I got home. I never told Grandma or anyone else about this, but she understood my need to do it. So, I took the Greyhound to Selma and found a woman who said Conrad's folks were all gone from their home place. She said they had gone except for his dad, who was a beggar down around the courthouse, so I went down there." Grandpa glanced at me, "You can see that Pettus Bridge people talk about right from the courthouse." He paused and took a couple of drags. "Anyway, I found this guy and asked him if he was Conrad Washington's father, and he said, 'Who's asking?' I said that I was in the war with him and that he was the bravest man I ever met. I said he was a stand-up marine. The man looked at me and nodded. I didn't know what I expected him to do, cry, maybe? But he just looked at me and said. 'Well, do you have any change'?"

Grandpa took a final drag and stubbed out his second cigarette. "I have been sad and disappointed in my life," he said. "But I think that was the saddest, and most disappointed that I have ever been."

That night I had the dream again, but this time it was different. This time I was walking down a country road, and I could smell lilac, so it must have been spring, and I could see two figures in the road ahead of me. I couldn't make them out, but then one was a person, and the other was a dog, and they were walking with their backs to me. And I could see it was Jane and Toby and I tried to run to catch them. They were walking slow, but no matter how much I tried, I couldn't run any faster. I couldn't catch them.

"Wait!" I heard myself say.

"Wait!"

That dream stayed in my head the next day, and during the drive with Mom and Dad to the airport, I couldn't shake it. We hugged and said our goodbyes, but when I got to the ticket counter, I decided to do something I should have done a long time ago.

A KISS GOODBYE

For those who have only journeyed to the Florida panhandle in the summertime, I suppose the notion of coldness might be hard to grasp. But, let me assure you by September, the clouds can come, and the wind can chill, and memories of walking on warm sands can be hard to recover. But sometimes cold and gray are what is needed and appropriate, and so it was when I landed in Pensacola.

I rented a car and drove through the rain to the naval station, where I checked into the Bachelors' Officers Quarters for the night. I changed into my dress blues, and as I looked in the mirror, I felt a lifetime away from the man who had come to this city so many months ago. I was a young and unsure man who wanted to be a navy flier. Now, as I looked at my wings and my ribbons from combat over Vietnam, I wished I could somehow do it over but with a knowledge of what had happened. I wished I could do it over again so I could savor it and save Jane. But, of course, none of that was possible. You may be able to make your own heaven according to Mom, but you can't make your own earth. I clamped my white cover on my head and walked to the administration building.

Pearl stood behind the desk just like she had the first time I saw her. Like she had on that day when I asked her about Jane and when she and Mrs. Howard had conspired to give me Jane's telephone number. Pearl started to cry as soon as she saw me, and I walked behind the counter and hugged her close.

"We thought you would come to the funeral."

"I didn't know she was dead."

"Who told you?"

I hugged her and sighed into her hair. "Jesus told me."

We stood like that, hugging, for some time, and I marveled at the steps that had put me on this path. It seems that during my life, unrelated events, many of them disappointments at the time, somehow coalesced and focused on the right direction, a better way. And now, dreams of a puppy from the past, Arlo's caution to savor,

Petty Officer Reese's lost arms, Mom's insight on heaven, all whispered to me. They whispered, and they said, "Taste the chocolate, Weenie." They whispered and said, "Live the life that blesses you; read your book's pages, Weenie."

Pearl and I stood there, hugging, and it was surprisingly comfortable. Although we didn't really know each other, our history was only the day she helped me get a date with Jane, our shared loss bound us together, at least in those sad moments. We didn't speak for the longest time, but when we did pull apart and wipe the wet from our eyes and the drips from our noses, Pearl told me what I had to know. She told me where I could find Jane.

I bought flowers at a grocery store and clutched them as I stepped out of my car. It had stopped raining, but the wind still held its chill, so I ducked my head against it and began to walk the rows.

That is why I didn't see Jane's grave until I was beside it.

To be honest, a part of me had hoped I wouldn't find it, that the story wasn't right, and Pearl had been mistaken. An irrational hope, I suppose, but one I carried until the stone stood before me. I glanced at it, then quickly shut my eyes, only to have them open and searching.

Why do we search for the pain we don't want to see?

My eyes found that pain in the etching of her name, which caused me to put my hand on the marble to steady my weak knees. There is a drama to my life, partly manufactured for sure, but also very genuine. And finding the resting place of this girl that I loved, this girl that I refused to let go, this beautiful young woman I had unabashedly positioned on a pedestal was something I had no way to prepare for. During my flight to Pensacola, I had thought of what emotions I might have, what actions I might take upon the discovery of Jane and seeing her name on the stone. And as the engines had droned, I had thought of an old book, my mother directed me to read for a dollar. It was when I was young and extremely interested in dollars and the treats they bought. The book was written in 1843 and entitled *The Various Writings of Cornelius Matthews*, and I had struggled with its ancient style and blurry test. But I had found a tale, "The Druggist's Wife," which held my attention due to its poignancy and sad charm. It was the story of a woman who searched for her husband's gravestone and how she wandered across the countryside looking for him. Rebuffed at every turn, she refused to give up until one day she found his resting spot. I remembered reading how a passerby later discovered her, fallen to her knees but still clutching the stone like a shrine. She was dead, but she was together with her love at last. I thought of the story as I, too, fell to my knees and clutched the stone of the one I loved, the one I had been searching for. I put my head against the cold wetness and felt the etching of her name against my cheek and sobbed in ragged bursts. The wet of the grass seeped into my trousers' knees and seemed to join the tears that streamed from my face.

"Jane."

"Oh, Jane."

I hunched there and hoped the rain would rinse away my misery but, glad that it didn't.

I was glad because misery was the fee for my broken heart, and my broken heart meant something remarkable had happened in my life. I thanked Jane for visiting me in heaven and that she needn't wait to enjoy the things paradise brings. I told her that when I came to heaven, I would have some great stories to share and wanted to hear what magical things she had done. I asked her to say "Hi" to Grandma and Toby.

My agony's rawness gradually lessened into an ache, and I knew it would always be with me. The hurt would be with me as a touch of melancholy, a cloud in my memory both soft and sad but a good thing because it would be a reminder of Jane and what I needed to do with my life. For our lives. For, unlike Cornelius's old woman, I didn't die there, and no one had to come and find my lifeless body, clutching my shrine. No, I eventually stood and whispered, "Goodbye, my love." I touched the stone a last time and resolved myself to get on with my life. I looked at my Jane's grave and slowly nodded as I recalled the Thornton Wilder quote in *The Bridge at San Luis Rey*. "There is a land of the living, and a land of the dead and the bridge between is love." I now wove that quote into my heart because I had been to the land of the dead when I had visited heaven. I had been there, and I had seen Jane there, and I knew at the right time it was a good place, and like Wilder, I believed that if someone were loved, they would always be in both lands. They would be in both places and never be forgotten, and I knew I would never forget Jane. Jane would always be with me.

I let the tears fall again as I said a final goodbye to my angel. And before I turned to go, I reached into my jacket and pulled out a shiny, aluminum-wrapped Hershey's Kiss and placed it on her stone.

Then, I drove back to the base.

THE JESUS EFFECT

October and the first part of November flew by, and the squadron flew a lot. We were headed back to Vietnam in January, so we had to work hard to compensate for the upcoming Thanksgiving and Christmas holidays. Despite the fact I had been home in September, I was ready to see the family for Thanksgiving.

Mom and Dad always made a big deal about holidays. A farm can be isolated and dreary, or it can be the center of vibrant and loving family traditions, and Mom, Dad, and Grandpa Two Bears had always focused on making our holidays something special to anticipate. The food was central, but I guess just being together was the best, especially now that we spend so much time apart. A huge event was the showing of family movies of Thanksgivings' past. Dad was an amateur camera buff and had a Bell and Howell Zoomatic with the eight-millimeter film. He had filmed all our holidays as far back as when I was five or six. That is how I recognized Grandma Catherine in my trip to heaven. After the holiday dinner and after the dishes, we would gather in the living room to watch the films.

Another tradition was to each say something we were thankful for during grace. I anticipated such practices and eagerly waited for this year's version. I think if farmers don't make a big deal about holidays, they might just wind up eating a lot and talking about pilgrims to the cows and chickens.

I often wondered what it would be like to celebrate a holiday in town, surrounded by other revelers and the sights and sounds of a full community. Militia Springs wasn't very big, but it was big enough to drive around and hear "Have a good Thanksgiving", see the pumpkins and gourds on the doorsteps, smile at the wreaths and early Christmas lights, and enjoy the kitschy stuff people put in their yards.

Mom and Dad picked me up at the airport, and we drove by the house Molly shared with two other college girls and got her. It was like the old days, except Molly was even more quiet than usual. I had been quiet in college, too, though. We hugged Grandpa Two Bears when we got home and fell into our comfortable family routine.

The next day we all stayed in the kitchen to "visit" while Mom and Molly did most of the cooking. Dad, Grandpa Two Bears, and I were enlisted to peel potatoes and make fresh coffee, but that was about it. Around noon, Mom announced that we should get dressed for dinner, so we did. We didn't get formal, but we had a tradition of wearing church clothes for the Thanksgiving meal.

I know that movies about Thanksgiving always have the fake family gather formally around the table while the father brings in a platter with a turkey the size of a collie on it. Well, we Kleegans fixed our plates in the kitchen to avoid the logistical nightmare of handling such a table-side carving then settled at the dining room table.

We bowed our heads, and Mom started the ritual of giving thanks. She was thankful for the health of her family. Dad, ever practical, was grateful for the milk prices, which sounded rather good the way he said it. Grandpa Two Bears was thankful for rain and America, despite her problems of late. It was Molly's turn, but she didn't say anything, so I picked up the cue and was thankful for Militia Springs and all of us.

The meal was delicious, and the company of my family made me warm and happy. I was genuinely thankful. It was like it always was and what I had anticipated. After we polished off most of the turkey and trimmings, we cleared the table. We watched Dad's home movies for an hour or so, and I sat next to Molly like always. I tried to poke some fun at her, but she wasn't having any of it. After the last film flopped in the disc, we took our own paths to digestion.

I was in the library upstairs when Molly ducked her head inside the door and said, "Talk?"

"Sure." I grinned and followed her downstairs and out the door. We walked across the yard toward the alfalfa field, and when we got to its edge, Molly stopped and leaned on the fence. I took her lead and did the same, and we gazed across the field of stubble and the remains of last year's hay crop.

"Nice day," I said.

"I'm pregnant."

The word "what" is used for two reasons. One is because you didn't quite hear what was said. The second reason is you heard what was said but didn't believe it.

I heard Molly fine.

"What?" I faced my sister.

"What?"

Molly didn't look at me, but I could see her shoulders shake, and I heard her start to cry. I reached for her and pulled her close and put my cheek against her head. She put her arms around my waist and cried. She cried steadily and softly like she had been waiting for a long time. My mind whirled with what to do, how to take care of my little sister.

What would Dad and Mom think?

I remembered how people treated girls that got pregnant.

Who is the father?

Molly stayed in my arms a moment longer, then she pushed back and wiped her eyes with the back of her hands.

"How far along are you?"

She sniffed and coughed. "Not long. A couple of months, I guess."

"Who is the father?"

"Caleb."

"Caleb! Caleb Hodges? I thought all of that Sons of Galilee stuff was over."

"It was over." Molly glared for a second, but her eyes lost their power. She looked away. "But then, he was here. I would see him in town. And he was so nice. At least at first."

"What does he say? About this?"

"He doesn't know."

"Oh." I looked back at the field. Then I turned to face Molly. "Is there a reason he doesn't know?"

Molly shrugged, and I took her hand, pulling her to me. I didn't know what to say. I didn't know what to do. I blurted, "Do you love him?" It seemed like a good question.

Molly grimaced and frowned. I thought it was an odd reaction, so I pulled her closer. "Did he do something to you?" Molly buried her head into my chest and hugged me tightly. I unzipped my jacket and put it around her while she cried.

"Do your friends know about this?"

"I don't have any friends anymore."

I let her cry into my jacket as I rubbed her back.

"Does anyone else know?"

"Just you." She whispered through her cry-rough throat.

I nodded and hugged her some more. My chin touched her head, and I smelled shampoo, and I thought of her when she was a baby, and Mom would give her a bath in the kitchen sink. Her hair smelled like shampoo then, too. I took a deep breath and let it fall out of me as I struggled to think.

"What do you want to do?"

Molly shook her head against my arms and kept crying, and I just held her. I heard the screen door slam and looked toward the house. Grandpa Two Bears stepped off the porch and smiled, but I put my hand up. He nodded and went back inside.

"Look, sis, this is probably the most important decision you will ever make. So, you need to think about it. I know you have. I know you have." I held her even closer. Toby flickered in my mind.

Toby? Why?

"You know, women are the only ones who can know what it is like to be in this situation. As hard as it is for you now, it is in some ways, so…so sacred. To give birth, to be someone's mother. So sacred. But…" I loosened my arms and held Molly away so I could see her face. "But that doesn't mean you have to carry the baby if you don't think it is right."

"I have had some time to think." Molly wiped her eyes and looked at me. "Thinking about this is about all I've done."

I nodded and softly gripped her shoulders.

"I." She looked across the field and wiped her eyes again. "I'm not sure I am ready to be a mother. Christ, I just turned twenty."

I swallowed and gripped her shoulders again.

"But that isn't all. It's not just about to have the baby or not." Molly pulled away and looked at me. "It's also about what people will think. If I abort the baby, nobody knows. Well, except you. So, it's not just a question of being ready to be a mother. There is also the question of facing the consequences, the shame, of being an unmarried mother."

I reached for Molly again, and as I held her, I marveled at how little I had thought about this, about abortion. Like Vietnam, it was a background to my college days, but I took little interest in it. It seemed that the folks who got excited about abortion were mostly angry women who threw it on the pile of other rights they felt denied. It felt like more of an anti-man thing to me. I did have a teacher in my sophomore American History class who took a period to discuss abortion in our country. She described it as something unwanted but positively not immoral, illegal, or impractical, given the drain that birth had on a woman's body. According to her, it wasn't until after the Civil War that abortion became demonized, and by the 1930s, it was mostly illegal with California and New York as the exceptions. Her talk was interesting, as it was all new to me, but I didn't think much about it since it wouldn't be on any test. And now, here was my baby sister, faced with maybe the most important decision she would ever make, and I hadn't given it a second thought. I felt a moment of shallowness, of shame, and shook my head. Vietnam, racial injustice, abortion, I hadn't given any of it much thought. What the hell had I occupied my mind with?

"At college, there is a program." I turned Molly to look at me. "I know about it because of my roommate's sister. It is managed through the student center, and they will fly you to New York to have the procedure done."

I couldn't even say the word abortion.

"It's legal in New York. I can work it for you. I will pay for it. If that's what you want."

Molly separated from me and walked to the field. She looked across it for a long time and, feeling the setting sun's chill, I moved to her. She shivered under my arms and then turned her face up to me, just like she had when I used to read her a story. Fresh tears rolled down her cheeks, "What will Dad think about me?"

"What?" I frowned.

"Mom will understand. Mom always understands, and I think she will agree with whatever I decide. Grandfather Two Bears will hate the idea of abortion but, he's my grandfather. He will find a way to love me, anyway."

I held Molly and nodded. "I know."

"But Dad...it will break Dad's heart." Molly looked up at me, tears running free. "You know it will."

"Dad will understand," I said but without much conviction.

"What if Dad thinks I am a whore?"

"Oh, Molly, don't say that."

Molly sobbed again, and I held her, filled with a new awareness that made me shake my head. Despite the things I had done, graduated from college, flew in combat, and survived a shoot down, survived being shot three times by a mad man, none of the decisions I had made thus far in my life was as delicate and essential as the one Molly now faced. I shook my head as I realized how quickly I had grown from someone too timid to offer an opinion on anything to a know-it-all willing to advise others on things I knew nothing about. I had spoken with authority about fatherhood to Reese, only to have him put me in my place with his rightful questioning. And now, I was advising my sister on abortion--a topic

I readily admitted I had thought little about. I had succumbed to what Grandpa Two Bears had described as the Jesus Effect. The Jesus Effect is when a person believes he can cause good by walking among the flock and saying profound things. I remember my Aviation Officer Candidate School class officer, Lieutenant Combs. He had walked into our sweaty and confused lives in his khaki uniform and had settled us down on the shiny tile deck and had looked at us and made us understand that leading our men was the primary reason for our existence. I remember his words as crisply today as when his bright eyes held ours, and he said,

"Can you put your men's interests in front of your own? Can you put their service of your airplane above your flight time in it?"

Whether intended or not, Lieutenant Combs had had a Jesus Effect on me, and from that instance onward, I wanted to be like him. And, here I was, being Jesus.

What in God's name did I know about a woman's thoughts? What did I know about something so life-altering as having an abortion? Molly had undoubtedly agonized over this and had done it alone. And here I was offering a solution out of my hip pocket. And why? Was it because I didn't want the shame of having my sister pregnant? That is…not married, and pregnant. I remembered Beverly Harden. Beverly was in my sophomore class in high school and went out parking with Shelby Weeks in his new Camaro. Beverly started to show by Thanksgiving and started her new year walking the halls with this bump on her stomach, and Shelby acted like he didn't know her. Everybody avoided her. I avoided her. She went from being my chatty girl pal, the locker next to mine, to nobody, and her dad moved them over to Gainesville. I don't know what happened to her.

"Look," I hugged Molly and put my face into her hair. "Look, we can figure this out. Just the two of us. No need to tell anybody until you want to. Just believe that whatever you want to do is going to be the right thing, Molly. I do know that."

"But what will they think? What will Dad think?"

"I tell you what. I will tee up the conversation, not referring to you, of course, but we can get a feel for this. We might be surprised; after all, this is the twentieth century."

"What if they all think that a girl who gets pregnant is a whore?"

"They won't think that."

As if on cue, Grandpa Two Bears swung the front door open. "Time for dessert."

Molly and I held hands as we walked to the porch, then she ran upstairs to fix her face. I don't think she wanted anyone to know she had been crying. I sat down, and Dad filled the pot, and the aroma of Maxwell House soon filled the room. Molly came down and sat next to me. "Good to the last drop," I smiled.

Mom made real whipped cream instead of the stuff you squirt out of a can, and we plopped creamy globs of it onto our pie. I was too full to eat, but I dug in anyway.

The pumpkin and apple pies were delicious, as always, and the table conversation spirited and fun. Molly didn't say much, so I covered for her with more than my usual tales of what I had been doing. Finally, I decided to test the waters.

"Hey, one of my buddies has a friend who is pregnant and is looking for advice. What should I tell him?" I glanced around the table, nonchalant, I hoped.

"Did your buddy get this friend pregnant?" Mom glanced at me and took a sip of coffee. "What is his motivation? It makes a difference."

"She shouldn't have gotten pregnant in the first place," Dad mumbled through his mouthful of pie.

I made a point not to look at Molly.

"He didn't get her pregnant. I think he just wants to help."

"I think she can get an abortion if she lives in California. Can't she?" Mom took another sip and nodded. "I think that is right."

"Yeah, I guess so." I reached for my fork again and glanced at Molly. She stared at her plate.

"So, why did he ask you for advice?" Mom frowned at me, and I was sorry that I had started the line of questioning.

"He wondered what my midwestern values had to say."

"And what do they say?" asked Grandpa Two Bears.

"I told him I hadn't thought much about the topic. I said I would ask my family at Thanksgiving dinner." I grinned and took a sip of coffee.

"I thought abortion would have been a centerpiece for discussion while you were in college," said Mom. "It is a pretty polarizing topic."

I shrugged, careful not to exaggerate my nonchalance. "Not for me, I guess."

"What about you, Molly?" Mom across the table. "What do your friends say?"

"Most of them say a woman should have a right to choose."

Grandpa Two Bears cleared his throat and made the click-suck sound. He made it whenever he was irritated.

"Choose what, exactly?"

"Choose to have an abortion, or not." Molly shrugged and dropped her spoon into her coffee cup. "The woman who carries the fetus should choose. After all, you always say, 'The guy with the shovel should decide if the hole is deep enough.'"

"But, what about the rights of the father and of the baby itself?" Dad frowned and poured himself another cup.

"I think the rights of the father have been about all that counts up until now," said Molly. "Hence, the new desire for women to have a definitive decision."

"And the baby?" Grandpa Two Bears leaned back in his chair and stared at Molly. "Who speaks for it?"

"We were taught conflicting things about this." I interrupted to take the pressure from Molly.

"Some are conflicted, I guess," grunted Grandpa. "I'm not. For me, life begins at conception."

"So, you don't believe in abortion at all?" Molly frowned.

Well, here we go.

"I think we all have the right to defend ourselves, so if carrying the baby would cause harm, then I think abortion is an option. And, by that, I mean emotional as well as physical harm."

"So, rape would or could be a reason for an abortion?" asked Molly.

I frowned. What did rape have to do with it?

"It could be. I think we all remember that your Grandma Catherine got raped by her father. So, we Kleegans have some personal history with this. Making a woman carry a child under certain circumstances could cause her immeasurable harm."

"But Grandma Catherine and you didn't abort her baby." Molly looked at him. "If you could have? If it had been your decision alone, would you have aborted it?"

"No."

Molly looked at Grandpa, and I saw her eyes searching him. Then, they dropped to the table. I don't know if she found what she was looking for.

We sat for a while in quiet thoughts, and coffee cups scraping saucers and our chair squeaks were the only sounds. I toyed with my spoon as I remembered that Grandma Catherine had carried her child, a little girl who died the day she was born. Grandma had been raped by her own father, but Grandpa Two Bears had married her anyway with the intent of accepting the child as his own. Grandma and Grandpa Two Bears named the girl Molly, the namesake of my sister, and buried her under a giant oak; thereafter called the Molly Tree. Grandma Catherine's mental decline began after that child's birth, although she did have my father a couple of years later. This was something we never talked about.

"I get the notion of a woman's privacy. According to the Saint Louis Post Dispatch, that is what this is all about," said Grandpa Two Bears. He looked around the table. "I think I get the reason women want to be able to control their bodies. God knows they have not been able to do that since humans have been on earth." He leaned back in his chair and nodded. "But there is something about robbing a child of the chance to live its life that bothers me, and, you see, I think that is the other side of the choice coin. For me, it isn't about whether a woman can choose; it is about whether or not a child can live out its life."

"Do you see a two-month-old fetus as a child?" I wanted to engage Grandpa to keep Molly from doing it.

Mom interrupted before Grandpa Two Bears could respond. "I don't think he gets to answer that question. The other side of the choice coin, as you put it, is who gets to decide what that two-months-old fetus is. I think the mother is the one to choose. The only one to decide."

"And what about when the pregnancy is at three months?" Grandpa Two Bears leaned forward. "We can hear a heartbeat then. As a society, we accept the absence of a heartbeat to indicate human death, but we won't accept the presence of it to indicate human life. Can a woman choose to terminate the pregnancy at five, six, seven months? Hell, if there is no basis for keeping the child alive, why not kill it after its born if it doesn't suit you?"

"Tobias! Shame on you!" Mom's eyes flashed as she glared at Grandpa Two Bears. "You know that if a woman chooses to terminate a late pregnancy, she must have one hell of a good reason to do it. Can you imagine the anguish she would go through? I mean, she has felt it kick. She would have felt HER BABY kick. To choose to terminate at that point would be devastating, but it would and should be her choice."

"Do you hear what you are saying?" Grandpa Two Bears stared hard at Mom, and I felt terrible. I wished I hadn't brought the subject up.

"You say society should give women the right to terminate life. And this is a life we are talking about and not some piece of fetal tissue. You are saying that even if we agree the baby is alive, a woman gets to terminate it?"

"I think women have made life and death decisions for a long time." Mom's eyes flashed as she leaned forward toward Grandpa Two Bears. She wasn't giving an inch. "Believe me, if a mother is going to end a baby's life, a baby that has kicked her and blessed her, it will be for a hell of a good reason!"

"I saw a thousand seventeen-year-old babies killed in the war," said Grandpa Two Bears. His voice shook. "They were children that we…all of us, put a man's uniform on, and took off to war. Every one of them had a life in front of him and then was unable to live it. Every one of them had a life, a precious life, that will never be known. So, I cannot abide by any decision that erases that opportunity for anyone."

He and Mom glared at each other, then both looked down.

Why did you bring this up? At Thanksgiving, no less.

We got quiet, and I again regretted raising the issue of abortion. Especially since I knew it was more than an academic topic for our family. Was it unfair for me to do that? We all have feelings, sometimes strong opinions, about things on which we don't have a whole perspective. I remember Mom talking about Mrs. Albertson, who said if she had a Mongoloid child, she would kill it. A few years later, Mrs. Albertson's daughter had twins and one of them had Down's Syndrome. Mrs. Albertson dotes on those girls, and, I think, especially on the challenged child. Mister Jonas, the Methodist preacher, used to rail against the sins of homosexuality. We all knew his son, Robbie, was queer. Robbie hung himself. Mister Jonas stopped preaching and moved to Springfield. Heck, people hate cats until the day they get a kitten.

"Well, maybe all of this can be avoided if the girls are just more careful." Dad picked up his coffee cup and took a sip.

"Was your mother not careful?" Molly looked at him, then swung her gaze to Grandpa Two Bears. "Wasn't Grandmother Catherine careful enough, Grandpa? When her father came for her when she was thirteen?"

"That's enough, Molly." Mom put her hand on Molly's arm.

"That's not what I meant," said Dad.

"Look," I interrupted. "I will just tell my buddy that he will have to talk this over with his girlfriend, and they will need to figure out what to do."

"You should have told him that in the first place," growled Grandpa.

"Dad, Mom told me you got a present for your birthday." I desperately needed to change the subject.

"That's right!" Dad's eyes brightened. He leaped out of his chair and strode across the dining room to the gun case. Taking a key from his pocket, he unlocked the door and brought out a shotgun. "It's a Remington 870, Mom got it for me for my birthday."

"You got it for you for your birthday," laughed Mom.

I was so glad the subject had changed!

"Well, anyway, you didn't mind." Dad laughed and carried the gun to the table. "Haven't shot it. Anybody up for testing it out tomorrow?"

"What's in season for hunting now?" I asked.

"Tin cans," laughed Dad.

"This model has been around since 1950," said Grandpa Two Bears. "Easier to load and handle than a Mossberg or a Smith and Wesson. It's a good choice, son." He nodded at Dad, who beamed. Dad only smiled when the subject was guns or cows, so this was a rare event.

"What's the bag limit on tin cans?" asked Molly. She didn't smile, but I was happy that she at least engaged in the conversation.

"As many as you can carry," said Grandpa.

TIME FOR THE CHRIST CHILD

I went back to San Diego but called Molly every week. I was unsure of what to do but certain that I should find a way to help. She was genuinely tormented by the decision to carry her baby or abort it. One day she would be upbeat, the next despondent.

I mostly listened during these conversations because my ruminations over the issue caused me to question the value of my advice. And, for that matter, I am not even sure what my advice would be. I know that on the days Molly decided to have the baby, she was the happiest. Maybe that was my biggest lesson about all this abortion stuff. Guys like me measure doctor business in levels of pain or danger. Abortion doesn't seem to offer much of either, so what's the big deal? Right? I mean stripping and having some guy scowl at your uterus would be bad, but is it any worse than have the flight doc stick his finger in your butt? So, I think that sometimes we believe women have abortions willy-nilly. My conversations with Molly changed all of that. Nothing willy-nilly about stabbing yourself in the heart!

Most troubling to me was the situation between Molly and Dad. They were alike in so many ways, chief among those was they were so introverted. I remember being in a barn for hours with Dad, and he wouldn't say anything except to the cows. Same with Molly. They were the kind of people who would disappear in a crowd of two! But just because they were both quiet and to themselves didn't mean that they understood each other. Or maybe they did but had no way to know it or show it?

The thing I hadn't understood until now, was how significant a role Dad played. Molly was so worried about what he would think. She agonized over the fear he would lose respect for her to the point that she lost sight of her most profound decision! I never imagined that a girl could get so hung up on what her dad thought, and that made me wonder and question how good of a dad I would be. I mean, I wasn't handling this situation very well, and I hadn't handled Reese very well either. I seem to suck when it comes to helping other people with big problems.

I told Molly I would be home for Christmas and help her if she wanted me to. She would be three months along by then...time to decide.

Dad and Mom picked me up at the airport, and Mom chattered away about Christmas plans as we drove. Dad was Dad, and the only sound that came from his driver's seat was when he put the turn signal on.

Click, click, click.

We got home in record time, and Dad and I found Grandpa Two Bears in the barn, bringing the cows in for milking. We had forty-two head, and they were fine cows, each averaging between five and six gallons per day. We set to the task of milking them, and it was a well-polished routine. It took around seven minutes to milk each cow, and we milked eight at a time, so the whole session took around ninety minutes. When the last cows were strapped to their milking machines, I left to find Molly.

She was in her room, listening to music, and didn't answer when I knocked. I gently pushed the door open and saw her sitting on her bed, looking out the window. She glanced up as I stepped in and immediately began to cry. I shut the door and quickly moved across the room as she stood. I hugged her.

"Hey, hey," I whispered. It's going to be okay. It's going to be okay."

"How is it going to be okay?"

"Because you are going to make a decision." I put my face into her hair. "An important decision, more important than any I will ever make in my life, but when you do, it will be the right decision. And we will all support you because we love you."

"Oh, Weenie." She sobbed.

"Shh."

"I'm going to ruin Christmas for everybody."

I frowned at her childish concern. "Christmas is about family. And family is about supporting each other."

Molly shook her head and sobbed, and I held her. Then she pushed away and sat back on her bed.

"Do you know what you are going to do?"

"No. Not yet."

God, she looks small.

"Is there anything I can help with?"

Molly looked at me and sighed, then buried her head into her pillow. I walked into the living room and saw Dad through the window. He was standing next to the tractor, so I grabbed my coat and pushed open the door.

"Join me?" Grandpa Two Bears sat on the porch, smiling up at me. He had on a jacket and held a pack of Luckies. He shook one out.

"A little later, Grandpa. I need to talk with Dad."

"I'll be here."

I grinned and turned back toward the barn. I crossed the yard and walked toward my father. I had no idea what I was going to say, but I knew I had to do something.

"Tractor not running?" I smiled at Dad as I stepped next to him.

He glanced at me and motioned toward his toolbox. "9/16s ratchet."

I looked through the box, found the head he wanted, and handed it to him.

Dad bent over the tractor engine and worked for a moment. "Spark plug wrench."

I found the spark plug wrench and handed it to him.

"Get up there and turn her over. Wait for me to say when."

I climbed up on the tractor and shivered as I sat on the ice-cold seat. "Will a diesel start when it's this cold?"

I could see Dad's shoulders jerk, and he grunted as he tightened something. He looked up, "Use the manifold heaters and turn her over."

I put the tractor in neutral, pushed the gas lever half-open, turned the key, and hit the manifold heater button. I held it in for about a minute, then depressed the clutch and hit the starter button. The engine coughed a couple of times then caught.

Dad looked up and smiled. "Good job."

I grinned, but as much at myself as to him. It amazed me how happy his praise made me.

We listened to the engine, then Dad gave me the cut sign, and I turned it off and hopped down.

Dad closed his toolbox, and I followed him into the dark barn. Milk, cows, bleach, hay, grain, and manure fused into a familiar scent that made me smile. It was the signature smell of a dairy barn, and it made me feel at home.

Dad put his toolbox on the shelf and turned toward me. "Something on your mind?"

I looked at him and nodded. "Something."

He looked at me, then frowned. "Let's take a walk."

Dad led the way, and we strolled around the barn toward the pond and the woods. I loved this walk, this part of our land. The hardwoods pointed their dark and empty branches skyward, but the dots of fir, pine, and cypress proudly stuck their green chests into the air to remind any observer that this forest was still very much alive. It was just quiet now, but alive.

Dad got us to the top of the pond bank, and we shuffled our feet in the dirt to turn, and side by side, we looked down upon the barn, fields, and farmhouse.

It was magnificent to me.

It made my chest tight because all I saw resulted from my family's hard work and determination. But more, it was part of me. I looked over the panorama of the blessing and knew that fixing the Molly situation was just as significant, more important than any of the stumps we pulled, fields we plowed, fences we built. But I also knew that this time, instead of handing Dad the wrench, it was my turn to fix the machine.

"Molly is pregnant."

I quickly glanced at Dad, fearful of his response. But so needful to know. A quick wish that I had not brought the situation up flickered. It flickered, then went out in a new wave of resolution.

Hand me the spark plug wrench, Dad.

I looked back down at the pastoral scene and waited for Dad. I heard him take a deep breath and then he sat down, so I joined him. He reached forward and picked up some dirt and rubbed it in his hand.

"Is she...is she, okay?"

"Yeah, Dad, she is okay. I mean, she is afraid like any young woman would be, but she is okay."

"And the father, any chance they will get married?"

"I don't think so, Dad."

"Do I know him?"

I felt Dad's eyes on me but didn't answer. He bent forward and picked up some more dirt.

"Caleb is the father."

"Caleb Hodges? From the Sons of Galilee?"

"Yes, sir."

"But...why?

"Dad, I think we know how. But I don't know why. I mean, I think Molly was lonely. I think she separated from her high school friends, and she was very lonely. I think Caleb was nice to her."

"Nice? Getting someone pregnant is a little more than nice!"

"Dad."

Why isn't she telling me this?"

"Why do you think, Dad?"

Dad glanced at me and frowned, then looked at his hands. He let the dirt fall through his fingers then slowly scooped up some more. And I realized that Dad might not know how to respond. After all, fathers and mothers don't have some automatic and extraordinary capability to know what to do or what to say.

We sat like that for a few minutes, then Dad pushed away from the ground and stood, and I stood with him. He wiped the dirt from his hands then brushed off the seat of his pants.

"Well, I better talk to her then."

"Dad." I looked at him, searching for what was in his eyes. They were hurt, and, yes, disappointed, but moisture in the corners softened their intensity.

Dad looked down the slope toward the house, then back up at me. He took a deep breath. "It'll be okay."

Dad walked down the pond's side, and as he strode across the barn lot, I watched him go. I figured he might need some time by himself. I just hoped to God that he could understand Molly. I hoped that he wasn't too disappointed with her. I knew he loved her; he would always love her. But sometimes love can't make the corner and gets hung up, and that is what I feared.

I stood at the top of the pond bank and questioned if I had done any good and knew my angst lay in the fact that I didn't know how Dad would handle the situation. I trusted him. If I didn't, I would not have broached the subject the way I did. I tried to imagine what I would do if the same thing happened to my daughter and me. But nothing came, and I shook my head. I walked down the pond bank then across the barnyard to see if Grandpa Two Bears was still sitting on the porch. I was not surprised that he was gone, so I went inside.

Mom and Grandpa were sitting at the kitchen table drinking coffee, and I could smell something wonderful in the crockpot on the counter.

"Come join us," smiled Mom.

"My butt got cold waiting for you on the porch," said Grandpa. He shivered and laughed then blew across the rim of his cup.

"Where are Dad and Molly?" I pulled a mug from the cupboard.

"I think they went for a walk." Mom frowned and looked at me. "Any idea why? Dad doesn't take walks."

I shrugged.

"You helped him start the tractor, didn't you?" Grandpa Two Bears' eyes caught mine. "Something about Molly come up?"

"No," I lied. But it was a good lie. "Maybe Dad wants to talk with her about Christmas presents."

"Ahh, that's probably it," said Grandpa.

I took my coffee up to my room and waited. Molly and Dad were gone for an hour or so, and when I saw them walking up the driveway, I smiled. They were holding hands.

Mom had a roast in the crockpot, the one she makes from the Betty Crocker cookbook. She uses a little horseradish to flavor the gravy, and Grandpa Two Bears always proclaims it as "darned good eatin'."

We took our places around the table, and after Mom said grace, we dug in with the intense energy of a family that shares but doesn't tarry. If you want that big old tater staring at you, you need to get it.

Molly sat next to me, and as she passed the cornbread, she smiled, edgy at the lips but calmed by absolute confidence in her eyes. I smiled back and knew that whatever she and Dad had discussed and agreed upon, or not, was most likely positive.

We gathered around the television that night and watched The Walton's and then Ironside. It was good to be home.

The next morning, I took a walk with Molly.

It was overcast and chilly, and there were enough flakes of snow scooting around to kindle my yearning for a white Christmas. I don't think I ever had one since it doesn't snow in Militia Springs until January, but thanks to television and Norman Rockwell, and maybe the poet, Robert Frost, and his snowy woods, I knew what to yearn for. So, I carried warm thoughts as Molly, and I bundled up and strolled down our graded gravel lane. I decided to let her speak first, but after a bit, and knowing Molly's penchant for quiet, I cleared my throat.

"I guess it went okay with Dad?"

Molly didn't answer right away, so I glanced at her, looking for a clue. Her cap covered her head, and I couldn't see her face.

I listened to the gravel crunch for a bit longer then glanced at her again. "How did your conversation with Dad go?"

Molly sighed, and we walked a bit further.

"Dad doesn't talk much," she finally said.

"I know, but the two of you had to have said something to each other."

"It was a lot like this," said Molly. "Dad came into my room and asked me to go for a walk with him, and we went down this very lane." Molly glanced around, then looked up at me. "We walked for a while, and I didn't know what to say, so I just kept walking. We got almost to the mailbox…"

"Down by the highway?"

"Yep. We got almost to the mailbox, and Dad turned to me and put his hand on my shoulder and said, 'I love you, Molly.' I started to cry, just like I am now." Molly's voice caught in a half chuckle, the sound when you try to make light of what you are crying about, but the reason for the crying wins. She wiped her eyes with the back of her coat sleeve.

"And he said, 'Whatever you may be going through, whatever you may be facing, just know that Mom and I are here with you.'"

Molly's tears came, and I took my sister into my arms and hugged her and smiled when I felt her arms go around me. We stood like that for a while, and then I stepped back.

"Good. That's good."

"I told him that I was pregnant. " Molly slipped back on the wet gravel. "I suspected that you had already done that, but I told him, and he just nodded. He didn't ask who the father was or any of that. He just nodded and hugged me, and after a while, he said, 'May I tell your mother?' I really started crying then, and he hugged me some more."

Molly wiped her eyes again, then shaded them with her hand as she looked up at me. "But you know, as bad as I felt about what was happening, I also felt good. Dad made me feel good, despite all of this."

I smiled and nodded.

"But I told him, No, I need to be the one to tell Mom. If she finds out from you, she will think I don't trust her."

I nodded again.

"So, last night after television, I told Mom. The rest of you had gone to bed, and she was cleaning up in the kitchen. I think she knew I wanted to talk with her about something. Moms are like that."

"And you told her?"

Molly nodded. "Yes, and after I told her, she hugged me and said, 'When you want to talk about what comes next, just let me know. '"

"I'm not surprised that Mom took it so well." I nodded.

"Oh, I imagine Dad told her," said Molly. "Just like you told him. I think sometimes we need to be warned about things so we can think about them a little. It doesn't take a long time, even for big things like this, but it does take a while to get over the shock. Besides, the last time you were here, you brought up abortion, and I think all of us have been thinking about it ever since."

"Well, I'm glad it's out in the open." I took Molly's hand and turned toward the house.

"Except for Grandpa Two Bears," she said.

"Yes, except for Grandpa Two Bears."

We walked back up the gravel path to the house and sat down to a lunch of leftover roast. I was anxious to see how Dad or Mom would tee up the conversation about Molly. Or maybe they wanted Molly to talk separately with Grandpa Two Bears. We had Christmas week to figure it out, and given the subject material, the timing for the discussion seemed especially crucial.

DOWN AT THE POOL HALL

That afternoon, Jimmy Wilson, Donnie Curry, and Paul Smart drove into our driveway. When I saw them, I remembered Mom mentioned she had seen Jimmy at the drug store and told him I was coming home.

Jimmy had been my friend since first grade. He was short, like me, and had limited athletic abilities like me. We shared many a bleacher seat and bag of popcorn in the guys-with-no-dates section of the stands and watched the heroes over the heads of those in front of us. Jimmy was smart and a loyal friend. He was an only child but said he avoided selfish and spoiled tendencies of that caste because of his inherently good nature, and the fact his dad paddled him when he acted up, which was about every ten minutes. Jimmy was the assistant pharmacist at the Militia Springs Drug Store.

Donnie Curry was a quiet, handsome, friendly guy who was a great athlete. He could also play the trumpet, much to my envy. Donnie was taller than me, about six feet, and, after college, worked at the school, which gave him time to hunt and fish, his true calling. He spent much of his time alone in the woods and seemed to like the animals' company more than humans'. Jimmy told me that is why Donnie liked me. At the time, I took it as a compliment. Donnie had a unique connection with the universe, all on his terms, that reminded me of Robert Redford in the new movie, Jerimiah Johnson.

Paul Smart was a slow, syrupy-talking ladies' man who was the Ozark version of Raoul Hungus. He was exceptional at disarming the girls with his charm and sincerity. And he was sincere in the moments he was charming. He was the kind of guy who had a girl in bed before she knew she was even on a date. Paul was slight but muscular and made his living building things. He could build a house from digging the foundation to shingling the roof. He was the only one of my friends that my dad made a point to talk with. Of course, Dad didn't know anything about Paul's libido.

The first time I described Jimmy, Donnie, and Paul to Cotton and Raoul, they asked, "Why on earth do they hang out with you?"

Paul drove, and Jimmy rode shotgun while Donnie and I sat in the back.

We had no sooner shut the doors when Jimmy turned around in his seat, "Want a beer?"

"Sure." I had usually declined to drink beer when we drove around in the old days, and Jimmy's question was as much a test as an offer for refreshment.

"I have Bud for the rich folks and Pabst Blue Ribbon. What kind do you like?"

"Do you have any hot milk?" I grinned and held out my hand.

"Good to see the navy hasn't turned you into a pussy." Jimmy grinned and handed me a Pabst.

We cracked open the cans and guzzled cold beer. Jimmy, Donnie, and Paul caught me up on what was going on in town, and Jimmy's retelling of the tale of how they blew up the Wiccan symbol on the square got me to laughing and wishing that I were closer to this place, and them.

We chatted on, and then Paul exclaimed, "You know, Kleegan, I was surprised when you joined the navy." He smiled at me in the rearview mirror.

"Yeah, it caught us all by surprise," said Jimmy.

"Total surprise," muttered Donnie.

"Why?"

"Because you aren't much of a risk-taker," said Jimmy. "The biggest risk you ever took was using a ballpoint pen to fill out the crossword puzzle."

Everybody laughed, and I did too.

"And what you did in Honolulu, you know, with the guy that shot you, was pretty much out of this world." Paul looked at me through the rearview mirror.

"We're proud of you, Weenie." Donnie looked across the seat at me. He had his usual, deadpan face, giving nothing to anyone. Donnie could have been staring at a deer he was about to bow shoot. But I could see a bit of something in his eyes, and it was the most emotion he had ever shown me.

I nodded and took a swig. God bless a can of beer when you need something to do with your face.

We drove around the town square a couple of times, holding our beer cans out of sight, of course. Then we moseyed out past the Sugar Shack to the Highway 5 intersection and turned right toward where old 5 crosses 14 and goes into Militia Springs. It was a loop that a fellow could make many times on a Friday or Saturday night. I decided to get some info on Caleb Hodges, so I took a swig and cleared my throat.

"You guys ever see that Caleb Hodges kid? I hear he is going out with my sister."

Jimmy turned in his seat and stared at me. I smiled at him, but he didn't smile back. I glanced at the rearview mirror to see Paul, but his eyes were straight ahead on the road.

What is all the drama about?

I looked at Donnie for a clue, but he was staring out his window. Jimmy twisted in his seat to look squarely at me. "She's with him, man. I mean, she is his girl. That's the word."

"She is?" I feigned surprise and took another swig.

"I keep expecting her to pick up an apron or an ax or something and join him in the commune." Paul's voice was strangely disapproving. I looked at him in the mirror, and he wasn't smiling.

"I don't know what is going on with them," said Jimmy. "I don't run in either of their circles. But I would be worried if I were you. The Galilee folk are nobody to mess with."

"I don't want to offend anyone," said Donnie. He rarely spoke, so I paid attention. "I don't know anything about Molly's relationship with him, but she needs to be careful. The clan men have a certain drive that could get out of control." Donnie looked at me and shrugged.

"Go ahead," I said.

"Well, last year Laura Buxton got pregnant by one of the men out there. The younger Dolan boy, I think. Anyway, the Sons of Galilee threatened to take her to court for the baby. Appears, they want rights over any baby sired by a clan male."

"What do you mean, rights? How can they do that?" I didn't want to appear too concerned.

Jimmy shrugged and took a swig of his beer. "Since this was a bit of local news, the Herald ran an article on parental rights, and according to what I read, the father of the child has equal rights to the kid just as if he were married to the mother. That means he has equal access to the child and decision-making for the child."

"What happened with Laura Buxton? Did she have to share the baby?"

Donnie raised his eyebrows and shrugged. "I talked with Jimmy Buxton, Laura's older brother. He said the clan lawyers made Laura out to be a slut since she wasn't married. They made the case she was unfit to be a mother."

I took another sip of beer.

"Yeah, doesn't make any sense, does it?" Jimmie shrugged. "Anyway, Laura's dad didn't want it to get into court, so he deeded sixty acres of forest he had over by Cowskin Creek to the clan. They backed off then."

"Jesus!" I began to grow more concerned.

"So..." Jimmy looked at me and frowned. "You did know about your sister and Caleb?"

"No," I lied. "But you can bet I'm going to ask Molly when I get back home."

"Well, you better be quick," said Paul. "I was riding around the square a couple of months ago, and I saw Molly get out of Caleb's truck and into that Fairlane your folks have. He sped off, but I tell you, she was crying, and it looked like her face was swollen."

"What!" I leaned forward toward Paul.

"Yeah, looked like he might have slugged her. I went looking for his car, you know because she's your sister and all. Anyway, by the time I got back to the square, Molly was gone."

I swallowed and leaned back into my seat.

"Be careful of the Sons of Galilee," said Jimmy. "They're trouble."

"How about if you guys take me home? I need to talk with Molly."

"Sure," said Paul. "It's beginning to rain anyway."

I looked at his eyes in the rearview mirror.

He frowned at me. "Hey, let us know if she is, you know, doing okay."

"Sure. I'll do that, Paul."

The guys dropped me off, and I hurried to Molly's room, knocked on the door, and when she answered, I walked in.

Molly smiled and leaned over to turn down her music. She was listening to records on a turntable she inherited from me when I went into the navy.

"No need to turn it down." I didn't want anyone else to hear me. I had considered asking Molly to take another walk, but it was raining too hard.

"What's up?" Molly frowned.

"Was Caleb ever rough with you?"

Molly stood and narrowed her eyes. "Why do you ask?"

"Some folks saw you with a bump on your cheek. You were crying."

"What folks?"

"That's not important. So, I ask again, was Caleb ever rough with you?"

Tears appeared in Molly's eyes, and she lowered her head.

"What is going on, Molly? What did he do?" I touched my sister on the shoulder, but she shrugged me away.

"Molly."

She shook her head, and I grabbed her. "Molly, did he do something to you? Did he hurt you?"

"It doesn't make any difference now."

She let me hug her and we stood like that for a while, long enough for the record to finish and hiss into the groove.

I kissed the top of my little sister's head, turned, and walked out.

"Going to take the car for a bit," I said as I strode through the living room. Mom, Dad, and Grandpa Two Bears were watching television. It was a Christmas movie, the one with Jimmy Stewart.

"Okay, but dinner is in an hour."

"Thanks, Mom." I pulled my coat off the rack, opened the door, and sprinted for the car. The key was always in the ignition, so I started the engine and headed toward the Sons of Galilee farm. I passed Paul coming the other way and for a second thought about enlisting his help. But, no, this was something I had to do alone.

The road was dark, and it was hard to see in the rain, but after some jostling and bouncing through deep ruts, I began to make out the lights through the trees. By the time I pulled into the yard, the dogs were out from whatever they hid under and were barking up a storm. I hoped they were barkers and not biters, so I opened the door and walked quickly to the big common house's porch. The door opened as I approached, and a figure stood in the frame.

It was Caleb.

I thought it was a bit of profound luck that the person I came to see would be the one to greet me until Caleb explained.

"We saw your car coming, and someone told me it was Molly."

"Well, it is Molly who I came to discuss." I fought for control of my voice. I had never confronted another man like this. Well, except for Vietnam, but then I had a gun in my hand.

"What about her?" Caleb straightened, and even in the dim light, I could see his eyes slit.

"I hear you roughed her up, and you hit her." I bunched my fists.

Caleb frowned and tilted his head as if to size me up, to figure me out. He took a deep breath. "I don't know what you are talking about."

"So, you didn't hit her?"

"Who do you think you are, coming to my house and accusing me of such a thing?" Caleb took a step toward me, then another.

"I am the brother of the woman you hit, that's who."

"Well, the brother of the woman, she had it coming."

My good friend, Raoul, rabid aficionado of world championship wrestling, lover of Muhammad Ali, and champion of Missy Sanders, once told me that when confronted by another man, especially one larger, there was only one thing to do. And that one thing was to hit the other guy first, preferably when he had his back turned. Caleb didn't have his back turned, but I did hit him first.

I think I was more surprised than he was, and I am the one who threw the punch! It was almost as if I willed my right fist to fly at his face. I mean, I didn't even consciously throw the punch. And it hurt like heck, but it felt good. It felt good, and as he stumbled back against the door frame, I found a dark side, a stranger, who had hidden in me all these years. It was the side of me that had bitten its lip when people had laughed at my name and sneered at my football uniform with its lack of game glory dirt. It was the quiet and obedient side of me that had previously accepted the edges of the crowd and the girls' down eyes but would do so no more. I hit him again, and I hoped he would get up so I could beat him forever. But as the beast rose in me, and as I drew back my fist again, I realized that I wasn't hitting Caleb for Molly. I was hitting Caleb for me, and that shocked and scared me, and I stepped back. Caleb lay there, and I could see the others in the open door with the fireplace's light behind their astonished faces.

"Touch my sister again, and I WILL kill you," I said, to explain myself.

I turned, and the dogs were quiet as I walked to the Fairlane. My hands shook as I turned the key, and they were still shaking when I pulled onto the square. I parked in the alley behind the Corner Store and slipped in the back door. Basil Starbuck had owned it forever and stood behind the counter.

"Pint of Jim Beam." I nodded toward the line of bottles.

"Why, Weenie, I didn't know you were a drinker," grinned Basil. He turned, grabbed a bottle, and slipped it into a bag.

"I don't drink much, Mister Starbuck. Got a cold coming on."

"Need anything for your hands?" Basil nodded toward me.

I looked at my fists and saw they were bleeding. "No, I had to open a stuck door at the farm. I'll be okay. Thanks, though."

"Sure, Weenie. You come on back."

"Yes, sir."

I walked out to the car and spun the top off the bottle. As I tipped it toward me, I thought about how many beers I had consumed that afternoon riding around with the guys. Was it a couple? Or was it more like six? Was that the fuel the dark side had used? I shook my head and took a long drink. Then I took another and drove around for a while, trying to figure out what had happened. I liked what I had done, but I still needed to figure on it some. I finally headed home, walked in, and hung up my coat. I could see Grandpa Two Bears sitting at the kitchen table talking with someone, but I hurried to the stairway toward my room.

"Weenie, where have you been? You missed a good dinner."

I hesitated at the foot of the stairs. The last thing I wanted to do was get into some long conversation. I just wanted to go to my room, finish my bottle, and get a grip on what I had done to Caleb. But it would be odd for me to just walk upstairs without acknowledging Grandpa, so I jammed my hands into my pockets and walked into the kitchen. As I turned the corner, I saw him with Mom, Dad, and Molly. They were eating chocolate cookies, the vast, soft, and beautiful Mom-made delights.

"Catch," said Grandpa Two Bears. He grinned as he tossed me one.

I instinctively grabbed the cookie but quickly cradled it in my hands to hide my knuckles.

"What did you do to your hands?" Grandpa Two Bears frowned as he looked at me.

"Uhh," I fumbled with the cookie, trying to hide my knuckles.

"Have you been in a fight?" Grandpa leaned forward and grabbed my hand. "That looks like a fight."

"Weenie?" Mom opened her mouth, but shock silenced her. She looked at Dad, who was frowning at my hands.

"Son?" Dad looked at me.

"Uhh."

"You haven't been fighting with your friends, have you?" Mom looked horrified. I mean, her son, Weenie, had never fought in his life as far as she knew. He wasn't a fighter. He was Weenie.

"No, of course not." I swallowed and looked down at my cookie.

"You weren't down at the pool hall, were you?" Dad glared at me, and I remembered when he caught me there when I was twelve. Dad thought pool halls were the devil's doing.

"Boys that hang out at pool halls flunk out of school, son. No good comes from wasting time in a place like this."

"No, Dad, I wasn't down at the pool hall."

Dad frowned, then looked at Molly. She had her head down, staring at the remains of her cookie. Dad's eyes flicked up to mine. He had a strange look on his face. "It was Caleb, wasn't it?"

"Caleb?" Mom frowned.

"Who?" asked Grandpa Two Bears. "You mean the Hodges boy?" He looked at me. "Why would he fight Caleb Hodges?"

I looked at my cookie again, then let my eyes go to Molly.

"Oh, Weenie!" Molly jumped from her chair and ran out of the kitchen. Mom frowned at me, then she stood and followed her.

"What is going on here?" Grandpa Two Bears glared at me. "What is going on?"

I took a bite but didn't taste anything. I shrugged again.

"Will someone please tell me what is going on?" Grandpa looked at Dad and me and frowned.

"Dad." I looked at my father.

"Molly is pregnant, and Caleb is the father." Dad looked at Grandpa Two Bears. "We just found out."

"What?"

I took another bite.

"What?"

"Molly is pregnant," I said.

"And how long have you known?"

"A couple of months" I looked at my cookie. "She told me the last time I was here. We didn't know what to do, so I made up that story about my buddy. You know, to feel you guys out about abortion."

"What abortion?" Grandpa Two Bears looked at me, then at Dad. "What abortion?"

"Maybe none, Grandpa." I shrugged. "Molly is trying to decide what to do."

"Then why fight her potential husband? I don't get it."

"Yes, why fight Caleb?" asked Dad.

"I heard he roughed her up some." I shrugged and glanced at my knuckles.

"What do you mean?" Dad stood.

"Roughed her up?" Grandpa Two Bears stared at me.

"I just heard he hit her. Paul saw her one night on the square. She looked hurt."

"He raped her, didn't he?" Dad put his fists on the table and glared at me.

"She didn't say anything about rape, Dad."

"We don't know that son." Grandpa reached for Dad. "Now, sit down!"

"Bullshit!" Dad jerked back. "If he raped her, I am going to..."

"Dad, Molly never said a word about rape!"

"Son, let's assume he didn't. What if Molly loves the guy?" Grandpa put his hand on Dad's shoulder. "What if Molly wants him to help her raise the child?"

Dad stared at Grandpa a moment, then took a breath and slowly sat down. He shook his head as Grandpa Two Bears patted his shoulder, then looked at me. "Does Caleb even know about any of this? Is he aware that Molly is pregnant and that he is the father?"

"I don't think so." Dad shrugged. "But, at this point, what difference does that make?"

"Do you have any idea what he will do, what the Sons of Galilee will do if they find out they have a Kleegan girl pregnant?" Grandpa Two Bears shook his head.

"What are you talking about?" Dad frowned and leaned forward.

"This thing with Molly gives them an opening into this place," said Grandpa. "According to Missouri law, Caleb has rights."

"What do you mean?" Dad frowned some more.

"The father has rights whether he is married to the mother or not. Once Caleb knows about the pregnancy, he could insist on being a part of the decision."

"I thought the letter you sent to the old man stopped him from taking any action against us." I frowned and looked at Grandpa Two Bears. Grandpa had given the letter to old Elmer Hodges as a warning to leave us Kleegans alone. My grandmother had written the letter, and it described how her father, Elmer Hodges, had raped her and impregnated her.

"Elmer died two months ago." Grandpa Two Bears stared down at his coffee cup. "We don't have any hold on them any longer."

"I didn't see any obituary in the Herald." Dad frowned.

"The Sons of Galilee don't do business with the Herald and don't make announcements like that."

"Then how do you know he is dead?"

"His son, Malachi, stopped me in the drugstore and told me he wanted to buy our thirty acres over by their hayfield. He told me the old man was dead, and there was no reason for hard feelings."

"What did you say?" asked Dad.

"I said, there was no way he was getting our dirt." Grandpa Two Bears leaned back in his chair and took a deep breath. He picked up his spoon and stared at it. "But now, I wonder." He frowned and looked at me. "So, when you brought all of this up, the stuff about your friend and wanting midwestern advice on pregnancy and abortion, it was all to get us to sound out on Molly. Right?"

"Yes." I nodded.

"How far along is she?" asked Dad.

"Coming up on three months."

"Jesus." Dad whispered and shook his head.

"But what will we do?" I frowned and looked at Dad and then Grandpa Two Bears. "What do we do if Caleb or the Sons of Galilee come after our property? Come after Molly?"

"Well, if that's the case we will do what a man has to do."

I started to ask Dad what he meant by that when I heard a sigh and looked toward the kitchen door. Mom stood there in the shadows. I couldn't see her face, only her silhouette, and didn't know how much of our conversation she had heard. Dad and Grandpa Two Bears squeaked their chairs and looked too. Dad stood, but Mom waved him away as she walked to her chair and sat. She had a sadness that made me want to reach her. To help her. She slumped with a weariness that I had no understanding of. I looked around our table in a kitchen where I had spent my entire life, and in the dim light, I saw in my mom and dad, and Grandpa Two Bears an understanding and an investment in life, theirs, and others, that made me feel like a child again. I knew nothing of sacrifice.

And I thought of Jane. I know that is odd, but I felt a sorrow for her because she woold never sit in her kitchen with her family. Jane would never be a mother. I put my hand on Mom's shoulder, and she reached for my fingers. When they touched mine, I squeezed and leaned over to kiss her cheek.

"How is Molly?" I asked.

"She is asleep. Or, at least, trying to sleep. She is ashamed and confused and..." Mom began to cry, and I gripped her shoulder, and I scooted my chair closer and held her. I looked into Dad's eyes, then to Grandpa, and saw their love and their worry. Sometimes I feel like I am in orbit around the world where I live, detached but safe. I like it out there, the delicious comfort of the uncommitted. But tonight, I wanted to be a part of all this family and hoped it wasn't the booze that prompted my slide into this maudlin capture.

I looked at my knuckles and right or wrong; tonight, I had fought for my family. For the first time, I had fought for us. Some might say I fought for my family in Vietnam, but it doesn't work like that. In Vietnam, I fought for the guys in the planes next to me and the guys on the ground we were trying to support. I didn't fight for any grand notion, just for the other guys. I left my orbit tonight, and I fought for Molly, and I fought for me. I fought for us. And I now wanted to own the angst and worry like the rest of them. I wanted to be a part of what we faced. For once, I didn't want to be a partially-interested-guy-off-to-college or a too-busy-to-be-part-of-small-town-stuff-naval officer. For once, I wanted the past and the here and now of my life as much as I wanted my future.

God, I hoped this wasn't just the booze!

That morning, I got up early and helped Dad and Grandpa Two Bears with the milking. I found myself paying more attention and more interested. I watched as the teats entered the suction cups, and I stood and looked at the cows, their faces, and their bodies, to see if they were doing okay. I hovered over our Holsteins' lines with a newfound attachment, and Grandpa Two Bears or Dad didn't have to tell me when the udders were emptying. I could see as they creased and shrunk, and I took the cows out and brought in the next set. I was in the moment in which I was living, not just passing the time.

Breakfast was cereal, and I sure didn't fault Mom for not cooking like she usually did. We only ate cereal when Mom was not feeling well, and the boxes were out on the counter. Like Dad, I chose Raisin Bran. Mom had shredded wheat with sugar. Grandpa Two Bears likes Post Toasties, but I think he eats them to remind himself he was a US Marine. Nobody really likes Post Toasties.

"So, what are we going to do?" Grandpa Two Bears asked through a mouthful of wet, brown globs.

"We are going to love her," said Mom. She looked around the table. "We are going to support whatever decision she makes, and we are going to love her."

"You know what I think about abortion," Grandpa snorted.

"Yes, we know, Tobias." Mom put her hand on his and patted it. "But what Molly thinks about abortion is what is important now. Don't you think?"

Grandpa Two Bears looked at her, then around the table at Dad and me. He took a breath and shook his head. "I love my granddaughter."

Mom patted his hand again. "More coffee?"

With that, we went through the motions of pretending everything was the same as it always was. I don't know; maybe things were the same as they always were, just with another challenge. But a good family can rise to a challenge. And we were a good family.

Around ten that morning, I saw Molly and Dad standing down by the gate. They were looking at the hayfield or the fall stubble of it, and Dad had his arms around Molly. Later, I saw Grandpa Two Bears sitting on the porch, and I started to push the door open and join him when I saw Molly against the awning post. I watched her strike a kitchen match and light his Lucky, and for a second, I felt jealous. Molly was in my spot. But as I saw Grandpa Two Bears take a drag and blow the blue circle, I smiled because it was for her.

On Christmas Eve morning, we gathered for breakfast. It was waffle morning, with bacon, my favorite! I think bacon is everybody's favorite, and the spirit of the pig was in the kitchen as we all noisily sat down and poured coffee and syrup. But just before I shoved a stick of wonderfulness into my mouth, Molly rapped her glass with a spoon. We all looked at her.

"I'm going to call it Catherine if it's a girl, and Tobias if it's a boy."

We stood and, in turn, hugged Molly. It was the first time I ever saw Grandpa Two Bears cry. I had seen him mist up a bit, but never a shoulder shaking cry. He excused himself and left the table for a while, but it was okay. It was good, in fact, and when he returned our farmhouse kitchen was filled with a happy family's excited words. I think we were all relieved, celebratory in fact, but I couldn't shrug off my concerns about how Molly was going to manage her life. Single mothers have a huge challenge, beyond anything the rest of us face. Single motherhood is a gateway to poverty that can become generational. But as I sat around our table and engaged in the various conversations and as I talked with Molly, I saw her rising. I saw my wonderful but quiet, sulking, and often rebellious and quarrelsome little sister glow! A daffodil at the edge of winter, maybe, but also a strong and determined young woman, the kind that built our country. The type that created all the nations. I began to think of the child as a blessing instead of a concern for alarm or burden and realized while single mothers do indeed face challenges, they only become insurmountable when the single mother is alone. Molly wasn't alone, far from it. She had all of us in her corner.

Suddenly, the entire Christmas holiday took on a special meaning for me, and I think for all of us. Molly's situation was in all our thoughts and unified us more than I could have imagined. The season's words and blessings that I had mouthed all my life but paid no attention to, now caused me to smile as they passed my lips.

RETURN TO 'NAM

The holiday ended all too quickly, and I found myself back on *Constellation* for a month at sea. It was our final preparation before deploying for a nine-month return to Vietnam. At this point, I had a significant leadership challenge.

I am the line division officer, a billet customarily held by a full lieutenant instead of a lieutenant junior grade like me. However, the skipper and XO believed I had potential and placed me in the job, and I love it. The line division is responsible for preparing the aircraft for flight, post-flight turnaround, and troubleshooting discrepancies. The division handles all aircraft ground movements, certifies the plane captains, and manages the squadron's support equipment. The foreign object damage (to engines) program, fuel, oil, hydraulic fluid, and oxygen surveillance programs are all in the line division. It's a big job, and since many of the division members are young men who are not yet rated, discipline can be a huge problem. The work is conducted in all weather, centers on the flight deck, and to say it is manual labor-intensive is a laughable understatement. If you ever see a newsreel of an aircraft carrier, the sweaty, dirty, tired-looking young men in brown shirts carrying chains and wheel chocks are my guys.

I also have the troubleshooters assigned to me. Troubleshooters are senior enlisted men who are experts in their ratings and possess quick and correct analysis skills. If an aircraft has trouble during the launch cycle, these men can offer suggestions to the aircrew and maintenance team about fixing it. Sharp troubleshooters will save a squadron from launching aircraft with sub-optimum systems or even from missing sorties. Petty Officer First Class Roy Simmons was my number one troubleshooter, and my leadership opportunity involved him.

It all began the first day of our month-long final at-sea period before the cruise. While the carrier sortied that morning, I was part of the group that remained ashore to fly our aircraft out to the ship.

Since all airwing pilots had to gain currency and the carrier needed flight deck room to operate, we flew the aircraft to the carrier in groups. I was sitting in the ready room when the duty officer, Sponge Moore, called me to his desk.

"Hey buddy, your man, Simmons, missed ship's movement."

"What? That's impossible. Are you sure?"

"Yeah, just got a call from the ship. He's UA." UA meant Unauthorized Absence, or as the Army would say, AWOL: Absent Without Leave.

"I don't get it." I frowned and shook my head.

"No shit," said Sponge. "The number one first-class petty officer in the squadron, our squadron Sailor of the Year. Heck, he was the Airwing Sailor of the Year. Hard to believe, man."

I was in shock. I mean, Simmons was a Rockstar if there ever was one. He was a shoo-in for selection to chief petty officer this year. "Do you have a recall number for him?"

"Let me see." Sponge grabbed a binder from the metal cabinet behind his chair. He plopped it on his desk and ripped through the vinyl-covered pages. I looked up just in time to see the skipper come in the back door.

"Quick, man." I walked behind the duty desk and looked over Sponge's shoulder.

"Here it is," pointed Sponge. "Looks like Simmons lives on base. Over behind the exchange."

I quickly scribbled the phone number and address.

"Sponge, do me a favor. Don't tell anyone you told me about Simmons. Okay? "

Sponge shrugged and grinned. "Sure, man."

I ducked out the front door to avoid the skipper, ran to my car, and headed to Simmons' house, praying that he was home, and wondering what in the heck could have gotten into him. I raced across the base and into the enlisted quarters' area. Following the street signs, I soon parked in front of Simmons' house and ran to the door.

"Petty Officer Simmons!" I knocked and ducked to peek into a living room window. The shades were drawn.

I knocked again, harder. "Petty Officer Simmons!" I jiggled the door handle. "Simmons!"

The knob clicked from inside, and I heard someone at the door. It swung open, and Petty Officer Simmons stood there in jeans and a sweatshirt.

"What's going on?" I glared at Simmons. "What are you doing?"

Simmons looked at me. There was no guilt or shading in his eyes. No weak smile or looking at the floor. He appeared confident and sure. If anything, Simmons looked resolute, and that confused me. He drew a deep breath, "Come in, Mister Kleegan."

I walked into the living room and saw his wife, Marilyn, sitting on the couch. I had met her several times at squadron parties and knew her pretty well. She looked like she had been crying.

"Marilyn," I nodded.

Marilyn dabbed at her eyes with a wad of Kleenex and pointed to a chair. I looked at Simmons, and he pointed to the chair, too, so I sat down.

"Mister Kleegan, can I get you some coffee or a coke? Water?" Marilyn's voice was thick and course.

"No, thank you, Marilyn," I sat forward and leaned my elbows on my knees. I looked at Simmons. "What's going on?"

Simmons looked at his wife, and whatever they shared caused her to start crying again. She got off the couch and walked across the rug. We both watched her disappear down the hallway, and I turned to Simmons. He looked at me a moment, then shook his head and dropped his eyes to the floor.

"We've been trying to have a baby for six years, Mister Kleegan." Simmons rubbed his palm with his thumb and then cracked his knuckles. He sighed and looked at me. "Marilyn's lost three babies." He shook his head, and I watched his eyes grow wet. "I mean, she's trying Mister Kleegan. She's trying."

"Is she sick? Do you need to take emergency leave? Is that what this is all about?" I felt better. Maybe Simmons wasn't in as much trouble as I feared. I swallowed and leaned back in my chair. Simmons had his head down, working his hands and running his fingers around his wedding band the way married men do when they are worried or don't know what to say. He made a few more circles on his ring then looked at me.

"Not exactly. Marilyn isn't sick in the way you might be thinking."

"Well, what then?" I leaned forward again. "You can't miss ship's movement without an awfully good excuse. You know that."

"I know that, sir." Simmons fidgeted with his ring again, and I began to grow frustrated.

"Simmons, for Christ's sake, what is going on? Did you hit her or something?"

"No, sir!" Simmons glared at me. "NO, SIR!"

"What then?"

"Mister Kleegan, she is crying because she feels responsible for me being here. Here and not on the ship."

I didn't know what to say. I was thoroughly confused. I looked at Simmons and threw my hands in the air.

"Sir, Marilyn can't get pregnant, so six months ago, we went to a fertility clinic. The one over at Scripps. We saw a Doctor Weston, and he said Marilyn had endometriosis. That is when the tissue that lines the uterus grows outside the uterus. We used my re-enlistment bonus and some money my dad gave us, and Marilyn had surgery, but the doctor said she had exhausted her body so much that she most likely wasn't going to be able to have a baby." Simmons looked down, and his shoulders shook, and I thought he might be crying. I swallowed again and frowned. I had hoped that Simmons was sick and unable to get to the ship, that their phone didn't work, and there was an explanation for all of this. But now I had no idea what was going on. Simmons took several deep breaths and wiped his eyes on the backs of his hands.

"The navy doesn't pay for anything like this, so we borrowed some more money from Marilyn's parents and agreed to fertility treatments. Marilyn began getting injections, and the doctor said that the next two weeks are critical and that if we didn't get pregnant, we never would."

"What does that have to do with you missing the ship?"

"Sir, I have to be here to get her pregnant."

I stared at Simmons and shook my head as I began to understand. Simmons needed to stay at home to make love to his wife to get her pregnant. My mind flashed on Molly and Grandma Catherine.

"Christ! Why didn't you come to me?"

"You were on leave, sir. I didn't know about the requirement to be here, and, you know, do my part, until a short time ago. I had hoped the timing would allow me to go to sea, and this would all happen after I was back home. But the doctor told us while you were gone. I did call your home number in Missouri, but you must have been out, and nobody answered. So, I went to Mister Macready and tried to explain it to him."

You went to Bo?" Bo Macready was the biggest dick in the world, and I had been on his shit list since joining the squadron. He hated me if he thought about me at all. The skipper had given him the job of maintenance officer, one of the best jobs a lieutenant commander can have because he wanted Bo to have one last chance for a career. The skipper was a thoughtful, kind-hearted man who was also a hopeless romantic. He had made me line division officer because "Weenie, I want to see you grow." But, despite the skipper's best intentions, the fact is that Bo was an idiot. He was a mean spirited, narrow-minded, selfish idiot. But he was my boss.

"Yes, sir. While you were home on leave. I visited him in his office and tried to explain our situation."

"What did he say?"

"He said, 'Do you realize how this will look?' He said, 'We will be the laughingstock of the airwing when everyone finds out we left our number one troubleshooter at home so he can fuck his wife.'"

"Did you tell him what the doctor said?"

"Tried to, but he just waved his hand and told me to get out."

I leaned against the chair and put my head back and thought of the conversation I had had with Grandpa Two Bears so long ago.

"Weenie," he said, "I want you to do one thing for me. No, not for me. I want you to do one thing for yourself and the sailors who will one day work for you."

"What's that?" I had asked.

"I want you to realize that you work for them."

Although I hadn't fully understood Grandpa Two Bears' words at the time, as I grew and matured as an officer, they began to make sense to me. In fact, they guided me. We tend to think of the navy, or any organization, I suppose, in terms of its product or its mission. We think of a squadron in terms of the aircraft we fly and what we do with them. But it is the men that count. It has always been the men. Well, and now the women. I looked at Simmons. He had his head down, still playing with the ring, and I wondered how old he and his wife would get to be. Eighty? Even older? Is a month at sea worth not having the chance of a child to spend all those years with?

"You are wrong, Petty Officer Simmons."

He looked at me and frowned. "Sir?"

"You did get in contact with me in Missouri. You called me, and you asked to take leave for an emergent situation with your wife."

"Sir?"

"I told you to put the leave request in my mailbox in the ready room, and I would sign it."

"Sir?"

I stood, and Simmons stood with me. "Get in your car and follow me to the personnel support detachment. It's far enough from the squadron so that nobody will see us. We will get a copy of a leave request there, and you fill it out and date it the day you called me. I will sign it and tell everyone I forgot to turn in the request to our squadron personnel."

"But sir..."

"No buts, Simmons."

"Won't you get in trouble?"

"I'm a lieutenant junior grade, Simmons. I have the right to be forgetful. Now tell Marilyn everything is going to be okay. Then follow me."

"Yes, sir." Simmons flashed a saucer-sized grin and ran for the bedroom. By the time I got my car started and backed out of his driveway, Simmons came out the door. He followed me to the personnel support detachment, and we filled out his leave request. I drove back to the squadron, snuck in the back, and slipped the request into my mailbox. I walked to the front of the room and saw the skipper's scowl.

"Weenie, do you know what the story is on Simmons?" He stood at the duty desk with Bo Macready. I glanced at Sponge.

"Sir?"

"Simmons missed ship's movement this morning."

I frowned for what I thought to be the right number of seconds and then opened my eyes as the moment of understanding hit me. "Oh, no, sir. He called me in Missouri and asked for leave. Just a second." I ran to my mailbox and retrieved the leave request.

"Here it is," I held the leave request up as I strolled back to the group.

"He asked me for leave, and I turned him down," scowled Bo. "He went around my back."

The skipper turned to me; a frown plastered his face.

"Sir, Petty Officer Simmons said he talked with Bo but was unable to give him all the doctor's information at the time. The doctor's diagnosis indicated continual bedrest for Mrs. Simmons for at least two to three weeks, and since Bo didn't have that information, I signed the request. And sir, Simmons has been grooming Petty Officer Hopkins as his understudy. You might have noticed during the last at-sea period Hopkins took a good deal of the leadership roles."

"Hmmm," the skipper pursed his lips and nodded. "Is Mrs. Simmons sick?"

"She has had very recent surgery, and there are complications to her full recovery. But we think she will be fine."

I could feel Bo glaring at me as I looked at the skipper. Over his shoulder, I saw Sponge stick out his tongue.

"Well, okay then," said the skipper. "Just hope Hopkins is up to the task."

"Yes, sir."

The skipper turned and walked to his seat to get ready for the flight brief. I looked at Bo and grinned. "Sorry, boss, my mistake about forgetting the leave request."

Bo glared at me, then turned and stormed out the door.

"Smooth," said Sponge. "Very smooth."

"Between just us," I said and took my seat for the brief.

The at-sea period was uneventful, and it was followed by a short, frantic, last-minute detail-filled month back at home base. I didn't ask Petty Officer Simmons about his time home; I was glad that he would make the upcoming nine-month deployment with us and that the rest was in God's hands.

Two days before leaving for deployment, Mom called. It surprised me since I had told her I would call her before I left.

"Mom?"

"Weenie, I just wanted to pass some news."

I frowned as a tingle of alarm swept me. "Oh?"

"Caleb Hodges was found dead today."

"What?"

"According to the sheriff, he was hunting and tripped over some rocks and shot himself in the chest."

"You have got to be kidding?" I almost shouted with happiness.

"I hate the wicked thoughts I have."

"Your thoughts aren't wicked, Mom." I gripped the phone, trying to understand my disappointment?

"It is a bit of a miracle. For Molly and us," said Mom.

"I just can't believe it." I swallowed and re-gripped the phone. "I mean, the timing is incredible!"

"Yes. But as much as I regret a young man losing his life, I still feel it is a miracle. And I'm not ashamed of it." Mom's defiance did not shock or surprise me.

"No, no. No reason for shame, Mom. Given the circumstances." I shook my head and barely heard her say goodbye. I hung up, slumped into my chair, and sat there for a long time, thinking about Caleb Hodges being shot. I sat there until it was long past time for bed as my thoughts ran 'round and' round.

Who shot Caleb Hodges?

Dad? Or was it Grandpa Two Bears? Or was it both and, if so, why didn't they include me?

All that night and for the next days, I couldn't get rid of a nagging suspicion as to the timely demise of Caleb Hodges, and I found myself thinking about Dad and Grandpa Two Bears. Strange, how so quickly and surely, I had disregarded the possibility of an accident. I wondered if I had just projected what I wanted to happen to Caleb on them. I mean, to be honest, I wanted Caleb out of the way.

What did I mean by that?

I wanted Caleb dead. I was reasonably sure he raped Molly, and I wanted him dead. Hell, sometimes I think I wanted to kill him myself. I remembered the face of the Vietnamese kid when I pulled the trigger on my .38. I could put a .38 against the man who raped my sister without any problem. And I remembered the adrenalin rush when I had punched Caleb. It had been so surreal and so wickedly uplifting. So, I wondered, did I want to know who shot Caleb because I wanted to sit on our porch or around our table and discuss it? Did I want to share the fact that while my last thought for solving Molly's situation was aborting her baby, my first thought for solving Molly's problem was killing the baby's father? Yes, it was unfair to Dad and Grandpa to think of them as murderers but not so unfair when I realize that maybe the only difference between them and me was that one of them got there first. And I wanted to tell whoever that was, that it was okay.

I couldn't fret over the situation long, though, since I was leaving on another cruise.

We set off in January, and despite the fact the Paris Peace Accords were signed on the 28th, we began conducting bombing missions in Laos and Cambodia as soon as we arrived off the coast. The peace agreement didn't include those two countries, so men and supplies were in constant movement along the Ho Chi Minh trail as it wound through Laos and Cambodia. Of course, this allowed the north to reinforce its positions.

Although I was now an "old guy," I felt the familiar thrill as I sat in the flight briefs, checked out my sidearm, and launched with a load of bombs and missiles. And I also enjoyed watching the new guys, the ones going feet dry over Indian Country for the first time, as they prepared for the flights. Like me, they had heard from their instructors and old-timers about flying in combat, and like me, their biggest hope was that they wouldn't screw up. I imagined what it was like for them to write the in-case-I-don't-come-back letters to their loved ones back home. The skipper suggested they do that the night before our first missions, and I smiled as I remembered writing to Jane. I wondered if any of the new guys had someone like her to write to. I hoped that they did.

We had been off the coast about a month when we got word the Khmer Rouge was closing in on Phnom Penh, so we had the mission to interdict their logistical lines. I crewed with Cotton, and we were to lead a section of Phantoms as part of a twenty-eight-plane alpha strike against a fuel staging base. Raoul flew with Chiquita Thomas, so named because of his massive nose, and they were our wingman.

We launched early in the morning, took on some gas, and headed as a giant gaggle toward the target area. Since we were "at peace" with Vietnam, we didn't worry too much about threats from the ground. Intel told us the surface to air threat from Cambodia and Laos was minimal, so we expected to roll into the target area unopposed, drop our bombs, and be back on the ship in time for a lunch cheeseburger.

All seemed to go as planned. But then…my radar warning gear began to pick up indications that we were detected. My AAA guns and SAM missile lights began to chirp and blink!

Then, the radio exploded with SAM calls!

I looked to my right and saw two missile plumes rising from the ground and then saw three more to my left! My warning panel glowed with missile guidance triplet warnings and the aural tones that indicated we were being tracked with missile lock on!

Cotton and I deployed chaff, shreds of aluminum and fiberglass, designed to trick radars, and jinked to break tracking solutions. At one point, I counted seventeen SAMs in the air, but we fought them off and pushed on. Two A-7 Corsairs and three A-6 Intruders were knocked out of the sky before we got to the target, but the rest of us delivered our ordnance and headed back east. That is when I looked out just in time to see Raoul and Chiquita's Phantom get hit. One minute they were off to my right; the next minute, all I could see was a fireball! Cotton and I turned back toward them, hoping to see some chutes, but the whole flaming mess fell into the clouds. We circled once while I screamed for Raoul over the radio. But the danger of flying over clouds in SAM country was real, and we had to leave.

I cannot explain the feeling of loss I had. The crushing, crushing loss of my best friend. The idea of losing Raoul was more than I could tolerate, and Cotton and I didn't say a thing the entire way back. We couldn't even look at each other after we landed. I think if I had looked at Cotton, I would have lost it.

That night, Cotton and I sat in our room and had a drink to
Raoul's memory. In fact, we polished off a bottle of vodka, and the
next day was a struggle like no other. There is nothing like a
hangover to make you wish you were as dead as the man you drank
to the night before and my alcohol induced depression pulled me
into a dark, miserable hole. I couldn't get Raoul out of my mind. We
had been through so much together; in fact, I felt I had grown up
with him in some ways. Or that with him, I had grown up. I started
to write a letter to Grandpa Two Bears about Raoul but couldn't get
through it. I kept seeing Raoul's goofy smile, and I just couldn't
write. I remember when my roommate, Jody, got shot down and
killed on my first Vietnam cruise and how I had told my skipper
that he was my friend. And my skipper had said, "They will always
be your friend, Weenie." I remember how sad that had sounded.
Then, my skipper was killed, and true to his word, he had been my
friend too. I began to regret the fact I had joined the navy. If I had
stayed at home, I wouldn't now miss Jody and Drifty, and the
skipper. I wouldn't be missing Raoul. I wouldn't be missing Jane. I
would be home, maybe teaching at Militia Springs High School and
living on the farm with Mom and Dad and Grandpa and Molly. I
wouldn't be out here missing people. I resolved to resign as soon as
my time was up. I would quit and go home where I belonged.

Three days later, a rumor came out of the intel spaces that we
had survivors from our raid, but no one knew if it was true or, if so,
who they were. A day later, we watched a helo land and out stepped
Raoul! The flight deck camera also showed Chiquita sitting on a
stretcher.

I started screaming and cheering as soon as I saw Raoul, and by
the time he got to the ready room, I was a complete mess. He
popped open the door, flashed that huge Raoul, goofy, big-toothed
wonderful grin, and said, "Boys, I just spent three days with a jungle
girl who had tits as big as watermelons!"

Of course, we mobbed him, and when Cotton and I finally got
him to the room, he told us the tale of how he had landed in his
chute, found Chiquita, and evaded capture by hiding in termite
mounds. I later read that there is a mound-building termite native to
the area but at the time wasn't too sure I believed Raoul. At any
rate, they were picked up by a South Vietnamese ranger unit and
hustled to the US embassy in South Vietnam. I never pressed Raoul
for details about the jungle girl. If Raoul said she was as he
described, then I believed him. It was more pleasant than termite
mounds.

That was the end of our combat sorties, and we fell into a routine of relative calm. Over the following days and weeks, I gained some perspective on my decision to leave the navy. Fact is, if I hadn't joined, I would never have met all the wonderful people I now loved, or I now missed so I wasn't going anywhere. I couldn't blame the navy for providing me the life that I sought. I was glad that I never wrote the letter to Grandpa Two Bears.

The rest of the deployment was uneventful, and the only real drawback was how much Cotton missed Melody. He was one sad man, and I felt sorry for anyone who had to leave a loved one behind for that long. I wondered how married men made it in the navy and thought of myself as lucky to be a bachelor. That was the first time I had ever thought about that.

We spent the rest of our deployment flying support for mine-clearing operations to clean up all the stuff we had dropped over the past nine years. It became arduous, and I was amazed at how focusing and purposeful combat had been, but now how boring and mundane flight ops had become. I realized that the excitement and focusing power of war has to do with the prospect of being shot and not the fact we logged it as a combat mission. And then, one night Big Daddy Towers and Andy Wayne got too low on their approach to the ship and hit the ramp. Their Phantom exploded, and a fireball swept them off, and we never found them. That event sobered me and reminded me that every flight off an aircraft carrier is a combat flight, the enemy just changes. I also realized that what I was doing was a privilege, and there was an art and a skill to maintain and so I got my perspective tuned and pressed on.

A letter from Molly surprised me. She had never written to me before, but this one made up for that because it contained the news that she and Paul Smart were getting married! I almost fell off my chair when I read that. Paul Smart! Christ! I mean, he was a great friend, but he was a ladies' man, a lothario, a Casanova. He wasn't a husband! Two days later, I got a letter from Paul.

Kleegan,

Your sister has probably written to you by now, so you know we are getting married. I wanted to ask you first since we are friends and all, but since you are gone, I asked your dad and Grandpa Two Bears. They were a little surprised but said, "okay." I don't want you to think I'm just fooling around. I really love her, man. I know I have a reputation for fooling

around, but I swear that ain't happening with Molly. See you
when you get back home.

    Smart

Mom wrote to me too! I never had so many letters on a cruise.
She told me about Molly and Paul, and I guess Paul had had his eye
on Molly for a long time but never could muster the courage to ask
her out. Mom said Molly was ecstatic and seemed to really love him
too. They wanted to wait for me to come home, but Paul insisted
that the baby be born to a married woman. Molly liked the idea also,
so they got married by the Methodist preacher in our living room.
Paul rented a house in Militia Springs, so the two of them made that
their home.

Two months later, I received a Red Cross message that Molly
had given birth to a healthy baby girl.

After nearly eight months, we turned east and headed back
home. We were approaching Hawaii when Petty Officer Simmons
pulled me aside. I was on the flight deck, enjoying the warm day
when he walked up and shook my hand.

"Twins," he said as tears streamed down his face. He held a slip
of paper in his hand and handed it to me. It was a class easy
message from the Balboa Naval Hospital in San Diego, and its short
message formed a lump in my throat.

Healthy baby girl and boy born 09/14/73 2047Z. Mother well
without complications.

I smiled and marveled at the irony--how the navy could describe
the most beautiful thing on earth in such drab terms. I grabbed
Simmons's hand to shake it, but he pulled me into a hug right there
on the flight deck.

"We will never forget you, Mister Kleegan. For what you did for
us."

"Any chance you will name that boy, Weenie?'

Simmons paused for a second, then hugged me a little harder.
"Probably not, sir."

We pulled into Hawaii the next day, and I found myself out with
Cotton and Raoul again, getting drunk again. And the following
morning, I strolled the same path I had walked the last time I had
been in Hawaii. I walked through the park and to the school where
I had been shot, but this time the children were not in danger. I
thought about Simmons and knew that I didn't need his children's
birth to validate what I had done. After all, all I did was forge a
government document by backdating it and encourage an enlisted

man to lie to his superiors. But as I strolled the sidewalk and smelled the gardenia, I felt better than I ever had.

THE GOOD ADMIRAL

I took some post-deployment leave home in Militia Springs and saw my new niece, Kate. She looked just like Molly with dark hair and gray eyes, and I was secretly relieved that Caleb's red was not evident. Paul was a little nervous when I first saw him, but I hugged him good and hard and told him I was super glad he was my brother-in-law. Molly paused her pursuit of a college degree until Kate was older. She had decided to become a teacher when she returned to her studies and planned to start with night courses in the fall. Some of the folks in Militia Springs did the math and wondered about the baby being born so close to a wedding, but they were too polite to ask, and the ones who didn't do math didn't care. So, it worked out okay.

I spent a lot of time with Dad during my short visit, and I think I had opened a long-needed door when I had told him about Molly's pregnancy. I also think he liked the idea of my bloody knuckles on Caleb's face. However, I did get some troubling news that Grandpa Two Bears was having difficulty getting around, and Doc Gentry had diagnosed Parkinson's. A specialist in Springfield confirmed it, and now Grandpa's stage one tremors had advanced to stage two slowness of movement. It wasn't a death sentence or anything, but danger signs did mark Grandpa Two Bears' road.

On my last day home, I had an opportunity to get some porch time with Grandpa. I had to find out about Caleb's shooting. It nagged at me, so after I got his Lucky fired up, and after his first smoke ring faded over the lawn, I turned to him.

"Anything ever happen about Caleb's shooting?"

"What do you mean?" Grandpa Two Bears glanced at me and frowned.

"Dad said he was shot on the thirty acres we own over by the Molly tree. He said the sheriff came out and talked with the two of you. You know since it was on our property."

"That's right," said Grandpa. "The sheriff did come out here."

"Hmmm." I nodded.

"He asked about you." Grandpa took a drag and squinted at me. "Said he heard you fought with Caleb before he died."

"Really?" I frowned.

"Said that witnesses saw you attack Caleb on his porch. But, he also said since Caleb was dead, he wasn't filing any charges against you for that."

I nodded and eyed my toe as I traced the grass under my feet. "Anybody ever make the connection between Caleb and Molly's baby?"

"Oh, there is always talk, I guess." Grandpa Two Bears took a drag, and I carefully avoided looking at his shaking hand. "But Paul's reputation as a ladies' man actually helped since people thought he had snuck in there somehow. The wedding pretty much cooled the rest of the talk off." I kept my eyes out on the field until I felt him watching me. I turned my head toward him, and he stared right at me.

"What is it that you really want to know?" he asked.

I looked at him, unsure how far to pursue my curiosity. After all, did I want to know how Caleb died?

"I guess I just don't believe in miracles. And Caleb's death was at least partly a miracle for us."

Grandpa Two Bears held me in his gaze for a moment, then took a final drag and snuffed out his smoke. He looked out across the field. "Miracle or not, he's dead. That's all that matters now."

The next day I flew back to San Diego and my life in the navy. It had taken on a familiar ring as Cotton, Raoul, and I had moved back into our snake pit in Pacific Beach. The timing worked well since the guys who rented it had left on deployment two weeks before our return. The owner was ecstatic to have navy renters and even helped us move in. Raoul and I went to MCRD the first Friday back.

A month later, Cotton announced that he and Melody were engaged, and soon he didn't spend any time at the house. Raoul and I saw him in the squadron, but that was about all. Then, he moved all his stuff to her place, and we had a spare room. Raoul wanted to turn it into a cool bar for hosting ladies. He even drew some pictures of what it might look like, but his ability to draw the Tiki motif made his idea look like a lopsided haystack. In the end, we just put our junk and dirty clothes in there.

Six months later, Cotton, Raoul, and I were selected for promotion to lieutenant, and we had a frocking ceremony in the ready room. Frocking is a navy tradition, whereby the squadron commander "promotes" an officer to his new rank before senate confirmation. The skipper held the ceremony in the ready room, and all the officers and chief petty officers were in attendance. Melody came and pinned on Cotton's "railroad tracks." The next day I took my dress blues to the exchange tailor shop and had the two gold stripes sewed on. They looked rather good, and I wore the uniform to the christening for Petty Officer Simmons and Marilyn's twins. The Simmons named their babies Grayson and Fern.

In June, Cotton received orders to the naval test pilot school in Patuxent River, Maryland, and Raoul received orders to the F-4 RAG, the training squadron, at Miramar as an instructor. I felt sorry about Cotton's leaving town, but that is part of navy life, and I knew I would see him again. We had a great going away party for him, and the day after he left, the skipper called me into his office. He and the XO told me the bureau had identified me as a "hot runner" and an excellent prospect to be an admiral's aide. They said my timing worked to be assigned to Rear Admiral Jay Jensen, and that he wanted me. I was happy to be selected and humbled to work for such an impressive man as Rear Admiral Jensen. The icing on the cake was their plan to detail me to Fighter Squadron 124, the F-14 RAG, at Miramar. I would transition to the Tomcat and then report to Jensen's staff in Virginia. It was a perfect plan, and I was ecstatic!

The squadron held a going away party for Raoul and me, and we left on the same day. Raoul reported to the F-4 RAG as an instructor in the Phantom, and I reported to the F-14 RAG as a student in the Tomcat. The squadrons were just down the street from one another, so we could even drive to work together on some days. Since I had already studied some of the training tapes, I quickly progressed through the self-paced syllabus.

Since I had over 600 hours in the Phantom, I understood the fighter mission, but the sheer capability of the Tomcat amazed me. Instead of expecting radar contacts at forty miles at best, I could see multiple targets seventy or eighty miles away. I could see airliners over 100 miles away! The Tomcat also had various systems, computers, and communications equipment that were light years ahead of the Phantom. I enjoyed my classes and flights, and the five-month syllabus whizzed by. When I finished my courses, I was ready to travel across the country to Virginia Beach, Virginia, to Rear Admiral Jensen's command. The hardest part of it all was saying goodbye to Raoul. He was indeed my best friend and confidant. He was the only guy I could tell Grandpa Two Bears level stuff to. So, we got drunk and said the sloppy but well-meant things guys say to each other in those situations, and the next day I nursed a hangover as I started my drive to the east coast.

Since the navy moved my stuff, I only had a suitcase in the Triumph as I took I-20, the southern cross-country route, east. The worst thing about the southern route is you spend a billion hours in Texas, which is psychologically depressing. After all, you know you can't get to Virginia until you get through Texas. And Texas is consumed by having the biggest stuff. Everything is the biggest! I saw the world's longest set of horns at Big Spring, a big soup can near Eastland, and a sign for a giant robot playground near Fort Worth. But I didn't stop for any of that "biggest" stuff. I was glad I was in a small car as an act of defiance, if nothing else. At any rate, I was happy to get to Virginia. I drove the 3000 miles in five days and checked into the Oceana Bachelor Officers' Quarters.

I reported at 0730 Monday morning and met the Chief of Staff, Captain Frost, who everybody called COS. You pronounce COS like the "caws' of a crow. I also met the twenty or so members of the staff. Rear Admiral Jensen was the wing commander for all east coast F-8, F-4, and F-14 fighter aircraft, and his office was located at Naval Air Station Oceana. Southeast Virginia is a hub of naval activity, and the biggest naval base in the world, Norfolk Naval Base, is located only twenty miles from Oceana. It is a similar setup to the one the navy has in San Diego with Naval Air Station Miramar near the North Island Naval Base.

The COS told me that Rear Admiral Jensen was in his first assignment as an admiral or flag, that he had been on the job for a year, and my job became available because his previous aide, Snake Hastings, was going to be an instructor at the Navy Fighter Weapon's School, called TOPGUN.

"Our main mission is to get resources for the east coast fighter community," explained the COS. "Replacement parts, depot priority, funding for fuel, and transportation are some of the things we get. But, as you probably know, the competition for money is fierce, and nothing comes without a fight."

"A fight?" I frowned, and the Captain smiled.

"Weenie, your first tour in a fleet squadron can be deceiving. When you needed gas or bombs or anything, it just appeared. You see, the fleet is operations-based, and everything flows to it. Here, nothing flows to us; we need to go and get it. To accomplish that, the admiral has all of us in a constant state of analysis. He is a metrics-driven man who is the most successful admiral in our wing's memory because he supports his arguments with facts rather than emotion. For instance, despite the fact the Vietnam War is over, he got our flight hour program fully funded because he cited safety studies that demonstrated the relationship between flight hours per month and mishap rates. He also believes that the aircrew retention problems are hidden because we are drawing down in force strength. The admiral believes that we will wake up in a couple of years with everybody getting out if we do not act now. He made a great argument to the CNO for an aircrew retention bonus, citing Fortune 500 statistics, and I think we are going to get it."

"Really? I can't imagine getting a bonus to do this."

"Me neither, but that is the way the admiral thinks." COS looked at his watch and smiled. "Time for you to meet him. You know each other, right?"

"Yes, sir, we flew together once."

Chief Cummings, the admiral's writer, ushered me in, and after shaking hands and small talk, Admiral Jensen leaned back in his chair and smiled.

"Let me tell you your mission, Weenie, and then you can discuss with the COS and others how to accomplish it."

"Yes, sir." I took my wheel book from my back pocket and snapped my ballpoint pen.

"Your mission is to ensure I am in the correct uniform or civilian dress and that I am never late. You will attend all meetings with me and take notes, as necessary. You will provide advice and honest thoughts when asked. You will carry and receive messages from and to my seniors and juniors when directed. You will act in total confidence and never divulge any of our conversations unless I specifically authorize it. Questions so far?"

I looked up from my note pad. "No, sir."

"Good. Now, some things you will not do. First, you are NOT a personal errand boy for me. You will not get my laundry from the cleaners, for instance. You will not go grocery shopping for me. If my wife, June, asks you to help her with something, you cannot do it unless I authorize it. June won't ask you, but I want you to know that you are an aide to my official duties, not some kind of modern-day house boy. And as much as I would like to have you shine my shoes, you won't do that either. If you spend any personal money on my behalf, you will present me with an invoice, and I will pay it immediately. You will work with Chief Cummings to ensure my travel plans make sense, and you will have our JAG inspect all claims to ensure I have complied with the spirit and intent of any law or regulation. That goes for the entire staff, by the way."

The admiral must have seen me frowning because he paused. "Questions, Weenie?"

"Well, sir, you are the admiral. Seems like a lot of rules for an admiral."

"Ahh," chuckled the admiral. "You see, there are many senior people that bend these rules to fit their interpretation, and that invites mischief. Flag officers must not only be above reproach; they must also appear to be above reproach."

I nodded and kept writing as the admiral continued to speak. After another fifteen minutes, he stood, and I did too.

"Weenie, when you meet Bones Sawyer, the intel chief, he will have you start getting a background check for a top-secret clearance. There are things you will see and hear that will require it."

"Yes, sir."

"And have one of the guys in operations take you over to the Tomcat RAG. They have agreed to put you on their flight schedule so you can maintain currency and proficiency in the airplane."

"Fantastic Sir! Thank you." I left the admiral's office and headed down the passageway to the operations and intelligence offices. This was going to be a great job!

That Friday afternoon, I went to the Oceana Officer's Club with the admiral, COS, and the other staff officers. It did not disappoint. Like Miramar, Oceana had a rich tradition of supporting aviators, including good booze and high camaraderie. I had also heard they had a back room for strippers. Whether that was true or not, I stayed in the main room with the admiral and the COS and watched the various officers approach him. Many were senior, captains, and commanders, but juniors also crowded around, and I could see the admiral thoroughly enjoyed their engagement. He was a very approachable person and would have earned Raoul's lofty praise, "not that bad for an admiral." But after an hour, he nodded towards the door, and I followed him out.

"Heading home," he smiled.

"Do you need anything, sir? Should I drive you?"

"No," the admiral laughed and shook his head. "Go back inside and join your buddies."

"You sure you want to leave, sir? The place is just now starting to boom."

"I'm not much of a boomer anymore, Weenie." The admiral chuckled and walked to his car. I watched him drive off then hustled to the back room. I squirmed through the crowd to the bar and ordered a beer and had just taken a sip when someone tapped me on the shoulder.

"Welcome to the east coast."

It was Jack Grant!

I almost spit my beer in his face.

"I think I got off to a wrong start with you," he smiled. "And I was a bit of an ass. Friends?" He held out his hand.

I was leery but smiled and shook. "Sure."

We spent the next hour talking, and he wasn't so bad after all. I was somewhat mystified as to his interest in the admiral's aide job, though. Most guys could care less what "the loop" did. I might have gotten a little tipsy because I did go on a bit about the value of an aide job to a navy career. Jack seemed genuinely interested, so it was okay.

Sunday, I headed up the coast to the Fort Story Officer's Club. It was the weekend afternoon place to be and rivaled Friday night at Oceana. There weren't any strippers, of course, but there were many young women, and that was what I was looking for.

I had been there about an hour when a group came in, and one of them caught my attention. And I don't know why. She wasn't some breath-taking babe or anything, but she was...well, she was pretty. No, she was more than that. She was, I don't know, classic? I don't know if that makes sense, but she was attractive in an enduring, timeless way. Sometimes I think about things too much, so I watched her a bit. She looked approachable, so I walked over and introduced myself.

"I'm Weenie Kleegan. This is my first time here, what's the deal with this place?" I couldn't believe I had introduced myself as Weenie. I usually say Win.

"Grace Sheehan," she replied. Her eyes were dark blue, almost violet, and her shy smile held vulnerability, which made my small ego smile back.

"My first time, too," she said.

"Sheehan? As in Vice-Admiral Sheehan, Commander of Naval Air Forces Atlantic?"

"The same." She rolled her eyes. "Are you going to run off now?"

"No," I laughed. "I have seen the admiral a couple of times. I am Rear Admiral Jensen's aide, and we meet with your father on occasion."

"Rear Admiral Jensen is a favorite of my dad's. He speaks highly of him."

"Well, I will pass that along. Would you like to dance?" I motioned to the floor where couples were gyrating and what I think of as flopping around. I couldn't dance a lick, well, I could slow dance because it was pretty much just clutching the girl and moving around.

I looked at Grace and reached for her hand, but she frowned and shook her head. "I don't dance much, maybe later? Something slow?" She smiled, and I felt she was sincere and not just putting me off. Maybe she couldn't fast dance, either? I really liked her.

I nodded and smiled and moved to the end of the bar. I wandered around and watched people dance for about thirty minutes. Most of the songs were the sort of funk stuff that everybody was playing now. I think it was God's punishment to us for letting the Beatles split up. Then, "First Time Ever I Saw Your Face" with Roberta Flack came on, and I searched for Grace. I caught a glimpse of her through the crowd, and she seemed to be looking for someone too. Maybe she was looking for me? Couples were starting to fill the dance floor, so I quickened my steps and smiled, and she came into full view. She was talking with Jack Grant!

"Hey Grace." I rushed forward, but Jack took her hand and moved toward the dance floor.

"Grace…"

Grace glanced at me and smiled, and I think I read a message. I think her eyes said, "Be patient. I was waiting for you."

So, I stood there and watched as Roberta sang my favorite song. It was the song that played over and over while I was at the AOCS club in Pensacola. It was the song that had reminded me of Jane, but I was now ready to have it remind me of someone else. I drifted to the back of the room, and Roberta's lyrics found me there, leaning against the wall and watching Grace.

I felt the earth move in my hand
Like the trembling heart of a captive bird
That was there at my command, my love.

And as I watched Grace smile up into Jack's handsome face, I felt my throat tighten. I swallowed as my old friend, despair, tapped on my shoulder. And when despair tapped it wasn't to dance.

I watched them until I saw Jack lead Grace out onto the back patio and then I slipped out the side door. I couldn't watch anymore. What chance did I have against somebody like Jack

Grant? Me with my scrawniness and everyday face. To make it worse, I had started wearing glasses again because I was tired of squinting. If a girl didn't like glasses, I might as well find out right away. I mean, Buddy Holly wore glasses. I read that James Dean wore glasses. Of course, he never wore them on the screen, so maybe he was like me. I slunk out to my car to drive back to my BOQ room but stopped at a 7-11 on the way. I needed some beer.

The next Monday, my first event was a meeting with the admiral, COS, commanding officer of Naval Air Station Oceana, and the commander of all the A-6 Intruder aircraft on base. The subject of the discussion was air discipline and safety.

"My office is getting daily calls about aircraft noise," said the admiral. "One farmer down in Pungo said a shark-looking aircraft flew over his field at treetop level, and it was so loud it broke the windows in his house." Admiral Jensen's eyes swept us. "When I look out over the runway," he pointed toward his window, "I routinely see aircraft coming into the break at well below 500 feet and well above 300 knots. That makes me wonder if our aircrews aren't getting a little too salty."

"Sir, with respect, we have been getting those calls since the navy built the air station." The F-4 RAG skipper, Commander Bob Sykes, made the comment. "And, sir, I bet you also came into the break pretty darned fast and low when you were a junior officer."

"True." The admiral grinned. He nodded but then frowned. "Hypocrisy is often the burden of leadership. Or the excuse for avoiding it." He smiled and leaned back in his chair. "I, too, violated the rules when I was young. But we also accepted a huge mishap rate back then. For instance, in 1954 alone, we lost almost 400 men and 800 aircraft, which was in peacetime training. We lowered the mishap rate 50% by the '60s and significantly lowered it by '70, but we still lose an unacceptable number of aviators each year, and the rate is going back up again, and that worries me."

"But, sir, noise complaints and a little flat-hatting don't necessarily mean people are unsafe."

"True, again," said the admiral. "But it does mean we have a break down in discipline, and I think you would agree that the loss of discipline in a military organization is inherently unsafe."

I watched the senior officers nod, but I had the feeling they were not convinced. The COS and I had discussed this, and we agreed the Vietnam years had ushered in a certain bravado and disregard for the rules in naval aviation and senior leadership, as well as the public, had primarily ignored or accepted aircrew antics. However, the sentiment was changing, and the public was viewing the military with new scrutiny. The military leadership was also becoming less accepting of what was once considered just the boys being the boys. The COS also said that, unfortunately, many squadron commanders and even more senior aviators wanted to ride the wave of ready room popularity that such hi-jinks spawned and were reluctant to crack down on violators.

The admiral frowned, leaned forward, and slowly looked at each of us. "I want you to get with your squadron leaders and take a turn on this, gentlemen. It is no lower than 500 feet and no faster than 300 knots coming into the break and no, absolutely, zero low transitions out of here."

I saw some frowns and clenched jaws. A low transition is a peacock event for sure. The pilot gets airborne but instead of elevating, remains low in afterburner until the end of the runway, then zooms into the vertical. The lower he flies, the more dramatic it is, and some squadrons even had a horizontal line drawn across their windows to show the "lowest so far" record.

"And I don't want any more unbriefed ACM."

ACM is an acronym for aerial combat maneuvering or dogfighting. It is supposed to be briefed in-depth, emphasizing what tactics and maneuvers to be used and specific discussions on what to do if you spin your aircraft. However, the fact is, fighter aircrew would often take advantage of "targets of opportunity" and attack aircraft they ran across in the training areas. I remembered my first flight in the Phantom, back in the old days. It was an unbriefed ACM hop against an F-8 Crusader.

"Sir, is there a reason for all of this?" It was Commander Sykes again.

The admiral looked at Sykes and took a deep breath. He leaned back in his chair again and slowly nodded. "You remember three months ago when we lost the A-4 and a Phantom? Four guys were killed."

"Yes, sir," nodded Commander Sykes. "Speculation is that they ran into each other in poor visibility. A freak case of bad luck."

"I just saw a report from FASTFAC, the fleet aerial surveillance guys. As you know, they record radar and radio transmissions in the training areas. The report has the transcript of a radio call from the pilot of the A-4 that says, 'Guns tracking, guns on the Phantom in the left-hand turn at 22,000 feet.'" The admiral took another breath. "It was made seconds before the loss of both aircraft on radar. So, I think they were conducting an unbriefed dogfight. And..." the admiral looked around the room. "I just read a flash message. You will see it by the time you get back to your squadrons. A west coast F-4 and a reserve F-8 from Washington, D.C. had a midair over Arizona. Phoenix ATC says they were heading in opposite directions on airways navigation plans under instrument flight rules when the F-8 suddenly deviated and dove toward the F-4. A radio call of, 'fight's on' was transmitted from one of the aircraft. In this case, the RIO in the Phantom survived, so we will get some more information, but it looks like an unbriefed event again." Admiral Jensen looked at Commander Sykes. "I want flight discipline, and safety stressed. I want you to do it now."

Two days later, a Phantom crashed into the water in Back Bay, killing the pilot and RIO. A nearby fisherman said he watched the plane streak over the water, getting lower and lower, shooting up a rooster tail of water behind it. Then, it just smacked into the bay.

That led to the admiral instituting a station-wide safety stand-down and rigorous enforcement of the published rules. Of course, one result was a lot of ready room grumbling and officer club fuming.

"Why is he such a pussy?" Jack Grant and I occupied a corner of the officer club bar, and each had a beer. He had continually sought me out, and we were now friends. I knew that he saw Grace, which bothered me much, but I also knew they wouldn't stay together for long. She wasn't right for him.

"What do you think? You're his aide. What's going on inside his head? Why is he such a prude?"

I frowned into my beer, not wanting to respond. A part of me knew I should defend my boss. But my junior officer blood, and the beer, made me remain quiet.

"Christ, he will probably outlaw the strippers in the back room next."

I could feel Jack looking at me. "What do you think about that, mister admiral's AIDE?"

I looked up into Jack's smirk. "The admiral is just conservative, that's all. He's a good guy." But even while I was speaking, I had my doubts. I mean, we had just fought a war over the skies of Vietnam, a war that was particularly dangerous to aviators, and we deserved to air it out a little. Besides, coming into the field at 450 knots and 200 feet LOOKED better, and I thought looking good was especially important.

"He is like all admirals," scoffed Jack. "If they were good guys before, and that's a big if, their balls shrink as soon as they pin that first star on."

"Come on, Jack." I was surprised at his tone. Before, he had seemed in awe of all admirals.

"And with each star that ball size goes down until they get the fourth and turn into completely nutless pussies."

I shook my head but had to laugh. Jack was funny, even if he was talking about my boss.

"You haven't lost your balls, have you?" Jack looked at me with a smirk. "Or has being an admiral's aide neutered you too?"

"I'm no different than I was as a squadron JO," I said.

"Well, then, let's have a shot of tequila to celebrate!"

I stayed in the club all during happy hour and into the night and loved the way the guys accepted me. They all knew of my background, heroics, or not, and nobody disliked me for being an aide. I even got into some animated discussions about how the admiral had overreacted and swore that I would talk to him about it. I would set him straight! This earned me thumps on the back and cheers and free beer. I barely remember going to my car and don't know why I even started it. The club was across the street from my BOQ room; I could have walked. But, instead, I started the Triumph and promptly ran it into a fire hydrant. The base shore patrol showed up, and someone helped me to my room, and the weirdest thing happened. While I took off my uniform, I cleaned out my pockets and threw a handful of change on the dresser top.

"I wonder if there are thirty pieces?" I laughed.

The next morning, I awoke with a massive hangover and showed up for work at 1030. The COS glared at me, but the admiral was busy and didn't say anything. I figured it was a cheap lesson learned.

The following week the admiral and I flew to San Diego for briefings with the famed TOPGUN school. The admiral's previous aide, Snake Hastings, was our escort, and he and I had gotten to know each other over the phone during coordination calls. He had told me some history--that the navy formed TOPGUN in 1969 due to the poor performance in aerial combat by navy fighter aircrew. We had barely a 2 to 1 kill ratio, which was not only far below our World War Two and Korean War numbers but also unsustainable. We would run out of fighters before they ran out of MIGS! The school formed to teach fighter maneuvering, missile employment, and aircrew coordination, and the result was a 12:1 kill ratio! The TOPGUN skipper was Lieutenant Commander Hawk Peters, and he provided a top-secret briefing on a program whereby TOPGUN pilots flew former Soviet MIG aircraft. They exploited the capabilities and limitations of the MIGs to refine naval aviation fighter tactics. It was a great brief, and I was very thankful the admiral had pressed me to get the proper clearance.

That evening, we had dinner at Hawk's house and Snake, and I strolled to the back deck to enjoy the southern California night.

"You know, the admiral was instrumental in getting the program you saw today started."

"He was?" I took a sip of Corona.

"Yep, against HUGE opposition, I might add. We can't talk much about it here, of course." Snake looked around the patio, then back at me. "But I can say the CIA was not happy with some navy pukes messing around with their toys. Many senior navy flags also didn't like the idea of junior officers involved with such a project."

"What did the admiral do?"

"Well, as you can see, the skipper of TOPGUN is a lieutenant commander. He doesn't have much firepower when it comes to high-level arguments. But the admiral was a senior captain at the time and worked in the navy operations offices in the Pentagon. He constructed a brief based on the benefits we would gain from such a program. He even briefed the Joint Chiefs. Anyway, you saw the result today."

"Wow, I had no idea."

"He's quite a guy." Snake nodded his head and took a sip. He looked at me and pursed his lips. "However, I hear from my east coast buddies that the admiral has turned into a wuss. That bothers me. He is anything but a wuss. You need to set those guys straight, Weenie."

I felt a sharp jolt of guilt. After all, I, too, had participated in such junior officer conversations, and indictments, in the Oceana bar.

"Lots of hate and discontent because of his flight restrictions," I said. "They even took the strippers out of the club."

"Really?" Snake frowned.

"Yeah." I took another sip. "I don't know if the admiral had anything to do with that, but they're gone."

"You know, I found that I had to defend him sometimes," said Snake. "I remember once I was in the back bar, and some dude came up and complained about the hours the commissary was open. Said the admiral didn't care."

"What did you say?"

"I cited a bunch of facts about what the admiral had done for the fighter community. I also told him that he should visit the base commander if he wanted to whine about the commissary hours. It's in his lane, not the admiral's."

"Gents."

We both turned toward the door. It was Hawk's wife, Ally.

"Time for dinner," she said. We followed her into the house, and throughout the evening and next day's flight home, I had a growing feeling of guilt. I felt like a disloyal prick.

A few weeks later, I sat down with the admiral to discuss my performance. Although my first fitness report wasn't due for months, the admiral felt it best to have discussions with each staff member periodically. Besides, if someone needed to move in a better direction, the admiral could give the required counseling before an official report. I admit I was a bit concerned. Not because of how I had performed but because of how I had not. Snake's conversation weighed heavily on my mind.

The admiral made me comfortable with some coffee and small talk. Then he leaned back in his chair and smiled.

"So, how do you think you are doing? How do you feel about this job, and what is going on?"

"I think I am learning the ropes," I grinned. "I'm starting to figure it out."

"I agree," laughed the admiral. "Remember what I said the mission was when you checked in? I haven't been late once, and I am always in the right uniform."

We both laughed, but the smile in his eyes and friendship in his face made me feel guilty again. He was such a great guy, and I had pulled a Judas on him. I had not supported him to my junior officer buddies when they had bashed him. I hoped he would never find out, and I pledged to make up for it.

"Weenie, I want to give you some words on leadership, if you don't mind."

"Of course not, sir. I will take any advice you give."

"But first, you talk to me about leadership, Weenie."

I looked up and frowned again.

"What is it? What is leadership in your view?"

"I don't know, sir," I chuckled nervously. "I guess it is doing the right thing."

The admiral smiled and nodded. "Sure. Sure, that is a part of it. But that is a result of leadership. Doing the right thing, you, or someone you direct or lead. Sure. But what is the watchword? What is the guiding execution thought?"

"Sir?"

"Weenie, leadership is a philosophy of life as much as it is a capability. And nobody is born with it, regardless of what you hear. Leadership is like medicine. It is something a professional must practice knowing that there is always something more to learn or do. Do you understand?"

"Not really, sir."

"Weenie, let me give you two words to use. Two words to guide you as you grow into a better leader. And don't worry, you will grow into a better leader. Weenie, those words are 'constructively confront.'"

"Constructively confront?" I frowned. I was confused.

"I don't mean getting angry. I mean, constructively confront. By that, I mean to be observant enough to detect a problem and care enough to do something about it. That is what I mean by the words constructively confront."

I nodded but was unsure what the admiral meant.

"The other day, when you and I went to the exchange, you dropped me off at the barbershop, remember?"

"Yes, sir."

"I turned to the parking lot, just as I got to the door and saw you walk past two sailors. All of you were in uniform, but neither of them saluted you, and you didn't stop them. Do you remember?"

I glanced at the admiral, then quickly looked at the deck. I remembered. But I had just had a conversation with Jack Grant about how big a prick most officers are to their enlisted men. "The navy made all of us pricks," Jack had said. I didn't want to be a prick.

I looked at the admiral and nodded. "Yes, sir."

"Why?"

I wasn't about to tell him the prick conversation, so I just shrugged. "Not sure, sir."

"Do you believe in our military tradition of juniors rendering salutes to seniors? It is a part of every military culture in the world."

"Sure. Yes, sir."

"Do you question whether you, Lieutenant Weenie Kleegan, is deserving of a salute from two sailors?"

"No, sir."

"Do you see what is going on here, Weenie?" The admiral leaned forward and clasped his hands in front of him on his desk. "I am confronting a junior officer on my staff who has a lot of promise but who could use some direction. We all need to be led and directed Weenie. And I am constructively doing this. Now, you might feel uncomfortable, but that is not because of my delivery but because of the nature of what we are discussing. With me so far?"

"Yes, sir."

"Young officers often have a difficult time constructively confronting their juniors. I struggled with it too. I think part of it is the ages are nearly the same; the other part is that you are hesitant to appear mean spirited."

"Yes, sir."

"Another group that is hard, ridiculously hard, to confront is our buddies. You have probably seen or heard your junior officer pals do or say things that are destructive-- untrue, hurtful. And when you witnessed those things, you knew it was wrong. But it is hard to confront such a situation. It is hard to lead in such a situation."

"Yes, sir." I nodded as I thought of my many conversations with my pals. Conversations that were wrong and untrue and opportunities and responsibilities for me to…confront them.

"Some people incorrectly think admirals and generals face the hardest leadership challenges. Sometimes I think the hardest situations are when two lieutenants are critiquing each other on a flight or when a brand new third-class petty officer leads two airmen on a maintenance task. The difficulty of leadership, or constructive confrontation as I have outlined it here, scales to all ranks. Nobody gets off. Nobody that wants to be a real leader that is."

I looked at the admiral. He was leading me, and I wanted to be led.

"One of the most difficult leadership challenges is parenting, and surely one day you will face that."

I nodded again.

"I suppose you know about my daughter, Amber?"

"Yes, sir." I knew that the admiral's daughter had died two years ago in a car wreck.

"On the afternoon before she died, she came to me and asked if she could sleepover at a friend's house. She mentioned a name, but I didn't know the girl or her parents. So, I said no. But Amber looked at me with her big eyes, her mother's eyes, and begged me. Weenie, I wanted to please her so much. She was sixteen and at that age when so many parents seem to separate from their children, and I didn't want that to happen to us. I had spent so much time away from her anyway. I wanted her to love me and think of me as the best Dad ever, just like you read on the T-shirts. So, I gave in, and she went to her friend's, and I got my wish. The last thing she said to me as she walked out the door was, 'I love you, Daddy.'"

I took a quiet breath and looked into the admiral's eyes. They were moist, and as he looked at me, I remembered my Grandpa Two Bears discussion about great moments in a man's life. He had told me that sometimes we are blessed with such moments, and if we act correctly, they can help us find a higher level. But I now realized that there are also great opportunities in a man's life. And this opportunity, this time sitting with this man, was a gift to help me grow into a better leader.

"The police called around two that morning, and when the phone rang, I knew what it was. I knew something had happened to Amber. And I knew that it was my fault."

The admiral looked out the window, and I could see him swallow and blink, and I knew he was having a moment with his story. I remained quiet, and finally, he looked at me.

"I should have confronted her, Weenie. Constructively, with words of concern and love, but I should not have given in. If I had done that, she would still be alive, and any grief or anger between us would have been long forgotten. I should have confronted her, but I didn't. Constructive confrontation is a responsibility, Weenie that many don't accept, and even if you do, the constant grind of it can wear you down. Weenie, I am telling you this because the art of leadership must be kept alive in our best young officers. I am telling you this because you must be one to hold that torch."

I spent an hour with the admiral that afternoon, and I think it was as blessed as anytime I have ever spent. It rivaled a session with Grandpa Two Bears. I knew that I was indeed in the presence of an incredibly special person, and I vowed to learn from him. More than that, I promised to deserve him.

Two months later, the CNO called. I answered the phone and almost choked when I heard his flag writer asked if Rear Admiral Jensen could hold for Admiral Holloway. In the navy, junior flag officers get on the line and wait for a senior to join. I gulped and mustered up my best big boy voice, "Certainly."

I ran across the passageway and knocked on the admiral's door frame. It was always open. He looked up and smiled.

"What's up?"

"Sir, the CNO's writer called. I told her you would hold for Admiral Holloway.

"Sure, you know what to do."

"Yes, sir." What the admiral meant was for me to be on the line taking notes. If Admiral Holloway asked if it was a clear line, that meant I should hang up.

I picked up the phone, and in seconds Admiral Holloway's voice boomed across the receiver.

"Jaybird! How are things in Southeast Virginia?"

"Well, better than they were for us in Southeast Asia!"

Admiral Holloway howled, and the admiral said, "Couldn't be better, sir. Thank you for asking. And for you, sir. How are things in the Pentagon?"

"Pretty much as you left them," laughed the CNO.

"That bad, huh?"

Both admirals laughed, and I held my hand over the mouthpiece and laughed too. I felt privileged. How many junior officers could be on a phone conversation with two admirals?

"Look, I called to tell you that you are on the two-star list. I wanted to be the one to let you know."

"Gosh, Sir, I don't know what to say. Thank you, sir."

"Don't thank me; it was your record that got you the promotion, Jay."

"Thank you, sir."

"How do you feel about this, Jay?"

"I feel humble, sir. I feel humble. And I feel lucky."

"Good. Great. Jay, that is the way I felt too. That is the way I feel now, humble, and lucky."

"Where are you going to send me, sir?"

"Where do you want to go?"

"Sir, I want to go to sea."

"I hoped you would say that. I am sending you to sea Jay, as Commander, Carrier Group Four. You will hoist your flag on *America* there in Norfolk."

"Christ, sir, that is fantastic! It is a dream come true. It is exactly what I had hoped for."

"Good, good. She is a great ship, and Airwing Six is a perfect complement to her. As you know, they just got the Tomcats."

"Yes, sir. I know."

"Congratulations, Jay. The flag detailer will be sending you a message within a day or two, but you can tell June the good news."

"Thank you again, sir. While I have you on the phone, may I ask who is coming in to replace me?

"Looks like the slate has Buzz Bass heading your way. Know him?"

"Yes, sir. I know him, or I know of him. He and I never served together."

"You have done a super job, Jay. The east coast fighter community is as solid as it has ever been; hell, it's better than any other naval aviation installation, and it is because of you. So, we could send an ensign in behind you, and it would be alright. No offense to ensigns, of course."

I heard them laugh and muted the receiver so I could laugh too. Then Admiral Holloway asked, "Is the line clear, Jay?"

"Yes, sir," answered the admiral, and I hung up.

The navy detailed Rear Admiral Jensen to be the commander of Carrier Group Four, and I pleaded with him to take me along as his aide. Admirals can do that if they want, but Rear Admiral Jensen refused. He told me that I had been on shore duty for a little more than a year, and he didn't want to rush me back to sea. He told me I should concentrate on serving Rear Admiral Bass, who wanted me to stay and take the opportunity to build flight time in the F-14.

While I was dismayed at the prospect of leaving the admiral, I admit I was glad to continue to fly the Tomcat. I was getting very proficient at operating the magic in the back seat. I was even happier to stay after I met Rear Admiral Bass. Shortly after the phone call with the CNO, he came to Oceana, and I had an office call with him. He stood when I walked into the room!

"Weenie, come on in. I have been looking forward to meeting you!" The admiral grinned and extended his hand. We shook, and I took the seat he motioned to, and the admiral sat on the edge of his desk.

"I am impressed with you, Weenie. Jay told me wonderful things, and, of course, I am familiar with your history. Your combat action in Vietnam, saving your pilot, saving all those kids in Honolulu. An incredible record for such a junior officer!"

"Thank you, sir."

"Very impressive!"

"Thank you, sir!"

"We are going to get along famously!" The admiral grinned again and took a seat behind his desk. "As for your duties, just continue what you were doing for Admiral Jensen, and I can always refine things as we go along."

"Yes, sir."

"Weenie, I am glad we are F-4 Phantom combat comrades. I think it is a bond that will make us a good team."

"Thank you, sir."

"And the fact that I am a pilot, and you are a RIO is going to come in real handy. We can fly together! I am still current in the F-4, and Admiral Jensen says you are too. You are current in the F-4 and the Tomcat."

"That's right, sir." I had maintained my currency in the Phantom and flew it occasionally with the F-4 RAG.

The intimacy of our conversation led me to ask a question that had always lingered.

"Sir, who was your RIO? When you shot down the MIG."

"Darby Collins." The admiral smiled and leaned back in his chair. "Darby and I were not usually crewed together, but we were that day. He was a good RIO."

"Do you still keep in touch?"

"No, strange, isn't it? After that deployment, I never saw him again. Have no idea what happened to Darby."

"Oh." I frowned.

"Hey, Weenie, we can't all stay together. It was a big war, and a lot of guys left when it was over."

"Yes, sir." I was disappointed. I wanted them to have maintained a lifelong relationship, one forged in combat over Vietnam. Kind of like the one I hoped to continue with Cotton.

Rear Admiral Jensen and Rear Admiral Bass had their change of command in building 23 at Oceana. It was designed for such events, and the crowd was overflowing. The CNO, himself, attended as the guest speaker, and I have never been so busy ensuring all the details were accounted for. The event went as planned with no significant hiccups, and I counted it as a major success. Of course, there was the one thing that kept me awake, which made me thrash my sheets. One of my tasks was to ensure all the admirals' wives and their entourage had seats in the front row, and on Mrs. Sheehan's list, I needed places for Grace Sheehan and Lieutenant Junior Grade Jack Grant. That depressed me to no end, and just after the national anthem and the prayer and as the crowd settled into their seats, my eyes found Grace. She was looking right at me when I saw her, and she smiled. And, of course, my heart leaped. Then my eyes moved to Jack. His eyes had found me too, and he put his arm around Grace's shoulders and smiled.

I smiled back and hoped my jealousy didn't show.

THE BAD ADMIRAL

The first Friday following the command change, I accompanied Admiral Bass to the Oceana Officers' Club. We spent a few minutes in the front room, as people came to "kiss the ring" and offer congratulations. We chatted for about half an hour, then the admiral sidled over to me and nodded.

"Let's go to the back."

"Sir, the…uh…dancer is back there now. I suggest holding off until she leaves."

"Why?" The admiral smiled. "I'm the one that brought the dancers back."

"Well, sir, I mean, Admiral Jensen would not consider it."

"I'M NOT JENSEN!" The admiral's face quickly flamed, but he caught himself and looked around as a nervous smile touched his lips. "Look, Weenie, I'm not a goody two-shoe like Jensen. I'm cut from a different cloth. So, let's get back there where the real party is."

"Certainly, sir. This way."

As soon as we entered the room, the crowd of junior officers roared and cheered. A huge smile plastered Admiral Bass's face, and he held his hands over his head in a triumphant clench.

"BUZZ! BUZZ! BUZZ!" The crowd chanted.

And guess who showed up right next to the admiral. Jack Grant, of course.

"We have a drink for you, sir." Jack grinned and grabbed the dancer. Her name was Bambi or Trixie, or something like that, and she leaned forward with a shot glass wedged in the cleavage of her huge, wonderful, and arching breasts.

The admiral reached for the drink, fondling the "fun bags" as Raoul described them in the process, and the crowd roared anew. The admiral deftly and slowly withdrew the glass from its twin masters and grinned broadly to the cheers.

"Now, that's the way to buy a man a drink!"

He threw it back and slapped the glass on the bar.

"Jack Grant, sir. Welcome home!" Jack extended his hand, but the admiral grabbed him in a bear hug.

"It's good to be back!"

I watched them for a while and marveled at how the admiral threw back drink after drink before his adoring throng of aviators. I can drink, but that guy was a master boozer!

I was three sheets to the wind when the COS showed up. He wasn't happy.

"Why aren't you watching him?"

"I am watching him."

"But can't you see he is getting plowed?"

"Sure, I can see that. But do you have any ideas on how to stop him?"

The COS looked at the admiral for a moment, then took a deep breath and shook his head. "We are in for a show, Weenie. Life as we knew it will never be the same."

The COS and I stayed and hovered at the edges of the admiral's party, and I admit I was jealous of Jack. He and the admiral seemed to enjoy each other's company immensely, and for the first time since I had joined the navy, I felt left out. I mean, even when I joined my first squadron in the Philippines so long ago, the duty officer had made me feel at home, part of the pack. But now, I had this feeling that I ceased to exist.

"I'll stick around and watch him," said the COS. "Go on if you want to."

I glanced at the admiral one more time and turned to the COS. "Thank you, sir." I went back to my BOQ room and thought about calling Grace. But I poured myself a bourbon instead.

The weeks went by, and the admiral and I fell into what I would call a working relationship, friendly but not close. It was nothing like the connection I had felt to Rear Admiral Jensen. I asked the COS if I had done something wrong but he just shrugged and said, "It takes time for an admiral to bond to a junior officer."

However, when we went to the club the admiral was never far from Jack Grant. Jack was always right there by his side with the drink or cigar or joke. Evidently, they had bonded! And that bothered me because I was no Jack Grant.

A month later, we began preparations for a huge political event in Pensacola. At least, was huge as far as Rear Admiral Bass was concerned. We were to fly to Pensacola for the winging of Senator Wolford's son, Alex. Senator Wolford was the most powerful politician in Virginia and chaired the Senate Armed Services Committee. He had a massive influence over the navy, and he and Rear Admiral Bass had grown into mutual fans. Senator Wolford had asked if the admiral would assist in pinning his son's naval flight officer wings, and Bass had giddily agreed.

We took a navy DC-9 to Pensacola, and the senator's contingent of friends and families nearly filled it! Shortly after landing at Forest Sherman Field, the admiral pulled me aside.

"Weenie, I need to borrow your wings."

"Sir?"

"I need to borrow your wings." The admiral held out his hand. I hesitated, then reached inside my jacket, unclasped my wings, and handed them to him.

The admiral looked at them a second, then smiled and clapped me on the shoulder. "Perfect, thanks Weenie."

There are no hard rules for a winging. Sometimes they are very informal, like the one I had in Flame's office in Glynco. No family or fuss, just pinning them on our chest with some words of encouragement. Other ceremonies are more elaborate, and the one we were attending was incredibly so. Everybody was in dress blues or suits, with ladies in delicate dresses and an overflowing crowd filled the auditorium. We stood for the national anthem, bowed for the prayer, and then the training squadron commander introduced Rear Admiral Bass. The admiral recognized the senator and others and spoke some glowing words about naval aviation, the fighter community, and the need for back seat warriors in today's complex battlespace.

The wings lay in a wooden box with a blue felt lining, and as a young officer stepped forward, the admiral called his family, and the winging took place with great fanfare and photographs. The senator's son was the last officer to be winged, and when he stepped forward, the senator and his wife accompanied him on the stage. But instead of taking the final pair of gold wings from the box with the blue felt lining, Rear Admiral Bass reached into his pocket and drew out a set of wings. My wings. He looked at them, and I saw him rub them in his hands. He rubbed them with a tenderness that begat great, personal significance. He rubbed them the way Grandpa Two Bears rubbed Grandma's ring. Then, Rear Admiral Bass lifted his face to the crowd.

"These wings used to belong to my best friend." The admiral looked down at the wings in his hand and took a deep breath. He shook his head and looked up at us.

"My best friend, my RIO, my cruise roommate. Like I said, my best friend."

I heard gasps, and I heard moans.

"The man..." The admiral paused and wiped his eyes. "The man who wore these wings, Darby Collins, was a warrior, a patriot, and a saint of a man. He died last year, and on his death bed, he asked if I would pass his wings to the next generation of fighters. He looked at me and said, "Bass, man, you get to see the best of them every day. Give these to somebody as good as we were."

The crowd fell silent, respectful, and hopeful. They yearned for that sacred set of words that would somehow capture the men in uniform, the gold of the wings, the solemnity and grandeur. And, I have to say, Admiral Bass might be the best elicitor of such emotions I have ever seen. He should have sold used cars or caskets. Anyway, as I watched him gaze out at the merging tears and the gasps waiting to leap from throats, I heard him say, "Darby told me that if I ever saw someone who embodied what we all did together over the skies of Vietnam, someone who had the passion for his nation and grit and guts...then, to give these wings to that man. And I think I see that in Ensign Lance Wolford."

Senator Wolford's mouth fell open in astonished glee, then his lips lit in a smile. Mrs. Wolford clutched his arm and dabbed at her eyes with her handkerchief. The trickle of a tear shined in the senator's eyes, then slowly edged down his cheeks. The crowd was silent, save for the sounds of swallows and low gasps.

But I was stunned! I mean, I was dumbfounded! The admiral's story, almost a soliloquy when he had shut his eyes and spoken of Darby, was so heartwarming and precious. But it was a fabrication. It was a lie meant to wring the emotion from the crowd and embrace him to the senator. The admiral told me he had lost sight of Darby years ago, and those were MY wings! The fact he said such a thing with me standing right in front of him. He knew that I knew the real story. How could he?

With the senator and his wife's hovering help, the admiral placed my wings on Lance's chest and shook hands, then embraced the young officer in an apparent moment of emotion. The senator and Mrs. Wolford crowded them, and the four hugged as the crowd clapped and cheered.

Later, at the reception, I found myself where they have the raw carrots and broccoli and cauliflower with the white, gooey ranch dressing. Nobody likes that stuff, but eating it is something to do until you can leave. I had just fixed a plate when I turned to find the admiral at my side.

"Thanks for the help, Weenie." The admiral smiled and grabbed my arm. "Lance, the senator, and Mrs. Wolford just had the experience of their lives, and you are partly responsible for it. The crowd got to see some of the passion of naval aviation, and it was a final moment in the sun for Darby, too. It was a win-win, Weenie and I thank you." He squeezed my arm, turned, and left before I could respond. I watched him enter the embrace of a group of guests, and as they grabbed for his hand and patted his back, I took a bite of broccoli. And, as I chewed, I thought of what I had just seen. True, the situation with my wings did provide richness to the lives of the Wolford's and to the audience of the winging ceremony. But the admiral offered that at the cost of the truth, and since I was the only one outside the admiral who knew, was that sacrifice okay? Was it alright to warm the hearts of all the people in the crowd at the expense of out integrity? Or was living with small lies that supported great opportunities some life skill that I needed in order to succeed? Was it something I needed to make it to the top?

A month after the winging, the admiral directed that we plan a massive, air station-wide event to support the Hampton Roads Polio Campaign. We conducted a small airshow at the field and asked the crowd to donate whatever they could. From the public view, the admiral was a saint. But I ran the public relations campaign, and I detected another purpose for the event. Posters with the admiral's face, begging for donations to "stop this scourge of polio" were everywhere, the admiral was on all local television and radio stations. We even placed calls to every member of the Virginia and North Carolina congressional delegations to ensure they were aware of our efforts. We raised thousands of dollars for polio, and that was a good thing. Heck, it was a great thing. But the admiral's reputation hugely benefited too. I had to admit that I was torn by him. Part of me despised his falseness and narcissism, but another side of me embraced his ability to produce good outcomes.

Months went by, and since I was a bachelor and still lived in the BOQ alone, I found myself supporting the admiral whenever he wanted. So, when the phone rang in the middle of the night, and the admiral called me to journey to a mansion in Broad Bay or a water-front estate in Great Neck Point, I was available. He would be slurring and magnanimous and drunk, and I would take him to his quarters and put him to bed in the guest room. I never did see the admiral's wife during these trips; in fact, I only met her once. She never attended any of the parties or functions.

I was also available to do all the personal things that Rear Admiral Jensen had told me an aide should not do. I picked up the admiral's dry cleaning, shined his shoes, went grocery shopping, even washed his car.

I also flew with the admiral, and we would take an F-4 from the RAG and fly local hops. He would make up his own rules on such occasions and just fly around sight-seeing, zooming the clouds, regardless of where the navigation routes might be. The first time I flew with him, we came into the break at Oceana at around 650 knots, just below supersonic, and at one hundred fifty feet! It was on a Friday, and when we got to the club, a crowd of adoring junior officers mobbed him.

In the meantime, the aircraft availability numbers began to fall. Rear Admiral Bass did not personally administer the programs and policies that Rear Admiral Jensen so painstakingly put in place. Those chores fell to the COS who, despite his efforts, was not the master that Rear Admiral Jensen had been. So, pressure on the money with no flag level support resulted in less money. Rear Admiral Bass did not interact with nor prod the various components of the naval aviation parts and supply system. He did not analyze the data. One morning during the daily staff meeting, he blew up when he saw the aircraft availability and other maintenance data.

"What is the purpose of this?"

"Sir," the COS frowned and shook his head. "Sir, this is to update you on our support for the fleet."

"The fleet?" The admiral pointed to a slide. "This says we have lost seventeen percent in our F-4 full mission capability rates."

"Yes, sir."

" Fix it. "

"Sir?" The COS frowned again.

"Fix the numbers. Make them the same that Jensen had. "

" Sir? "

"Look, nobody cares about these numbers. They just become part of some meaningless, low-level brief in the Pentagon. I ask you what real difference do numbers make?"

"Sir?" The COS frowned again. I looked around the room. Everyone frowned.

"In the big picture for naval aviation, what real difference does this data on the F-4 make?"

"Sir, the data indicates we do not have…"

"NO!" The admiral looked around the table. "I want all of you to think about the big picture; not this small, tactical world that seems to seize you. I need you to think bigger than that. What good is an F-4 against the Soviets or the Chinese? I mean, they are our global competitors, not some sideshow like Vietnam. Vietnam is over. Do you see us dogfighting Russian MIGs over Eastern Europe?" The admiral leaned back and shook his head. "It will never come to that. The battle, gentlemen, is right here in the United States, and it is a battle for dollars. The surface and subsurface navy, the air force, and the army are competitors for defense dollars, and we need to ensure that naval aviation gets its fair chunk. Your previous boss spent countless hours developing these programs and managing this data and wringing every bit of capability out of the supply and support system. Great! But for what? You see, gents, I am not a manager. I am an inspirer! I am a leader! What naval aviation needs is not a tinkerer but a larger-than-life personality that can command a national, hell, a world stage. Rear Admiral Jensen was a nobody in the big scheme of things. He is unknown outside of the navy and has no real ability to help us. Don't you see, that is why I do the things I do. So, don't show me meaningless data on the F-4 that indicates I am not successful. Talk to me about how we can support the navy and the nation. We work directly for Vice Admiral Sheehan, the three-star, help me support him. Bring me ideas on how we can better position naval aviation and carrier operations all over the world, not just some F-4s in Oceana."

"But sir." I shook my head. "The mission of this command is clearly stated on numerous documents. It says our mission is to support the east coast fighter community, not world-wide naval aviation."

As the admiral stared at me, his mouth hardened into a thin line of disappointment. His eyes indicated surprise that I would speak up. "Lieutenant Kleegan, you are my aide, not my scold. Our mission is what I say it is. Managing a few numbers for the east coast fighter community isn't big enough for me and if it isn't big enough for you then you are in the wrong place." Rear admiral Bass glared at me a moment longer and then looked around the table.

"Clear the room."

The chairs squeaked as we all stood to go.

"Not you, Kleegan."

I remained standing while the others filed out, and when the door shut, I chanced a glance at the admiral. He was glaring at me.

"You are my aide. Kleegan, that is a privileged position, and I am surprised your time with Rear Admiral Jensen did not make that privilege clear. You see, when an aide supports his admiral, people assume it is because the aide is not only loyal but also because he knows something they do not. They assume the aide is privy to something, and that is why it is such an esteemed position. Admirals take aides inside the circle, Weenie, inside the circle of power, and that is a place very, very few people have entered. So, when you question me, particularly in others' presence, the aide and admiral relationship is turned upside down. We both lose because of it. Do you understand?"

The admiral's voice was now soft, and when I glanced into his eyes, I saw sincerity. I realized that I had not only fallen short of defending Rear Admiral Jensen to my junior officer buddies, but I had also failed Rear Admiral Bass.

"Yes, sir." I felt like crap. I was a shitty aide.

"Don't turn your back on me like you did on Jensen."

"Sir?" I was shocked! How could he possibly know about any of that? I mean, the only guy I ever confided in about my reservations had been... I took a deep breath...had been Jack Grant.

"Yes, sir."

"Good, you can go now."

My relationship with the admiral became increasingly forced and sterile. Our morning staff meetings became less and less about support for our fighter fleet and more about a higher-level naval aviation strategy and Geo-politics. For instance, despite our Tomcats' engines' problems, he resisted highlighting the deficiencies and demanding change due to what he called "ambiguous congressional support." Instead of the COS and the maintenance and supply officers doing the briefing, Bones Sawyer, the intelligence officer, led the way. I was confused, and so was the staff, and I don't think any of us understood what we were doing. But I certainly wasn't going to say anything. The admiral's mission for the command was not to "produce the best aircraft for the best aircrew in the world," as Rear Admiral Jensen had said. I came to believe that Rear Admiral Bass's mission for the command was him getting more stars on his collar, but I think he genuinely felt that was not so much selfish as it was necessary.

Despite my concerns, I felt obligated to support the admiral, he was my boss, and I was his aide. So, one day I knocked on his door while he was having his lunch. He always ate alone, and I hoped he would give me a few moments.

"Come in." I heard his voice, gruff, and muffled with food.

"Sir, could I get a minute while you eat?"

The admiral frowned but motioned with his fork. A piece of lettuce pointed toward a chair, so I sat.

"Sir, I have thought about your comments to the staff and me. About our thinking about the big picture."

The admiral nodded and added a forkful of tomato to his mouth.

"Sir, as you know, when carriers depart the east coast, they routinely steam straight for the Straits of Gibraltar, enter the Mediterranean and chop to Sixth Fleet."

I suppose it is possible to chew thoughtfully, so I continued when I saw my boss nod.

"And requirements, largely due to the Israeli-Arab situation, keep us inside the Med until we return home."

The admiral shrugged and took another bite.

"But the threat to us is not the Arab world, but the USSR and its backyard is the North Atlantic. Second Fleet is responsible for the North Atlantic and, as you know, Vice Admiral Calhoun, a fellow naval aviator, commands Second Fleet."

Rear Admiral Bass put down his fork and leaned back in his chair. I had his full attention.

"I have prepared a few slides that depict a multi-carrier battle group operating far into the North Atlantic, beyond the Greenland, Iceland, UK gap and close to the USSR. It could demonstrate pressure that naval aviation could put on the Soviets to support NATO land operations across Europe."

"We have done that before." The admiral took a sip of tea. "It is a vulnerable place to be."

"Yes, sir, but we haven't done it with the F-14. I have designed a plan whereby Tomcats take cap stations hundreds of miles from the carrier, defending against the Soviet cruise-missile attacks from mainland bombers. My plan uses carrier launched A-6 tankers, our E-2 for battlespace command and control, so we don't need the air force. We also execute the plan with zero emissions from the carrier."

"How is that possible?"

"Sir, I have developed a navigation grid using the Tomcat's inertial navigation system. The RIO displays it on his Tactical Information Display, let me show you."

The admiral put his plate to the side of his desk and pointed to a sheet of legal paper.

I put an X in the middle of the bottom, "this is the carrier." I then drew a line to the top of the paper, "and this is the threat axis where the Soviets will most likely attack us, I will use 090 for this example." I drew three lines on each side of the threat axis that fanned out as they went to the paper's top. "Using 090 as the threat axis, the lines on the right are 100, 110, and 120. The lines on the left are 080, 070, and 060, do you follow me, sir."

"Yes, go on."

I continued. "Sir, every fifty miles from the carrier will be described as a letter. The cap station fifty miles away along the threat axis of 090 is 09 Alpha; at 100 miles, it would be 09 Bravo. The cap station fifty miles further out would be 09 Charlie. The cap station 200 miles out would be 09..."

"Delta," said the admiral.

"Exactly. So, let's say an F-14 stationed at 09 Bravo sees something 150 miles away from him, he would say, '09 Bravo is hot for 09 Echo.' "He would transmit this over the grid frequency but encrypted. So, the Soviets wouldn't understand even if they heard something. The E2 would hear that, and he could direct another airplane in the grid to replace 09 Bravo at his old cap spot, and he could call the carrier and tell them to launch another fighter from the alert. All of this would be encrypted."

"Does anybody else know about this?"

"No, Sir. I put it together in my room at the BOQ."

"Hmmm," the admiral leaned forward and stared at the drawing.

"Sir, if we put two carriers together, we would have four F-14 squadrons to man the grid and two battlegroups worth of Aegis cruisers to support the carriers' defense. We would also have six bomber squadrons that could launch. That is a potent threat, and I think it would pressurize the Soviets to divert resources away from NATO and central Europe. It would make naval aviation a key player against our most formidable foe. Of course, this works against the Chinese, too."

"Could you develop some graphs and facts? And add some notes so I can study this further."

"Of course, sir. I will have it for you tomorrow."

"This is great, Weenie. By the way, what are you calling this concept?"

"Not sure, sir. Right now, I am calling it Vector Logic."

"Vector Logic. Sounds good. Thanks, Weenie."

A month later, I was on a plane to Roosevelt Roads Naval Air Station in Puerto Rico. Carrier Battle Group Four was conducting a fleet exercise that involved not only aircraft from America but also submarines, surface ships, and P-3 anti-submarine planes. Rear Admiral Bass had persuaded Vice Admirals Sheehan and Calhoun to allow him to be an observer for the exercise. He told them it was because he wanted an opportunity to gain a fleet-wide understanding of the navy's fighter requirements. However, I knew Rear Admiral Bass wished to use the exercise to support his personal mission of greatness and, more importantly, relevance. So, my tasks were to secure the visiting flag officer VIP cottage on base, rent the admiral a car and get him a hotel room off the base. That final task puzzled me until the admiral explained.

"Weenie, there may be press interest from the local newspapers, and some do not have the credentials to get onto the base. I want to ensure Puerto Rico is always available for this large-scale fleet training, so I want to include all their voices. I need a room off the base, someplace nice where I can hold meetings and other functions."

"Yes, sir? Should I use your credit card? This doesn't seem like something the navy will pay for."

"My wife took the card, and she is on a trip to Florida to see her parents. Weenie, could you put it on your card, and I will pay you back."

I hesitated a second. The admiral had a way of forgetting about the five, ten, twenty dollar "loans" I had given to him in the past. I had stopped asking him for them because the subject made him angry. But he was my boss.

"Sure. Yes, sir."

I took the navy C-9 connector flight from Norfolk to Roosevelt Roads and had some time to think on the way to Puerto Rico. My job as an aide to Rear Admiral Jensen had been uplifting, and the more that I was around him, the better of an officer I became. He was an inspiration, and I think all the staff felt the same. But now all of that had changed, and I was often confused by Rear Admiral Bass. I wasn't sure how to feel. The more I was around him; the more dismal I felt because deep down inside I didn't trust him. I also didn't respect him or believe in him, and the worse part was I was sure he felt the same way about me. So, I was now in a survival situation whereby I had to make it through the remaining year until I rolled back to sea duty.

I napped on the plane, and during my semi-sleep, my mind wandered to Grace Sheehan. Why? I have absolutely no idea. I don't know what's wrong with me; I mean, I occasionally meet someone and then, after a few moments, can't get her out of my mind. The same thing happened with Jane. And now, Grace was on my mind, and as I droned toward Puerto Rico and my assorted duties, I remembered our chance meeting the previous day.

I was in the Oceana Navy Exchange, buying a birthday card for the admiral's wife. I had reminded him of her birthday last week, but he forgot, so I was purchasing it. I would deliver it to her with two dozen roses that afternoon.

"Hey, Weenie."

Of course, I recognized Grace's voice! I turned and smiled into her eyes. I had forgotten how clear and kind they were or, maybe, I had remembered, and that is what sent the shivers up me.

I smiled wider, "Grace. How are you?" I reached for her hand.

"I'm fine."

Her hand was small, and I swallowed as I felt its warmth.

"Shopping?"

Of course, that was an extremely goofy thing to ask. Why else would she be in the exchange?

"Waiting for Mom, she is in the commissary."

"Oh, I see. How have you been?"

"Okay," she nodded.

"Have you been back to Fort Story?" I knew she had not because I had gone there every Sunday for the past six months looking for her. Jack was never there either, which had always made me hopeful. If only Grace would show up.

"No, I haven't gone back since I saw you there that day."

"Me neither," I lied.

Grace smiled at me again and turned to leave.

"Would you like to get a cup of coffee sometime?" I fought to keep the plea from my voice.

Grace opened her mouth, and I saw her throat contract in a swallow and knew she didn't want to have coffee with me.

"Weenie, Jack Grant, and I are engaged."

I swallowed yet again and forced a smile. "Congratulations, Grace! That's great! He's a lucky man."

Grace hesitated and started to say something, but I saw discomfort in her eyes.

"Hey, you don't want to miss your Mom." I grinned and patted her hand. "Congratulations again, Grace. I wish you and Jack the best."

The beautiful eyes held me; then, they were gone.

And I awoke to hear the attendant announce our final approach to Naval Air Station Roosevelt Roads.

I completed all my tasks, and when the admiral arrived on the shuttle from Norfolk, I met him with his rental car and keys to the VIP cottage and his off-base hotel suite.

"Weenie, a family friend, arrives at the airport in San Juan this afternoon, and I need you there. Make a sign that says, Charley, and wait at the gate. It's an American Airlines flight from New York City."

"Yes, Sir. Charley, it is. The hotel room has one king-sized bed. Do you want me to get another room or a rollaway bed?"

The admiral seemed puzzled, then smiled. "No, let me worry about that later."

"Yes, sir."

I helped him get to the VIP cottage then shoved off for San Juan.

Charley turned out to be Charli, a beautiful young woman, and I got the feeling she was not quite the family friend that the admiral said she was. Despite my trepidation and feelings of being complicit in something wrong, I drove her to the hotel and left her there. That afternoon, the admiral called me to the VIP cottage, and I met him on the outside patio.

"Discretion is part of your job title." The admiral smiled and handed me a beer. He was wearing a tropical shirt and shorts and looked every bit the man on vacation.

"Of course, sir." I grabbed the beer and took a sip.

"Charli is important to me, Weenie. So, we need also to protect her identity, the fact that she is even here, from everyone."

"Sir, we spent quite a lot of time and effort to get the local press, even some national outfits, to focus on us. I am curious as to why you are taking the risk of having Charli here."

"Charli IS the press," smiled the admiral.

"Sir?"

"Charli works for the New York Beacon. She is covering the story. She will tell not only the value of what the navy is doing but also my value to the navy. Why did you think I brought her down here?"

"Well, sir. I wasn't sure."

The admiral looked at me and pursed his lips, the way he does just before he fires off a line of contempt. He narrowed his eyes, then nodded.

"Good. Now, I hear the club has lobster night tonight. I need you to get me two of the biggest ones, get all the stuff that comes with them too, you know, the veggies. And get me a bottle of cold, white wine. They must have something decent in the club. I need it for dinner at seven."

I fought a frown. I had planned on dining at the club with my buddies from the ship and airwing staff. We had all worked hard to coordinate the exercise, and tonight was to be our celebration.

"Just put it all on my bill. I'll square up with you when we get back."

"Yes, sir."

"And, Weenie, I want to fly in one of the events tomorrow. Make it an F-4 flight with live ordnance. And not too early. If you know what I mean." The admiral winked and clapped me on the shoulder.

"Yes, sir."

Part of the exercise involved the ship defending herself from air attacks, so some of the airwing planes had flown off and based at the air station. They would fly training hops and drop bombs on the ranges and serve as attackers against the carrier.

I turned to go, then hesitated. "Sir, you know there are only a few live bombing flights, one for each squadron. They planned on letting their junior aircrew drop those bombs. You know, to get the experience."

"And?" The admiral scowled and put his hands on his hips.

"Well, sir, I just think…"

"I DON'T CARE WHAT YOU THINK, KLEEGAN!"

I stepped back, stunned at the outburst. The admiral's face was red, his eyes wide, and he jabbed a finger at me.

"I'M GETTING PRETTY FUCKING TIRED…" The admiral paused and took a breath. He looked down, shook his head, then raised his eyes to me. "I am getting tired of your attitude, Weenie. You continually put on this air of criticism, of superiority. Like you are better than I am. It is getting pretty stale."

I swallowed and nodded. "Yes, sir."

"Now do as I say," he turned and left the room.

I did as the admiral said, bought the lobster dinners and the wine, and took it to his hotel room shortly before seven o'clock that evening. I hoped to drop the items off and dash back to the club to be with my mates, but the admiral insisted I stay and serve Charli and him. So, I performed the silent butler chores all evening as the admiral did not bring me into any of their conversations. It was humiliating and boring, and I think he did it to put me in my place.

The next morning, the admiral and I briefed with the other members of a four-plane flight with the mission to deliver live ordnance on the target at Vieques Island. I manned up early since I needed to preflight the ordnance as well as the airplane. The admiral's habit was to wait until I finished, then arrive, hop in, and start the jet. Unfortunately, we had a generator that would not stay online, and that delayed our take off. We eventually got it fixed, but not until the other three aircraft in our flight had already departed. Vieques is only five miles away from the Roosevelt Roads airfield, so as soon as we were airborne, I gave the admiral a southeasterly heading to fly. It was extremely hazy, and we could not see the island. However, the admiral banked sharply to a northeast heading, and I keyed the ICS.

"Sir, we are heading too far north. Come starboard, come right."

"I know where Vieques is," he snapped.

We continued to fly in the wrong direction, and I lowered the radar to scan low to find the island with my pulse system. The admiral switched the radio to the target frequency, and we could hear the other aircraft make pattern calls.

We continued to fly above the clouds, and I was sure we were far north of the target. Then, the admiral's ICS announcement confused me.

"Got it, on the nose, combat checklist."

"Sir, it can't be…"

"Damnit Weenie, I see the target. Give me the damned combat checklist."

I read the checklist to him, and he armed the weapons and banked to the south.

"Looking for the roll-in point. Do you see the other aircraft?"

"No, sir." I frantically scanned the sky, then a break in the clouds allowed me to see below us.

"Rolling in," said the admiral.

"SIR, THIS IS NOT VIEQUES! THIS IS THE NORTH ISLAND!"

"What?"

"SIR, THIS IS CULEBRA. ABORT! ABORT!"

"What?"

"ABORT!"

The admiral pulled up from his dive-bombing run, and I looked down. Culebra's beautiful beaches and blue water were now clear of any haze.

"Aircraft over Culebra, this is Roosevelt Roads Control. You are well outside of the training area. State side number and intentions."

"Don't say anything," said the admiral. "I'm turning off our squawk."

"Sir, fly 170."

For the first time in the flight, the admiral did as I directed. He pulled the nose to 170. But he also descended to get lost in ground clutter so the radar couldn't follow us. With the IFF squawk turned off, we would "disappear."

"Aircraft near Culebra, state side number."

I remained silent, and we flew south until we spotted Vieques. The admiral slowly climbed to the pattern altitude, and we joined the other three aircraft. We eventually delivered our bombs and returned to base as a four-plane division.

As soon as we landed, the admiral pulled me aside. "Get on the next connector to Norfolk. I don't need you here anymore."

"Sir?"

"You're piss-poor navigation almost got me fired. I do not need you here anymore. Report to the COS and wait until I get back. And call your detailer, you're fired!"

To say I was stunned doesn't begin to capture my feelings. I mean, the situation was surreal to the point of being unbelievable, except it was really happening and happening to me! I packed my gear and flew back to Norfolk, then reported to the COS in his office.

"What the hell happened down there?" The COS scowled and pointed to a chair.

I sat and told him the complete story, not only about the flight but also about Charli.

"That's not the same story he just told me on the phone."

"Well, sir, who do you believe?"

The COS looked at me a moment then shook his head. "The admiral is going to give you an unsatisfactory fitness report. Do you know why he is so vindictive?"

"Sir, I think when I question some of the things he does, he feels insulted. He believes I think I am better than he is."

"Well, do you?"

"Sometimes, I do."

The COS shrugged. "Well, no matter now. He is going to nail you with that report. I will try to talk him out of it when he comes in on Monday, but it's likely going to be bad. I will call the head aviation detailer. He is a buddy of mine, and maybe he can help."

"Yes, sir." Dazed, I walked out of the COS's office. How was this happening to me? How did I go from a hot burner and front runner to cashiered and finished? I hung around my BOQ room all weekend, afraid to show my face in case word of my failure had somehow gotten out.

On Monday, I walked into the COS's office, and he told me to close the door and sit.

"So, it's over here? I'm fired as the aide."

The COS nodded. "Afraid so, Weenie. I'm sorry." He picked an envelope from his desk and handed it to me. "This is your final fitness report. The admiral left it; he is not going to discuss it with you."

I took the envelope and opened the report and scanned the front. The admiral marked me at the bottom of the scale in all categories. The narrative on the back was devastating.

I got sick as I read some of the passages.

This officer does not understand the basic requirements to be an effective naval officer. He is immature yet arrogant and elitist and is incapable of serving even at his current rank.

I would gladly serve as president of any board or proceeding that seeks to demote or remove this officer.

Most strongly suggest he not be promoted!

His aviation skills are non-existent. His navigation errors nearly cost civilian lives, and he fails to communicate with controlling aviation authorities.

I shook my head and looked at the COS. "Can't I write a letter and explain this? Tell my side of the story?"

"Sure, you have that right. But it's an admiral's word against a lieutenant's. Who do you think they will believe?"

"But you know some of the things he did. You could back me up."

"Not really. I can say I think he is selfish, narcissistic, foolhardy, bombastic, and a total asshole. But all of that will be viewed as my opinion. None of it will be worth anything because the admiral can always say your mistakes occurred when I wasn't with the two of you."

"So, what can I do? Quit? Resign?"

"You can always resign, but not for a couple of more years. You still owe time for your wings. Weenie, the word of an admiral on a fitness report, is powerful. It has a massive influence on promotion boards. I talked with my friends in the bureau, and their advice is for you to volunteer for some hard sea duty where you can compete in a large group and come out on top in your next fitness reports. That may negate some of the effects of this."

"You mean like go back to a squadron? For a second sea tour." I brightened. That sounded mighty good.

"Weenie, as you know, your first operational tour in a squadron is to grow into a naval aviator, and the first shore duty tour develops you as an officer. The second sea duty tour, the one you are now facing, is really for the navy. If you are lucky and good, that second tour can be back into a squadron as a seasoned hand, a junior officer leader."

I thought of Arlo Grundeen.

"But in your case, that second sea duty tour means ship's company."

"Ship's company? You mean in a non-flying job?"

"Yes, I mean to be a catapult officer, for instance. *America* has an opening now, and they need someone badly." The COS leaned forward and handed me a slip of paper. "This is your detailer's number, call him."

Since I didn't have an office desk anymore, I went to my BOQ room and called my detailer. He was a lieutenant like me named Tobin Riley.

"We heard you might be calling, Weenie, and glad you did. I have a hot fill and need you to get to *America* as soon as you can get trained. She is on deployment to the Mediterranean."

"But, Tobin, ship's company? I don't get it. What happened to all the flying jobs?"

"Look, Weenie, Gus Sweeney is the fellow you are replacing. He stepped out into the landing area just as an A-7 trapped, and the arresting gear cable cut his left leg off at the ankle and his right leg off mid-thigh. AIRLANT sent some guy on their staff out there to cover for him, but we need somebody to take the job. So, it is my highest priority fill."

I felt numb. I could not believe I was having this conversation. I was a fighter guy for God's sake, hand selected to be an admiral's aide, and now I would be a ship' s company puke?

"Are you sure there aren't any second tour squadron jobs open? I have Vietnam combat experience, you know."

"Weenie, I know all about your career, and you do have an impressive record. That is, up until a few days ago. Man, you ran into the Buzzsaw."

"The Buzzsaw?"

"Yeah." I heard Tobin laugh into his phone. "Buzz Bass lives by his rules. If you align with those rules, he loves you. If you are disloyal or any kind of threat, he gets rid of you. That's the way he operates."

"Threat?"

"Come on, Weenie. You know that aides get to see and hear stuff nobody else can. That makes them powerful but also vulnerable, and both of those things can make you a threat to a guy like Buzz Bass."

"But how can that be?"

"Hey, if you would have toadied up to him, did what he wanted, we wouldn't be having this conversation. All the stuff you hate about him would be left in the wake of your trail to the next job."

"So, what are my options?"

"You would do anything to go to a new F-14 squadron, right?"

"Well." I shifted the phone to the other ear.

"Right?"

"I guess so."

"So, you have to fix yourself. You ran into an ass and got stunk up. No problem: the navy is also full of great guys, and one way to get that stink off is to be a catapult and arresting gear officer on the USS *America.*"

I could see Tobin beaming as he worked to hook me on his line.

"I don't know what to say. I have never given one second's thought to serving on a carrier except to fly."

"Nobody does, Weenie. And then, something happens, and you are having a conversation about it with a guy like me."

I remember seeing the catapult officers in the wardroom, and I remember my respect for them, with all they had to do in the rain and cold and all. But, still, I was in the plane, and they weren't. Up to this point in my military career, I didn't have much time for anybody who wasn't in an airplane. Well, except for Grandpa Two Bears, but he had been a US Marine. I thought naval aviators were heroes to the nation, especially after Jody and the skipper, and Drifty had gotten killed. And now I was going to be one of those grimy, rained on, wind-blown, non-flying slugs?

"Look, Weenie, you have one real choice here. Either accept these orders and go to *America* with a positive attitude or don't accept them and go like a sour puss. Either way, I am sending you there. This job is critical, and I have to fill it, and you are the guy to do it."

"Jesus," I shook my head. "Has an admiral's aide ever been demoted to cat officer?"

"Don't know," said Tobin. "But given what I have seen, you might consider it a promotion."

"So, there is no way out of this?"

"Well, the captain of the ship may not take you. He has that choice, you know."

"So, it is possible that I might not make the cut for being demoted from admiral's aide to catapult officer?"

"It's possible."

"Can you give me a week or so"?

"Not really. My next class for cat officers is in three days, and the ship needs its relief right away. The fill-in from the AIRLANT staff leaves when the ship gets into Naples. That is where you will join her. We need you, Weenie, you are valuable to the navy despite what your admiral might have written."

"If you say so." I took a breath and started to hang up. "Hey, Tobin, just out of interest who is coming in to take my place? To be Rear Admiral Bass's aide."

"It was an easy fill for us," said Tobin. "The admiral recommended Jack Grant, and we will roll him into the job Monday."

"Jack Grant." I shook my head. "Good choice," I said. I hung up and started packing my stuff.

CAT OFFICER KLEEGAN

I wanted to take some leave and go home and see my family. Lick my wounds among friendly faces. But the navy was insistent that I get through the catapult and arresting gear course at Lakehurst and hustle to *America*. So, I journeyed to New Jersey and drunk from a firehose for two weeks. It amazed me how little I knew about the systems that had launched and recovered me. I had just trusted them to work and had planned to pull my ejection seat handle if they didn't.

US aircraft carriers have four catapults, two located in the front, or bow, of the ship, and two located in the middle or waist. Cat one is on the right side of the bow as you look forward, and cat two is on the left side. Cat three is on the right side of the waist, and cat four is on the left side. Each cat has a pair of long, metal tubes located underneath the flight deck into which steel pistons slide.

The pistons have a metal connector on top, which fits through a slot in the tube and juts up through the flight deck and attaches to the aircraft. The connection may be with a rope and harness system for older aircraft or a nose launch bar on the newer planes. A metal holdback fitting is used to attach the airplane to the deck so the pilot can go to full throttle and not have his feet on the brakes. When the catapult fires, steam from the ship's boilers is injected behind the pistons, propelling them forward. This breaks the holdback fitting and accelerates the aircraft to flight speed. For instance, an F-4 Phantom can be accelerated from zero to 140 knots in about two seconds with such a system. The amount of steam to be injected depends upon the aircraft's weight, configuration, wind, temperature, and how much the catapult has elongated due to repeated firing and operation. Catapult officers reference a binder with bulletins for each aircraft under all conditions and use them to determine the steam setting. They then ensure an enlisted crewmember inserts the correct pressure into the system.

While we are called cat officers, we are also in charge of the arresting gear. Each carrier has four arresting gear engines for regular operation and one additional engine for the barricade. The barricade is a twenty-foot-high nylon webbing that can be rigged across the flight deck to snare aircraft that cannot catch a cable due to a tailhook malfunction. Each engine connects to a steel cable that stretches across the deck, and when an aircraft tailhook engages the cable, it reduces the aircraft speed with a ram and damping system. An arresting gear crewmember sets each engine for the specific aircraft that is landing next.

The launching sequence is most critical to cat officers because it is when pilots have little control. They are at the mercy of the system, so cat officers must ensure the aircraft are correctly placed on the cat and configured for the flight with wings in place and flaps down. Once the cat officer confirms the aircraft weight with the aircrew, he references the correct bulletin and directs his crewman to dial in the steam setting. The cat officer makes visual contact with the pilot, raises his hand, and shakes his index finger to signal the pilot to go to maximum power and cycle his control surfaces. Troubleshooters and other squadron personnel ensure that the aircraft looks safe to launch and signal the cat officer with a thumbs up. In the meantime, the cat officer checks the deck in front of the plane and rechecks the wind and steam settings. He looks at the pilot, and when the pilot is ready, he salutes or turns on his lights at night. The cat officer returns the salute, kneels, touches the deck, and the enlisted deck edge operator hits the fire button. As you can imagine, much can go wrong in such an operation, but the truth is that nothing does go wrong. Not very often anyway, and catapults generally work one hundred percent correctly one hundred percent of the time if everybody does his job.

The crew that works with the catapult officers are aviation boatswain's mates. Their skillset ranges from maintaining and servicing the complex electrical and mechanical systems to grueling manual labor under dangerous and extreme conditions.

I met the ship in Naples, Italy, and reported to the quarter deck. An airman picked me up and escorted me to the division office. There, I met a second-class petty officer named Bodle, who told me he was the PPO.

"PPO?"

"Yes, sir, the police petty officer."

I frowned since I had no idea what a police petty officer was but didn't want to start my cat officer career with a question to the first person I met, so I took a seat. I watched Bodle make a pot of coffee and found him a sinister-looking fellow with dark hair and eyes so black they didn't appear to have any irises. He just had two black spots in his head that made me uncomfortable when they grazed over me. I sat for about ten minutes until Lieutenant Commander Dick Parker came in and ushered me into his small office. Dick led the division, and the other two cat officers, lieutenants like me, were Trace Collins and Mick Service. Lieutenant George Smith, a former enlisted man, was our maintenance officer. Chief Petty Officers Tommy Amos, Matt Bower, and Otis Mays provided our deck plate leadership with the crew, which numbered two hundred and six.

"Know what happened to the guy you are replacing, Guy Sweeney?"

"Yes, sir. I heard he stepped out into the landing area and had his legs cut off."

"Guy was a great officer and my best shooter. But Guy got a letter from home, and his not-so-great wife told him she was leaving. Guy couldn't get her out of his head, so he absent-mindedly walked into the landing area."

I frowned and leaned back in my chair.

"I'm not telling you this to scare you."

"Well, you are."

"I am telling it to remind you never to lose your focus up there. As an aviator, you took the shortest route onto the deck, flew your airplane, then took the shortest route off the deck. Now, you live up there. You work up there from the beginning of flight ops until the end, and it's hot, its cold, it's loud, it's sharp, and it's unforgiving to guys with their heads up their asses."

"Yes, sir."

"By the way, what did you fuck up to come here?"

"Sir?"

"Kleegan, nobody becomes a cat officer because they don't like flying anymore. They get assigned to this job because they fucked up. Or, in my case, they quit and then came back in. So, what did you fuck up?"

"I pissed off my last boss. He was a rear admiral."

"You were an aide, then?"

"Yes, sir."

"Well, this is about as far away from an aide job that you will find, so hopefully you won't get your panties in a bunch when you get your hands dirty." Parker leaned back in his chair.

"Sir, I was raised on a farm. I can handle the dirty hands."

"Good." Parker looked at me, then smiled. "And forget the sir stuff. Call me Dick."

"Yes, sir."

"How long did you last as the aide? I always wondered what it would be like to be one."

"I lasted a year with my first admiral and only three months with Rear Admiral Bass."

"Oh, yeah, who was the first?"

"Rear Admiral Jensen."

"Jensen? Our Jensen? The battle group commander here?" Parker leaned back and raised his eyebrows. "Does he know you are here?"

"No, and I hope he never finds out."

"Why? If you did good with him, maybe he can get you out of here. Get you back into a squadron."

"The last thing I want to do is have him come and bail me out. No, I screwed up, and I must fix it."

"Mister Parker."

We looked at the door; a sailor stood in the frame. "Sir, Jenkins won't get out of his rack. He just lays there when I try to get him up."

"BODLE!" Parker looked past the sailor into the office. I heard a chair squeak, and Bodle's face appeared over the sailor's shoulder.

"Get Jenkins out of the rack."

"Do you care how, sir?"

"No, just get him up."

I could see the coffee machine from my chair and watched Bodle pick up the pot. I didn't think Bodle was the kind of guy that would take a cup of coffee to wake someone up, but then, maybe that is what a police petty officer does. I looked back at Dick.

"What's the story on Jenkins?"

Dick had his head down, writing on a pad of paper. He jotted some notes then looked up.

"Jenkins is one of those guys who has figured out the navy has no answer for someone who just quits. Occasionally we get guys like that, people who joined the navy to avoid the draft and now want out by any means. We have already busted Jenkins to E1, taken his pay, put him in the brig for three days of bread and water, restricted him to the ship, written him bad conduct evaluations, the whole schmeer. But Kleegan, if a guy wants to quit, there isn't much to stop him." Parker put his pen down and leaned back in his chair.

"Why don't you just kick him out of the navy?"

"Oh, come now, Weenie. Mother navy doesn't want us to give up on her children. No, Jenkins must stay until our leadership efforts turn him around, or until his enlistment ends, or until he deserts."

I heard a scream from the passageway and the sound of scuffling. I jumped from my chair and looked out into the office to see Bodle dragging someone across the deck with one hand, the empty coffee pot in the other.

"He burned me! He burned me!"

"Get up, Jenkins!" Bodle kicked the man in the side.

Dick brushed past me into the office and stood over the man. "Get up, Jenkins, or I'll have Bodle put another pot on you."

The man struggled to his feet, tears running down his face. I could see the wet stain of coffee smoking on his shirt and pants.

"Bodle, call the ship's XO and have somebody run this report chit to his office." Dick handed him a slip of paper. "I want to see if the captain will hold immediate mast and put this piece of shit in the brig again."

"Yes, sir." Bodle picked up the phone, and I went back into the office with Dick. A few minutes later, Bodle stuck his head in the door.

"Sir, the captain is ready for mast on the bridge. They say to get Jenkins up there now."

"Bodle, get some dry clothes on him and get to the bridge. Be sure to wear a cover and make sure Jenkins has one too."

"I don't think he has a cover, sir."

"Then staple a fucking napkin to his head."

"Really?" It was the first time I had seen Bodle smile.

"No, Christ no! Borrow one from somebody but get him to the bridge."

"Yes, sir."

"Come on, Kleegan, let's go."

I grabbed my cover and followed Dick to the bridge. We entered and waited behind the navigation tables until Bodle came in with Jenkins. The ship's master chief petty officer stood by the captain's chair, but he walked over when he saw us.

"Sir, are you here with Jenkins?"

"Yes, we are master chief."

"Very well, follow me, sir." Dick and I followed the master chief to the captains' chair. He looked up from a packet of messages and nodded.

"Captain, Lieutenant Commander Parker here for mast for Airman Recruit Jenkins."

The captain glanced at Dick and held up a piece of paper. "This all true? We've been on deployment for 124 days, and this guy, Jenkins, has been UA thirty-five times."

"Yes, sir."

"Bring him forward."

We turned to see the master chief and Bodle walking forward with Jenkins between them. I looked at Jenkins and bit my tongue. He was dressed in a set of green, army fatigue trousers held up by a piece of rope and a blue short-sleeve uniform shirt. His footwear was a pair of flip flops, and a filthy dixie cup cap sat on the top of his head. I heard Dick mutter a quiet, "Fuck."

The three marched forward until the master chief commanded, "Halt," followed by "Hand salute."

Jenkins saluted and stood at a semblance of attention.

The captain looked at him, and I wondered what could be going through his mind. I mean, I had been to many captain's masts, and usually, the skipper reads the charge and asks the man if he has anything to say and how he pleads. He also asks if anyone has something to say, and that is a good time for a division officer or chief to say positive things about the sailor. The skipper then provides guidance and concern, announces guilt or innocence, and the punishment. But Jenkins made this all a joke.

The captain looked at Jenkins, looked at the report chit, and then went back to Jenkins. He took a deep breath and sighed.

"Guilty, three days bread and water. Get him off my bridge."

I followed Dick back to his office, and we took seats. "As you can see, it's a little different than squadron life." He laughed and rocked back in his chair. "Most of these kids are great. Hardworking, bright, eager to please and do the right thing. But then, some aren't. You work around them until one way or another, they are gone."

Later that day, I met the other officers and the chief petty officers and got a set of yellow flight deck jerseys with the words CAT OFFICER stenciled on them in black letters. I also got a yellow flight deck flotation coat, a green plastic cranial with goggles, and some leather gloves. That and a pair of wash khaki trousers was my flight deck uniform.

While the shock of my fall from grace numbed me, I didn't have time to dwell on it or feel sorry for myself. I had to get qualified to assist my fellow officers so that they could take time off the deck.

Cat officers must conduct various administrative and management tasks when not on the flight deck, and each of us lieutenants had nearly seventy sailors to lead.

The other cat officers took turns, taking me up on deck to observe and learn and get on-the-job training. I did that by understanding and then mimicking their launching techniques. The chief petty officers and first-class petty officers tutored me on mechanics and procedures, and after a week at sea, Dick qualified me to shoot alone on the bow in the daytime.

I was shocked at how gratifying it was. It reminded me of how I felt when I drove the hay bailer by myself for the first time, but this had a ton more risk. The worst thing that could happen to me bailing hay was a busted bale or a three-legged dog. Here, I could kill people. As a backseater in the F-4, and now the F-14, I was always with the pilot. The ultimate decisions and responsibilities for the airplane lay in the front seat, not with me. But now, for the first time in my military career, I stood alone to decide if an aircraft was ready to launch or not. Oh, I had a lot of help with the cat crew and others, but at the end of the day, I was responsible. I was the one that touched the deck. It was a humbling feeling, and I found myself grateful for the experience I had so fervently and ignorantly wanted to avoid. And my relationship with my enlisted men changed too. I had always seen them as people who worked for me, but not with me. I mean, the squadron enlisted men were maintainers for the most part, and I didn't carry any tools or work on the aircraft. But here, on this deck, we worked shoulder to shoulder. When an A-7 turned its exhaust on us to taxi up the deck, we all grabbed a pad-eye to hang onto. When it rained, we all got wet. At the end of the launch, we all carried the shuttle to the side, and we all ensured hatches were closed, and the landing area was ready. We all did it together, officer and enlisted.

I also found that an aircraft carrier can be a cruel and unwelcoming place if the officers let it be that way. The laundry would come up wet; the galley would close before the end of flight hours, the commodes would plug, the mail would languish in the post office, all manner of torment would prevail unless an officer with a passion for his men stopped it. I wish I could say I found this through epiphany, but the truth is I learned these things from my chief petty officers who looked to me to intercede on the men's behalf. And I found that it took not only passion but also unrelenting determination and guile to budge those who loved their power of "No" or who didn't care. As the days flew by, I became more efficient in my topside duties, and I also became a master at cajoling, threatening, and leveraging on behalf of the men. My previous squadron life was so insulated from these things, and when I think about it, I know why. A fighter squadron has roughly the same number of enlisted men as our division had here on America. But we also had ten chief petty officers, senior chief petty officers, a master chief petty officer, and thirty officers. We had two navy commanders in the CO and XO, all ready to right any perceived wrong. A squadron also had the weight of the airwing and its leadership behind it.

America spent three weeks at sea, and I became qualified on the waist as well. I enjoyed the job and the men. Jenkins came out of the brig, and even he began to show up for work. He wore that makeshift uniform when he did, but he did make muster. He reminded me a little of the Klinger character in the television show, MASH, but more pathetic than funny.

Aside from the brief meeting at the captain's mast for Jenkins, I met the ship's skipper, Captain Tyndall "Hose" Compton, the day before pulling into Cannes, France. I was launching on the waist that morning, and after shooting an F-14 from catapult three, nearest the tower, I hopped across the shuttle track where an A-6 tanker was turning up on catapult four. I waved my fingers in the air...but something was wrong.

Something is wrong!

I couldn't figure it out...but something was just not right. The pilot saluted, and I returned his salute. The troubleshooters had their thumbs up in the air, I glanced at the tower, and the green light was on; I knelt to touch the deck.

Then I saw it! I crossed my hands over my head, the signal to suspend the launch. The aircraft was now at full power; only the holdback fitting kept it from rolling forward. I directed the topside petty officer to run out in front of the plane and then signaled the deck edge operator to maneuver the shuttle aft so the launch bar would spring free. If the cat fired at this point, the topside petty officer would get killed, and the jet would go into the water.

The launch bar popped free, the shuttle maneuvered forward, and I ran out in front of the airplane, motioning the pilot to throttle back.

The boss called on my headset.

"What's wrong, Weenie?" He sounded annoyed.

"Sir, his flaps are up."

"What?"

"Sir, his flaps are up. If I had launched him, he would be in the water."

I motioned to the pilot to put the flaps down, and he did. Then, I shot him and proceeded with the rest of the launch. After the last aircraft took off, I helped the crew push the shuttle cover into place, then ran back to the fantail and served as the arresting gear safety observer for the recovery. I found it odd that we took the COD, the logistics plane, first. Typically, it was the last plane in the recovery. Maybe they had mail! When I returned to the office, Bodle told me the bridge called, and the skipper wanted to see me.

A summons to the bridge would have caused me to go into a panic at an earlier time. But my exposure to naval leadership as an aide had seasoned me, and it also allowed me to put this into perspective. The skipper had no doubt watched the launch and noticed me suspend the A-6 tanker on cat four. He probably wanted to talk about that. So, I cleaned the grit off my face, combed my hair, and climbed the ladders to the bridge. When I walked in, I saw the air boss, Commander Phil Mason, and his assistant, Commander Mike Dobbs, talking to the captain. He sat in his bridge chair on the port side of the island. I walked to a point where I was in the periphery of the boss and waited. He quickly noticed and waved me toward him.

"Skipper, this is our newest shooter, Weenie Kleegan."

"Good afternoon, sir." I nodded to the boss, then to the assistant, "Sir." I reached my hand forward to the skipper and nodded again. "Good afternoon, captain."

The skipper smiled and gripped my hand. "Good to have you aboard, Weenie. I have heard good things about you. That was great work you did out there on cat four. Those boys would have been in the water if it weren't for you."

"Thank you, sir, I have been trained well."

"Maybe so, but the three of us and a bunch of other folks were also looking at that A-6, and we didn't notice it. It's our job to watch out too. But you did, and I want to thank you. You saved some lives, perhaps, and for sure, you saved us a terrible blemish on what has been a great deployment so far."

I nodded and swallowed but didn't speak. The fact that the ship's skipper would acknowledge that he, too, had missed something took my words away.

"Skipper, we need to get to the tower to start the next launch. Request permission to leave the bridge." The boss saluted.

"Absolutely," the skipper smiled and returned the salute.

I turned to leave with them.

"Come alongside, Weenie." The skipper motioned me to his chair, so I moved next to him.

"The XO and the boss briefed me on your situation. The thing with Rear Admiral Bass."

"Yes, sir." I tensed and waited for his critique.

The skipper looked at me and pursed his lips. I held his gaze and waited. His eyes were friendly, and I hoped that he was too. "I know Rear Admiral Bass."

"Yes, sir." I gulped.

"What happened?"

"I didn't meet his expectations, sir." I continued to hold the skipper's gaze. He studied me a moment, then took a deep breath and slowly exhaled.

"Ironically, he just trapped in the COD. I welcomed him aboard just a minute ago."

"Sir?" I couldn't believe it.

What was Rear Admiral Bass doing on *America*?

The captain must have read my mind. "Beats me why he is here. I guess we will all find out later."

"Yes, sir." I nodded and took a step back.

Welcome aboard *America*, Weenie. You did well today."

"Yes, sir, permission to leave the bridge."

The skipper waved and looked down at a folder of papers on his lap. I exited the bridge and headed down the ladder to get ready for the next launch.

That afternoon, I focused on my duties and refused to let my mind wander. I didn't want to wind up like Guy Sweeney. However, once below, I couldn't help but think about Rear Admiral Bass. I just hoped I wouldn't have to see him. I launched two more events then headed to the office to work on enlisted evaluations. I walked down the starboard side on the O3 level, and as I got to the blue-tiled area of the admiral's spaces, I saw Jack Grant. He was standing in the passageway with a bowl of popcorn in his hands, evidently getting ready for the nightly movie. If he had not been looking right at me, I would have ducked down a side passageway. I smiled as I came toward him, noticing his crisp, khaki uniform with the gold aiguillettes around his left shoulder. The ones I used to wear. I watched his eyes as I drew closer. They initially widened when he recognized me, but as he took me in, my dirty yellow flight deck jersey and khaki trousers with the black knees from kneeling to shoot, my grimy face and hands, my greasy hair, his eyes crinkled into a smirk. I shifted my helmet to my left hand so I could offer him a shake, but as I did, he gave me a curt nod and pushed open the door into the admiral's mess. I continued to the office and my paperwork.

CANNES

The morning *America* pulled into Cannes, we cat officers decided to
have breakfast together, so Dick, Trace, Mick, and I met down in
wardroom two for some chow. I had learned a little about each of
my mates, but I had not had time to really "jell" with them. I looked
forward to going ashore together. Besides, they were old hands at
Mediterranean cruises and were familiar with Cannes.

Like me, each of the others was "flawed" in some way. Parker
had gotten out, Trace was a RA5C Vigilante pilot whose aircraft had
been retired, giving him no squadron to go to, and Mick was, well,
Mick was Mick. He was rough around the edges kind of guy who
would be your first pick for support in a bar fight. But the navy
wasn't drinking.

We had the eggs, pancakes, and bacon with a gallon of coffee,
and the conversation was a mix of what we had done on the flight
deck and what we would do in Cannes. Mick had just started an
animated description of the women of France when the air boss
came in. He had a grin on his face, and as he approached our table,
we stood.

"Weenie, the flag secretary, called, and the admiral wants to see
you. I guess he found out you were onboard."

"Yes, sir. When…"

"Right now." The boss pointed to the door.

"Boss, have breakfast with us." Dick gestured to my seat.

"Can't. Got a damned meeting in fifteen minutes in wardroom
one."

"What kind of person would call a meeting the first morning in
port?" Mick frowned and shook his head.

"An admiral kind of person," said the boss.

I hurried out of the wardroom and up the ladders to the O3
level. I hoped I wouldn't run into Rear Admiral Bass or Jack Grant.
Christ, that would be depressing. I wanted to enjoy my time in
France. I reached the blue tile area and entered the admiral's office.

His flag secretary motioned me forward, and I followed him to the admiral's cabin.

"Sir, Lieutenant Kleegan, to see you."

"Absolutely!"

I entered the room as Rear Admiral Jensen rose from his chair to meet me. His handshake was hearty as always, and his smile made me feel welcome, as always.

"Take a seat on the couch." The admiral motioned to a sitting area, and I sat down.

"Weenie, I am a bit angry at you." The admiral smiled. "Why didn't you tell me you were on board?"

"Well, sir..."

"I feel guilty," interrupted the admiral. "I should have checked up on you after I left. I assumed you were still at the wing with Rear Admiral Bass. That is, until this morning, when he told me you were no longer with him. He said his new aide had seen you. That is how we knew you were here."

"Yes, sir. I saw him last night in the passageway."

"What happened, Weenie? I didn't press it with admiral Bass, but I am interested. You were moving hot when I left." The admiral's smile disappeared as he leaned back on his end of the couch.

"I confronted him." I looked at the admiral. "But not constructively enough, it appears."

The admiral smiled and nodded. "Even the most constructive confrontation doesn't guarantee a positive outcome. I'm sorry, Weenie."

"I'm not, sir. I like this job, which surprises me. I never considered being a cat officer would be very fulfilling. I always thought it would be something dreadful to get through until it was over. I was wrong."

"So, you don't want me to pull any strings to get you out of here? Or at least inside? The assistant navigator job is coming open. It is one of the most prestigious jobs on a carrier for a lieutenant."

"No, sir. I like it outside."

"I hoped you would say that Weenie. I hoped that your positive attitude hadn't dampened."

"No, sir. But, out of curiosity, what brings Rear Admiral Bass out here? That isn't usual, is it? You never visited a deployed carrier when you had his job."

"No, it isn't usual." The admiral frowned and shook his head. "He gave a brief to Second Fleet about how we can operate north of the GIUK gap and put pressure on the Soviets. He even had a scheme of some sort on how to use the F-14s to defend the carrier. I hear a concept got to the CNO, and he wanted some fleet perspective, so Rear Admiral Bass is out here to discuss it." The admiral narrowed his eyes. "Did you have anything to do with his brief?"

"No, sir. I did mention the concept to Rear Admiral Bass before I left."

"The concept?"

"Yes, sir. I went over it with him during lunch one day. Do you want to hear it?"

"Sure."

I got a piece of paper and drew the same plan I had for Rear Admiral Bass. We discussed it for several minutes.

"How did you develop the idea?"

"Well, sir, I am an avid reader, and since I lived alone in the Oceana BOQ, I had a lot of time to read. I found many articles on the subject because, as you know, we have been interested in the GIUK gap since World War Two. Today, it's the only way into the Atlantic for the Soviet Union, and they want that route to be able to threaten our east coast with ballistic missile submarines. If we bring our ships into the gap to keep them out of the Atlantic, they plan on using attack submarines to take those ships out. If we bring in carriers with their formidable anti-submarine capabilities, they plan on attacking them with air-launched cruise missiles from their bombers. So, it was somewhat of a no-man's land for us until the F-14 came along."

"With its long-range, great radar and the Phoenix missile."

"Yes, sir, exactly."

"So, you developed a concept to use the Tomcats to break that stalemate?"

"Yes, sir."

"And that is what you briefed to Rear Admiral Bass?"

"Yes, but I hadn't developed the details of execution yet. I have worked on it quite a bit since I left the wing."

"Sir." A lieutenant with aiguillettes stood in the doorway. "The brief is scheduled to begin in five minutes. It is up in wardroom one."

"I'll be right out." The admiral stood, and I scrambled to my feet.

"Weenie, I think you should come with me. Stand in the back but take mental notes. Second Fleet asked me to evaluate this concept if I could, and I want to do that. He wants me to take a hard look and give him some input. So, I need all the eyes on this I can get."

"Yes, sir."

"The complication is it is just a concept for now, and I need to get to the details of execution to see if it works."

"Yes, sir."

The aide led us forward on the O3 level, sailors, and officers giving way as we filed past them. I broke from the admiral and entered through the back door, slipping in as everyone was coming to attention.

The place was packed! I could see the ship's captain and the airwing commander sitting next to the air boss. All the squadron commanding officers were there with ship's company officers from operations, intelligence, navigation, and supply. The admiral's staff was present, and I could see Rear Admiral Bass and Jack in the front row.

Rear Admiral Jensen wasted no time and grabbed the mic. "Gents, take a seat. I realize this is the first morning in port, and many of us have wives and sweethearts waiting for us. But I have been directed by the Second Fleet commander to receive a concept brief and evaluate whether we can test it during the next at-sea period. That is only six days away, so that necessitated getting a head start this morning. Rear Admiral Bass is familiar to many of you, he is the east coast fighter wing commander, and he will give the brief. Buzz, you have the floor."

The admiral handed the mic to Rear Admiral Bass, who motioned to Jack, and a slide with the words VECTOR LOGIC popped up on the screen.

I almost fell over!

For the next thirty minutes, Rear Admiral Bass showed slides that depicted the very brief I had given him during his lunch. He even used the same sentence structure and the same threat axis of 090! I couldn't believe what I was seeing. I thought he had audacity when he took my wings to give to the senator's son, but that was nothing compared to this. He was using my work to make himself look like the next Admiral Nimitz! However, things soon started to heat up.

"Do you execute this out of cyclic operations, and if so, what is the cycle time?" The airwing commander asked the question.

"I will have my aide answer those types of questions. He is an F-14 pilot and was a key person in developing this plan." Rear

Admiral Bass nodded to Jack, who took the mic. Jack looked nervous, and that made me happy.

"Yes, sir, we intend on executing this with normal cyclic operations supplemented by alert launches."

"What kind of cycle time will you use? We normally run ninety minutes here on *America*." It was the air boss's turn to question Jack.

"Ninety minutes should work." Now Jack looked EXTREMELY nervous. I was beginning to enjoy the show. A ninety-minute cycle would never work, and the boss quickly took exception.

"But is a ninety-minute cycle time flexible enough? Once we launch an alert, won't that screw-up everything? What if you need to launch while setting the deck for the next event?" The boss wouldn't give up easily.

"Well, sir, we will just have to fit the alert launches in." Jack gulped and glanced at Rear-Admiral Bass, who was staring at his feet.

"What about nighttime? Will you still operate in EMCON, or will you use normal case three operations?" It was the captain's turn.

"Well...uh." Jack looked at Rear-Admiral Bass and shrugged.

I saw Rear Admiral Jensen frown as the room erupted in confusion.

"How in the world are we going to do this?" It was Captain Swenson, Rear Admiral Jensen's operations officer.

Rear Admiral Jensen stood and looked to the back of the room where his eyes found mine. "Weenie, do you have thoughts or input on this?"

Everybody turned, and I saw confusion in their frowns.

I heard someone say, "He's just a cat officer."

Rear Admiral Jensen smiled at me. "Come on up and help us out."

I strode to the front of the room, and the admiral handed me the mic.

"Well, sir, to answer the boss, I think a flexible version of cyclic operations will support this concept, but it would be a shorter, forty-five-minute cycle time. We can call it battle flex deck."

"Forty-five minutes! But how can we do that?" asked the boss.

"We can never stay on schedule," said the navigator. "We cannot recover PIM because we will be constantly in the wind launching and recovering."

"No, sir," I said. "It is not as difficult as it first appears. A larger number of short cycles allows us to have smaller launches and recoveries. True, it will be more difficult for the deck handlers, but it will allow us to quickly get into and out of the wind. Also, all the F-14s, A-6s, S-3s, the E-2 could launch as a double or even triple cycle, so their scheduled recovery will be an hour and a half after takeoff." I watched some heads begin to nod, so I continued. "Night operations will be more difficult, sure, but we can keep our EMCON status by relying on the E-2 Hawkeye to provide situational awareness and battlespace management. For instance, let's say the F-14 out on O9 Echo launched on the first event and had a scheduled recovery time on event three. But we want him to stay on station because his relief didn't launch or the tactical situation changed, or something like that. The E-2 would use a covered circuit and direct him to the new recovery time four and call the ship for a tanker launch if one isn't airborne. He would make that call but the ship would not answer. She would remain silent. We have a lot of options with this." I saw a lot of heads nodding, and the captain even smiled.

"So, is this just a fighter thing, or does the rest of the airwing count?" The skipper of one of the A-7 squadrons asked the question. He looked disinterested but pissed, a familiar naval aviator feeling. And I understood. After all, thus far, we had not talked about the attack community. There were two squadrons of A-7s onboard and an A-6 squadron, and they were not to be taken lightly.

"Oh, no, sir. We will need the entire airwing. What we are talking about here is only the defensive plan. In a real-world scenario, we would need S-3s and the helos to work with battlegroup destroyers and even land-based P-3 Orion's to blunt the Soviet submarine threat. We would need you and the A-6s to defend against any surface attack the Soviets may mount. Of course, you represent the only offensive capability we have. No, sir, this will be a total naval aviation effort. All of us will be involved; fortunately, we have a lot of flexibility due to the wing's composition."

"We have enormous flexibility." Rear Admiral Bass interrupted and looked around the room as he nodded. He seemed to want to regain his authority and confidence, and I could tell he was trying to bridge into my conversation. A piece of me wanted to expose him for the fraud he was, but a more mature part of me realized that would do no good.

"Rear Admiral Bass is correct," I said. "I discussed this with him while I was still on his staff but had not developed these final execution plans."

"That's right." Rear Admiral Bass looked at me for a second, wary and uncertain, but then he turned to the crowd and clenched his jaw, "That is exactly right."

"And night ops?" The captain narrowed his eyes. He looked at the admiral for a moment, then at me.

"Yes, sir. Once again, we will use the E-2, so we don't have to turn the TACAN on or clutter up the radio. Unless told otherwise, aircraft will leave their cap station before their scheduled recovery time and will be vectored by the E-2 to a point where they will intercept the final bearing seven miles behind the ship. They will descend to 1200 feet while doing this, and once they fly into the cone of the instrument landing system, they will fly their ILS needles like always until they see the meatball. Nobody will be talking. The LSO will flash his lights once to signal cleared to land."

"That's right," said Rear Admiral Bass.

The captain nodded as did many in the room.

"But won't the Soviets be able to pick up the ILS?" The ship's intelligence officer had his hand up.

"Yes, sir, but the detectable signal is fairly narrow, and it is a risk we will just have to take."

"It's something we plan to analyze," said Rear Admiral Bass. He had regained his confidence and the initiative.

I surveyed the room and saw many nods, and the conversation was more excited than chaotic. I smiled and continued, "Of course, there are many details that Jack and the admiral's staff can work out with you, but we can do this."

"We can do this!" Rear Admiral Bass jumped up and reached for the mic. But he wasn't as quick as Rear Admiral Jensen, who stepped forward and grinned at me.

"Thanks, Weenie, glad that you could help." He winked and whispered, "Now that is constructive confrontation!" I grinned back, and he turned to the crowd.

"Okay, lots to think about." He looked at Captain Compton, "Hose, I hope that the duty sections can begin to shape this concept into a solid brief by the time we head back to sea. Rear Admiral Bass and I would like to see it in a couple of days."

"Yes, sir," said the captain.

We jumped to attention, and as the admirals left, the skipper turned to me. "I imagine that met Rear Admiral Bass's expectations." He grinned and headed for the door.

I waited in the wardroom for a few minutes to let it clear, then headed to my room to change for liberty. I was going ashore with the other cat officers, and we were going to see the French Riviera!

I walked a few frames and turned toward my room when I saw Jack Grant waiting for me. His face was grim and his eyes dark with rage.

"You made me look like an idiot!"

"I saved your ass, is what I did!" I stepped nose to nose.

"Don't blame me if you don't know what you are talking about."

"You fucked me, Kleegan, and I will never forget it!"

"I saved you, Grant, but I plan to forget that as soon as I can."

Jack glared for a second longer, then stomped down the passageway. I smiled as I watched him go.

It had been a good morning! I had eaten bacon, constructively confronted Rear Admiral Bass, set my hero, Rear Admiral Jensen, up for success, and had a face-off with my arch enemy Jack Grant...all before going on liberty in southern France!

The brief caused me to miss the first liberty boat, so Dick and Trace had already left to meet their wives on the beach. Mick was gone too. I thought it was so cool to have people meet you on deployment. My two WESTPAC Vietnam cruises had port calls a million miles away from home and unfamiliar places to Americans. But cruises to the Mediterranean were not that far away, and the locals even understood English! So, to have your sweetie meet you in a place like Cannes was so romantic. I couldn't believe the navy could even conceive of allowing it to happen!

I changed into my civvies and started to leave when I heard the knock at my door.

"Weenie, I need a little help."

Rear Admiral Jensen's aide stood in the passageway. He extended his hand. "Bob Evans, we haven't met."

I shook and smiled. "What can I do?"

"Weenie, I have a bit of a problem. A personal problem, and I hope you can help."

"Come on in." I backed into my stateroom, and Bob followed me. He took a chair as I flopped onto the edge of my rack.

"Weenie, Jack Grant, whom I think you know, contacted me and asked me to take the barge ashore to meet some visitors, friends of

Rear Admiral Bass and Jack." Bob leaned forward and took a quick breath."

"Okay, what can I do?" I frowned.

What was he doing here? What did he want with me?

"You see, I can't get away because, well, this barge run is supposed to be kept secret from Rear Admiral Jensen. He will want to know why I left the ship."

"I don't get it." I frowned again. "Why are you taking the admiral's barge on some secret run? I shook my head and stared at Bob. "Why are you setting yourself crosswise with your boss, to help Jack Grant?"

"Oh, come on, Weenie. It's an aide thing. Aides help each other."

"Bullshit, Bob! An aide's allegiance is to his boss, not to another aide." I stood, "I can't help you with this, Bob. I have to get to the beach."

"Please, Weenie." Bob stood and touched my arm. "You have to help me. I'm trying to get into the F-14 community when I roll out of here. Jack can make that happen through Rear Admiral Bass."

"Why can't Rear Admiral Jensen help you?"

"I got into trouble with some of the staff. I screamed at one of the enlisted men's wives because she spilled spaghetti sauce on my uniform. I had had too much to drink and anyway, Rear Admiral Jensen was furious, but he's not going to fire me. But I can't ask him for any favors." Bob looked at me. "Jack can help me. Please, Weenie."

I slumped to my rack and shook my head. What a mess. I looked at Bob, "I take it that these visitors aren't the kind to bring back to the ship?"

"Oh, God, no! The more discreet you can be, the better."

"What kind of visitors are they?" I frowned at Bob.

"You know, Rear Admiral Bass," was Bob's lame reply.

"Okay, let me change into my white's."

"No need to change, Weenie. Just find the visitors, two women, and tell them the admiral and Jack will be along in a minute. Tell them to sit tight. You can send the barge back with the coxswain and go on your liberty. No need to return with it."

"Okay, is it ready?"

"Yes, they will pull it up to the fantail when I tell them."

"I'm heading there now."

The liberty boats docked against a floating platform called a camel, and the admiral's barge was waiting for me when I arrived. I waded through the line of enlisted men waiting for the liberty boats and jumped onboard. As I turned to tell coxswain to shove off, my eyes panned the sailors in the line, young faces, many going on liberty in France for the first time. I yelled up to the petty officer of the watch.

"Send me fifteen men from the enlisted line."

"What?" The petty officer of the watch frowned. The officer line had precedence for departure on liberty boats.

"Send me fifteen men from the enlisted line. Send them NOW!"

"Yes, sir."

As I watched their gleeful faces descend the ladder, I began to feel better. At least something good can come out of this trip.

The men herded by me, shouting and happy to be off the ship. They took their places in the barge's plush seats, admiring their accommodations of royalty, and I smiled and ordered the coxswain to the beach. Men parted the lines, and we started the fifteen-minute trip to the shoreline. I looked over the group of men and smiled again until I saw Jenkins! Jenkins? How in the hell did he get out of restriction? How did he escape from Bodle and get to the liberty line? Well, it was time to end this foolishness! I stepped forward toward the cockpit and tapped the coxswain on the shoulder but then, I turned and looked at Jenkins.

Heck, twenty years from now, somebody will ask Jenkins if he was in the navy, and he will say yes. And when they ask him if he ever visited any foreign countries, now he could say yes to that too. Who knows how important that will be to him then?

At least he was in proper liberty attire, and, at least, he was on time! I looked at him and shook my head. He gave no indication that he saw me, but he did hide behind the man next to him.

"Yes, sir," replied the coxswain.

"Best speed," I said.

America's anchorage off Cannes was not far from shore, the blue, clear water was calm and in no time we were approaching fleet landing. The admiral's coxswain was very skilled, as expected, and he deftly maneuvered us into position. I stepped off the barge, shook hands with the Cannes Navy League's protocol officers and leaders, and explained that Admiral Jensen would be along momentarily. I wound through the small crowd, wondering how I was going to find the visitors since I didn't have a description. Luckily, they found me.

"Excuse me, but did you just get off that little boat?"

I stepped back as a buxom and exotically beautiful woman smiled at me. "Yes," I couldn't help but smile back.

"Where is Buzzy? Isn't that his boat?"

"Ma'am?"

"Where is Buzzy? The admiral of the fleet." She pointed at the barge. "This is his boat."

"Ma'am, do you mean Rear Admiral Bass?"

"Yes, of course, Admiral Bass." She turned and yelled at a younger woman. "Roseanne, I found them."

"And Jack? Where is Jack? He promised he would be on the first boat. He said he would be on his admiral's boat."

"Well, ma'am, Jack, and the admiral are still onboard America. They have important national security details to solve; then they will come ashore. They told me to tell you to just sit tight, and they would be along shortly."

The woman frowned and pouted her large, puffy lips. "Buzzy said to talk with no one. I guess you're okay. But we will wait at the hotel up the street, right there." She pointed to a building with French and American flags. "We are at the Radisson Blu. Tell them that Fontana and Roseanne are waiting."

"I will be sure to tell them."

I shook my head as I watched them stumble over the cobblestone in their heels and marveled at how Rear Admiral Bass could have so little regard for the oaths he took to his wife or the navy or to any sense of decency.

And, then there was Jack Grant, following in his footsteps.

I told the coxswain to return to the ship, then headed up the street. Mick had told me to veer to the left as I came out of the port area and meet him at the L' Alba Restaurant. I walked north and smiled as the smell of perfume hit me. Perfume is one thing you don't realize how much you miss until you get off an aircraft carrier and smell it again! It is so wonderful after a near-total immersion in Right Guard and foot power.

I walked toward the Radisson Blu with fingers crossed that I would not see Fontana and Roseanne again but as I closed, I noticed someone in the café window. She looked familiar, sitting there in the lobby.

It was Grace!

I approached her from behind so she didn't see me, but I could tell she was studying the waterfront. The back of her neck and movement of her face showed me the way of her thoughts, and I knew she was looking for Jack. I knew she hoped that any minute, maybe this second, her Jack Grant would emerge from where he had been and come to her. I decided to quickly walk on and get to some hard-earned liberty with Mick. But then I thought of Fontana and Roseanne and wondered what would happen if they ran into Grace? What if they told Grace they were waiting for the admiral and Jack? I slowed and looked back. I could see Grace clearly now, and when she touched the handle of her coffee cup, I saw her hand tremble and pause, and I saw her frown as she lifted to sip. I could see she was worried he wasn't coming. I felt so sorry for her as she blew the heat from her cup, knowing she wasn't trying to cool coffee but give herself a segue to understanding. I wanted to run away from her. I wanted to turn and run because I could not do her any good; I couldn't solve any hurt coming her way. I could not help her. But then she turned and saw me. She smiled, and I saw relief in her eyes. I saw her mouth my name through the window.

"Weenie?"

I waved and sighed and walked up the steps into the hotel lobby. "Grace! Wow! Wow! What are you doing here?"

She stood, and I wasn't sure if we knew each other well enough to hug. She answered that by holding out her hand. I took it, then we sat.

"Waiting for Jack?"

"Yes," she smiled and looked over my shoulder like she expected to see Jack behind me. Her eyebrows knotted in a touch of disappointment, then she looked at me and smiled again. "I didn't know you were on Jack's staff. I thought you were gone somewhere."

I smiled and instinctively reached for her hand. She didn't respond, so I withdrew and put my hands in my lap.

"I am on *America's* staff, you know, the aircraft carrier. Just a coincidence that Jack and the admiral are here."

"I hope you aren't still in trouble." Grace frowned and looked down.

"Trouble?"

"Yes," she looked up at me. "Jack said you had made some charges to the government credit card for personal reasons. So, the admiral had to let you go and hire him."

"I see." I shook my head. "That was all a mistake, and I cleared it up. I'm not in any trouble."

"Oh, that is great, Weenie! I must admit, when he told me, I didn't believe him." Grace reached her hand across the table, and I quickly slipped mine into hers. I didn't clutch it or anything creepy, just kind of laid my hand into hers.

"I only met you once, well, twice counting the exchange," Grace laughed. "But I am a good judge of character, and I doubted you did anything dishonest."

I looked into her eye and smiled. The irony of her words, "I am a good judge of character," caused me to shake my head, and I squeezed her hand just a bit. She pressed back, and as her lashes closed in a brush against her cheeks, I felt a rush of something for her. Pity, maybe, but more. But I knew I didn't deserve to feel anything more.

"Jack and the admiral are delayed. They gave a superb brief this morning, and I think the battlegroup commander is going over some refinements with them.

"Really!" Grace smiled and squeezed my hand again.

"Yep! I think we are going to take their ideas and develop them for our next sea period."

"Wow, that is great! Isn't it?"

"You bet it is. It isn't often that somebody comes up with an idea that changes a whole at-sea period for a carrier battle group!"

"Oh, I hope so," said Grace. "I hope it works for Jack."

Grace smiled, and at that instant, she seemed so vulnerable. More even than before and I wanted to help her or protect her somehow.

"Does Jack know you are waiting? Surely he must."

"He doesn't. Do you think he will be surprised?"

"Oh, I am sure of that," I said.

"Do you think he will be pleased?"

Her question surprised me. It was a glimpse into their relationship that she probably didn't mean to offer.

"How could he not be pleased?"

Grace smiled and sighed. "I hope he isn't long. I have a place rented in the Cap D' Antibes Beach Hotel."

"Cap D' Antibes? My roommate has been to southern France many times, and he says Cap D' Antibes is beautiful."

"Oh, wonderful," said Grace. "I found it through a travel agent and booked the coziest little room. I wanted to surprise Jack and just be here when he came ashore. I guess I will just have to wait for him."

I thought of Fontana and Roseanne. They could pop out at any minute, and sooner or later, the admiral and Jack would be along. Heck, they might be on the barge heading this way now. The idea of

Grace interrupting the reunion of those four made me shudder. "I tell you what, let me help you get your bags to your hotel and then I will go back to the ship and tell Jack where you are."

"Are you sure? I mean, you are on liberty."

"I have plenty of time to see France. Come on, let's get your things."

I helped Grace with her bags, and we walked to the train station, where we bought tickets for the short ride around the coast to her hotel. I helped get her luggage into the room, then headed back to the pier. The barge wasn't there, so I waited for an hour and took the next liberty boat to the ship.

Once on board, I changed into my uniform and went to the flag spaces to tell Jack that Grace was waiting for him. Predictably, he wasn't there. So, I left the message with the flag secretary, including the hotel's address in Cap D' Antibes. I then went to CVIC, where I found an airwing team busy working on battle flex deck and vector logic. A lieutenant commander from one of the F-14 squadrons was in charge and quickly told me he didn't know squat about any of that vector crap. As you can imagine, he was glad to see me. I helped his team develop the plans, finally hitting the rack around midnight.

Mick and I met Dick and Trace and their wives for dinner that night, but I spent the next three days of the in-port period working on the plan. I didn't see Jack, assuming he was with Grace, and I hoped she was happy. On the evening of the third day, I went ashore by myself. Mick was off with a girl he had met, and after wandering the streets for a bit, I found myself on the train to Cap D' Antibes. I planned to drop by Grace's hotel, not to go in or anything, but to see if everything was okay with her. I would just stroll by or buy ice cream from the vendor out on the street and see if I could get a glimpse of her. I suppose this kind of thing isn't normal, but nothing about women and me is normal. I've heard a baby duck will imprint on what it thinks is its mother and follow it forever. I must be part duck, because I sometimes imprint on a girl that I think is special, and, well, follow her forever. I wondered if someone found the piece of chocolate I left on Jane's headstone and if they ate it or threw it away.

I got off the train and walked to the Cap D' Antibes Beach Hotel. Grace had booked a room with a beach view, and I was careful to stay out of sight of its windows. I certainly didn't want to take the chance that Jack would see me and blame Grace somehow! I sat on the beach for a while, and I bought some ice cream, pistachio, and it was either very good or I just thought it was because I was in France and on liberty. But, after two hours, I couldn't stand it any longer, so I walked to Grace's door and knocked. I figured if Jack answered, I would say I was there to tell him we had finished the plan, and we were on schedule to give it to the admiral tomorrow afternoon. I would ask him to be sure to be there and leave.

I knocked again, and Grace answered, and as soon as she saw me, she crumpled against the frame and started to cry. I stepped in and drew her to me and held her. She sobbed into my chest as I gently rubbed her back, and we stood like that for some time. I felt a surge of both angel and demon as I stood there, knowing that I was right to drop by and comfort Grace, but also knowing that there was an advantage for me now. I waited for her to speak.

Her sobs diminished, and she pulled away and looked at me with wet, puffy eyes.

"Would you like to sit down?" Grace motioned to a small sitting area by a window. "I have some beer in the little fridge." Her voice was thick and hoarse.

"Sure," I took a seat and looked out at the beach. It was late afternoon but still filled with people, and I smiled when I realized I could see the ice cream stand after all. Behind me, somewhere in the room, I could hear a radio. It was playing softly, and I looked up as Grace joined me. She had two French Kronenbourg's in her hand, so I took one, sipped, and waited for her to speak. She sat and looked out the window, then back at me.

"I saw you."

I frowned and cocked my head.

"I saw you on the beach with the ice cream."

I grinned, shrugged, and took another sip.

"I hoped you would come in."

I swallowed and looked at her. Grace glanced down at her lap for a second, then back to me. "Jack showed up the first night and stayed only an hour. Said he had to go back to the ship because he was planning something important for NATO. He said he wasn't sure when or even if he could come back." She looked at her lap again. "I don't think he wants me here."

"Oh, Grace." I started to say something like, 'I'm sure he does,' but that would be a lie. Instead, I awkwardly leaned toward her and touched her wrist.

"I saw him last night." Grace looked at me, her eyes growing wet. "I couldn't stand it here, waiting. I took the train to Cannes, and I saw him and the admiral at the Radisson Blu." A tear rolled down her cheek. "They were with two women, getting into the elevator."

Grace looked down again, and I could see her shoulders shake. I scooted across the settee and put my arm around her. There wasn't anything to say. At least, nothing I could think of. The only thing I could do for her was to listen. She cried for a while, then straightened, and I moved to my side of the settee.

"The first day we were married, after the honeymoon, Jack played golf with his friends. His friends and the squadron skipper and the admiral. Can you believe it? The first day of our marriage!" She shook her head and dabbed at her eye with a napkin.

I took a sip and looked at her. I hoped I had an *I'm here to listen to you as much as you want* look to my face. Because I was.

"We were married only a month before he began pressing me to ask Daddy if he would help Jack get promoted early to lieutenant commander."

"He had just made lieutenant." I shook my head.

"Jack is on his own timeline. I haven't asked Daddy yet, and I don't want to. But he will keep pressuring me." Grace looked out the window and sighed. "Sometimes, I think the only reason he married me was to get ahead in his career."

I looked out the window too. I wanted to commiserate with her but throwing gas on this fire would do no good. She didn't need my help to know who she had married.

"This isn't the first time I saw Jack with another woman. I was in the Lynnhaven Shopping Center about six months ago, and I saw him, and her." She took a deep breath and sighed again.

"Oh, I love that song!" Grace stood, walked into the kitchen, and turned up the radio. It was "As Time Goes By", with Louis Armstrong.

"*Casablanca.* Great movie!" I smiled as she returned to the settee.

"There is just something about this song…" Grace stared off into the beach again, and we listened.

You must remember this; a kiss is still a kiss.

A sigh is just a sigh:

The fundamental things apply,

As time goes by.

And when two lovers woo, they still say I love you,

On that, you can rely…

We sat in silence, each in our thoughts and, perhaps, a little in the other's and listened to Louie. I, too, loved the song and had for a long time. When it was over, Grace hopped up and turned the radio off. She fetched two fresh beers.

"The song is melancholy, almost haunting, isn't it?" I looked at Grace as she sat.

She frowned and cocked her head. "What do you mean?"

"When you say the words, 'as time goes by' you are initially in the present as you say, 'as time,' but then when you say, 'goes by,' you connect to the past. It's nostalgic, a continuing history, almost. Do you understand? Am I making sense?"

"It might be nostalgic because it was written back in the 1930s." Grace took a sip.

"Perhaps, but I think it is more than that. To me, at least. It is almost a refrain to remember that time does go by. It doesn't stand still for anyone or any reason, and we don't have much of it on earth. We can't waste it."

"Wow, you get that from Louie Armstrong?" Grace laughed, and for the first time that evening, she seemed a little happy.

"Why do you stay with him?" My forwardness shocked me a bit, but evidently not enough to shut me up. "You could be wasting the best part of your life."

Grace paused and lowered her bottle. "Maybe I can't help myself." She took another sip and narrowed her eyes a bit. "Why are you here? What part of your life are you wasting?"

I stared at her for a moment, then sighed and looked to the beach. I could feel her eyes on me, so I looked back at her.

"Maybe I can't help myself."

Grace smiled, then leaned across the settee and kissed me. And her kiss was all I had hoped it would be. But as much as I wanted to stay in her embrace, I knew better. I knew better, and I also suspected that soon she would be uncomfortable, so I let my lips part from hers.

"As I said, maybe I can't help myself."

Grace nodded and looked out the window. A tear formed in the corner of her eye, and just before its silvery trace threatened to expose her, she reached up and brushed it away.

"Why did you marry him?" I asked.

Grace continued to look out the window, but her chin trembled, and more tears formed, tears she couldn't just brush away. I grabbed a tissue box and placed it next to her on the settee. Grace plucked one and dabbed her eyes.

"I loved him, or at least I loved what I thought he was."

"And what was that?"

Grace took a deep breath and glanced at me; then she returned to the window and its openness. She stayed there for a while longer, then sighed and looked at me.

"I have been calling two o'clock in the afternoon 1400 since I was five."

I grinned and nodded. "Military brat, huh?"

"Military brat for sure. On steroids!"

It was good to see Grace laugh. "I grew up on a farm, so I can't relate. It must have been a pretty rigid environment though, shining brass all day."

Grace laughed again. "It was all I knew, so it was okay. But it did set in me certain expectations. Expectations for my life, what I wanted."

"And what was that?"

"The same as you; happiness, fulfillment, success."

"How has that worked out?"

Grace flashed a quick smile, the kind people use as a pause, a thought collector. She looked out the window again. I followed her eyes, but there was nothing there. She wasn't looking; she was searching. I took a sip of beer and watched her until she turned her head and looked at me.

"Did you know that I sat next to the vice president of the United States when I was in college?"

I smiled and shook my head.

"It was at a party in honor of Admiral Rickover, and my dad introduced him for his speech."

"Wow! That must have been something."

"Not really. Rickover speaks like he will stab you any minute, and the Vice President was Spiro Agnew, and he resigned a month later for felony tax evasion."

I choked and spat my beer on my shirt. Grace laughed and handed me the tissue box.

I dabbed at my shirt and grinned at her. "Still, sitting next to the vice president…"

"And that is just it." Grace looked at me, but her smile was gone. "Sitting next to…not by mind you, but next to the vice president…that does sound grand, doesn't it? And I think that is what I wanted. I wanted to sit next to the rich and famous and have everyone see me there and then talk about it. You know, just drop it like during tea with my girlfriends.

"Oh, look at that scone. Why I do believe it's the same one that the vice president likes."

I frowned and put the beer-damp tissue on the table.

"You see I didn't care who the vice president was or who any of them were. I just wanted to be a part of the grandness of it all. I think that is what I have wanted all my life. My dad was a three-star admiral, and that rank is close enough to the sun to tease you to try to fly up to it."

"Until it melts the wax, and your wings fall off?"

"Grace Icarus?" Grace shook her head. "Maybe, but I wasn't worried about that. I knew I could handle the heat. I just needed the right wings, so that is where Jack came in."

"You make yourself sound Machiavellian."

"Machiavellian means cold and rational." Grace chuckled. "I'm not so sure what I did was rational. I mean, I was just a kid that observed success and wanted some for my own. The paths I saw seemed to work, so I started on them. My status climbing desire wasn't as direct as it might sound," said Grace. "It was like the smell of liver and onions. Even if you don't like it, once you are around it awhile, it doesn't smell anymore."

"Did your mother teach you this?"

"Like I said, not directly. It was something that I just observed. Like sending thank-you notes depending upon rank and not the gift."

"And getting back to Jack? Did you ever love him?"

"I loved him enough to marry him."

"What does that mean?"

"It means that he filled the need I thought I had. I loved that he did that."

I felt sorry for Grace before I came, and now, I think I felt even sadder for her.

"But when I first came in, you cried when you said you saw Jack with another woman. Doesn't that prove you have a broken heart? Doesn't that prove that you love him?"

"It proves that I don't want him with other women."

I nodded and took a sip. The beer was warm, so I sat the bottle on the end table. I looked back at Grace.

"Did your mom love your dad? Or was it the same as you and Jack?"

"I think they accommodated each other. Love is pretty complicated, Weenie, despite how much we try to simplify it."

"So even if you like the smell of a rose, after a while, it doesn't smell anymore?"

"Something like that."

I nodded and stood. "Got to get back to the ship."

"Thank you, Jack." Grace rose from the settee, took my hand, and smiled at me. Then she stood on her tiptoes and kissed my cheek.

I turned and walked out the door and down the street to the train station. And as I rode to Cannes, I didn't know if my time with Grace did her any good. I wasn't sure if it helped me either. Since I had no real reason to visit her, I had no calculus for its success. I hopped off the train, and as I walked back to fleet landing and the liberty boat, I realized that my love life was okay. I was okay. Even if love weren't the center of my life, even if I may never be the male role in a magnificent romance story, a story at least as remarkable as what I saw in eager eyes and shaking hands after each mail call, I could still have romance at the edges of my life. And there it would be something always mysterious. It would be something mysterious and wanted, and if it were never gained, it would at least be looked for. And maybe seeking is what we all want. Because when we find, then, well, then something else happens. Hopefully, that something is good, but if not, I didn't want to be like Grace. I wanted always to smell the rose.

I went to the beach for half of one day with Mick but spent the rest of the in-port period working on the plan. We briefed it to the two admirals the afternoon before leaving Cannes, and I was surprised when the commanding officer of Tomcat squadrons invited me to fly in the exercise. Since I was current in the airplane, I asked Dick, and he said to go for it.

We started the exercise the second day at sea, and I launched on the third event. It was my first hop off the ship in the Tomcat, but once I got the inertial navigation system to align, it was pretty much the same as the Phantom. My pilot was a lieutenant commander named Bugs McKee, and he was a great help getting me through the peculiarities of the Tomcat. The threat sector was 260, and we were assigned 25 Delta, so we flew to our cap point at 200 miles. We orbited a couple of laps, and I contacted a target 150 miles down the bearing line. I called it the E-2 over the covered frequency, expecting a "Roger, airliner, disregard and remain clear." However, moments after I called, the E-2 came on the air and ordered me to intercept and rendezvous. That surprised Bugs and me, but we did as instructed, and I locked the target, and we headed toward it. We were twenty miles away when Bugs said he had a "tally," and I was surprised. It must be a big target! We flew closer, and at fifteen miles, he transmitted over the covered frequency, "Two Five Delta is tally on a TU-95 Bear Bomber, angels 40, heading 093."

The TU-95 is a large, four-engine bomber that the Soviet Union had been flying since 1956. It was routinely used to search for American aircraft carriers because the Soviets got nervous when they didn't know where we were. Their goal was to find us and overfly the carrier before our knowing we were there. In this case, we were escorting them over 300 miles from the ship, and I don't think they knew where it was yet! We flew up next to the Bear, and I could see a crewman looking at us from the observation window behind the cockpit. He smiled and held up a Playboy magazine centerfold. I gave him a thumbs-up, and he gave me one in return, and Bugs and I broke off to a more lethal tail position. It would be harder to shoot down a guy that likes Playboy, but, if we had to, we could do it better from behind.

We followed the Bear around until another Tomcat relieved us and headed back for our recovery.

The exercise lasted for two days, and by all accounts, it was a success. The captain came up on the 1MC and told us how great we were, and Rear Admiral Jensen called me into his office and told me how much help I had been. He even wrote me a letter of appreciation for my personnel jacket. Rear Admiral Bass and Jack were also in attendance, but I decided not to look at them. That was the only time I saw Jack since our spat in the passageway. He never showed at any of the working sessions for the plan, and I have no idea if he ever visited Grace after that one night. Rear Admiral Bass and Jack flew off in the COD the day after the exercise, and a couple of months later, as we were heading back home, I heard our training had been deemed a huge success and that Rear Admiral Bass was now known in naval aviation as a tactical genius. His plan had ensured the first Tomcat intercept of a Soviet Bear bomber and over 300 miles from the carrier! The F-14 bubbas also told me the admiral had let Jack go, so I guessed he had served his purpose.

WHATEVER HAPPENED TO CALEB HODGES?

The cruise finally ended, and we pulled into Norfolk, where I got a room at the BOQ and retrieved my Triumph from storage. I planned to find an apartment and expand my social life, but I needed some time to decompress so I booked a flight to Militia Springs. I had received a couple of letters from Mom on the cruise, but they didn't have a lot of detail, so I was eager to see how everybody was.

Dad picked me up at the airport, which was a surprise. He looked a little older but as healthy as ever. I hoped I looked that good when I was forty-four. I felt lucky to have parents so young, only eighteen years older than me, and a vibrant and healthy Grandpa too!

"How did you get drafted to come and get me?" I grinned as Dad and I hugged.

"Grandpa Two Bears was taking a nap, Paul and Molly were looking at a new back loader, and Mom was watching little Kate, so that left me. Besides, I wanted you to see my new pickup!"

We walked to the parking lot, and sure enough, there sat a brand-new Ford F-150. It was a beautiful truck, red, with a long bed. Dad threw me the keys, I put my bag in the back, and we hopped in. Dad liked a manual shift and four-wheel drive, so I shoved the stick into gear, and we headed for home.

"Baby Kate keeping you folks busy?" I grinned across the bench seat.

"Christ, that child never stops. And she's smart too. You can't just put her in a corner or something or tell her to color. She insists on engagement; she's a firecracker."

"So, not like Molly?"

"Not at all. Molly was sensitive and liked her alone time. So were you if you had a book in your hands. But Kate is much more extroverted."

I was going to ask, "Do you think she gets that from Caleb" but, thankfully, I didn't.

"And Mom? Doing well?"

"Doing exceptionally well."

"How about Paul and Molly?"

"Thriving as far as I can see."

I looked at Dad, expecting him to say something about Grandpa. I looked back to the road, then glanced at Dad. "And Grandpa Two Bears?"

"He took a spill the other day."

"A spill?"

"Yes, we were on the square, over by the hardware store. Grandpa tripped and hit the sidewalk. Bumped his head, too."

"But he is fine, right?"

"He's fine. Just getting older."

I shook my head and gripped the wheel. My thoughts of Grandpa Two Bears were of a man in full, a man in complete control of himself and his surroundings. Anything less was unimaginable.

"And the new sheriff came by the other day."

I looked across the cab and frowned. "New sheriff?"

"Yes, Lutie Collins, you remember him?"

"Sure."

"Appears the Sons of Galilee never bought the story that Caleb somehow killed himself with that 12 gauge. They think someone shot him, and since it was on our land, and he was seeing Molly, it was one of us."

"What?" I almost ran off the road. "But that was almost three years ago."

"Yep."

I glanced at Dad, and he nodded and pursed his lips. "Seems that Malachi Hodges, Caleb's father, and some of the others have been imagining things and poking around. They keep bringing up the fact that you fought with Caleb just before he died."

"But I was in California."

"Yes, but we weren't. Sheriff thinks your fight shows a family hostility. The sheriff also said that Malachi found some man who claims to have seen a truck by the road's side the day Caleb was killed. The description fits my old truck, of course."

"Do you remember being out there on that Saturday?"

"Heck, no, son. This all happened a long time ago. I can't remember where I was last week, let alone back then."

I nodded and drove some more. "Has anybody made the connection between Molly's baby and Caleb? I mean, do people think it is Paul's?"

"I don't think anybody outside the Sons of Galilee gives a hoot."

"But they are nosing around it appears."

"I don't believe they have pieced it all together yet. Besides, Missouri law does not require paternity tests, so they will never prove anything, anyway."

We drove for a couple of miles, but as I was descending Dogwood Hill and close to the farm, Dad cleared his throat. "That fella, the Sons of Galilee, found thinks he heard two shots."

"Two? What does that mean?"

"According to the sheriff, it indicates that Caleb didn't stumble and accidentally pull the trigger, but somebody shot him. Shot him, then fired a shell through Caleb's gun to make the story right."

"Does the sheriff believe that?"

"Not sure. He was coy. I guess he has to be, being he is the chief lawman in the county."

I stared ahead and focused on the curves as we went down the hill. But my mind did whirl as I kept thinking of Dad the night I said Caleb had roughed up Molly. The night he found she was pregnant by Caleb. I kept thinking about the dark in Dad's eyes.

"A man's gotta do what a man's gotta do," he had said.

"Do you think somebody shot him?" I glanced at Dad, then back to the road. In my periphery, I saw him turn toward me. I glanced at him again, and he looked startled. I returned my eyes to the road and continued to drive. Dad sat still for a while, maybe a half-mile.

"The sheriff questioned all of us. He said to let him know when you were back in town. He wants to question you too."

"Again, I was in California when Caleb was shot."

"The sheriff just wants to find out what you remember. Wants to know why you two were fighting. But, son, don't go down some rabbit hole of what ifs. Don't do a lot of speculating with him."

"What do you mean?"

"I mean, I think the case of Caleb Hodges needs put to rest."

Dad's words confused me, but I didn't say anything and just kept driving.

We arrived at the house in the early afternoon and I had barely gotten out of the car when Paul, Molly, Mom, and little Kate surrounded me. We hugged all around, and I felt that familiar swell of love in my chest. But, of course, someone was missing, and I looked to the porch. There stood my Grandpa Two Bears. I walked to him as he stepped off the porch, and I hugged him. The familiar smell of tobacco and old spice put another smile on my face, but I was surprised at how thin he felt. He was a bag of bones!

Walking into the house, we began the rapid-fire question and answer sessions we always had when I came home, and since everybody was okay and the farm was doing well, our conversation soon turned to the community and other people. I found that my friend Jimmy Wilson had moved to Kansas City and had gotten engaged. Donnie Curry had also found a girl that lived down by Dora and had gotten married. I guess he had someone to hunt and fish with him. I was glad Paul was there but felt a little guilty around him. I used to come home from college and find the box of my old toys in the closet. I would take them out and hold them, not to play with them but to remember playing with them. Recently, I had developed a nagging guilt that I was executing a version of that with Jimmie, Donnie, and Paul. When I came home now on leave, was I taking my old friends out of the box like I had the toys? Did I take them out, not so much to be their friend, but to pretend like I was for a while?

As I said, I was sure glad Paul was in my family now.

That evening we sat around the kitchen table like we always do, and we started talking about Caleb Hodges and the sheriff. I watched Molly during the conversation, concerned about how she might react to talk about her baby's father's death, but she didn't seem any more bothered than the rest of us. She and Paul just sat there holding hands.

"Is the sheriff suspicious or just gathering information?" I filled my glass with iced tea and looked at the others.

"I can't tell," said Dad.

"He does have a way of thinking out loud that makes him appear to be piecing something together." Mom frowned and nodded.

"And that is a bit unsettling," added Molly.

"How so?" I took a sip of tea.

Grandpa Two Bears leaned forward. "Lutie was sitting here last week with all of us at the table and said, 'You know, most hunting accidents occur when one hunter shoots the other by accident.' He said, 'It's very rare for a single hunter to shoot himself and when he does it usually is in the foot or hand or something.'"

Grandpa Two Bears sat back in his chair. "The sheriff said that he looked through the past editions of the Douglas County Herald. They have it on microfiche now, and he went looking way back."

"He said he found only one case of a hunter killing himself," interrupted Dad. "The hunter had evidently tossed his shotgun up a slippery hill, so when it discharged, it was pointed back at him, and only a couple of feet away so it nearly cut him in half. But the sheriff said it looked like this shotgun was eight feet or so from Caleb when it went off."

"Well, that would be impossible to tell if the blast wasn't aimed right at him," said Paul.

Everybody nodded, and I found myself nodding too. We seemed to be defending ourselves. It was an odd feeling, and I didn't know what to make of it.

The next afternoon the sheriff came out, and I went for a walk with him at his request. He repeated what my family and I had talked about earlier around the kitchen table, but then he stopped and squinted at me. "Weenie, is there some connection between Molly, her daughter Kate, and Caleb? I mean, the word is Caleb and Molly were seeing each other, then next thing I hear is she gets married to Paul Smart two months before the baby is born. Doesn't that seem a bit odd to you?"

"No, not really?"

Lutie pursed his lips. "Then why did you get into a fight with Caleb? Or, from what I hear, attack him on his front porch?"

I figured Lutie would get into this with me and had worked up a reason for the fight.

"I heard his Dad, Malachi, was badgering Grandpa Two Bears about selling him some land. I went to talk to Malachi, but Caleb stopped me. We got into an argument, and one thing led to another."

"And you hit him?"

"He said some pretty mean things about my Grandpa." I nodded toward the house.

"And it wasn't about Molly?"

"No, why would we fight over Molly? I mean, they weren't seeing each other anymore."

The sheriff nodded and put a friendly hand on my shoulder, "Sorry, Weenie, I know how much you love your granddaddy. But I had to ask."

"No problem, Lutie."

The sheriff looked across the woods for a moment, then shook his head and turned to me. "I just wish someone in your family had an alibi. I mean, besides you." He shook his head again. "Grandpa Two Bears was in the barn with a new calf, your dad was off in the truck, but he isn't sure where he went that day. Your mom was home alone, and Molly was driving around in the Fairlane, alone."

"Well, that sounds like a normal afternoon at my house."

"I suppose so," nodded Lutie. "I suppose so."

DOOLY

My job as a catapult officer was exciting while on our deployment, but now we were at home, it was an administrative chore. No airplanes to launch, only paperwork. And working with aviation boatswain's mates can be a challenge because they tend to get into trouble, and trouble means even more paperwork. Not all our men were problems, of course, only the obligatory ten percent. But ten percent of two hundred and six is twenty-six, which is a handful for four officers. The result was that our division took part in every ship's captain's mast. The term captain's mast had always intrigued me. I knew it came from the old days when an offending sailor would be hauled in front of the captain, who would hear the story and declare punishment. It all took place at the base of the ship's mainmast where all assembled to hear. And to be forewarned. So, the modern-day incarnation was how I knew Airman Dooly so well.

I am the bow cats officer and, therefore, responsible for the crews that run catapults one, and two, and Airman Willis Dooly was one of my men.

Dooly was one of the most likable guys you could meet. He was a jokester and always had a big smile and a "How are you doing, sir?" He eagerly and readily pitched in regardless of the task. Dooly was tenacious and courageous, and one job he really liked was to be the holdback man when we launched the F-8 Crusader. Once the Crusader was on the catapult track, a chain attached to the deck was connected to the airplane's underside using a holdback fitting designed to break when the catapult fired. The crewman who made that connection had to lie on the track, inches beneath the afterburner of the F-8, and hold the fitting steady while a nylon harness was attached to the airplane's hardpoints. This harness connected to the catapult shuttle, which ran along the catapult track. The holdback man held the fitting as the catapult officer signaled the pilot to increase power. Crusaders tended to slide sideways on the greasy deck during this part of the sequence, so the holdback

186

man had to be nimble to avoid being crushed! Once the Crusader was at full power and the fitting and bridle were tight, a fellow crewman would kick the holdback man's foot as a signal to roll away from the airplane. When he was clear, the cat officer would signal the pilot to select afterburner. Once that lit off, the cat officer shot him. The holdback man had arguably the most dangerous job on the deck, and Dooly loved it!

However, he also loved beer and carousing, and when the ship was in port, or off duty at home, he was continually late for muster. Dooly was busted in rank and fined and restricted to the ship. However, I still loved the guy for his work and his whole attitude toward others and tried to stick up for him when possible.

I remember one day, Dooly went to mast for the offense of being late to muster. The captain knew Dooly too, as he had observed him down on the deck during flight operations and remembered my praise for his work ethic during earlier mast appearances. So, after the JAG officer read the charges, the captain asked Dooly to explain himself. I genuinely think the captain hoped Dooly could get himself out of trouble.

Dooly grinned up at the captain and said, "Well, sir, it's like this. I was sitting at the bus stop over by the barracks, and a mother goose came out of the brush, and she had five or maybe six goslings right behind her. They were really cute, sir, and they waddled in a row, and when I saw them, I just knew one would get under the tires of that bus, so I got that mother goose to follow me with a sandwich that I had, and she did, and I led her and the goslings all back to the bush and when I turned around the bus was gone!"

I choked back a laugh as Dooly looked at the captain with all the big-eyed sincerity of a child with chocolate on his fingers. The captain looked at me and asked, "What do you think, Lieutenant Kleegan?"

I said, "I believe him, sir."

"So, do I," said the captain. "Case dismissed."

A year later, I was on my second deployment as a catapult officer, and during a night launch, I saw Dooly for the last time.

I was launching on the waist, and my last airplane was an F-14 that couldn't launch for a maintenance problem. The F-14 was right in the middle of the flight deck, and I stood next to it, waiting for the plane to taxi clear of the landing area. Dooly ran to me and asked me if the launch was complete, and I told him, "Yes" and "Wrap the deck." Dooly grinned, gave me a thumbs up, then ran to the crew. As I stood by the F-14, I saw out behind the ship, the lights of an A-7 on final approach. I remember thinking they will wave him off for sure. There was no way we could clear the deck in time for him to land. I walked to the other side of the F-14 to ensure the shuttle cover was in position, and the launch hatch cover was secured and glanced up.

The A-7 was coming in to land!

I looked at Dooly and frantically waved my arms, but he must have seen the A-7 too because he was already running to the crew. They were milling around at the side of the deck, evidently unaware of the danger. Dooly shooed them into the catwalk, then turned and ran back toward me. I heard a massive explosion, and the canopy of the F-14 beside me whipped off the plane into the night, and then the ejection seats fired. The seats' movement must have jammed the throttles forward because the engines staged into afterburner, and the airplane lurched toward me. I flung myself to the deck and away from the tires and felt the afterburners' heat torch by me. I rolled onto my back just in time to see the A-7 fly over the top of us, and the F-14 swerve toward Dooly. He picked up a tire chock and threw it under the left tire. It bounced back, so he picked it up and crawled next to the rolling tire and shoved the chock at it. The chock bounced back again, and the Tomcat's shoulder missile rail caught Dooly's float coat. I staggered to my feet and screamed as I saw him struggle to get free. He was half-carried and half-ran as he pulled at his jacket. He pulled and pulled at his coat. He was still pulling as he and the Tomcat went over the side.

Our helo picked up the pilot and RIO from the F-14 and we caught the A-7 in the barricade. We searched for Dooly for two days, but never found him.

I find myself thinking of Dooly. I think of him and wonder why he didn't stay in the catwalk with the others. He was safe there. Why did he run to me, and why did he try to stop the Tomcat with the chock? That was an impossible task.

I wrote his mother a letter.

Dear Mrs. Dooly,

By now, you will have received word about the death of your son, Willis. I hope that the delivery of that message was as decent as possible, and I pray that God has now somehow given you the strength to bear this impossible sorrow. I know that it will be the whisper of God, and not the words from me or any of us here, that will help you move forward from your sorrow, your always sorrow, to some beautiful memory.

Mrs. Dooly, I had the very distinct honor to sail with your son, and I hurry to tell you that I found him to be a most exceptional shipmate. There was no harder worker on the ship, and Willis had a ready smile, a strong back, and a sharp mind, and he used these tools to serve his nation. He used them to help all of us on USS America, and his efforts ensured we did our duty.

I was with Willis when he died, and I must tell you that he died a hero in the most real sense of the word. I say that because I think a true hero dies risking his life while trying to help others. And Mrs. Dooly, Willis did just that. He died, saving his shipmates. He died saving me.

I certainly can't tell you why God took your son. But here in the Catapult and Arresting Gear Division, we speak of the God of Steam and Grease because it is steam and grease that runs our world. I think that the God of Steam and Grease has a catapult in heaven, and I think he needed your son to go and run it for him. I sure hope so, Mrs. Dooly. Because one day, I, too, will go to heaven, and I will need Dooly to watch over me. Like he did here.

Very Respectfully,
Winfred Kleegan
Lieutenant, US Navy
USS America

Despite the horror of losing Dooly and the arduous nature of the work, my job as a catapult officer was a blessing. I had the opportunity to work with young men whose families didn't have the money to put them in college or didn't have the grades or sports pedigree to get a scholarship. They were so young. So young, with few choices, and the navy was fortunate to be the choice they made. Like Dooly, some of them were trouble, but they were also heroic and just looking for a little respect. When I told my family about Dooly, this was before he died, Mom couldn't understand why we weren't mad at him with as much trouble as he caused us. But I told her that when someone causes themselves more trouble than they cause you, it isn't anger you feel but frustration. I told her about Jenkins and the fact we all felt anger toward him because Jenkins was lazy and worthless, at least when he was with us. Sometimes people deserve forgiveness, and we forgave Dooly for being Dooly. The navy is fortunate for their Doolies and if you ever see a movie or an illustration in a book that depicts a sailor up in the rigging with the wind blowing hard or one racing into a fire with nothing but an ax in his hand, then you will understand why.

We continued the deployment for two more months after Dooly's death. An investigation revealed that the landing signal system had been turned on without the landing signals officers on station. The A-7 pilot didn't realize the deck wasn't clear until too late, and there was no one there to wave him off. We were just lucky he didn't try to land. He would have hit the fully loaded F-14, and, hell, we would still be putting that fire out.

I finished the cruise and a few months later, transferred off America to my new job as an instructor in the F-14 RAG at Oceana. The captain ranked me the number one lieutenant out of eleven, so I successfully got my career back on track! Due to my work on the Vector Logic exercise, I was assigned as the tactic's development officer at the RAG. I liked this opportunity because it gave me a chance to build flight time and experience in the Tomcat and ingratiate myself into the fighter community.

INSTRUCTOR DUTY

My second month in the squadron, I took a cross country training flight to San Diego and visited Raoul. He had just received orders to one of our F-4 squadrons in Japan. Of course, Raoul was excited, so I mailed him a copy of James Clavell's Shogun, as a gift. Clavell had recently published the novel, and it was about a shipwrecked British seaman who washed up on the shore of feudal Japan. The book was all about Samurais and had generated a lot of buzz.

I landed at Miramar Friday afternoon, and that night Raoul made a Japanese dinner in honor of my visit and his new move.

Raoul is one of those people we all know who is impossible to embarrass, and I think we at least secretly admire them for that. I know I respect Raoul for it and although I think it is a trait of the lower animal kingdom in many ways, it gives humans so afflicted a certain power over the rest of us.

Raoul's date, Maria, answered the door and sat me on the living room couch with a glass of Tsing Sao beer. She looked lovely in a floral kimono that she said she rented from a costume shop in University City. Maria was a Filipino but did not seem a bit worried about crossing any Asian cultural lines, and when she informed me that we were having Chinese stir fry, my only answer was, "Of course."

I expected Raoul to make a grand entrance wearing some version of samurai clothing, perhaps even with a sword of some sort. Plastic, I hoped. So, when he walked in as a sumo wrestler, I was floored!

Raoul had not gone to the expense and hassle of renting a sumo outfit, even if you could do such a thing. He had simply taken a large towel and wrapped it between his legs and around his waist. Thank God, he had the sense to wear some skivvies!

Raoul had constructed a Sumo wrestling area in his small backyard and the circle on his lawn still smelled of spray paint. After he sanctified it with some sake and a Corona he asked me to honor him in manly battle. I demurred, so Raoul performed some sacred moves for Maria and me but they were really just him screaming fake Japanese stuff, raising his legs, and stomping. I think he had been drinking, maybe for some time. Thank God, he tired of it after a while and we squatted on the floor to eat our stir fry. Maria excused herself to go to the kitchen and when she later walked out the door, Raoul shrugged and looked at me. "First dates need to be tender, Kleegan."

I am sure we violated every rule of Nippon that night, but we did drink a lot of sake.

The navy promoted me to lieutenant commander, and I put the gold oak leaves on my collar in a ready room ceremony. My skipper assigned me as the assistant ops officer, and I thoroughly enjoyed it. Well, I enjoyed most of it. When I took a new pilot to the carrier for his first night landings and catapult shots, I wouldn't say I felt joy. It was more like apprehension...or, maybe, terror. A pilot qualifies on an aircraft carrier by getting so many graded landings and proving that he can fly a safe aircraft and follow the LSO's instructions.

Initial qualification happens during basic flight training command, and all carrier landings are in the daytime. The first time a pilot sees the deck at night is in his first fleet airplane, and the Tomcat was a challenge for sure. Pratt and Whitney engines took some time to spool up so a pilot could "get behind the power curve" if he didn't anticipate correctly. Also, the Tomcat is large with a long wingspan, which makes it critical to not only fly on the glide path but also right on the centerline. It is a beast to bring aboard, and that first landing with a new guy on a dark night is just short of frantic. Of course, the "reward" for those white knuckles is the next catapult shot.

To qualify, the pilot needs six good night landings so, cat shots are part of the deal to get us back out there for the next attempt. My greatest fear during the night cat shot is that we have a fire, or compressor stall, or some other engine failure because that emergency, so close to the water, requires immediate and correct actions by the pilot to survive. If he doesn't get the nose up to establish a positive climb rate, we crash and die. If he freaks out and pulls the nose up more than ten degrees, we roll off into the "dead" engine, and if I don't eject us at the very beginning of that roll, one or both of us will die. There is a World War Two-era quote, variously attributed to war correspondent Ernie Pyle and other chaplains and generals that goes, "There are no atheists in foxholes." I don't know who said that line, but I will tell you there are no atheists in cockpits either. I pray before each cat shot, just in case one of our Pratt and Whitney twins takes the night off.

The only fly in the ointment was that Jack Grant was also an instructor at the RAG, but since I was in the operations department, I made sure we were never on the schedule together. So, the next two years sailed by. I did see Grace at squadron events and admit I thought of her often. After that night in Cannes, I considered her as a friend, a fragile friend. And I worried about her, given Jack was such a selfish jerk. I caught the news that she had a baby boy she named Christopher.

I did well in the RAG and got a good fitness report from the skipper, then headed off to my department head job. I looked forward to the challenge of going back to a sea duty squadron, and this was a pivotal time in my career.

As the head of either the operations or maintenance department, superior performance is a prerequisite for screening for command and getting your own squadron. You will never get a command if you don't get ranked number one out of the four department heads. That competition will force the best to the top is both a strong and weak assumption in the navy's promotion system. The strength is that it forces the commanding officer to rank officers against each other, and the process of doing that is a worthy one. The skipper must look at each man in the eye and tell him where he fell within the group and why. It provides a formal venue for the skipper to address performance shortfalls and recommend solutions for improvement. However, the weakness is that the process assumes no commander's bias and that every squadron's group of competitors is equal. I was savvy enough to know this, so when my detailer began talking to me about where I might go, I could parry his initial punches. He first wanted to assign me to VF-1 on the west coast. I pushed off from that opportunity.

VF-1 was one of the first F-14 squadrons, and the navy had front-loaded it with talent to the point that they had superstars practically sleeping in the passageways waiting for their turn at maintenance or operations. Getting lost in the crowd is a good thing if you are on a bombing mission over Vietnam, it is not a good thing if you are trying to survive the department head rat race. My detailer next wanted to send me to VF-143 in Airwing Seven. It was an east coast squadron so that I would stay at Oceana, but the skipper was an infamous prick named Red Bannister. Red had his two favorites-- Squeezer McGinnis, and Bunny Smith-- lined up for the number one tickets, so breaking into the top of that crowd would be impossible. Besides, Jack Grant was going to 143 for his department head tour, so I did not want to go there. In the end, my detailer sent me to the Ghostriders of VF-142, the other Tomcat squadron in Airwing Seven. So, I would be in the same airwing with Jack Grant after all.

I also received the joyous news that Cotton was coming to my squadron to be one of the other department heads! I asked the executive officer if we could share a two-man stateroom, and he agreed, so Cotton and I were once again going to be roomies. He and Melody came by the house and stayed for a couple of days while looking around for a home. It was wonderful to see them again, and the fact that Melody was pregnant made it even more special. The best part of their stay was that I had a breakthrough of sorts with her.

I felt uncomfortable around Melody, and it was my problem, not hers. She was gracious and friendly, but I got a vibe from her that made me feel odd. I felt like she didn't expect anything or want anything from me. It is hard to explain but most people I am around, especially friends, make me feel like they need something from me, maybe only a smile or an opinion, or an agreement. Something small, but enough to make me feel like I am a part of their lives. But I don't get that from Melody. On the second day of their visit, I realized that I felt like a stranger around her.

Plus, she had these beautiful, light amber eyes, and I swear she could look inside my head with them.

Then, a miracle happened. On the afternoon of that second day, we were standing in the kitchen, and Melody was making some guacamole. I have no idea why people eat that stuff. It must be some guilt Californians feel for stealing Mexico. Guacamole is one of those things that people must eat if they are in California, and if you are from the Midwest, you best, By-God, eat it, or you will be labeled as some doofus from the sticks. It's like when I first went to the beach in Pensacola, and everybody was eating oysters and someone, I think it was Raoul, handed me one. I had watched people throw that snot down their throats and "wow" and "gosh" and say the emperor doesn't have any clothes for a while and knew enough to slather it with cocktail horseradish sauce and chase it with a cracker. I said it tasted mighty good, but the truth is I just like horseradish, and I like crackers. I was eating the snot to be sociable. It's the same for me with guacamole, except I had never actually eaten it.

Anyway, Melody turns around and holds out a chip with some of her dip on it. "Does this taste okay?"

I hesitated because I was now caught in the classic "jaws of a dilemma." I had heard that phrase all my life, and now, here in my own kitchen, I was in them. If I said, "I don't like guacamole," it would seal me forever as a white guy that can't dance OR eat guacamole. In California, no less. If I took a bite and said, "Yes, this is great," she would use those light amber eyes to see into my head, and that would seal me forever as a white guy who can't dance and who is a liar. I was faced with two equally bad choices. I was doomed.

I swallowed and took the chip and looked at Melody, and at that second, our eyes met, her amber orbs found me, and I realized she really, really wanted me to like it. But she didn't want me to appreciate it for me; that would be too personal. Melody wanted me to enjoy it for her, the creator of the goop masterpiece. She was proud of the green goop! Realizing that I was facing not guacamole dip but a point of honor and being a nobleman of midwestern values, I puffed out my chest and bit into the dreaded chip.

"Best guacamole I have ever tasted," I said.

From then on, Melody and I got along fine.

I knew most of the guys in my new squadron, and I quickly fit into the group. I also was heartened by the skipper and XO, who spoke enthusiastically about their plans for me. They told me that I would start as the administration officer but would most likely move to ops or maintenance in about a year. I felt some relief to know a plan directed my career rather than just luck and timing.

Also, I knew I also had to transition from being a junior officer, a JO, to a senior squadron leader. This task required a resolute sternness when it came to supporting squadron rules and procedures without becoming a dick. I had seen many lieutenant commanders that, once the gold leaf was on their collar and the stripes on their sleeves, conveniently forgot the JO hi-jinks of their past and became holier than thou dispensers of blah from the jar of "wouldn't-it-be-wonderful." They would ruefully shake their not-yet-even-gray heads and stroke their barely thirty-year-old chins and refer to the JOs as "those kids." They reminded me of the college frat guys I saw that smoked pipes and took themselves so seriously while forgetting that they had gotten falling-down drunk just the weekend before. So, the trick was to lead the JOs in supporting the squadron's mission instead of trying to beat, trick, or shame them into submission.

Shortly after joining the squadron, I got a surprise call from Grace Grant! I felt an immediate pang of guilty pleasure at the sound of her voice. I knew our relationship would always be limited to friendship, but perhaps I could save her from her past, and Jack.

That pleasure disappeared when I heard her sobs and learned that her son, Christopher, had died. I met her near the beach, and we sat in her car, and Grace cried until I thought she was going to just die there beside me. I have never imagined such sadness, such abject defeat, and I think much of it was because she felt no way to share her sorrow. Losing her son had never been in the dreams that took her to the sun.

There is a sweet and safe time in your early life when sorrow is best, and maybe only, shared with your mom and dad. But later, when you are older, the time comes when you also need a companion, and I think that is what Grace needed. I believe that is why she sought me and gave me the honor of being her shoulder that day. And it was an honor, and I was so grateful that I had the decency to recognize it as such. I knew she would find no solace in Jack. I don't think he could feel sorrow for anyone but himself.

MISSY

A week later, I visited the navy exchange to check out some new Bose speakers. I don't know much about music machinery, but all the guys in the squadron talk about Bose as the thing to get, so I was there looking.

I don't spend that much time listening to music anyway, except for when I am home at night on the weekend. Then, I am usually drunk, and it doesn't make any difference what speakers I have. So, I was mostly passing the time when I heard a female voice behind me.

"Hey, sailor!"

Grace flashed through my mind, and I smiled and turned around to stare into the eyes, of...Missy Sanders.

"Missy!" I grinned and rushed to hug her. I hadn't seen Missy since leaving Miramar years before. "What are you doing on the East Coast?"

"I am flying for VF-43."

"Towing the banner?" VF-43 was the adversary squadron at Oceana that flew A-4 Skyhawks and T-38 Talons to simulate MIG tactics. They also supported fleet squadrons by towing a gunnery target banner. I assumed that since she was a woman, that is what she did.

Missy's grin disappeared, and she cocked her head.

"Sorry, I didn't mean to insinuate..." I felt my face grow hot.

"The navy lets us chicks fly tactics missions too." The grin returned. "If we can qualify, of course."

"Sorry, I haven't kept pace with what you gals can do these days."

"You mean what us gals may do." Missy laughed as I remembered my favorite teacher, Mrs. Decker's, voice.

"Can refers to ability. May refers to permission."

"There aren't that many of us gals to keep up with, especially lieutenant commanders like me. Most leave after their first tour."

I nodded and smiled. Missy looked great, and for some reason, that made me nervous. She had always been a pal, and I had seen her as such. But this woman standing in front of me was a little beyond pal material.

"One of these days, I'll catch you up on the exciting world of female naval aviation. I am in the BOQ."

"Sure," I grinned.

She winked, turned, and left. I watched her go and went back to perusing the Bose speaker choice. But as I read about woofers and balance and degrees off azimuth, I wondered if I would call her. I mean...to catch up.

I thought about Missy the rest of that day, and on Friday, I did call her. Her "Hello" was bright and cheerful.

"Hey, did you really want to catch up?" I felt like I was back in the eighth grade.

There was a split second's hesitation that I interpreted as distrust followed by a falsely supportive, "Sure!" It was like when the flight surgeon asks, "Ready to bend over?" And you answer, "Sure."

"I mean, there is a lot to catch up on. What about tonight? I mean, you probably have a date, though."

She hesitated again. "Actually, I don't have a date. I just got here, so I haven't met anyone yet. But, hey, I am in the BOQ. Pick me up across the street at the officer's club lobby at seven."

"See you then." I hung up and felt instant remorse. Well, maybe not remorse, but unease. What was I getting into? What was I doing asking a girl pilot out? I mean, they were off-limits, unwelcome sisters. Their efforts at manly things like flying airplanes were to be tolerated but not accepted. So, what was I doing?

I worried about my date with Missy all afternoon, and I almost called her to cancel. What if somebody saw me? What if someone saw me going out on a date with one of the girls? Everybody in naval aviation knew Missy. They would look at me and give me the eye roll and the smug grin. The grin that asked, "What's the matter, Kleegan? Can't get a date with a real woman?"

I was still agonizing when I pulled the Triumph into the officer's club parking lot. I quickly surveyed it and felt a bit better when I didn't see any cars I recognized. Most guys don't go to the club on a Saturday night anyway. Certainly not for dinner, unless your wife is bored enough with you to eat there. I got out and headed toward the lobby.

What's the matter, Kleegan? Can't get a date with a real woman?

I took a breath and pulled the door open. Missy stood at the bar, chatting with some guys in golf clothes. I recognized them as fellow pilots in Missy's squadron. I swallowed and walked toward her.

"Hey."

She turned and flashed a smile. It was momentary, gone in a second, but while against her lips, it was shy and touched with fragile doubt. That made me more comfortable.

As I approached, her smile widened and became less intimate, and by the time I reached her side, the fragility and uncertainty were replaced with the rollicking looseness of happiness in crowds. I was no longer "alone" with her.

"You know the guys?" Missy opened her arm to present the group.

"Sure," I grinned, and the men returned my smile and nod.

"I hear you are taking our mate out on the town?" A pilot I recognized as Squinty Thomas smiled.

"I think we might go to the beach."

Squinty looked at me a moment and nodded his approval.

Did I see jealousy?

Jealousy changed everything. It made Missy desirable. It made me enviable.

"Ready to go?"

"Sure, see you guys later."

Missy and I walked out of the bar, and I led us to the Triumph. We drove to the beach, and since Missy wore her hair short, the ride in my convertible didn't mess it up much. At least, she didn't seem to mind, and since she was a pilot, she couldn't mind, and the thought of that both gladdened and bothered me. We ordered shrimp and crabs at a local restaurant, and, despite knowing Missy, I entered the negotiation of discovery that typified all my first dates, not questions as mundane as about weather, maybe, but not much more.

"How's the navy treating you?"

"Good enough to stay in." She smiled and took a sip of beer.

I nodded and bent to my crab, working it to get the meat. I didn't think about the women in the navy much, but when I did, I wondered why they stayed, why they put up with it. Women weren't really on the team, the operational team. I sensed Missy looking at me and felt awkward, so I cussed the crab to fill the space between us.

"I stay in because I like the navy."

I looked up as my face flushed. Missy knew what I was thinking, and she most likely knew why.

"I like the navy. I sometimes wish I could love it as you do." Her face froze as she realized she had said too much.

I nodded and began working on my crab again.

"You know, I volunteered to go to sea in a non-flying billet. I told my detailer I would take anything to get to sea, but he turned me down."

I looked at Missy again, and her eyes hardened above her sip of beer. "I volunteered to even go to Korea. Nobody volunteers to go to Korea."

We both laughed, and I took a swallow as Missy pulled the shell from a shrimp and plopped it into her mouth. Her eyes smiled above her chewing, and I waited.

"The navy finally let me go to Iceland for two years."

"How was that?"

"About like it sounds."

We laughed again, and I felt the ice, and not the kind in Iceland, begin to thaw. Isn't it strange that when you are just casual chums with someone, the temperature never gets to the ice-forming stage. It stays at the pleasant, noncommittal temperature of *whatever*. I guess it is just the nature of the human beast.

We had some more beer, and before I knew it, we were back at my house.

I have a three-bedroom cottage a block from the beach that I bought with my "boredom bonus," as Raoul called it. And he was right. I saved most of my money because I have no life. I rarely dine out or even go to a movie and have no expensive vices or tastes. Booze is cheap in the exchange.

I didn't buy the Bose speakers.

Raoul proclaimed me the most boring man in the world and once told me, "Weenie, in a Haagen-Dazs ice cream world of fifty flavors, you are one scoop of vanilla."

"Wow, this is nice," said Missy as we walked through the front door.

"Thank you." I smiled the pride of homeownership that is America's dream, and eagerly gave Missy a tour of my palace. I don't have much furniture, but I have a couch, and Missy settled on it with a beer. I flipped on my reel-to-reel player, and the bass guitar and keyboards of Marmalade's Reflections of My Life came on, and we settled back in that post-dinner, drunkish reflection stage.

"What kind of missions do you fly for 43?"

Missy shrugged. "All of them. I don't have any girl limitations if that is what you are asking."

I nodded. "I just wondered. As I said, I don't know what you gals are up to these days. You know what you can do and all. Oops! What you may do and all." I grinned and bent to picking at the label on my bottle. I knew I was showing interest in something I hadn't given a second thought.

"I guess I like dogfighting the best."

I glanced at Missy and saw the challenge in her eyes.

"I know you fighter guys don't like the idea of a woman doing that kind of thing. After all, it's for manly men, right?"

"It takes a lot of strength to fight an airplane." I frowned at my whine. "A hard seven G turn can take it out of a person."

"I know. That is why I like the A-4. If I can get your Tomcat to slow down with me, I only have to pull a couple of Gs."

I frowned again and picked at my bottle. I did not like what I was hearing from her.

Missy chuckled. "If I were a guy sitting here and said that what would you think? I can see you brooding over there."

I instantly thought of Grandpa Two Bears, who once told me, "Weenie, brooding doesn't mean you are thoughtful. It just means you can frown to yourself."

I glanced at her and chuckled too. "I guess not much. Not anything bad that is." I took a sip. "But then, you're not a guy."

"Right. But you see, I'm not trying to out-man anybody, Weenie. I can't beat any of you in an arm-wrestling contest." Missy stared at me. "But I do know that if one of you comes next to me and slows down, I can trim the elevator on that little jet to give me even more pitch, and if I can get the slats to extend together, I can roll 720 degrees a second. I can glom onto you until I kill you."

I swallowed and took another sip of beer.

"Now pretend that I'm one of your buddies. How does all of that sound?"

"Pretty good," I guess.

"But not pretty good coming for a girl, right?"

I shrugged.

"So, to answer the question you asked earlier. "The navy is treating me okay. But that isn't really what we are talking about. It is all of you guys that aren't treating me well. And I don't think that is ever going to change."

I just looked at her and nodded.

"I can't go to the briefs or de-briefs of any flight. The skipper doesn't want anybody to know a girl is flying one of the planes. My callsign is never used, and I don't say anything on the radio that the Tomcats can hear. I use our squadron frequency for safety of flight and tactical calls. After all, there is nothing like a girl's voice calling guns on a Tomcat to cause panic."

"What is your callsign?"

"Beaver."

I almost threw up my beer.

"What?" I thought of Cotton.

"I kind of like it," laughed Missy. "I gave it to myself. It is hero, anti-hero, don't you think?"

"I think you are right," I laughed.

I felt something change at about that time. Or maybe evolve? I don't know, I just began to feel differently about Missy, or perhaps I was starting to realize she was an actual woman instead of, at best, a novelty. She wasn't one of those corncob pipes they sold down at the Lake of the Ozarks, cute but not usable. I guess the question was could she be everything a guy was in the cockpit but at the same time give up nothing of her womanhood? Was that even possible?

We continued to talk, and the beer changed to coffee, and then I looked out the window, and the sun was coming up. It was the first time I had shared a sunrise with a woman. All the other times, the few other times, I had awakened midmorning with the girl already dressed and gone.

I asked Missy out for the following Saturday, and to be honest, I didn't know why. I wasn't smitten like I had been with Jane or ensnared like with Grace. Unlike them, I hadn't fallen for Missy at first sight. I hadn't fallen for her at all. Yet here she was.

But my Missy thoughts were not romantic. Far from it, because she wasn't the center of some dream as much as she was the center of a quandary. You see, Missy Sanders made me face and challenge my disdain for women in naval aviation. After all, it is so much easier to dislike them than it is to dislike her...fill in the name.

So, here I was, strangely drawn to someone who I wanted to dislike but didn't.

That Saturday, we went to The Raven on the beach and then did a pub crawl along the boardwalk. Funny, when I am alone with Missy, none of that woman in naval aviation stuff enters my mind. I just have a remarkably good time. She is smart and funny. She is pretty.

Then, I see her in the officer's club with a bunch of the guys, and somebody starts "talking" with his hands the way pilots do. The way pilots do whether the fly F-14s, or I suppose Arlo's crop-dusters. Then she raises her pilot's hands and I watch her from the edge.

NO MAN IS A RACIST IF HE CAN LIE

My quandary with Missy evolved into a relationship of sorts. Despite my feelings about women in naval aviation, Missy was attractive and smart and fun. I liked being with her. My love life was pretty much a blank page, save for my moments with Jane, so Missy brought me the female companionship I needed.

A part of me wished for love. A part of me was glad it was more a case of happy convenience. Besides, she and I had more in common than I wanted to admit. I don't know, for whatever reason, I decided to take her home with me to Militia Springs for Christmas. It was the first time I had ever taken a girl home. Of course, Mom insisted that she sleep in Molly's old room.

"You can stay together in your room if you get married," she explained. The fact that she even mentioned the word "married" made me laugh.

Everybody loved Missy, and when my old pal, Paul, dropped by with Molly and Kate, he sidled up to me and whispered, "I'm glad you're not gay after all."

Grandpa Two Bears was especially taken with Missy, and I think he saw in her what a grown-up version of his Molly might have been. The Molly that he and Grandma Catherine lost at childbirth. The namesake of my sister, Molly.

Christmas morning, we went to the monastery like we always did and sat together on those cold benches and listened to the monks and their beautiful music. I liked the tears Missy shed as she listened. Being a man, I hid my moist eyes, so she couldn't see.

It was a perfect trip home except for one small blip. We were sitting around the dinner table on Christmas day, and Mom said," This is so nice. Weenie, you and Missy need to take one of your Tomcats out here every weekend."

"That would be great," I said. "We need to get Missy qualified in it first."

"Well, you're qualified," said Molly. "You fly it, and Missy can come with you." Molly never quite understand what I did.

"I'm not a pilot," I shrugged.

Molly frowned and cocked her head.

"He just sits in the back," said Missy. She glanced at me, grimaced, and quickly took my hand.

I squeezed her hand to show no hard feelings.

"Yep, he just sits in the back." I grinned and looked around the table, but everybody was in their thoughts. Their eyes were not on me and didn't see my hurt. All except for Grandpa Two Bears, who held me in a steady gaze. That afternoon Grandpa pulled me outside for a smoke and a talk. Everybody else was taking a nap so I pulled on my coat and followed him to the porch.

Grandpa's breath fused with his Lucky's smoke but a circle wheeled out of it like always. He glanced at me and grinned, "For you."

I smiled and nodded.

"I like your girl."

I nodded and shoved my hands deeper inside my pockets. "Not sure what she sees in me."

Grandpa took another drag and slowly blew out the smoke. He looked at me. "Security."

"What?" I frowned.

"Security. You are someone she can trust. I imagine a woman in her position might need that more than anything."

"What do you mean?"

"She is virtually alone in a man's world. Probably doesn't feel all that much wanted. I think that story you told me, the one about Nolen Roundtree and that fellow Grant says it all."

I had told Grandpa about how Jack Grant had tricked Missy into believing Nolen Roundtree liked her. I told him how Raoul and I had come to her rescue.

"Maybe." I wasn't sure if I liked the role of security blanket. Although, I was pretty sure I was dating Missy for convenience and that wasn't much different.

A month after Christmas, I left for a six-month deployment, and leaving Missy was sadder than I had imagined. Before this, going on a cruise had been a time of anticipation, excitement for the upcoming adventure. But this was different, and I was surprised. I mean, we weren't even engaged. I didn't feel like talking about it with Missy, so I just pretended that leaving her was no big deal.

"Don't let them see you whistle while you pack," was the joke that went around the squadron. But there were times when I lay awake at night, when I felt the warmth of her next to me and heard her soft breathing, that I developed a new-found appreciation for all my fellow sailors who had left the ones they loved on the pier.

Missy didn't talk about it. I assumed it was just my problem.

A month into the cruise, my sadness at leaving Missy was replaced by the joy of deployed squadron life. Having Cotton as my roommate made it even better, and I also felt happy for him because we had twelve Black officers in the airwing. A tiny percentage, but at least he wasn't alone.

A winter cruise in the Mediterranean isn't pleasant, but it is better than any season off the Vietnam coast, so I enjoyed myself. My earlier Med cruises as a cat officer allowed me a familiarity with the ports, and I took advantage of that to lead Cotton on liberty. He carried me back aboard a couple of nights, but, hey, I brought him out of Vietnam, so it wasn't any big deal.

Midway through cruise, our sister squadron, VF-143, had a brouhaha that catapulted my nemesis, Jack Grant, to success. Like me, he was stuck in the admin officer job as a first department head, but, unlike me, he had no prospects for ever getting ops or maintenance. The 143 skipper, Red Bannister, had his two favorites, Bunny Smith, and Squeezer McGinnis, installed in those jobs. Bunny would be first in line to get the number one fitness report, and Squeezer would move up for the next one. The timing of that plan would freeze old Jack out because he would leave the squadron before he ever got a chance as a major department head. I knew all of this because the 143 JOs hated Jack as much as everybody else did, and they talked to our JOs who spoke to me. But that all changed the night Red got drunk and crashed his Tomcat while landing in Italy. The later investigation revealed that he, Bunny, and Squeezer, had been drinking that night in Red's stateroom and had done so practically every night of the cruise. The airwing commander fired Red and kicked the other two off the ship. That allowed Jack to move up to be the squadron's operations officer with a shot at command. A genuinely horrendous proposition for naval aviation.

Missy and I wrote regularly and I got a letter almost every mail call. I have to say I thought of Missy a lot, but when she came into my mind, usually at night just before I fell asleep, I was still more confused about us than missing her. I knew that my trouble with Missy was due to my ego and what some might think of as old-fashioned thinking. But was my dislike of women in naval aviation wrong? I mean, what did they bring to the game that wasn't better done by men? After all, was all social change a sign of progress, or was it just a weak bend to pressure? I would always drift off with the issue unresolved.

Toward the end of cruise, on the day we pulled out of Haifa, Israel, the skipper called me to his stateroom, and I knew it was to tell me I would take over operations. Joe Jacoby, the operations department head, had left the squadron during that in-port period, and I knew my time had come. I was a little surprised that the skipper hadn't told me earlier.

"Come in, Weenie." The skipper pointed to a chair by his folding desk, and I took a seat. I had expected the conversation since joining the squadron and worked to keep the eagerness out of my smile.

"Look, Weenie, I am going to give operations to Cotton."

I blinked as my head blew off!

"Yes, sir."

Ready to bend over? I heard the flight surgeon ask.

"I know I promised it to you, but, well, I think this is the best move for now. Don't worry; we will get you your chance soon."

"Yes, sir." I stood.

"Well, no need to leave." The skipper frowned, and I could tell he wanted to have a more significant discussion. I think he had prepared for such a thing.

"I don't think there is much more to talk about, sir. You told me Cotton is getting operations."

"Well...sure. Yes, Weenie. Yes, I guess that is all."

"Yes, sir. Permission to leave, sir?"

"Well, yes, sure."

I turned and walked out of the room. My face burned as I headed down the passageway and to the nearest flight deck exit. We were between launches, so the deck was quiet, and the ship, out of the wind, was eerily calm. I heard a signal flag snap above my head but kept my eyes down to hide my disappointment.

I also fought the darkness that was filling my mind. The darkness of my thoughts that questioned why I was not chosen. The darkness that suggested the skipper picked Cotton because he was Black, and the navy needed Black leaders. After all, I had been successful in my navy career, and the skipper had all but promised me operations. Now, without a word of counseling or warning, he had given it to Cotton. Why? Was he that much better of an officer than I was? Or was he just a better color?

My darkness turned to anger, and I was grateful for the open space of the deck. Our ready room discussions on race equality, led by the executive officer, had all been easy to support, pablum to slurp. But diversity is only a great concept if it doesn't affect you.

But, as I stomped off my anger, my mind settled down. After all, who is to say Cotton doesn't deserve the pick? After all, he is one hell of a pilot, officer, and leader. What if he is part of some plan that the skipper has with the bureau to finally get a Black commanding officer in the fighter community. Wasn't that worth disrupting a fellow named Kleegan's plans? And why didn't I have a conversation with the skipper about all of this, instead of abruptly leaving his stateroom?

I felt disappointed because I had always thought I was above this kind of negativity. Even in college, when I first met Blacks, I had an innate desire to be fair to them, although I never knew what "being fair" meant. I resisted any feeling of guilt because I wasn't guilty of anything.

I took a deep look at the rolling sea and, finding nothing there, headed to my stateroom. Cotton was at his desk when I walked in, so I gave him my biggest grin and offered him my hand.

"Congratulations, roomie! I hear you got ops!"

Cotton stood, and even in the semi-dark, I could see his eyes search me, looking for my true feelings. He took my hand and shook it. "The skipper just told me. I had no idea."

"You earned it, man."

"No hard feelings?" Cotton's eyes remained wary. "I mean, we talked about you getting ops."

"None! You are the man for the job; just tell me how I can support you. I am really happy for you, roomie." I wasn't totally lying. Not totally.

We grinned and clasped in a bear hug, then went off to chow. I was outwardly happy, even buoyant, but inwardly I was conflicted. I could not rid myself of the certainty that somehow Cotton had taken my spot. I had this vision of a giant ledger with the tally of a million harms against Blacks on one page and only one or two marks on the other, and I was on that page. That night, as I lay in my rack, I realized that despite what I had thought of myself, open-minded and generous, I knew that my generosity was mostly due to the fact I was willing to do good and be fair because it wouldn't cost me anything to do so. I remembered Sunday school when in Luke,

John the Baptist said, "Whoever has two coats must share with anyone who has none." But, what I wanted to know, John, is what if you only have one coat? I felt that the operations officer's job had been my one coat, and the skipper had given it to Cotton.

I fought my jealousy, and as I watched Cotton grow into his job, it killed me. Whenever he stood in the ready room during our meetings and discussed operations, it killed me, and operations ran the ready room, so Cotton was the squadron's central point. As admin officer, all I could talk about was paperwork. Cotton must have felt something was up because he kept a distance from me. Even when we were together in our room, he held a distance and maybe I did too. It bothered me but not enough to honestly embrace what had happened.

During the last week of the cruise, as we sailed home, the skipper called me into his stateroom.

"Weenie, I am making you the maintenance officer as soon as we get home. Take some leave and be prepared to come back and get us through the turnaround."

"Thank you, skipper!" I kept my face straight, showing no emotion. Petulance is best savored when confused with stoic professionalism.

The skipper frowned, and I knew he expected a different response. I almost smiled but held it to punish him.

"And I want to thank you for how you took the news, you know, that I was giving ops to Cotton instead of you."

"It was no problem, skipper." I lied.

"Well, you couldn't help but be disappointed, and I am proud of the way you handled the situation. A lot of guys would have had a difficult time with it."

"Thank you, skipper." I smiled and accepted the praise I didn't deserve.

"Weenie, I wanted to talk with you the day I told you about giving ops to Cotton, but you left before I could. I think you were shocked by the news and needed some time to recover."

I didn't answer.

"You see, I got word from fighter wing that we are going to get new block F-14s as soon as the cruise is over, so I changed the plans for you from ops to maintenance. I knew you could handle any disappointment, but more importantly, I need my strongest guy for this transition, and I know you are that man. It will be a huge challenge."

"Thank you, skipper." I fought to keep a straight face. I had had two coats, after all.

We shook, and I left the skipper's stateroom in a daze. I wanted to talk with Cotton and make up with him and tell him how much I had hated the fact he got ops. How much I had viewed it as my job to get. I wanted to tell Cotton that I wanted us to be like we were before.

But I couldn't.

If I did that, I would admit I was like everybody else who thought Black achievement was rigged. Even if I knew I was like everybody else, it was possible that Cotton didn't know. Maybe we could go on like before.

But Grandpa Two Bears' words kept trilling my mind: "No man is a racist if he can lie."

LONELY BUT NOT ALONE

A post-deployment fly-in at Oceana is a festive affair whereby all the F-14s from both Tomcat squadrons and the Intruders from the A-6 squadron fly across the field in formation. They then separate into smaller groups and land. Many family members and friends wait at the flight line, which is a joyous and emotional event.

But it can also be awkward. I had now completed five such cruises and had seen five such reunions and had seen my squadron and shipmates meet their loved ones. Healthy relationships can grow even more vital during such separations, but weak ones can disintegrate. It first appears with the letters not coming, continues with the troubled in-port phone calls home, and ends its painful evolution in false and fleeting smiles and empty, cold hugs. Then, somebody moves out.

We parked our jets, and once all of us were chocked and chained with engines winding down, we stepped out to meet our friends and families. I saw Missy at the edge of the crowd and shot her my widest smile. After we shut the engines down and climbed out, I headed toward her. And, as I drew near, I remembered the quote, "If two lovers can remain friends, either they never were in love, or they still are."

And I knew that we never were.

I hugged her with an awkward but expected wariness, and I wasn't surprised by her aloofness. In fact, I welcomed her distance as it put us on an equal footing of sorrow rather than some one-sided guilt.

"Welcome home," she said as she looked up and smiled.

"It's good to be back," I replied.

We hugged again, and despite the tepid nature of our reunion, I felt happy that I had someone there. I had never been met before. Well, there was one time when Arlo Grundeen hired a hooker to meet us at our fly-in back in the Vietnam days. Arlo was my pilot and believed in sharing everything. It was before he married Wanda, of course, and the hooker's name was Lady Marian. I still remember how it felt when she had hugged me and kissed my cheek. Phony doesn't mean it wasn't real.

Missy had to go back to work, so I went home, and that night we went out. It was friendly, but only that, and I think we both knew it was over, that our relationship was more a functional courtesy than anything intimate.

I decided to go back to Militia Springs on leave, and I would go without Missy. We had continued to drift, and, like birds on a wire, we remained next to each other, waiting the thing that would cause us to fly apart.

The farm has always been a place of comfort for me, and Militia Springs was a host for so many wonderful memories. I am fortunate that my life spark began there, but I am also nagged with a feeling that I should come back to Douglas County. The notion of me moving back to that little town would be laughable if it weren't so persistent and if it weren't accompanied by a sadness that pulls at me and evokes a fear that every day I stay away is a day that I have missed something important. I fear that I am missing being a part of America that is comfortable with itself. I fear that I am missing being a part of America that moves at a pace slow enough to stop on the sidewalk or in the field and say "Howdy" and really want an answer. Melancholy is the word I settle on when I get this way, and it is a good word, but it is not enough. Because I wonder that like the characters in Hemingway's *The Sun Also Rises*, am I just going through the motions of life and not living it? I worry that while the novel's Brett and Jake and Mike found temporary happiness in alcohol and sex, that I am using alcohol and my career for the same thing. But worse, when I refer to the Bible, Ecclesiastes 1:5, and the passages that gave Hemingway his novel's title, I find the sun also rises means that whatever we do, win, or lose, it doesn't really matter because in the end, the sun just rises again and the world goes on. So, if that is true, it is our responsibility to get as much out of our lives as we can because once it is gone it is gone. Or as Raoul told me, "When the merry-go-round goes by it doesn't make any difference if you get on the red horse or the blue horse, just get on and enjoy the ride as much as you can until it is over."

Mom and Dad bought a new Ford Fairlane from Don Sally at his sales office just off the square, and they drove it to the airport to pick me up. They looked well in their mid-fifties-going-grey, and our conversation was both exciting and comforting.

I sat in the back while Dad drove. Most folks take US Highway 60 through Mansfield and then down Highway 5, but Dad always took 65 to Ozark and then Highway 14 over through Sparta and down the Dogwood Hill to home. He said he "liked the country of it."

Kate surprised me how big she had grown, and Paul and Molly looked happy and content, and I was glad for that. Paul's construction business was going strong, and Molly was a math teacher at Militia Springs High School. They seemed to enjoy their lives.

Grandpa Two Bears looked frail and moved with hesitation, but his mind seemed sharp as ever. It was good to be home.

I spent ten days on the farm, and ironically the closer I got to my family, the more I felt apart. One night we watched Steinbeck's The Red Pony on television, and I had to get up and walk out. Despite the fact the Tiflin family groused at each other, at least they were actively taking on life together, and Robert Mitchum's Billy Buck taunted me. He was integral to the family he worked for; he was part of it, despite the fact it wasn't his family.

Everybody was engrossed in the movie, so I quietly slipped out the door and plopped down on the porch.

It was a beautiful night, and I sat and listened as the pond frogs piped their background to the wind sighing over the alfalfa. I heard the screen door squeak and glanced over my shoulder to see Grandpa Two Bears shuffling toward me. He was seventy-five now and entitled to a shuffle, and he grunted as he put his hand on my shoulder to step off the porch. Once settled, he reached into his shirt pocket and took out his pack of Lucky Strikes. I kept a batch of Mom's blue-tipped kitchen matches in my pocket for just such times, so I scratched one against the concrete. I let the phosphorous burn to clear flame, held it, and Grandpa Two Bears lit his cigarette.

For some reason, the circle he always blew, was a blessing.

"For you," he would say.

We sat for some moments, enough time for the frogs to realize they hadn't croaked anything in a while and re-start their songs.

"You are missing a good movie."

"I've seen it." I glanced Grandpa's way and saw the red glow of the cigarette. It brightened as he took a drag, and for a second, I could see his face. His eyes were friendly and kind as always, and even though I had come out to be alone, I was glad I wasn't.

"Something wrong?"

I sighed and shook my head. I looked out at the dark for a while and smelled his smoke. I turned to him. "I don't know; concerned, I guess."

"Concerned about what?"

"That's just it, Grandpa. I shouldn't be concerned about anything."

"Things okay with Missy?"

I shrugged. "Good as can be, I suppose."

Grandpa grunted and shuffled his feet.

"I'm not sure if there is anything there anyway?"

"Oh, that's a shame. We all like Missy. We like her a lot."

"It's just that, I'm not sure she is right for me. I always thought I would know instantly. Like with you and grandma."

"And you and Jane?"

"Yes," I nodded.

"What isn't right about her? Or do you even know?"

I glanced at Grandpa again and sighed. "Well, a part of it is… I think it is because she is in the navy. Part of me just doesn't like the idea of a woman in the navy. And most of my friends feel the same."

"But what about it, don't you like? Do you not respect her?"

"I don't know, Grandpa." I shook my head.

We sat in silence for some moments, and I heard Grandpa clear his throat.

"We sure respected the nurses."

I frowned and looked at him. He glanced at me, and another drag lit his face.

"We didn't take women in uniform all that serious. In retrospect, it was a disservice to them. But, for us, at the time, the bar for respect was high and narrow. There was only one bar, courage in combat. Well, that and integrity. Doing what you say you will do."

I nodded. "I guess we all have bars for respect."

"Yeah. Yeah, we do." Grandpa took another drag.

"Why nurses?"

"I think that in the back of all of our minds and the thing we dreaded even more than death was to be crippled. To lose legs or arms, or to be blind. You see, when you are dead, you still matter. Or you mattered. But when you are a cripple, you are just somebody's problem. And to tell you the truth, when I visited guys in the hospital, I couldn't wait to get out of there. But our nurses had to deal with that all day, every day."

I thought of Reese.

"But at least the men they dealt with were alive, Grandpa. They still had a life they could live."

"The nurses thought so. Even if the guy had given up... the guy they pulled out that stinking bedpan for... had given up, the nurses hadn't. They had seen a hundred broken men, and they believed one day the broken man they now tended would realize that he had to live the life that now lay in front of him. Not the one he had before. So, the nurses changed pans and applied bandages, and gave pills. And they cleaned the wounds but what they really did was keep the men going long enough for them to adjust their bar. To get it down where they could limp or crawl over it. Or whatever they had to do. I couldn't do what the nurses did. That is why I respected them."

Grandpa Two Bears reached over and touched my shoulder. "I imagine Missy is also doing something you couldn't do."

"Grandpa, I respect women, but they change everything. The whole environment, the feeling in a squadron, is built on guys being guys. A ready room is a man's place and has been since we started flying off carriers. Women just ruin all of that."

"Maybe so," grunted Grandpa Two Bears. "Maybe so, but none of that sounds like a good reason to exclude them, does it?"

"Easy for you to say. You didn't have to put up with them when you were in the marines."

"True, we didn't. But times were different then, besides, slogging around in the mud and heat is physically demanding. Maybe part of the reason we didn't have women was that not many wanted to do what we had to do or could physically do it. It might not be the same for flying an airplane. Besides, who knows, one day you might need them just to get enough people to keep the military running. There isn't a draft anymore."

"Look, Grandpa, a part of me wants just to say, "What the heck? Let them come in. But another part of me resists it mightily. Like we are giving something away."

"What would you be giving away?"

"Well, our culture of men working together to fight an enemy, for one."

"I understand that, and I don't trivialize it. But, Weenie, much of our history has men and women fighting together whether the enemy was weather, disease, locusts, rocky soil, or Indians. I imagine the women are going to have to earn what they get in the navy. I don't think much will be given to them. But the real question is, how do you feel about her? Put all this women-in-the-navy stuff aside and ask yourself what you feel about Missy? What if she was a civilian? Would you feel the same?"

"I don't know. She isn't a civilian. I can't separate the two."

"Well, son, I wish you luck figuring all of this out. You surprise me a little, though. I mean, you are such a thoughtful young man, you always have been."

"I never had anything like this to be thoughtful about." I was surprised at the edge in my voice.

"Is this what you have been moping around about? You have been moody and quiet since you got here."

"I guess so. I mean, the center of my life is the navy now. But you know, Grandpa, that might be wrong."

"So, you are saying that if you were less navy-centered, Missy wouldn't be a problem?" Sometimes Grandpa Two Bears looked at me like I was six years old. This was one of those times.

"Uhh." I shrugged.

"That doesn't make much sense, Weenie. Lots of people have trouble with their relationships because of their jobs. But most of that is because the job takes them away from their loved ones, not because it brings them closer."

"But Grandpa, that is just it." I hated it when I whined. "The navy IS my life. It is the only thing I have ever been good at. I wasn't a high school football star like you and Dad. I wasn't popular. I studied hard, and people liked me, okay, but I was a nobody. The same for college, I was a nobody. Then the navy came along, and I AM good at it, and I AM somebody. I love the history and heritage of naval aviation. I'm in the same profession as the heroes at the Battle of Midway, and I just don't think women are part of that."

"Weenie, the service can never be your whole life. Hopefully, you will live a long time so think of the navy as a vehicle for this part of your life, not as an end-all. Heck, you met Jane because of the navy. You met this girl, Grace? You met her because of the navy."

"But Jane and Grace aren't IN the navy."

We sat there in the dark for a while, and I lit another cigarette for Grandpa. He inhaled and blew out a ring. "For you," he said. He always said that when he blew a smoke ring.

I glanced at him but said nothing.

"Why did you leave the movie and come out here by yourself? To think about this, Missy thing?"

"Not exactly." It amazed me how Grandpa could read me. I looked at him, a dark shadow on the porch, "I feel like I am missing out on something, something that is important." I shrugged. "Something that, once gone... it's gone. I just, you know, feel hollow. The movie made me want to be by myself."

"Makes sense."

"It does?" I frowned and turned toward him.

"Sure, I think all of this is connected. You are struggling to figure out what your life is, what you want it to be. Your navy life is successful but, perhaps, incomplete. And let's be honest, military life is stressful. Every day of it is stressful. Here, your home is where you were safe and comfortable; your friends still live here. Despite your comments about being a nobody in high school, we both know that isn't true, or you wouldn't seek refuge here. I think it is natural for you to be pulled back to where you feel you belong. Where you were part of something that has roots. Remember, when you leave a little place for a bigger one, you can expect to get lost. What you must do now is figure out what your life is and what you want it to be. Then you need to go and live it."

"Easy to say, Grandpa."

"Yes, it is. But, Weenie, that also means you must have the courage and the patience to let other people live their lives too. Don't underestimate the danger of not letting them do that because it will turn people that should love one another against each other. Don't begrudge Missy for living her life as a navy pilot."

I was grateful for the dark on the porch. It hid my face. After a few more minutes, Grandpa snubbed out his smoke, patted my shoulder, and shuffled back inside.

The next morning, I drove Mom into town to get some supplies at the grocery store. We discussed my night's conversation with Grandpa Two Bears.

"Grandpa is exactly right! It is up to us to understand what parts of our life we can control and what we cannot. Sure, we must seek what we find elusive, but we cannot dwell on a never-ending search for our life's purpose if it causes us to miss what is in front of us. The Though Shall Not Covet commandment was written for a reason, Weenie, which all fits into what you and I have been talking about."

I drove while Mom sat next to me. I glanced at her, "What do you mean?"

"Living your own life has a value now and in the future. You remember when I told you that God's greatest gift is that we can make our heaven?"

"Sure."

"Well, some folks will need help with that. Babies that die, for instance. So, we need to live our lives to the fullest, live the best ones we can, so we can share that with our family and friends in heaven."

"So, when I see Grandma or Jane, I will be able to share my life's experiences with them and make their heaven more whole."

"That's right, and I think that is a major reason why God doesn't want us to commit suicide. We not only give up on our precious lives when we cut them short; we also limit the wonderful things we could have done and been part of."

"Then, why does God let people do it? Why do babies die if that is the plan?"

"Do you remember Mister Robey's science classes?"

"Sure, I remember he smelled like cigars most, though." We laughed, and Mom patted my knee.

"Do you remember a quote he might have used? The one from Einstein that went, "Energy cannot be created or destroyed, it can only change from one form to another"?

"Sure."

"I think that he was right. I think the world we live in is full of energy and some of it is good, and some of it is bad. And I think God needs a lot of good energy to balance out the bad. When good people die, their good energy fights the negative energy. I think a baby has such a strong and wonderfully pure energy that sometimes God needs it. I know this might sound cruel to you, but it is the only explanation I have."

"Does the baby grow?"

"What?"

"In your example, does the baby that dies grow?"

"I think its spirit, its soul grows and mingles with those who loved that baby. So, yes, it grows."

"So, you don't just think that crap happens?"

"No, remember that I once told you that God is practical. "Crap happens" is not the strategy of a practical God."

The leave was over too soon, and I was back in the squadron. Missy and I continued to date, but we didn't discuss our situation. We didn't admit there was a problem and that surprised me. I thought women had a need to talk things out, desire for closure. But maybe not. Or maybe the ones who joined the navy to become pilots did not. Maybe Missy's arsenal included the ability to act like a man, even if it wasn't productive.

For passion, I met secretly with Grace.

My liaisons with Grace were not about sex; we met in libraries and coffee shops and other public but out of the way places, and I found it refreshing to talk with someone so desperate for friendship. I would have thought such conversations would be unbearably depressing, but with her, I had such a feeling of being needed that it overcame everything else. It was the first time that I felt truly needed, and the idea that my presence made a critical difference in someone's life inspired me. When Grace described the grief for her lost son, it was such an open, transparent, total cry of loss that I felt as if my heart would burst. Instead of recoiling or running away from her angst, I found myself reaching for it. And when she told me about finding a little dog, Harley, she called him, and how that surprise gift from God...and she was adamant that was who it was from... so filled her life it made me want to hear more. In later meetings, she told me how Jack had turned away from the pet and was embarrassed that it was a poodle instead of something more manly. I suppose some of my joy came from the reinforcement that Jack Grant was every bit the ass and jerk that I thought he was. And I felt guilty for that joy because I knew that Grace was paying the price for it. But despite what therapeutic value I might have had, the one thing I could not do for Grace was to save her from her depression. I could be there for her. I could talk and listen. But I could not stop her disease. And maybe the ultimate irony of it all was that despite how my relationship with Grace was beneficial to her, it was also a Godsend to me.

IF I HAD A DOG, IT WOULDN'T LIKE ME

The squadron began to receive the new block airplanes, and my job as maintenance officer made for long days and sleepless nights. It was a nightmare performing all the transfer and acceptance inspections and other tasks while executing a robust operational schedule. At times, it pitted me against Cotton. You see, Cotton's job was to train all the aircrew to the highest level of proficiency, and that required a lot of flight time in well-maintained airplanes. Ideally, maintenance supplied the right number of planes to fill the flight schedule, but Cotton was so aggressive I often thought he didn't understand the pressures we were under. It didn't help that I had never resolved my issue with Cotton's selection for the operations job. Or how I had handled it and the thoughts about Cotton that I had had. I had never pulled him aside and had that frank and honest discussion about what had happened. So, there it hung, a low hanging beam that I had to consciously remember to duck whenever I was with Cotton.

It is a mark of honor never to miss a scheduled sortie, so I decided to pattern my old mentor, Rear Admiral Jensen, now a four-star admiral, and constructively confront Cotton. I pulled him aside from the morning meeting, and we walked out to the flight line. It was early, and the aircrew were manning for the first launches of the day.

"Cotton, my guys have been working full shifts and a lot of weekends since we came off cruise. You remember when we came back from our first cruise together? We went to a four-day workweek for about six months. My guys need a break."

Cotton turned to me and smiled. "I remember."

"I was going to talk with the skipper but thought it best to speak with you first."

"I appreciate that." Cotton nodded, then frowned. "But, Weenie, the skipper allowed so many of our pilots and RIOs to extend for the last cruise. As you know, they all bailed out since we came back and we have had nearly a complete turnover in our aircrew. Weenie, all of those new guys need to get trained for the next deployment."

"I understand that, I do." I put my hand on Cotton's shoulder and was grateful that he didn't flinch. "But our receipt of new airplanes complicates that. I know we can't go to a reduced workweek, but if you can find a way to shave off some of the daily requirements, we would appreciate it."

"I'll do what I can." Cotton smiled again. We shook, and he walked back to the hanger while I strolled the flight line. And as I did, I thought of the look in his eyes, the look he had just given me as we had just talked, and I wondered if my eyes had been as his were. Were my eyes also those of only a colleague and nothing more? Cotton and I had become special friends during our first cruise together and had cemented that as roommates. But now? I shook my head as I continued to walk among our airplanes. I feared that I had let something terrible happen.

That night, as I tried to fall asleep, a memory refused to let me slumber. It was the image of Cotton and me with Cotton lying in a bed in the ship's infirmary. We had been rescued, and he was recovering from the beating the Vietnamese had administered with their gun butts. He was in pain and moaned with each movement. But he had opened his eyes and said, "Thanks for getting me out of there."

That was it; that was all he said before he fell back asleep. But the look in those eyes, the reaching to me, the pure and total honesty of them. The giving of those eyes had shaken me. I don't think I realized it at the time; I know I didn't. But now, as I remember, I think it was at that moment that Cotton and I had become something special. We became what all the Bro movies try to achieve, but we had done it for real. And now, I had thrown it all away because I couldn't take the idea of him beating me, and why was that? Was it because I could only be friends with people I felt superior to? Wow, that was a change from my high school and college days! Everybody I knew in those days was better than I was at almost everything. I think my navy success had, in some way, contributed to the situation. When I was a nobody, I remember being happy as such. I didn't have to worry about disappointing anyone, at least at school. And the same happened in college. I was a nobody and got my quiet, good grades and slumped along in wonderfully cocoon-like anonymity. But the navy was different. Almost from the first, I had succeeded. I was a four-bar in Aviation Officer Candidate School. I was ranked the number one ensign and lieutenant junior grade in my first squadron. I had had a hiccup with Rear Admiral Bass, but I more than made up for it as a catapult officer. I was the number one lieutenant wherever I was assigned, and everything had worked. I was somebody! I am somebody! But now I worry always. I am petrified that I could lose it all and become nobody again, and I think that would kill me.

Cotton was true to his word, and the operational demand for aircraft lessened. We had time to groom our planes for the upcoming tactics development program with the Bandits of VF-43, Missy's squadron.

All Oceana based Tomcat squadrons went through the program, and the Bandits graded our flights. The better we did, the more points we accumulated towards the Battle E award, given annually to the best unit within a competitive group in the navy. Ships, squadrons, all sea-going units vied for the honor. Our competition was all the other Tomcat squadrons on the east coast, but first and foremost, our sister squadron. I could not bear the thought of them, and, of course, Jack Grant, beating us.

I was crewed with Mike White, callsign Magwai. He got the callsign while on a cruise and in port in Palma De Mallorca. Palma is in the sun-splashed Spanish Balearic Islands and is a bit of heaven in the sand. The story goes that Mike was joining his squadron mid-cruise, and the carrier had pulled into Palma for liberty. Mike checked into his squadron, and, of course, the JOs took him out on the town. They plied Mike with welcoming shots of stingers, and he got pretty tanked up. When he was introduced to the commanding officer, he reached out his hand and mumbled, "Migg whidd," just as he threw up all over his new skipper.

"What did he say?" The skipper is reputed to have asked.

"Mike White, sir," came the answer from one of the JOs.

"No," said the skipper. "No, he said Magwai."

So, here I was flying with Magwai.

The first flights against the Bandits are tutorial and meant to get the Tomcat pilots and RIOS familiar with the MIG surrogates; the A-4 replicated the MIG-17 and the T-38, which patterned the MIG-21. They were old technologies, but when adequately flown, a real handful for Tomcat pilots. The A-4 was relatively slow but could turn on a dime and cling on to a poorly flown F-14. The T-38 was faster than the A-4 and had a knack of arriving at a firing position unseen.

The king of the Bandit lair was Hokie Bond. Hokie was a farm boy from Oklahoma who didn't look at all the part of a fighter pilot.

He was barrel-shaped and thin-haired and eschewed the in-vogue workout and gym regimens. He looked more like a guy from a doughnut commercial than a fighter pilot, and that is where his strength lay. He was remarkably approachable and had a gentle way of telling you how bad you were that left your ego intact. Hokie was an incredible pilot, and the word was that if a Bandit showed up on your six and you couldn't shake it, then Hokie was driving.

Since Missy was a Bandit, I good-naturedly, but intently, pressed her for any advantage she might offer for my squadron. Her only advice was, "stay fast, get your kills, and get out."

The second week of tactics training took a serious tone since that was the graded part of our training and each Tomcat section of two planes faced two Bandits with the results of kills recorded for grades. We did well, exceedingly well, but so did our sister squadron; Jack Grant's squadron. By the end of the second week, we knew we were tied.

The last day was pivotal, and both squadrons were tasked to fly a two versus unknown to see which outfit was the best. A two versus unknown was extremely difficult because we didn't know how many bad guys were out there. We were just given a vector toward a threat sector, and we had to figure out what was in it. In that way, it mimicked the real world and forced us to be more conservative. However, if we were too conservative, we might just fly around at high speed and not shoot anybody.

On the other hand, the danger of turning with the bogy you saw could get you killed by the one that you didn't see. Our squadron did great, but so did Jack's, and we figured we were still tied. My section was last to fly, so Magwai and I led our wingmen against the bandits. Ironically, Jack Grant led his squadron's section.

We did some excellent radar work and quickly found two Bandits up at 45,000 feet. We soared to get them, but I was suspicious and kept lowering my radar antenna. Sure enough, I found two more Bandits ten miles behind the leads but down at 5,000 feet! We shot the high two and flew past them, screaming downhill to the trailers. I was still suspicious, so I kept searching. I was rewarded by finding two more bandits at the very left edge of my radar and down at 1000 feet. We shot both bandits at 5,000 feet, turned hard left and dumped the nose to get the bogies at 1000 feet. We shot one and one escaped. In the end, we scored five kills out of six opportunities!

Later, in the debrief, we found that Jack and his section had also done very well against the same scenario and killed five Bandits.

Jack and his section were accelerating away until an A-4 appeared off Jack's right side, and for some reason, he turned into it. It wasn't long before Jack was in a desperate fight for his life and everybody suspected it was Hokie driving the A-4. It had to be Hokie because the A-4 saddled up on Jack and gunned him.

I was elated! We had won the competition, and I was doubly happy because Jack Grant had lost for his squadron.

I drove to VF-43 to pick up Missy. Her car was in the shop, and I had given her a ride to work that morning. I ran upstairs to her office space but paused when I heard voices from inside the room.

"Missy, it was an incredible piece of flying." It was Hokie's voice. "The Tomcats were free and clear; all they had to do was keep going. But you showed up and supplied a learning point that will most likely never be forgotten. You tempted a fighter to turn into you when he didn't have to, and he paid the price. It was an invaluable lesson! Missy, you are one of the best pilots I have, and I wish we didn't have to keep that a secret…." A roar of laughter and clapping interrupted him. Evidently, the Bandits were assembled behind the door.

"No problem, skipper," said Missy. I could hear her over the sound of the cheers. "I understand where we are."

"Here's to the gal that gunned the Tomcat!"

As the cheers erupted anew, I turned and headed down the stairs. I waited in the parking lot for fifteen minutes, and to tell the truth, I was strangely conflicted. A part of me was so proud of Missy and so glad that she was the one that shot Jack and gave us the win. But another part brooded as I paced back and forth between the cars. I fretted because I didn't like that a woman had beaten a man in aerial combat. Even if it was a woman I cared for and a man I loathed. How sad was that?

I didn't mention anything to Missy, I just picked her up in her cubicle, and we headed for her house. We talked about our great victory, and she told me that the Bandits all had a lot of respect for us. I glowed when she told me my radar work on the last flight was the thing of legends. But I didn't say anything to her about her prowess as a pilot, or the fact that she manhandled a man.

MAKERS MARKED

I began to drink more. I didn't drink heavily at the club; I saved that for home with my music and thoughts. Getting drunk is fun, and that is why I like it. I like the euphoric feeling I get as the alcohol takes hold, and it is the only time when I am not worrying. I'm not a nail-chewer or anything, but I do "grind." By that, I mean, I am always working at some problem or worry in my head. Alcohol takes that grind away and lets me imagine what life could be. After a few drinks and while deep into, say, some Rolling Stones, I imagine things like shooting down MIGs or becoming a commanding officer or standing in front of some crowd with everybody clapping. When I start thinking about Jane, I know I have had too much, but I keep drinking until I cry. Strangely, the crying is good because it is shedding emotion, and even if I only share it with Mick Jagger, it makes me feel connected to something. All of this gets me to the half of the bottle and to sleep.

Missy shared my bourbon with me when she used to come over. Well, she would have a sip. Missy preferred wine, and she didn't drink much of that. In fact, toward the end of our relationship, she would leave if I had more than two bourbons. In the end, I guess I liked Mister Makers more than I liked Missy Sanders. I have read that drinking alone is a sign of being an alcoholic, and I worry about that some. But what is a guy that lives alone supposed to do? Go to the street and ask people to come over?

"Hey, buddy, would you like to come home with me so I can drink?"

I remember our Catholic chaplain on my first Vietnam cruise. My skipper, who lived alone as a perk of command, said the padre used to knock on his door and ask to come in. The chaplain would ask the skipper if he had any booze because he didn't want him to drink alone.

225

So, I drink alone, and I am not sure it isn't by choice. After all, do I drink to be alone, or am I alone because I drink. Kind of a twist on the chicken and egg thing.

My job as the maintenance officer kept me engaged, and I eagerly faced each workday. Even with a hangover, I found energy in my challenges, and one incredibly daunting problem turned me into something of a hero. The F-14 community was plagued with a weakening and cracking of main landing gear struts. Of course, these were the supports for our tires and had to absorb the shock of landing.

Unfortunately, the entire community was forced to inspect after every landing and had to do a drop check after every ten landings. A drop check requires maintenance to put the airplane up on jacks and cycle the landing gear up and down. You can imagine that while deployed on an aircraft carrier, this is a crushing requirement. Drop checks are conducted in the hanger bay, and that places a considerable burden on the ship. I began to research the problem, and through diligent work and some luck, I traced all the known cracked gear to a single supplier, DeWitt Machining from Clinton, Arkansas, specifically their lot numbers 107 to 412. I showed my data and analysis to the skipper who ran it to the airwing commander, who took it to the fighter wing commander. Soon, my work was in the hands of the Navy's Air System Command. Main landing gear supports from those lots were identified and directed for removal and replacement. The problem went away, and I received a navy commendation medal from fighter wing. Despite the fact Cotton had been a department head three months longer than me, I felt I was in a good position for the number one fitness report when the skipper left. It was critical because it was the final opportunity for Cotton and me to get that all-important ticket. We both would detach before the next annual report, so it was a do or die situation for command.

Saint Patrick's Day in 1986 fell on a Monday, and I liked that because it was an excellent excuse to drink on a weekday. I flew a hop during the day, and the oxygen from my mask revived me from my mild hangover. After work, I headed home to get a nap. At thirty-six, I was at the party crowd's far edge and had trouble staying up into the wee hours. I awoke at seven and listened to tunes while I drunk a six-pack. It helped me get loose enough to talk to chicks, and I went out around nine.

The oceanfront has many watering holes, so I parked on Atlantic Avenue and started bar hopping. Like most towns, every bar is an

Irish bar on March 17, so I didn't have any trouble finding a party. The Virginia Beach area also has a significant college population that brings enormous energy to weekday celebrations. Soon, I was in an animated conversation with some girls from Old Dominion University. They seemed interested in me, which I found refreshing, so I kept buying them all drinks. But after a ton of beer, I had to take a leak, and when I came back, they were gone. I had a couple of Guinness Stouts and decided to leave, but it took me a while to find my car, so it must have been close to two in the morning when I started driving home. I woke up some time later in a cell in the Virginia Beach police station.

The bad news is that I didn't remember getting stopped, but the good news is that I didn't crash or anything and was courteous to the policeman. They let me out the next morning on my own recognizance but issued me a ticket for driving under the influence. The navy pretty much looked the other way for such things, if nobody was hurt, and if your skipper didn't hammer you. The only problem was paying the fine. I figured it would be a cheap lesson for me to clean up my act. However, the skipper had a different take. His twin sister had been killed by a drunk driver when they were only 20 so he had a very dim view of driving under the influence. He called me into his office that Friday, a week prior to his change of command, and informed me that he had intended to give me the number one fitness report but that my DUI forced him to reconsider. He told me he would not put any adverse comments in my report and hated the idea of one mistake changing the course of my career, but he could not in good conscience rank me as the best department head. He said he would rank me as number two, so I might select for a non-operational command and would promote to commander for sure. I kept quiet during the session; what could I say? I had bilged myself and had no one else to blame.

"I'm sorry about this, Weenie, I really am." The skipper's eyes were sincere. "I don't know what kind of problem you have with alcohol. I mean, there is some talk about hangovers and such, but I never paid attention to it. But, Weenie, if you have a deeper problem than just one, unlucky night, I suggest you visit the base chaplain. He has a program that covers all manner of personal issues; you should check it out."

We shook, and I told the skipper, "Thank you, I will" with absolutely no intention of doing any of that kind of crap. However, I didn't have anything to drink that weekend, the first time since I could remember and considered giving up booze. Maybe God had given me a message.

The skipper gave me my fitness report, and, sure enough, I was ranked number two. Number two sounds good, but when you consider that each squadron generates a couple of number one fitness reports each year, and squadron commanders stay in office around fifteen months, there is no room for a number two to be competitive. So, it was a sad affair in his office, as we both knew my chance for an operational F-14 command was nil. I avoided Cotton since there was nothing to say to him.

I wanted to talk to Grace. For some reason talking with her makes me feel better. I suppose that is selfish, given her problems with losing her son, Jack, anxiety, and depression. But she calms me and makes me feel relevant. I called her number once and almost said her name when Jack answered. Fortunately, I had my wits about me and just hung up. According to the rumor mill, Jack had already received a number one fitness report, so he would get command of a fighter squadron. The absolute unfairness of it angered me to desolation, and I found myself ripping the wax off a new bottle of Makers. Jack and Cotton, one a hated foe and the other a former best friend, would wear the command button as a sign of honor and privilege, and I would not. And I hated them both equally because of it.

"Black is Black" was playing when I passed out.

Monday, I called the duty officer and told him I had an intestinal virus and could not come into the squadron for the week. I planned to stay home and drink and listen to my music. I didn't want to go to the squadron anymore. I didn't want to be in the navy anymore. I opened a fresh bottle of Makers and planned to drink it while watching "Hollywood Squares." I liked the show, especially Paul Lynde.

I had never been a day drinker, even to get over a hangover, so I fixed some coffee to watch my show. It was only 1030 when it ended, so I flipped through the channels looking for something to occupy the time. An old movie named The Lost Weekend caught my eye. It starred one of my favorite actors, Ray Milland, and I was surprised I had never seen it. I eyed my Maker's bottle sitting on the counter, waiting patiently with its promises of euphoria and contentment, and turned up the volume.

Sometimes God does listen. And sometimes He eavesdrops, and I think that is what He did that morning. I hadn't asked for any help, but I think He gave me The Lost Weekend anyway. A part of me wanted to turn the movie off once I saw it was about this writer, Don, who was a pathetic alcoholic. But I didn't. Something made me watch it; I suppose just to see how it ended.

I saw a lot of me in Don, and Milland did a marvelous job in the part. At first, I offered haughty chuckles to Don as he frantically searched for his hidden bottles but soon, I wasn't laughing anymore. I was disgusted with Don and his weakness. He was a liar and a cheat and would do anything to get a drink. He treated his best friends, people that loved him, like crap. And when he told Helen and Wick that he is two people: "Don the writer" whose fear of failure causes him to drink and "Don the drunk," I felt myself fall. By the time Don dropped his cigarette into his whiskey glass to signify his resolve to get sober, I was sobbing. My Maker's bottle heard me and called to offer its help, but I resisted and forced myself to confront "Weenie the naval officer" and "Weenie the drunk."

It is hard for me to imagine a movie could have such a profound effect, but I think The Lost Weekend was only the door to an epiphany that had been gathering for a long time. Like Don, I had hidden my drinking from others, and like Don, I had tried to hide it from myself. I spent the afternoon and evening in frank reflection, and as the hangover wore off and was replaced with a freshness of mind and purpose, I began to feel the need for help.

The next afternoon, I put on a fresh uniform and headed to the base chapel. I parked my car and hurried in only to be met by a crowd as they were leaving. They were in groups of two or three and were animated with their excitement. Evidently, I had missed something good. I shook my head and walked into the room. Maybe they had another meeting later in the week.

There stood Reese! I almost didn't recognize him with his beard. If it weren't for the metal hooks, I probably wouldn't have.

"Mister Kleegan!" Reese smiled and kept his dark eyes on me as he slowly walked across the room. He gently embraced me, the kind of sincere hug that old friends with a past in misery might share. Although I had only seen him the one time in the hospital, it seemed proper and right. He must have held his hooks away because I didn't feel them against me. I stepped back to see him better.

"What are you doing here?" I was genuinely glad to see him.

"I guess the real question is, what are YOU doing here?"

"I, well, I…"

"Too bad you missed the class. It was a good one. You did come for the class, didn't you?"

Reese smiled when I didn't answer and nodded toward the library. "There is a coffee pot near. Let's grab a cup and catch up."

I thought about leaving, hesitated, but instead found myself following Reese. He led me to a small room with a refrigerator, sink, and coffee pot, and I watched as he poured the steaming liquid into two cups. His hooks had rubber edges, and he seemed at ease with his task. Reese handed me a cup, and we sat down.

"It is terrific to see you again, Mister Kleegan."

"I wondered what happened to you." I was telling the truth. I took a quick sip. "I told my mother about you one night."

"Oh?"

"I told her that I had failed you." I swallowed as I looked at Reese. I don't know why I blurted that.

Reese frowned and slowly shook his head. "On the contrary, Mister Kleegan." He sipped from his cup and looked at me. "On the contrary."

"Well, it was a long time ago." I smiled and shrugged.

Reese nodded, and I found myself needing to hear more.

How had I helped him?

"What did you mean by 'On the contrary'?"

Reese looked at me for a moment, his face set in a frown. He nodded and took a deep breath. "I was in a bad way back then. I think you saw that. I was in a state of shock, I mean, I had just lost my arms. I had no idea how I would live the rest of my life." Reese was looking at the table between us as he spoke. He swallowed as he seemed to collect his thoughts.

"I stayed in the hospital for a month, then went home. I was afraid of what Delores and the girls would do when they saw me when they saw what had happened to me. But Mister Kleegan, they were good to me. They didn't stare or anything. Dolly, my youngest, just asked, 'Does it hurt, Daddy'? I remember when she asked me, and I just said, not anymore, honey."

I fought the tears in my eyes and took a quick sip of coffee.

"They were okay, but I wasn't. So, I started smoking a little marijuana. It was easy to get, and I was still getting my navy paycheck, so money wasn't a problem. Delores had her job too, so I was able to buy cocaine a little later. And I bought a lot of it, booze too. Cocaine makes you thirsty, man." Reese laughed and looked up at me. He must have seen the wet in my eyes.

"Delores never gave up on me, Mister Kleegan." He took a deep breath and tapped his cup with the end of his hook. "She kept after me, not nagging, but just talking. She would hold my hooks, Mister Kleegan, and she would look into my eyes, and she would tell me that she and the girls loved me and that I had to empty the garbage bag."

I felt a tear trickle out of my eye and quickly caught it with the side of my hand. I made it look like it was part of taking another sip.

"And Mister Kleegan, it was on one of those nights, when the girls were in bed, and Delores was holding my hooks that I remembered the note you left for me at the hospital. The one you gave the nurse to hold for me. I looked through my old things and I found it, Mister Kleegan."

Reese smiled and gently placed a hook on the top of my hand, then he reached into his back pocket and deftly brought out his wallet. He opened it and took out a piece of worn paper. He smiled again and looked at me and began to read:

"The world breaks everyone, and afterward, many are strong at the broken places. But those that will not break it kills. It kills the very good and the very gentle and the very brave impartially. If you are none of these, you can be sure it will kill you too, but there will be no special hurry. "

Reese looked at me, "And I knew that I had to acknowledge my brokenness, or the world would kill me, Mister Kleegan. It would kill me and in no special hurry."

Reese carefully put the paper back into his wallet, then handed me a napkin, and I dabbed my eyes. He grabbed one for himself. We both half-laughed as we wiped, and Reese cleared his throat. "The thing that got to me was that I realized that I had believed you that day, Mister Kleegan. Somewhere in my mind, I believed you enough to get the note and to read it. Then I believed that I could fix myself, that I could make myself stronger, that I wanted to make myself stronger again. Eventually, I went to school and found I was good at sharing that strength with others."

Reese stood and grabbed the coffee pot. He filled our cups again, then took his seat. He let out a breath; it was loud as if to say, "Now, that is that."

"So, Mister Kleegan, did you come to check out a book from the library? To see the chaplain, or was it something else?"

I looked into Reese's eyes. They comforted me, surprisingly so, and I didn't feel weak or fragile. I suppose men can share tears if for the right reasons.

"I drink a lot, Reese."

"Many do, Mister Kleegan."

I let out another breath, and it was my turn to stare at the table. "I ruined my career with the stuff." I looked up, "Got a DUI."

"Anybody hurt?"

"Just my career."

"Well, that is a bit of a blessing."

I nodded and took a sip.

"You lost your arms; in fact, you lost them protecting Mister Crosby." I looked up. "I didn't lose anything, Reese. How did I let the world break me? Christ!"

"Your mind thinks you did."

I looked at Reese and slowly nodded. "Evidently."

Reese stood and reached out his right hook. "Stay for a class, Mister Kleegan. If you want."

I did as Reese suggested and found a place in the back of his meeting room. A crowd packed the place, and Reese electrified it with his uplifting message. He even mentioned me, and as the group turned and politely clapped, I offered a slight wave.

I had many talks with Reese and others over the weeks and found that alcohol abuse takes many forms with many bad outcomes. He told me that since I did not have any reaction or withdrawal symptoms when I stopped drinking, it meant I did not have a physical addiction. But that didn't mean my emotional addiction was any less powerful or devastating.

A month after my first meeting with Reese, I drove to the squadron to call my detailer. When he answered, I asked what I could do.

"You mean besides pray?"

"Yes, besides that." I could see him chuckling in his cubicle in the Navy Annex as he stared at the microfiche that represented my life.

"Well, with a number two, all the number ones are ahead of you. That doesn't leave much, maybe something in the training command. Maybe."

"Is there anything I can do?"

"Probably not, realistically. I mean, well, wait. Wait a minute; I will be right back."

I heard him lay his phone down and shook my head. I wanted a drink but quickly threw that thought aside. That was the last thing I needed.

"Hey, Weenie, there may be a chance."

"Really?" I gripped the phone and swallowed.

"Yeah, maybe. You see, there is one thing that could save you: to work for a four-star aviator. You've been an aide, I see. For Admiral Jensen, right?"

"That's right."

"Well, he is in Stuttgart, Germany. He is the deputy commander of European Command, and he is looking for an aide. If he takes you, and if he likes you, he can make it happen."

I swallowed again and gripped the phone. I took a breath and let it out slowly.

"Weenie, what do you say? I can give his staff a call today."

I took another breath and shook my head. "I can't do that."

"What do you mean? Germany is great, everybody says so. And, it says here in your record that you aren't married, so there is nobody you have to convince."

"I just can't do that. That's all."

"Well, if that's what you say, then, okay. But you aren't going to screen without something like this, Weenie. You need a miracle, and Admiral Jensen is it."

"I appreciate it and thank you." I hung up and leaned back in my chair. I couldn't let Admiral Jensen save me. He would find out about the DUI, and he would know that he was supposed to be some sort of lifeline for me. I didn't want to put a great man like the admiral in a spot. I couldn't do that to him. If I didn't screen, then I didn't.

I went home and thought about having a drink. I found my hidden bottle of Maker's and felt the smoothness of the glass against my hand. The understated tan label with its black lettering called me, and I glanced at the clock to see if it was drinking time. Then I put the bottle away.

The next day was Saturday, and just before noon, the phone rang.

"Kleegan," I answered.

"Weenie?"

"Sir." I gripped the phone. It was Admiral Jensen!

"What are you doing at home? The Soviets don't take the weekend off!"

I laughed and swallowed. Evidently, he had found out about my situation.

"Weenie? You still there?"

"Yes, sir, I'm here. It is great to hear your voice, sir."

"How are you doing?"

I didn't know if he meant in general or if he knew I had wrecked my career. "I'm okay, sir."

"Good. That is what your skipper said. I called the squadron yesterday, looking for you."

"You called looking for me?" It must have been when I was visiting Reese.

"Yes. I'm a little disappointed in you."

HE DID KNOW. He knew about the DUI.

"Well...sir..."

"I called PERS 43 to see if they had some names for an aide and found you had turned the job down. What's the matter, don't like wiener schnitzel?"

Maybe he didn't know.

"Oh, no, sir. It's not that." I laughed.

"You know you don't have to wear those leather shorts if you don't want to."

I started to laugh but choked and coughed. I gripped the phone harder.

"You okay, Weenie?"

I placed the phone on the cradle to hang up, but I snatched it back at the last second.

"You okay, son?"

"I...I..."

"Look, Weenie, I want you to think about the job. Take the week if you need to. But if you decide to take it, there will be no drinking. Not anymore. And that is something to consider in Germany. Beer is the national beverage here, and the social pressure to drink large amounts of it is extreme."

"But sir."

"No need to talk about anything now. If you want the job, we can talk about everything once you are here. Call your detailer and let him know."

"Sir..."

"Call your detailer, Weenie. And make the right choice."

"Yes, sir."

EL DORADO CANYON

The United States European Command headquarters is located at Patch Barracks in Stuttgart, Germany. The commander, a four-star officer, is simultaneously the Supreme Allied Commander Europe within NATO's military alliance. In deference to the NATO obligation, the commander resides in Belgium while his four-star deputy commander resides in Stuttgart. Admiral Jensen was the deputy, and Stuttgart was my next duty station.

I took the Delta Airlines non-stop from Atlanta to Stuttgart and arrived, disheveled and red-eyed, around midmorning. A driver met me and, after waiting for an hour to get my bags, zipped us to Patch, as the base is called, and the Bachelor Officers' Quarters. The driver waited while I took a quick shower and put on a fresh uniform, then he drove me the short distance down the hill to the headquarters.

Admiral Jensen looked the same, maybe a little grayer at the temples, and his broad smile made me feel welcome. We had coffee as he explained his requirements, which were like our previous aide/senior relationship. The most significant difference was in scope as the admiral represented the United States across Europe and much of Africa. That put him in a delicate and possibly adversarial conflict with the state department and its set of ambassadors as well as the four-star commanders leading the Army, Navy, and Air Force in Europe. Since he was the deputy and not the commander, his chosen tool was more a carrot than a stick, requiring delicate and nuanced leadership. As I listened to him explain the challenges, I thought of his conversations about constructive confrontation as a leadership technique. I knew why the admiral was where he was. He was perfect for this job. He didn't mention anything about what brought me to Stuttgart.

I settled into the job quickly and meshed with the admiral's staff, especially his executive assistant, a USAF colonel named Bill Morris. I think Bill appreciated my willingness, and capability, to take ownership of the tiny but critical details in the admiral's daily schedule. He appreciated the extra steps and effort I took. For instance, I would not only provide a bio for each visitor during the day; I would also research with the staff historian and others to find any valuable information. When the Lord Mayor, Herr Fritz Ganz, visited, I provided the admiral a datasheet of the mayor's plan for the city. That enabled the admiral to discuss what the mayor believed to be essential and ask how the US military might support him. It was a marvelous, energetic, and productive meeting and Colonel Morris beamed at me. I even provided the admiral information that Lord Mayor Gantz had recently acquired a Weimaraner and was an avid hunter. This led to a spirited discussion about hunting in Germany, and the relationship Germans had with their gun dogs.

A month after I arrived at European Command, terrorists bombed the La Belle Discotheque in West Berlin, killing one US soldier and two other civilians while wounding 229 others. The US quickly tied this to Libya, claiming to have "exact, precise, and irrefutable" evidence of the involvement based upon intercepted cable transcripts from Libyan agents in East Germany. The day after the bombing, the admiral called me into his office.

"Weenie, I need you to travel to England, specifically Royal Air Force base Lakenheath."

"Sir?"

"We are making plans to attack Libya, and for now, the air force planners at the 48th Tactical Fighter Wing have the lead. They deny needing any help from the navy, but I'm not convinced. I want you to go as my representative and get a feel for what is going on. I don't like being kept in the dark."

"Yes, sir." I frowned, and the admiral leaned forward.

"Do you remember our failed attempt to rescue our hostages in Iran?"

"Sure, sir. Six years ago, it was an embarrassment."

"It was a fiasco. And it was followed by that shit-show we had in Grenada and the bombing of the marine barracks in Lebanon, and the shootdown we had in the Bekka Valley in Lebanon."

"Yes, sir, when Mark Lange was killed, and Bobby Goodman was captured."

"Right, and Jesse Jackson rescued them. Christ, you know you have failed when Jesse Jackson is your rescue plan."

I frowned and nodded. I had never seen the admiral so agitated.

"Weenie, do you realize our only victory since Vietnam was when the two Tomcats shot down those Libyan fighters."

"Yes, sir," I grinned. "I even had one of those Navy 2, Libya 0 buttons. I still have it on my flight jacket."

The admiral smiled for a second, then his scowl returned. "Weenie, we cannot have another failure. We cannot goon this up so, get to Lakenheath and see what you can find out. You spent two deployments off the coast of Vietnam; you probably have more combat planning time than any of those guys."

"When do you want me to go, sir?"

"I have a C21 leaving in two hours."

"Yes, sir."

"Weenie, if you need to communicate, use a secure line."

"Yes, sir."

I landed at RAF Lakenheath at eight that night, and a driver took me to the BOQ. Somebody got their wires crossed because instead of a standard room, they gave me the visiting flag officer's suite! There was even a fruit basket with a card that said, "Welcome to the United States Air Force's Finest Base in Europe." Some colonel signed it. I looked longingly at the little bottles of liquor in the cabinet and cold beer in the fridge but grabbed an orange juice instead.

The next morning, I ate one of the pop tarts from the overflowing bag of geedunk they gave me and made some coffee. It was instant and tasted as bad as navy instant coffee, which made me feel at home. At seven, a driver arrived, and I went to the operations center, where I found a flurry of planners. It was just like navy planning; except they had a lot more room and people. I walked around, trying not to look like a spy until some enlisted man with about fifty stripes on his arm told me the operations officer wanted to talk with me. I followed him to a large office where I found a pinch-faced lieutenant colonel who eyed me like I was stealing girl scout cookies from an orphanage. He motioned to me, and I sat in front of his desk.

"Look, Kleegan, we got the message from your boss. Said he was sending a rep to see if you can help. Of course, you can't."

I nodded and stared at the man. He gave me the stink eye for a few moments, kindling my memories of playing "stare" in grade school, then yelled into the adjoining room. "Pool, get in here."

Seconds later, a tall, red-haired captain limped into the room and swayed to attention.

"Yes, sir."

The lieutenant colonel motioned to me. "Take Kleegan here to watch our planning. Stay with him at all times."

"Yes, sir."

"Get out, both of you."

I popped out of my chair and followed Pool out the door.

"Nice guy," I said as we walked toward the planning tables.

"Yeah, he is quite the dick, isn't he?" Pool looked at me and grinned, and I felt a kinship beginning to build.

We slowly circled the tables, and Pool tried for calm as he explained what the officers were doing, but the place was a frenzy of yelling and arguing. Everybody was running around with their hair on fire, and then I found out why.

The plan called for twenty-four F-111 aircraft from RAF Lakenheath and five EF-111 jammer aircraft from RAF Heyford to fly 3500 miles around France and Spain through the Straits of Gibraltar and into the Mediterranean to their attack profiles into Libya. So far, France, Spain, and Italy refused overflight permission, so the aircrews would have to inflight refuel four times each way! My flight planning experience caused the hair on the back of my neck to stand up because that kind of logistical stress introduced so much opportunity for failure.

"Wow," I said, as I listened to Pool. "I've never seen anything so complicated, and that is just getting to the target area. Once the shooting starts, it should really get interesting."

"No, shit," muttered Pool.

We watched for a while longer. Then Pool took me to the officer's club for lunch. Over a club sandwich, Pool told me he broke his leg while skiing in France, which took him out of the mission. Like the navy, a flier out of the mission is of no value except for doing goofy stuff like shepherding a spy around. We went back to the planning rooms for the rest of the day, and after we changed, Pool took me to a pub for dinner.

I ordered a double gin and a glass of water, and Pool got a Guinness. As soon as the drinks arrived, I excused myself, went to the head and emptied the gin down the sink. I replaced it with tap water and rejoined Pool, who was guzzling his stout. I ordered two more "gins" and passed them off into my water glass when Pool wasn't watching. He drunk a couple more ales, and soon he was giddy. I felt like a spy.

"Are any of you concerned about the mission?" My question was meant to be innocent, and I looked into his reddening eyes with a manufactured frown. "I mean, I saw come combat in Vietnam, and this looks difficult."

"I noticed your uniform," said Pool. I had worn all my ribbons on purpose, hoping to get some traction with them. It appeared to have worked.

"I've done my share of planning," I said as I drained my glass of water. "But nothing this elaborate and risky." I motioned to the waiter and held up two fingers.

"Sure, it concerns us," nodded Pool. "A few of us were in Vietnam. Not me, of course, but a couple of the colonels. But this thing, just the sheer distances involved, yeah, it has us concerned. Just think of it. Almost thirty aircraft have to tank four times each just to get to the target. That means all that gas-passing stuff needs to work perfectly. Then, we must get to the targets without getting shot down, find the targets, and hit them." Pool shook his head.

"Have you guys ever done anything like this before?"

"Yeah, kind of." The waiter brought our fresh drinks, and we each took one. Pool took a sip of his ale and looked at me.

"The 20th Tactical Fighter Wing rehearsed using ten aircraft. Seemed to go okay." He took a bite of pretzel, then frowned. "However, they were flying the E model, and we have the F with its new targeting system. It is a bit of a mystery at this point."

I nodded and fished a pretzel from the bowl in front of me.

"We have had a lot of availability issues too," said Pool.

"Like what?" I took an innocent bite of pretzel.

"Oh, you know, problems with bomb release, lots of electrical issues in this new jet. All kinds of issues." Pool frowned and looked at me. "You guys have the same, right?"

"Oh, yeah," I grinned. "We have all kinds of problems too."

Pool nodded and took a sip. My comments weren't entirely true. Most of the Tomcat quirks had been worked out, and the A-6 and A-7 aircraft were reliable bombers. The F-18 Hornet was too new to offer many problems.

"The Pave Low targeting system in the F model is brand new, and we are still working the bugs out of it. We have had a lot of training missions where we couldn't find the target or couldn't release the practice bombs when we did." Pool looked at me and shrugged. "And the rules of engagement we have, you know, to avoid targeting civilians, makes it nearly impossible, I think. I mean, thirty-five hundred miles is a long way to fly for a no-release."

The next afternoon Pool let me use his secure phone, and I called the admiral. I made sure no one was listening and told him about the plan and Pool's comments concerning the F-111 availability and the rules of engagement concerns. I told him the air force had done a dress rehearsal but with a different squadron and different aircraft. Admiral Jensen seemed extraordinarily interested and asked me to repeat myself several times. That meant he was taking notes himself on a clear line instead of having Colonel Morris or somebody take them. I stayed another day, then flew back to Stuttgart.

The next day, reps from Sixth Fleet, USS *Coral Sea,* and USS *America* journeyed to Lakenheath to partake in the planning for an operation named El Dorado Canyon. The navy would provide A-6, A-7, F-18, and E-A6B aircraft from the carriers for the strike mission and F-14 Tomcats for combat air patrol if any MIGs flew.

On April 14, the plan commenced with the jamming of Libyan radar sites, followed by the navy hitting Benina Airfield and Benghazi Military Barracks. The air force targeted the Aziziyah Barracks in Tripoli and the Sidi Bilal terrorist training camp.

Many considered El Dorado Canyon a success, and President Reagan garnered widespread support for his actions. We get BBC television in the command center and watched a visibly shaken Mummar Ghaddafi denounce the attacks. But besides spooking the strongman in Libya, the reality of our success was more sobering. Of the twenty-four-air force F-111s scheduled, eighteen made the mission. Seven missed their targets, six did not drop for mechanical and rules of engagement issues, and one was shot down. So, four of the air force attackers hit their targets. On the navy side, fifteen A-6s participated, with twelve hitting their targets while three aborted. While that sounds good, the fact is the navy used dumb bombs on an airfield and barracks while the air force was still perfecting its new Pave Tack system to deliver precision-guided weapons. A side-by-side comparison of performance was not possible.

That said, Admiral Jensen was very pleased with me and told me it was my report that spurred him to insist the navy take part in the plan and that if that hadn't happened and the air force had acted alone, it would have been a disaster. As it was, the general success of the raid covered up many of the problems. The admiral asked me if I wanted him to write a letter to the command screen board. My timing was off because my next fitness report from him would come after the command board met. I told the admiral I appreciated it but didn't think it was right for him to do that, and I wanted to make it on my own.

GABY

Germans have a constant intensity on their faces, and when you pass them on a sidewalk, or anywhere, they always look like they are late for something. Since being on time is sacred to Germans, the stern face is God-driven. However, if you do take the chance and stop one, and get him or her to break allegiance to the clock, you will find Germans are almost universally eager to help and assist. Whenever I did flag one down, I struggled to speak German to them, but through their confused frowns, I think they appreciated my efforts. I also found that no German could say my nickname, Weenie, without grinning nervously. I remember standing in the headquarters when the admiral introduced me to the Lord Mayor.

"This is my aide, Weenie Kleegan."

"Veenie?"

"No, Weenie. Weenie with a W," smiled the admiral.

The Lord Mayor pointed to his crotch. "Weenie, like in schwantz?" Of course, he followed this with hysterical laughter.

Although I was tied to the admiral's schedule, I did have opportunities to drive around the countryside, and it is easy to see why Germans are so proud. The entire country is a series of picture postcards with real people living in the idyllic scenes of villages, ancient churches, mountains, beautiful valleys, and the coast. The Germans revere the earth and take close care of their environment. They also take pride in what they own, and each house I passed was immaculately kept.

German food is what we would call comfort food back home, and they serve it in large portions. Germans don't waste a lot of energy flitting around the beautifully presented, but pigeon-egg size entrees the French hover over, for instance. They provide delicious food for real people who are late for something. On such a journey through the countryside, south of Stuttgart in the village of Nurtingen, I met Gabrielle Schaffer.

It was Saturday and delightful, so I had stopped for a late lunch at an inn that featured a second story dining area, overlooking the Neckar River. I had stopped once before, but it had been closed. I didn't want to miss a second chance, so I hurried in.

Looking through the menu, I hoped it wasn't the beautiful swans at the river's edge that prompted me to order the salad with turkey breast strips, but I did, and I attempted it in German. Of course, my German is the Nordic version of pig Latin but without the rhyming rules. It is a mixture of anything that sounds foreign.

"Escusa, ich bin ein Putenbrusten salat."

German waiters are much like French waiters but without the pretense of patience. The late-for-something look on their face is real, and their glare underscores the fact they are salaried and not dependent on your tips' crumbs.

"Escusa? Escusa? Was ist das?" He seemed incredibly angry.

"Uhh..." I gulped.

"Was moechten Sie?"

"Uhh, ich bin ein Putenbusten salat." I stammered.

The waiter threw up his hands and turned to walk away when I heard a voice behind me. "He wants a salad with turkey breast strips, Erich."

The waiter looked past my shoulder and frowned.

"You understood him." It was a female voice, in accented English. "Don't be such an ass."

I started to turn and look at my savior, but the waiter sighed and glared at me.

"Dressing?"

"Vinaigrette."

The waiter scribbled and turned on his heel. I shifted in my chair to see who had saved me. For a second, I was startled! I was looking at Meg Ryan! Or someone who looked a lot like her. I had seen Meg Ryan in the movie, TOPGUN, and I had a crush on her, and now here she was looking right at me.

I envied Tom Cruise as I turned around. "Thank you."

"You told the waiter you were a turkey breast salad," the Meg Ryan look-alike smiled again. "Not that you wanted one, but that you were one. He knew what you wanted, but sometimes Erich is a jerk. It is just his nature."

"You must come here often?"

"You could say that. My family owns this inn. Erich is my brother."

"Ahh, I see." I smiled. "Well, thank you again."

"Of course." She shrugged, but her grin lingered a millisecond longer than required, and I took that as a chance. And it was indeed a chance because she was clearly out of my league.

"Do you mind if I sit with you for lunch?" I swallowed. It would be an awkward meal if she said "no," and I had to eat my dead swan salad with my back to her.

"Sure, why not?"

I quickly took the seat across from her and fought not to mess with the silverware. "How do you know English? You speak it so well."

"I am a Russian spy, I learned it in the Soviet tradecraft school."

I looked at her for a second and must have blinked, or maybe my mouth fell open because she suddenly laughed. "I am just kidding."

I laughed too, but my face felt hot.

"I took English in school and later in university. I work the international section of our Deutsche Bank here in town, so I get to practice a lot." She extended her hand, "I am Gabrielle. Gabrielle Schaffer. Call me, Gaby."

I hesitated. How should I identify myself?

Weenie, like in schwantz?

I couldn't bear the thought of her laughing at me, so I said, "Winfred, Winfred Kleegan."

I steeled for the inevitable frown followed by the scowl and "Winfred? What kind of name is that?"

"Winfred," she said. "What a lovely name."

I looked as deep into her eyes as I dared, looking for evidence of the joke, the gathering around the iris's that would foretell her sarcasm. But…nothing?

"It sounds German, are you German?"

"No, most likely Irish, but I am not sure." But as I answered, I could barely contain my glee. Gaby was the first person in my entire life who liked my name. I don't even think Mom liked my name. "Winfred is a good name. A solid name," she would say. But I don't know if she liked it.

And it was the way Gaby had said, "Winfred". It sounded robust and earthy but also…also almost exotic. I mean, she had mixed the *f* and the *r* with just a hint of *w* to make a name that sounded like it belonged to a man holding a sword.

"What brings you to Germany?" She looked at my hair. "US military, I guess?"

"That's right, I am stationed in Stuttgart, at Patch Barracks."

"Hmm," Gaby nodded and looked up as Erich brought our food. My salad was a mound of lettuce, carrots, hard-boiled egg slices, and turkey breast strips. Gaby had a plate with two wieners, potato salad, and a crusty roll. We dug in, but she caught me, eye-balling her food.

"Do you want to try the wiener?"

"No," I smiled. "I'm sorry. It's just that when I was a kid in school, every Thursday we had wieners and sauerkraut. The wieners were boiled and were these pale, limp little things in pinkish water. The sauerkraut was something they found in a can, I suppose, and the school cooks just heated it. It was hideous, and I didn't know any different until I got here."

"So, you have sampled our wurst?"

"Yes, and your schnitzel, rump steak, schweinshaxen, and maultaschen! It is all wunderbar!"

"I'm glad you like it." She smiled. "And Germany? You like it here?"

"I think if I didn't live in the United States, I would want to live here."

"Why?"

"Because I grew up on a farm. I respected and loved the fields and the woods and the animals before I respected and loved anything else."

"And now? Now that you are a military man, a man of the city, what do love and respect? Weapons and the concrete?" Gaby's eyes toyed with me.

"I still miss the farm." I looked at her and swallowed, knowing I was being tested, wondering if I had passed.

Gaby nodded, and a smile swept the intensity from her eyes. "Sometimes I wish Germany were one big farm." She picked up her fork and stared at the tines. Then looked at me. "And we were all still farmers."

"Maybe you just wish things were simpler. Is your life that complex?"

She looked at me for a long second, then shrugged. "Maybe."

We continued to eat and talk, and when Erich brought the check, Gaby shooed him away. I expected her to grab her purse and run, but she made no effort to leave, so I found myself blabbing. I told her about Militia Springs and my family. I told her about our milk cows and how I joined the navy. I even told her about Jane. I don't know why. I don't have a clue why.

But Gaby brightened as I talked. "So, it seems you know what love is," she said. "You know what it is to love someone and be loved by them, yes?"

I shrugged. The word love, the thing I was in a melancholy and often ridiculous quest for, now made me uncomfortable.

"That is very important, Winfred." She said my name in that magical way again. "I think if we have a chance to love, we need to take it. I know my parents forbade me to have boyfriends in school. They did not want me to waste time with boys that wouldn't mean anything to me."

"I can understand their concern. You are a beautiful woman." I swallowed and hoped I didn't sound too forward.

Forward or not, Gaby smiled and told me about growing up in her small town. There were many similarities to Militia Springs, of course, but her upbringing in post-war Germany was much different than my idyllic youth. Her story was about hardship and strife and uncertainty, and she told it with the downcast and occasionally pleading eyes of someone who believes, at least in part, that what she suffered she brought upon herself. Or, at least, her people did. I found myself growing attracted to her in that way when you don't quite understand or believe what is happening. I felt myself fearing that if I thought this afternoon's pleasure too much, I would wake up tomorrow and remember it all differently. I would remember Winfred was just Winfred.

"Perhaps I could call you? On the telephone."

"Perhaps," she smiled.

"Could I have your number? I can call tomorrow if it isn't trouble."

"Sure, that would be okay," Gaby smiled again and scribbled a number on the back of the check I didn't pay. I glanced at it and put it in my pocket. "Until tomorrow."

"Until then."

I turned, and Erich glared at me as I walked out the door.

I called Gaby the next morning, and we agreed to meet that afternoon for coffee at a little café in Sindelfingen, just south of the base. She was already there when I arrived, so I took a chair at her table.

"Would you say my name, please?"

"What?" Gaby's smile erased her frown.

"I'm not a narcissist. But, you see, I have never liked the sound of my name. Not until yesterday."

"Of course, Robert."

I stared at her and gulped.

Was she thinking of someone else?

"I am just playing," she laughed. "Thank you for inviting me to coffee, Winfred."

Aha, there it was! Winfred!

I smiled and nodded. "Thank you, Gaby. And thank you for coming up here from Nurtingen."

"I don't live in Nurtingen; I live here. I was in the inn because my parents needed help getting ready for the morning opening. Erich isn't much good sometimes."

"Great, it will be easier to get together," I blurted. Thankfully, Gaby's head was turned as she signaled to the waiter.

We both used a lot of sugar and milk in our coffee, and we each ordered a slice of apple streusel. And, like the day before, I got lost in her. I don't mean lost like confused; I mean lost like absorbed. Instead of lost in thought, I was lost in Gaby. Sometimes I hate myself for being such a pathetic romantic. Sometimes I love myself for it. I wasn't sure which this time.

I didn't get to see Gaby again until the next Friday when we met at the SI Centrum. I offered to pick her up, but she said it would be better to meet me. The Centrum was about the only place in town I had visited. Since I didn't drink, I didn't party with the other guys much; besides, they were all married. I was also tied to the admiral's schedule, so I spent most of my time at Patch in the headquarters or the admiral's chalet. He lived in an 11,000 square foot mansion in one of Stuttgart's most exclusive neighborhoods and entertained many nights of the week.

We met at the Sonder bar. It wasn't as loud as the Churchill or as rowdy as the Dubliner, and I wanted to talk with her. I ordered a Pilsner, and so did she, but after ten minutes, I noticed she hadn't taken a sip yet.

"Do you want something else?" I motioned to the beer.

"Oh, no," she smiled. "I'm just not much of a drinker." She nodded toward my untouched glass. "How about you?"

"I guess I'm not much of a drinker, either."

"Then what the heck are we doing in Germany?" We laughed, and I touched her hand.

"And in a bar in Germany."

She didn't move her hand, so I kept mine there for a few moments, then moved it. I didn't want to be creepy.

I saw Gaby the next night and either called her or saw her every night for the entire summer. I even took her to Patch, and we ate pizza at the café next to the Swabian events center. Gaby took me to her small apartment in Sindelfingen, and we had schnitzel and some German pasta called spaetzle.

I think I was falling in love with her.

No! I had fallen in love with her! From the first time I met her. Now, I just savored the *falling* part of love. And, I think, relished the *being*.

Each military branch at European Command has a birthday ball where we dress in our finest uniforms, and the ladies wear formal gowns. They are fun events, and the army and air force even have a band they bring in to put on a big show. The navy doesn't have such a thing, so we usually have some sailors sing or something. The marines just get drunk.

October 13 is the navy's birthday, so I took Gaby to our ball. Since I hadn't met her parents, she asked me to pick her up at their home in Nurtingen, so I felt spiffy as I parked in front of the address she had given me. I wore my blue mess dress uniform with miniature medals and wings, the golden cummerbund, waist jacket, pleated shirt, and slacks. I arrived at six to give us plenty of time to get to the ball at seven, and Gaby's dad met me at the door. He was a distinguished-looking man despite the bags under his eyes. I think all people who own restaurants or inns have bags under their eyes. He introduced himself as Dieter and led me into the living room, where I met Gaby's mother, Irmgard. Dieter offered me a beer, but I declined and took a seat.

Erich walked in as I sat, and spat, "Too good to drink German beer?"

At first, I thought he was kidding, so I smiled. But Erich's eyes were dark, and his face mean. I frowned and stood.

"No, of course not."

Erich glared at me and snorted. I was confused by his hostility.

"Erich, I think you should leave." Irmgard rose from her chair and pointed toward a door.

"Why? I don't want to miss seeing the princess."

"Erich, we do not need this." Dieter motioned to the door.

Erich glared at me for a moment, started to say something, then stomped out.

"I am sorry about that," said Dieter. "Erich sometimes has...has...schlect laune."

"He says Erich sometimes has a bad mood," said Gaby. I looked at the stairs as she came down. Forgetting Erich and his mood, I beamed.

Gaby was beautiful! Her light brown hair was up, exposing her delicate neck and ears, and she wore a pale blue gown that accented a body that was perfection. I walked to her, and she held out her hand, so I helped her step to the floor. I leaned forward and kissed her lightly on the cheek. "You look wonderful!"

"Oh, Gaby!" Irmgard rushed to us, and I stepped aside so the mother could gush over daughter, which she did.

I glanced at Dieter, who was giving me the once over. He had an odd look in his eyes. I couldn't quite tell if they said approval or if they hid a desire to stab me. So, I just smiled and looked at Gaby.

"Shall we?"

I led Gaby to the door, paused for her to hug her mother and father, then we headed to the ball.

Since it was chilly, I had the top up on my Triumph, which also allowed us to talk while driving. By the time I got to the ball, I knew that Erich and Gaby had been at odds since they were children. In a nutshell, Erich was the younger and felt entitled and that Gaby got in the way of that entitlement.

We had a glorious time at the ball, and the admiral went out of his way to compliment me while June insisted that Gaby sit next to her. Gaby seemed to enjoy herself, and when the band played the slow songs, her hand led me into a world of enchantment that I had wanted for so long.

Two weeks later, Gaby invited me to have coffee at her parent's house. Erich wasn't there, which I was grateful for, and it was a very relaxed time. I spent several minutes with Dieter, sitting in the back yard, and I felt he was warming up to me.

I visited for coffee again a week later, and Dieter showed me his small workshop where he made furniture. It was a dark space and might have seemed drab if it were not for the homey smell of new wood dust and polish and the beautiful creations. Dieter showed me tables and chairs, and he had the sheepish but proud demeanor of a man who did not want to brag but had to. He had to because his hands and the wood made him so happy and fulfilled. And as Dieter explained how he wove the grooves and ridges into a table leg, I felt a growing kinship. We talked a lot during these sessions, strangely, not about Gaby, though. I assumed he was protecting her privacy, that she should be the one to divulge her life's details to me, and I appreciated that.

One day Gaby invited me not to afternoon coffee but to dinner, and I could tell by the way she asked me that it was a big deal. She was nervous and hesitant and made me feel like we were heading for danger instead of dinner, so I enthusiastically accepted to make her feel better.

Fortunately, the admiral was not entertaining on that Saturday night, so I had the day to think about my dinner date and what to expect. I knew that Erich would be there, of course, and to anticipate his surliness but hoped that I could grow closer to Dieter and Irmgard. After all, I loved their daughter!

I arrived at seven and soon sat to a beautiful dinner of rouladen and mashed potatoes. Rouladen is a small beef roll cooked in a sauce with onions and mustard with pickles to give it a tang. It was delicious! Erich was drunk when I arrived, and he hit the wine bottle hard throughout the meal. That said, he was quiet, and I took that as a blessing.

"Would you take a small schnapps?" Dieter looked at me and smiled. "Schnapps after a big meal is a tradition in Germany." He laughed and clapped me on the shoulder. "It settles the stomach." Irmgard and Gaby had taken the dishes to the kitchen, leaving us three men at the table.

"Of course," I smiled. I would at least take a sip to show my gratitude.

Dieter stood and walked to a side table. He pulled a bottle and three small pewter glasses from the shelf. Deer carvings adorned the glasses, and I could tell they were important to him.

"From my grandfather." Dieter looked at a glass, smiled, and put it in front of me. He filled it with liquid, then did the same for Erich and himself.

"Prost!" Dieter held up his glass then drained it in one gulp. I saw Erich do the same, so I took a small sip.

Dieter looked at me, expectantly, so I smiled and said, "Delicious!"

"Again? Oh, I see you still have some." Dieter filled his glass and Erich's and then leaned back in his chair. He had a content and a happy look, and I felt welcome.

Gaby and Irmgard joined us, and I was surprised that Dieter didn't offer them a schnapps.

"No schnapps for the women?" I grinned at Dieter.

"We prefer ice cream," said Irmgard. "Would you like some?"

"Sure," I smiled.

"First, finish the schnapps," said Erich. He glared at me as he leaned forward.

I took another sip and smiled at him.

"Finish it!"

"Erich, enough! Winfred can drink what he wants." Dieter put his hand on Erich's shoulder, but Erich shrugged it off.

"Here, men drink schnapps! They finish the glass they are offered!"

"Erich, enough!" Irmgard leaned toward her son.

I picked up my glass and drained it. It tasted like medicine and if drinking horrible tasting things made me a man, I was now manly.

"Another! Fill your glass again!" Erich pointed to the bottle.

"No, thank you."

"Erich, enough! Dieter glared across the table.

"I will get the ice cream." Gaby stood.

"Oh, aren't you sweet?" Erich looked at his sister. "The princess doesn't drink schnapps now. You used to drink it, remember? You used to do heroin, remember?"

"Erich, quiet!" Dieter stood and grabbed Erich by the shoulder.

"Ask your girlfriend how she knows English so well?" Erich angrily jerked his dad's hand away. He staggered back and stuck his chin out. "Ask her what she was doing before she moved to Sindelfingen!"

"Erich!" Irmgard slapped the table.

"Your little princess is a drug addict! She is also a felon!"

"GET OUT!" Dieter grabbed Erich by the shoulders and spun him around. He shoved him out the door, and I heard Gaby cry and run for the kitchen. Irmgard followed her, and I stood at the table, shocked at what had just happened. I looked toward the door, hoping Gaby would return but knowing she wouldn't. After a few minutes, I heard a door open, and Dieter returned, motioning for me to follow him. We walked through the kitchen and out into the small garden, and Dieter pointed toward a metal bench. We sat quietly for some moments, then he reached into his breast pocket and pulled out a pack of Marlboro cigarettes.

"Do you know this cigarette?" He showed the pack.

"Yes," many of my friends smoke it."

"Would you like one?" Dieter held the red and white package for me to see.

"No, no, thank you."

Dieter shrugged, plucked a cigarette, and put it between his lips. He clicked a lighter, and I smelled the familiar smoke.

We sat for several awkward minutes, and while Dieter smoked, my head spun.

What in the heck had Erich been talking about? Drug addict? Heroin?

He must really hate his sister to make that kind of stuff up. I suspected Dieter invited me to the back yard to explain what was going on with Erich. Otherwise, he would have asked me to leave. But the fact that he wanted to explain it to me was gratifying. I appreciated the fact our relationship had gotten that far.

"Gaby makes terrible choices in men."

I frowned and sat straighter. I was expecting a discussion about Erich.

Dieter glanced at me and took a drag on his cigarette. "I don't mean you, or at least I don't think so. Not yet anyway." He let the smoke out of his lungs as he talked, and I could see his words.

"Thank you. I guess." I frowned again.

"When she was only sixteen, she fell for an American soldier who was no good, and I could see that from the day I first met him. Selfish, arrogant, he felt like Germany owed him something. His name was Peter, and he was twenty, and we warned Gaby and forbade her from seeing him. But she wouldn't listen. Erich warned her." Dieter looked at me, "Winfred, you must know that Erich's intentions are good. He did not handle himself well tonight, but please know his intentions are good." Dieter stared at me, but I frowned and sat back.

"What are you talking about? Do you mean Erich was telling the truth?"

Dieter looked at me and nodded.

"Gaby told me she and Erich always fought since they were children."

Dieter frowned and shook his head. "They were the best of friends when they were children. They were inseparable. It was only after Gaby started ruining her life, that they fell apart."

I took a deep breath.

WOW!

"It began with marijuana, I think. I could smell it on her when she came in. And she changed. He changed her. He made her like him-- selfish and arrogant, and believing that everyone owed her something. She insisted on speaking English in our home. You notice that Irmgard and Erich and I also know English, we need to speak it. We get so many American tourists at the inn."

Dieter looked at me with wide eyes, and I could see he wanted me to understand.

"Gaby had been a great student, a wonderful daughter, but she became this slovenly, lazy...thing. She lost her way, and finally, Peter was arrested and taken away, and we thought Gaby would be okay. But Peter's friends took over, and she began to spend all her time with them. And they had the hashish and the cocaine and the heroin."

Dieter turned to face me. He took a final drag and flicked the cigarette onto the grass. "We tried, and we tried, and I found a counselor, and there are programs to help people like Gaby, but she refused. She became pregnant, a baby she wisely aborted in my opinion." Dieter leaned forward with his hands together between his knees. He shook his head and stared into the dark grass. "She broke Erich's heart and her mother's." Dieter leaned back and looked at me. "And when they found her bringing heroin from Turkey and put her in prison, she broke mine."

"Gaby was in prison?"

"Yes, for four years."

"Jesus," I whispered. I glanced at Dieter. "How long has she been out?"

"About two years now. Gaby struggles, but she gets better. And despite the fact she broke all of our hearts, we still love her. But we cannot forget, Winfred. She seemed okay before when she clearly wasn't. And now, she has another American." Dieter leaned against the back of the bench and crossed his legs. "She has you. So, maybe you can see why Erich is so angry."

"I think I understand."

"Of course, she told you none of this."

I shook my head. "She told me she had learned her English at the university and that she speaks it so well because she works in the international division at Deutsche Bank."

"She does work in the international division of Deutsche Bank," said Dieter. "She works there as a cleaning person. Jobs are hard to get here in Germany, especially if you have a drug record."

I shook my head again and slumped back against the bench. I was drained; in fact, I was beyond that. I was at the bottom of my life.

Dieter stood. "I will tell her that you have gone. No need for you to say anything to her. After all, it doesn't make any difference if she understands or not. You can't possibly want anything to do with her now."

I stood and followed Dieter through the kitchen and to the front door. I didn't look back as it shut behind me.

THE BROKEN PLACES

It's not that I hadn't realized how badly I had fallen for Gaby, how much I loved her. I knew that. I knew it when I would wake up and she would be my first thought, the reason that my mouth creased into a morning smile. I knew I had fallen for her because she was always with me, a part of my mind sometimes at the edge and sometimes alone in the center, and I knew it when those thoughts of her caused my throat to catch. I knew I had fallen for her but what I didn't realize was how much hurt I could feel, or how complicated and rich those layers of misery could be, when I lost her.

The pain from lost love is simple, really, compared to the pain of deception. Losing my Jane was a heart wrench, but at least I had one left to beat after she was gone. But this thing with Gaby, and I will call it that, a thing, left me in a state of dark bewilderment. At first, I didn't want to think about what had happened and plunged into my work with near manic diligence. At least, I thought of it as diligence, and I arrived hours before anyone and worried over details and points of precision and stayed long after everyone had left. When security told the admiral that I worked until two or three every morning, he asked me if something was wrong. I told him everything was fine. But on those lonely nights, I began to allow myself into the dark and never satisfying world of why? Why had she done this to me? I forced myself to remember every lie and every smile and began to guess the point when the lie began. I tried to remember what I was doing at those points and how she had made me feel. And sometimes I think Gaby started her conversations as the truth but then let the lies in. And I had believed all of it. I had loved all of it.

So, I was in a dark place when I got Mom's early morning call. I assumed it was about my missing Christmas this year.

We had the routine of me calling her and the family every Sunday. I called at around eight in the evening, my time, in the early afternoon in Missouri and not a time of cow milking or interruption to church. So, when I heard her voice, I bolted upright.

"Mom?"

"Weenie, Grandpa is in the hospital. He had a stroke, and you need to come home."

"Is he okay? Will he be okay?" I felt sick.

"He asks for you, Weenie. Hurry."

I couldn't sleep so I took a cab to the airport and found an early morning flight to Heathrow in London. I spent the next six hours frantically searching for a plane to the States and finally landed at Springfield Airport following an overnight flight to New York City, then on to Missouri. The taxis lined outside the baggage claim, and I hailed one to Barnes General Hospital. I must have fallen asleep because the next thing I knew the driver was shaking me awake. The woman at the desk told me Tobias Kleegan was in room 414.

Grandpa's room was so dimly lit that I stumbled over a chair leg as I entered. I quietly pulled the chair next to Grandpa's bed and strained in the dark to see him. I figured he was asleep. I started to shake him but didn't, a little annoyed that he was alone. It surprised me that Mom, Dad, Molly, and Kate weren't here. But as I leaned back and sat in the dark, I surmised that they had been here since the beginning, so maybe they were getting something to eat.

Weariness pulled at me and the past sleepless weeks and exhausting trip from Germany now conspired against my eyes. I couldn't keep them open. The coffee I had been drinking now lay heavy and sour in my stomach, and I felt nauseous and strangely weak. I wanted to get up and get a drink of water, but I was so tired. I was just so tired. My head bobbed but I fought the exhaustion and jerked myself up straight. I wanted to be alert when Grandpa woke up. I felt my head nod again. Maybe, just a short nap...

"I'm glad you could make it."

"Grandpa?"

"I waited for you."

"Grandpa?"

"I waited for you." His voice was so small and far away.

"I know Grandpa; I'm here." My voice was small too.

"I'm sorry about Jane."

"It's okay, Grandpa."

"I think maybe you couldn't see Jane because God wanted you to find Gaby."

"Grandpa? Did mom tell you about Gaby?"

"I think that is why you have been searching. You were supposed to find Gaby."

"I found her, Grandpa. I found her."

"I know, Weenie."

"I love you, Grandpa."

"I know, Weenie. I know."

"I love you, Grandpa."

"And I love you."

"Weenie, the alcohol wasn't for you. It was never for you."

"Grandpa?"

"It was for her. It was so you could understand Gaby."

"Grandpa? Grandpa?"

"Wake up, Weenie."

I jerked my head up and squinted against the bright light. Dad shook my shoulder. "Wake up, son."

"Weenie, Oh, Weenie." Mom rushed forward, and I struggled to my feet. I felt like I was drugged. Mom hugged me, and I could feel her wet eyelashes on my cheek. Then Dad was hugging me. Molly and Kate joined our group, and we were all hugging and crying.

"I am so sorry you were too late," said Mom. Her voice was muffled into my shoulder, and I wasn't sure I heard her.

"What?"

"I am so sorry you got here too late. Grandpa died about an hour ago."

"What?" I swallowed and slowly relaxed my hug. Mom, Dad, and the others let their arms drop, and I could see the red in their eyes and sag of their faces.

"He tried to hold out for you, son," said Dad.

"He kept saying he had to talk to Weenie," sobbed Kate.

"But." I looked toward Grandpa's bed. In the light, I could see the sheet drawn over his head.

"I'm glad you could at least sit with him for a few minutes," said Molly. "I'm sure he knew you were here."

"Weenie, Grandpa Two Bears was probably looking down on you. He is looking down on all of us now," said Kate. She looked up at the ceiling and smiled through her tears.

"I am sure you are right!" I grabbed Kate and hugged her. "I am sure you are right." I looked at Grandpa's form and closed my eyes.

Had he been here with me?

Did he say the things I thought I heard?

Or...?

I let Mom and Dad lead me out of the room, and we sadly trooped to the car. Dad drove, and I sat in the back between Molly and Kate. I was in a state of shock, I think. And extreme exhaustion. I hadn't slept in weeks, and the flight from Germany was one coffee after another. Despite my fatigue, I could not fall asleep. I kept thinking of Grandpa's words, and what surprised me the most was how normal it all seemed. Even now, knowing that Grandpa was dead when I talked with him didn't alarm me or seem particularly strange. I think it is because I always thought of him as near mystical. It was Grandpa who had read to me about dragons and giants and bears named Poo. It was Grandpa who had explained the seasons and solar system and all other things of mystery and awe. So, it was fit for Grandpa to find a way to reach me, to tell me what I needed to do.

The following week was one of misery as we Kleegans grieved the loss of our beloved Grandpa Two Bears. I had never imagined a life without him. I was completely unprepared for the reality of never talking on the porch with him, never lighting his cigarette again, never hearing the click-suck sound when he was irritated. And, of course, there was the loss of Gaby too. I could at least share my sorrow of losing Grandpa with the family, but my loss of Gaby was a private grief I kept for me. I wanted to tell Mom and have her help me with it, and I knew that she probably could. But it seemed so selfish, given what she had on her plate. Dad was his usual stoic self, an oak but not a shoulder, so Gaby was alone with me. It was a week that seemed endless.

Finally, under the Molly Tree, we buried Grandpa Two Bears next to his beloved Catherine and daughter. And there is one good thing about death, I suppose, and that is the new burial of a loved one makes the ones first there not seem so lonely.

I flew back to Stuttgart on Saturday, and that Monday, the admiral called me in. After condolences, he told me the command screen board had met but that I wasn't on the list. I would have to wait until next year to see if I would get a command. The admiral told me he wanted me to take the rest of the week off, rest, and get well from my loss. He invited me to his house for Christmas, but I told him I wanted to be alone.

That night as I sat in my room at Patch Barracks, I fought great despair. I had been depressed in my life, and indeed, I had felt beaten, sometimes overwhelmingly so, but this blackness pulled me lower than I had ever been. I had lost my life's true love; I had lost the dear mentor of my life; and the navy didn't want me either. At least not to command a squadron.

The Maker's Mark bottle that I had stashed in my dresser, under my never-used summer shirts and civilian socks, whispered to me. It reminded me how I liked to peel off the wax top and roll open the cap and pour heaven over some ice. It promised first euphoria and then the maudlin embrace of the weepy remembrance of good times. I thought about how great it would be to get genuinely drunk because I wanted to be drunk enough to fully explore how miserable I felt and let it all fall upon me. I wanted to laugh and cry and shout and cry some more.

But there was another whisper in my ear, a slight rustle, barely detectable and hoarse as the air wound through its old throat. And as this speck of bright light grew in my dark mind, it reminded me that the promises of my wax-topped friend were false. More importantly, it reminded me of the goodness of me. And I needed, I craved to hear that message and the whisper knew I needed to hear it and the whisper was good, and it was familiar and comforting.

It was Grandpa Two Bears.

And as I felt myself sink, as I felt myself break, Grandpa's voice became louder, and I found myself strangely glad that I was at this low, low point. I was pleased because down here I could hear. Down here, the sounds echoed off the walls of my trough and into my mind, and it was hope rising above despair that became the vehicle for Grandpa's message.

"You were supposed to find Gaby," he said.

"You were supposed to find Gaby."

And I realized for the first time that the love I had sought and the loneliness I had found in that pursuit were but the hounds of my hunt. They were the flushers of my game and the preparers of my battlefield and meant to get me ready to fight.

ICE CREAM

The next morning, I dressed in civilian clothes, hopped into the Triumph, and drove to Sindelfingen. It was chilly but clear, so I took the little back road, Pascalstrasse, into town. It took longer that way, but it also gave me time to think. I had considered calling Gaby and asking her to explain herself, but I knew I had to see her face to face. What I had to know could not be carried through fiber lines or over a plastic handset.

It was seven in the morning, still dark, when I pulled into the ally by the rear door to the Deutsche Bank. I knew Gaby got off of work at half past seven, or at least that is what Dieter had told me, so I turned off the ignition and sat for a moment. I wasn't sure what I wanted. I mean, what could I want from a girl who had spent four years in jail for felony drug trafficking? What could I want from a girl who had lied to me about everything? What in the hell could I want from a girl who had gotten pregnant and then, apparently, just walked away from that too? Why in hell was I here?

I sat for a few minutes and listened to the car engine tick and shook my head against my futility.

I think what I wanted, why I was here in this alley, was because I sought some clarity. Had my heart been all that wrong? If I had loved Gaby before I found about her past and, if I loved the woman in front of me, then wasn't that the one I was supposed to love? Not the one from some time before. I mean, was I now supposed to tell her about my DUI and how much I had loved to drink myself into tears with my Rolling Stones?

I took a deep breath and wished that I could talk to Grandpa Two Bears. I really needed some porch time but he wasn't whispering to me now. While I knew his silence was good, a sign Grandpa now trusted me to do my part, I still walked to the rear door of Deutsche Bank with no clear understanding of what I wanted to happen. I just knew I was supposed to find her. And despite the fact I had known her for several months, I knew that I had not done that. I had not found her.

I swallowed and waited, half-hoping she wasn't there or that she was already gone but praying that she was still inside.

I heard footsteps from inside, then the knob's metallic click, and as the door swung open, I looked into Gaby's eyes. They brightened at the instance of surprise but quickly clouded, I assumed, at the thought of confrontation and the dreariness of explanation. In that instant, that part of a second, I knew what I wanted and why I was there. And that is the opportunity I took.

"You never came back with the ice cream."

"What?" Gaby's voice was small in its unsureness. She frowned and cocked her head.

"The ice cream. The last time I saw you, in your house, you said you would get the ice cream. I have come for it."

"Ice cream. You have come for the ice cream?"

"Yes. Any flavor will do."

Gaby's hands flew to her face, and as she began to sob, I stepped back and she stepped out of the door and the heavy door clicked closed. I took her into a gentle hug and as I smelled the bleach and cleaning fluid I think I loved her more than ever. "I prefer vanilla because it goes with everything."

I held her like that for a long time, and as I did, I remembered how much I liked to hold her, and I told myself that feeling is the only thing of her past I needed to know. All the rest was, well, in the past. A couple of times, Gaby started to speak, to explain, I imagine, but I shushed her quiet. But as I held her, I knew there were still demons, unspoken and unexplained, that would find us, just as I found her, and they would be no small challenge. If the wax bottle could whisper to me, the manner of Gaby's intoxication could purr to her, and we would have to be strong to find the good voices, the strong voices.

Over the next days and weeks, Gaby attempted to speak about her past, but when she did, I would shake my head and hold her hand and say, "If you need to explain to yourself, then go ahead, but there is no need to explain to me." And slowly, I think she began to gain confidence again, in herself, in us. Then, one day she said," But I need to explain to you." And so, began her story.

Gaby did not tell it in one sitting. Over time in teary bits and struggling pieces she bled her tale--the one I also knew, of the promise and ultimate deceit of addiction. Hiding in the woods and smoking marijuana was exciting and fun, and it countered the discipline and order of her home. Dieter and Irmgard arose at four every morning to begin the baking and food preparation, and by six, Gaby and Erich were helping too. Then it was school and homework and drudgery until time to run into the woods again.

She was sixteen when she met Peter, a dashing and handsome American soldier who always had money and marijuana, and he stole her heart. In Germany, school children followed two routes, one to a vocation or the second to university. Gaby's grades allowed her to enter university, but she abandoned that for Peter.

"I did not run from anything bad," Gaby said. "My mother and father gave me so much, and Erich was a good brother. They all loved me, too. The problem was not with them; it was with me."

Gaby would have moved out of her home if Peter had a place to go, but he was in bachelor housing at Patch. He told Gaby he would marry her one day, and they would live in a beautiful house, and soon he gave her a taste of cocaine. And that is when a want became a desire which became a need. With heroin, the need became her life.

"So, in some ways, I had no choice," said Gaby. "When Peter was arrested, my source went away, and I became frantic. I found Peter's friends, and when they told me to bring heroin in from Turkey, I did it."

"Is that when you hit bottom?" I asked.

"No," she smiled. A sad smile. "That day in Istanbul. When the door shut behind me, the first day in prison, is when I hit bottom. It was the day I prayed for every next step." She looked at me. "I had never prayed before."

Four months later, I asked Gaby to marry me. I didn't get down on my knee or anything, we were sitting in her living room, on the couch that her mom gave her, and I just asked her.

And she asked, "Are you sure?"

Gaby took my hands in hers and didn't look at me. I could see her swallow and when her shoulders shook, I knew that she was crying. But after a while, she looked up, and her eyes had a pain in them. They had remorse and hope and a plea. Perhaps, even a prayer. I knew she wanted me to say "yes" to her question but I knew she needed me to take ownership of my answer. She had to give me a way out of something that she hoped I didn't take.

"I'm sure." As I hugged her I never felt surer of anything. Anything I had ever said or done or thought. I hugged her tightly. Then, we called her parents.

Since I had six months left on my tour in Stuttgart, we decided to wait to get married. I wanted the ceremony in front of my family and friends in Militia Springs, and Gaby and her parents wanted to visit the states, so everybody liked the plan. I also knew that given Gaby's past difficulties, many of her childhood friends had abandoned her, and their parents had severed ties with Dieter and Irmgard. A wedding in the States had a lot of upsides.

A couple of months later, the command screen board met, and the admiral called me into his office and informed me I was on the list. I would get an F-14 squadron to command! I was so emotional when he told me I nearly broke into tears and later, in my room, I did.

My lows had been so low!

I had lost my career, my girl, my grandfather. I had lost myself. The world had broken me, and I had known that I had to fix myself again. And I had. And I had. My resurrection began when I listened to the whispers of my Grandfather Two Bears, and I stood again when I found Gaby. I mean, really found her. And now, I had my career back!

The expression, "I am on cloud nine", is used to express happiness, and it is generally attributed to the meteorology community who would describe clouds with a number. A cloud with a nine would be very high and near heaven.

I was on cloud nine after the admiral told me about screening for command, and the days sailed by. Gaby and I looked forward to our move to the United States, and every night we would talk about what it was like and what we were going to do together. I was in heaven. Until the admiral's executive assistant, Colonel Morris, called me into his office.

I took a seat in front of his desk, but my grin dropped off my face when I saw his expression. When your boss looks mad, it means there is something you can probably talk your way out of. When he looks sad, it means there is something so wrong even he can't talk your way out of.

The colonel looked very sad.

"Sir?" I swallowed.

"Weenie, intel tells me you are in the process of updating your top-secret clearance."

"Yes, sir, it's been five years. I filled out the paperwork a couple of weeks ago. Is it lost or something?"

"There is a problem with it."

"What? What kind of problem?"

"It has to do with Gaby." Colonel Morris looked at me. He had met Gaby several times; we had even attended a party at his house on Floridastrassee, the cul-de-sac on Patch, where all senior officers lived. "You are getting married, I believe."

"Yes, sir, when I take leave and go home."

The colonel nodded and leaned back in his chair. He closed his eyes and slowly let the air out of his lungs. Then he looked at me.

"Weenie, when we do a background update on an officer serving in a foreign country, even a friendly foreign country, we take extra measures. We have access to partner security agencies, INTERPOL, etcetera."

I looked at him and nodded. I felt something terrible was about to happen.

"Gaby has a criminal record, you know about that, I hope."

"Yes, sir."

"It is a felony criminal record, Weenie." Colonel Morris's chair squeaked as he leaned forward. His face was stern. "It deals with drugs and prison."

"Yes, sir, I know."

"Didn't you realize we would find out about this? Or did you think it would go unnoticed?"

"I didn't want to drag her name into the dirt, sir. I didn't want any of you to know about it if I could avoid it. Gaby is different now; that stuff happened when she was just a kid."

"It didn't happen that long ago, Weenie."

"Sir, you aren't going to tell the admiral, are you. He and Mrs. Jensen think the world of Gaby."

"Weenie, this is more of a problem than disappointing the admiral and June. This situation can, and probably will, derail your clearance. If you can't keep a top-secret clearance, you can't become a commanding officer."

I looked at him as nausea crept up my gullet.

"What can I do?"

"Well, not get married is one thing you can do."

"Sir?"

"Weenie, I'm not sure if there is a way to get your clearance now. Not if you have a foreign-born wife and who committed a felony in a NATO country."

"What if she isn't my wife but lives with me?" I asked. I was desperate.

"Weenie, this is the US Military, not the Playboy Club. Cohabitating with a person, not your spouse, is frowned upon, and the more senior you become, the more serious that frown becomes. Besides, anyone that lives with you is subject to the clearance requests."

"How much time do I have?"

"Oh, Weenie, letting this thing ride out isn't a good idea. It isn't going away, you know."

"Yes, sir, but sometimes security clearances get hung up."

"Well, it's true your current clearance is still active until somebody rules it isn't. I'd say you have a couple of months, max."

"Who makes that decision?"

"The paperwork from here would go through the navy to DoD CAF."

"What's DoD CAF?"

"It is the Department of Defense Consolidated Adjudications Facility."

"You aren't going to tell the admiral, are you?"

"No, not unless I have to. But if the intel shop here believes you are hiding something, and they bring in the Navy Criminal Investigation Service, I will have to tell him."

"Yes, Sir. Do you think they will do that?"

"I'll talk with Colonel Thomas. He is the J2, as you know. He runs the place."

"Thank you, sir."

"Weenie, let me give you some advice."

"Yes, sir."

"If I were you, I would think long and hard about how much Gaby means to you. You are thirty-six years old, right? When do you go over twenty for retirement?'

"In six years, sir."

"The navy will let you hang around for that even if you can't get your clearance. But you won't be allowed to do anything. Is she worth that risk? And if you think she is, how are you going to feel at night when you come home?" Colonel Thomas leaned forward and stared at me. "What are you going to talk about, Weenie—look honey, I got another paper cut?"

Since I had been frowning from the minute I had sat down, my face knew what to do through all of this. But my mind didn't, my heart didn't. I didn't know what I was going to do.

"I don't know, sir." I stood and stumbled out of his office.

AREN'T YOU THROUGH BREAKING ME YET?

That evening, Gaby called. I prided myself on not letting my desperation, my angst, enter my voice. But when she asked about our weekend plans, I forced a cough and told her I thought I was coming down with a cold. She sounded dejected, and I felt like a heel, but I just didn't want to see her now. I would have picked up the phone and called Grandpa Two Bears if he were still alive. I swear I would have.

I slumped in my chair and held my head in my hands.

Christ, I finally resolved the two quests in my life. Must I have to choose between them?

I had found my love. I had been looking for Gaby since I was old enough to realize I didn't want to spend my life alone. I just didn't know her name yet. And along the way, Jane had blessed me with the assurance that the search was worthwhile. Grace had blessed me with the knowledge that the road to love had forks in it, and many paths might be worthy. And now, Gaby blessed me with who I had been seeking.

I had secured my career. I knew I wanted to be a commanding officer since I reported to my first squadron and saw Skipper Hudson in action. He was such a strong, smart, kind man. I wanted to be like him, and I know he is why I decided to make the navy a career. That understanding didn't happen suddenly but came to me over time, and I knew I craved that same influence. I wanted someone to want to be like me just as I had wanted to be like him. More than anything in the world, I wanted to stand in front of a group of patriots and have them see me as their leader and my selection for command of a squadron gave me the opportunity to earn that trust and respect. But now that might be gone.

I fell asleep wondering and praying, anguishing.

The following day, Friday, I felt sick. I almost called in to take off, but I sat at my desk, dreading the phone's sound every time it rang. Thankfully, the admiral was fully scheduled with phone calls and meetings and needed minimal support. I called Gaby and left a message that I had a cold and would call her when I felt better.

I went home and fell into a dark hole. It reminded me of when I had watched *The Lost Weekend*…except that I didn't have any alcohol to numb me. I just couldn't see staying in the navy as a nobody. And as an officer without a clearance, that is precisely what I would be.

Friday night, I had a dream that I was back in high school in the marching band. At first, I was smiling and admiring my band uniform. It was blue with gold trim, but then we were marching in the rain, and everybody was playing their instruments, but I didn't have one. I just had my hands at my lips like I was playing the flute, but I didn't have a flute. And everybody was pointing at me and laughing, and I moved my fingers faster and faster.

"Did you get that uniform in a whorehouse?" asked my dad and I had awakened in a sweat.

Saturday, I felt even worse, and I thought maybe I did have a cold. I thought about buying some of that Dayquil stuff but decided against it. I think it's full of alcohol, and I might wind up drinking the whole bottle. So, I hung around my room and watched the Armed Forces Network on television. AFN has perhaps the worst programming in the world and is preoccupied with the avoidance of impropriety. No cussing, no gore, no flesh. Mostly old sitcoms and western movies. I am surprised they didn't dress the horses in pantsuits to hide their legs.

But the television was just background to my tormented thoughts. Tormented because they were selfish thoughts of what I might have to give up. I could not walk away from the navy, I just couldn't! I could not live my life as a nobody again, not ever, which was so unfair to Gaby. But was it unfair? As I sat in front of *The Golden Girls*, I found myself questioning her. How could she have been so stupid? So weak! How could she have fallen so far that she was snorting cocaine and shooting heroin? Who does that? I'll tell you who does that. Idiots do that! Losers do that! Losers who aren't worth throwing your life away for! By the time I went to bed, I had resolved to call Gaby the next day and call the wedding off.

Of course, I didn't sleep, and all the next day, I sat in a state of torpor. And when my brain did work, I reached for the phone to tell Gaby the bad news. I even dialed her number once but hung up on the first ring.

I was dozing in my chair when Mom called. It was around six in the evening, noon her time, so I walked to the wall phone. I hesitated as I reached for it because I did not feel like talking to anyone.

"Weenie?"

"Hey, Mom." I forced an upbeat tone.

"Hi, Weenie, how is Germany?" Mom's voice picked me up. Her voice always picked me up. Maybe that is why I answered. Selfish again.

"Okay. What's going on there?"

"Well, that is why I called. Molly is pregnant! She and Paul are going to have a baby. Isn't that great!"

"That's fantastic!" I slid down the wall and sat on the floor. "Please tell them congratulations for me. I will write a note tomorrow."

"I'll do that. Molly told me they had tried for a couple of years and had all but given up hope. But it was important to them and, you know, Paul is your age, and he wanted to have a child of his own. He loves Kate, don't get me wrong. But you know."

"I know," I frowned.

"How is Gaby?"

"She's fine, Mom, just fine."

"Good, great. Well, all is well here. I just thought I would give you the great news."

We talked for a few minutes longer, then hung up and I slumped back to my chair.

Her good, great news further depressed me. It was like Molly and Paul's life was one bookend, and mine was the other. Life was in the middle. But as I sat there in my misery, I slowly realized that I was at one of those blessing/curse divergence points. And despite that I often used the idea of a blessing and a curse in my life's assessment, I hated the phrase. Is it a blessing, or is it a curse? Make up your mind. It is just a more romanticized way of saying yes and no, and if something is both yes and no, then it is nothing.

Yet here I was. At a point in my life where a single decision would definitively lay out the course of the rest of it. But, in a way, it is a blessing to be given such a point, such a choice instead of having someone else make it for me. Maybe that is why I couldn't reach Grandpa Two Bears now. He was gone and I had to figure this one out for myself. The blessing...or curse... was not the choice but the living with it.

I awoke at around three in the morning and sat up with a clear resolution that I didn't have to choose. It wasn't a blessing or a curse; it was just a glitch. A momentary distraction. Why must I select between two of my life gifts, my wife, or my career? Who says I must?

I couldn't sleep, and when morning finally came, I went to the intel spaces and found Colonel Thomas. He looked annoyed when I knocked on his door but motioned me in.

"What can I do for you, Weenie?" He had a wary look that all professional intelligence officers have when their senior's emissary shows up. They have that look because their entire careers are built on looking for what is wrong. They look for clues to disaster and deception. They look for the code to crack the cipher because they know if Pearl Harbor happens on their watch, they will swing for it. So, the colonel looked at me askance because he was expecting me to bring him a problem.

"Sir, I need to speak with you about my clearance."

"What about it?"

My heart leaped. If he didn't know, then maybe there wasn't a problem. "Well, sir, I am separating soon to go to my command training track, and my clearance update is critical. I just wanted to know if there was any problem."

Colonel Thomas frowned. "Christ, Weenie, we don't have time to worry about that?" He took a breath and shrugged. "There was something about your girlfriend in the file, I think." He threw his arms in the air, then leaned forward. "Do you realize the new Unified Command Plan puts 350,000 US troops in Europe? We are now responsible for supporting the biggest US force anywhere in the world since the end of the second world war. We have the responsibility now for almost all of Africa, even below the Sahara! The Russians hate us, even if we are locked into missile negotiations. I don't trust them for a second, and believe me, my search for their trickery is never-ending. And by the way, the Red Brigades, The Red Army Faction, a shit-pot full of Palestinian terrorist groups, are still trying to kill us off. They haven't gone anywhere. So, Weenie, I have a lot to do. I looked at the paperwork; it looks okay to me, I forwarded it without objections."

"Oh."

"Does the admiral want anything?"

"Uhh, no, sir."

"Good, now get going. I have work to do."

"Yes, sir." I hopped up and ran to my office. I wasn't sure how to feel. I wasn't off the hook, but then, I wasn't snared either. I spent the day and all that week in agony, every day expecting

Colonel Morris to call me in and tell me to turn in my access card and badge.

"No, the admiral doesn't want to see you," he would say.

Then the week dragged into another, then another, and I began to make plans on moving back to the states. With Gaby.

We flew to Norfolk and moved into my house near the beach. I had rented it to a navy man and his wife while I was in Germany, and he had taken great care of it. I hadn't taken much, but uniforms with me to Stuttgart and Gaby didn't have many possessions, so our move was quick and easy. Since I had to get requalified in the F-14, my first task was to check into the RAG at Oceana and then take leave to get married. A personnel clerk handed me a note directing me to call on PERS 43. That excited me because once an officer screens for command; he is assigned to come in behind a sitting executive officer as his replacement when he moves up to command. That plan of assignment is called the slate, and it wasn't set when I left Stuttgart. I found an empty desk and dialed the number on the clerk's note. I was soon talking to Captain Dudley Wright, a great guy, and superb pilot.

"Weenie, it's great to have you back in the stable."

"Thank you, sir, it is great to be back in the Tomcat community."

"We thought we might have lost you when you didn't screen last year. Looks like God and sanity won out this time."

"Well, thank you, sir."

"Do you have a preference?"

I knew it was a trick question, so I said, "No, sir, whatever fits your scheduling. I do own a house in Virginia Beach, so an East Coast squadron would make my logistics easier."

"I understand you know Cotton Crosby?"

"Yes, Sir. I got commissioned with him. We served together in two squadrons and were roommates."

"He asked for you."

"He did?" I frowned, but it was from guilt, not disappointment. I didn't think Cotton and I had that relationship any longer. I thought I had ruined that.

"Yes, he called me and asked for you if you were available and would take the job."

"He is in 143, isn't he?"

"Yes, the Pukin' Dogs."

"I would love to go in behind Cotton."

"Okay, then consider it done. Congratulations on your selection for command, Weenie. It is great to have you back with us."

MR AND MRS KLEEGAN

The Militia Springs Methodist church is located north and east off the square and is set in a residential area with the parsonage next door. It is a small church, the one I attended whenever I was home, and where I wanted to introduce Gaby to my community. Gaby's parents flew in from Germany, leaving Erich behind to run the inn, so I got them a room in the Militia Springs Motel. They planned to tour the United States for a month before returning home. Molly was the maid of honor.

My best man selection was not as easy. My friend Jimmy Wilson was an obvious pick, but so was Paul. He had rescued Molly by some notion. And, then there was Raoul. Raoul had transitioned to the Tomcat following his tour in Japan and had done well. In fact, he had been selected for command by the same board that picked me! He and I stayed in touch; in fact, we spoke by phone weekly. Of course, when I called him, he was happy to hear I was getting married.

"Do you need a best man?" I could see him grinning into his phone.

"Well, uhh…"

"Maybe you folks use a best cow down there?" His chuckle didn't help. "I know where I can get a chicken suit. Best chicken has a ring to it."

"Stop it, Raoul."

"Okay, best man then. Do you need one?"

"I…I have a high school friend…"

Raoul must have detected my conundrum. "Look, Kleegan, if you have a high school friend who you can trust not to steal your ring, then ask him. After all, you are getting married in Militia Springs to connect with the place, right?"

"Well…"

"So, ask him. I'm coming anyway."

I called Jimmy, and he readily accepted my request to be my best man. I also called Melody, and we had a friendly chat. I knew Cotton was at sea as the executive officer of his new squadron, and they would not be able to attend.

All the planning made me remember the wedding of Cletis Browning. Cletis was a romantic, which is dangerous for an Ozarkian because the image and notions that seem so extraordinary in books and movies can become untethered in the woods. Cletis was to marry Nancy Downs, who did not have the imagination to match Cletis's or the energy to fend off or even modify his ideas. She did not challenge Cletis's vision to get married at their family farm, nor his idea to gallop out of the woods just as Nancy was drawn forward in a carriage. When I heard Cletis's plan, I winced with concern. Public ceremonies that rely on animals and children often go awry.

I attended the wedding with Jimmy, Donnie, and Paul, and the guests sat in plastic chairs that Cletis had borrowed from the Lion's Club. Of course, their feet buried unevenly into the soft ground, which caused much grousing as everyone had to contort and squat on their shanks.

Someone installed a piano on some pallets, and when the musician struck up the chords of "Here Comes the Bride," Nancy's carriage appeared from behind the barn. The scene was a bit corny but well-intended, so people only snickered to themselves.

As the carriage rolled to a stop, Nancy's father helped her down, and the proceeding appeared to be going off without a hitch. However, at that moment, the two beagles that were in some way a part of the wedding caught the scent of the white rabbit that was also, in some way, central to the affair and bolted toward it. The white rabbit scampered under the royal red ground cloth that Nancy was supposed to trod as she walked to the preacher and her husband to be. At that moment, Cletis galloped out of the woods on a white horse. The wedding colors were red and white, so Cletis wore a bright red suit complete with a red cowboy hat and boots. My first thought was not of a gallant man riding to his lover but of a ketchup sandwich, only funnier. The wedding beagles bored under the red carpet in earnest pursuit of the wedding rabbit, and their commotion caused the buggy's wedding horses to rear. That spooked Cletis's white wedding steed and caused him to buck. Chairs flew, and people ran, and the wedding piano fell off its pallet.

I smiled as I thought of Cletis and Nancy, and I was glad that Gaby and I were having a more traditional ceremony. I stood at the front of the sanctuary with Jimmie, Raoul, and Paul at my side and smiled as Gaby entered the church. Dieter escorted her and I let my eyes fall to the crowd and to my family in the front rows. I took a deep breath and made myself forget the phone call from Colonel Thomas. The call I had received an hour ago. He had been frantic to reach me.

"Weenie, your clearance has been rejected by DoD CAF. If you get married or have any relationship with Gabrielle Schaffer, you can forget squadron command."

And then, Gaby was by my side. Her dad lifted the veil and I looked into my lover's eyes and smiled.

WHEN COTTON WAS KING

The commanding officer of a squadron is called the CO or the skipper and the number two leader is the executive officer and is called the XO. I remember the day I told this to Gaby, shortly after we were married.

"Why isn't the executive officer called the EO.?" She frowned and tilted her head in that cute way I love.

"I don't know." I smiled and tilted my head the opposite way. "Remember, this is the navy. It doesn't have to make sense; it's just the way it is."

Gaby narrowed her eyes. "Do you find comfort in that?"

"Most of the time." I smiled again.

Another unexplained tradition is that the CO writes with a red pen when he edits documents or makes notations on the message board, and the XO—me—uses a green pen. That makes sense because it allows any observer to know whose opinion is being expressed and agree with it. On my first day in the squadron as the XO, Cotton gave me a handful of green pens and a smile.

"I hope you don't have to rescue me again." He was referring to the time when we were shot down over Vietnam. I had chased away his captors and carried him to the helicopter.

"Same here." I smiled, referring to Cotton's acceptance of me as his number two even when I had a question about my security clearance. Working with Cotton was a joy, and the fact we had been shipmates and roommates gave me a measure of him that allowed me to be more supportive than if we had been paired as strangers. I'm not saying he is stodgy or predictable, but I do believe I know how he thinks and how he wants things done. I ensured our spaces were inspection ready, our troops were well supported, and our officers toed his line. I did not hesitate to direct our personnel to get a haircut, adjust an incorrect uniform or lose weight, and I plunged into the tedious but critical administrative details that, if left undone, expose the squadron to all sorts of mayhem. Poorly crafted messages and missed deadlines can hurt a peacetime fighter squadron as much as the MIGs could in combat. But that said, Cotton could still surprise me. One such time was the callsign incident.

Naval aviation callsigns are a part of our culture, and we usually get them during our first fleet squadron tour. The junior officers, the JOs, will start calling you something, and it will stick. Sometimes an officer will arrive at the squadron with a callsign and keep it if the JOs think it fits. Sometimes the callsign is just a modification of a name, like "Weenie". Often it is assigned to celebrate some shortcoming, mistake, or perceived weakness. There are few rules for callsigns. They must be short enough to be barked over the radio, and they must be clean. The clean part has always been a challenge, and occasionally inappropriate names would crop up. I mean, a callsign of Master when your last name is Bates or Pussy when your last name is Licker can be challenging to look at when it is stitched together on a flight suit. Or on the canopy sill of an airplane. But I was a bit overwhelmed when the Deputy CAG, a smallish, Heinrich Himmler-influenced former Hornet pilot, called Cotton and me to his office and asked us to change our callsigns. His name was Brian Collins, and his callsign was Fang. But the JOs called him MOL, an acronym for Meaning Of Life because the DCAG appeared to have a unique insight on that-- given the gravity and self-importance of his every utterance. Fang/MOL also had a near mindless embrace for anything that smacked of "political correctness." Although only 5'6", he enjoyed the advantages of looking down on the less progressive. So, his glare was cold and straightforward when we knocked on his door. He told us to come in but didn't offer a seat.

"I need you both to pick a new callsign. Tell me what it is and if I approve it, you will get rid of Cotton and Weenie immediately." He waved his hand to dismiss us, but Cotton spoke.

"I'm sorry?" Cotton took a deep breath and leaned his head forward. It was his fighting pose.

Fang/MOL frowned an impatient tug to his lips. "Skipper, I don't know the genesis of Cotton, but I find it extremely offensive. The fact that a Black officer such as yourself uses it is beyond untoward." He looked at me. "And Weenie is a clear and revolting reference to men's genitalia. Again, extremely untoward."

Untoward was the new word replacing "incorrect" or, even more clearly, "wrong." Admiral Kelso, the CNO, had used it, and now all bootlickers used it too.

Cotton leaned forward a bit more. "First of all, Sir, Weenie is a nickname my XO has been called all of his life. It is short for Winfred, a portmanteau of the names of favorite uncles, and his mother and father gave it to him."

I was blown away by Cotton's aggressiveness. I was also surprised at his use of the word portmanteau, but suspected Cotton did it to knock the DCAG off his stride. Kind of like how William F Buckley would use his vocabulary to get an advantage over his opponents.

Cotton continued, "I have met Weenie's father and mother, and I know them. So, I will not direct him to change his callsign. And secondly, Cotton is a nickname I chose to honor Ms. Dorothy Cotton, who, I am sure you know, is one of our civil rights activists and leaders and a confidant of Doctor Martin Luther King. Doctor King asked her to help set up the Southern Christian Leadership Conference. But I think her biggest contribution was her creation of the Citizenship Education Program." Cotton straightened and took a breath. "Because it was designed to register Blacks to vote."

Life-long followers of whim can easily be influenced. So, the currents of culture-change in naval aviation had easily pushed Fang/MOL to his position of moral superiority. However, such people can easily topple when a real symbol, perhaps even victim, of the oppression they claim to champion challenges them. Fang/MOL's heretofore-smug mouth fell open, and his eyes widened in surprise and alarm. As the vanquisher of demons, he had not expected any pushback from his sanctimonious demands.

"You are familiar with Dorothy Cotton?"

"Well, yes. I mean no, but I have heard the name." Fang/MOL appeared to shrink behind his desk.

"Surely, sir, you are familiar with Doctor King, the Southern Christian Leadership Conference, and the Citizen's Education Program."

"Absolutely! Well, Doctor King." Fang/MOL swallowed.

"Sir, I would like to send some materials to you to read, if you don't mind."

"No. I mean, yes, absolutely I would love to read the materials." Fang/MOL sprang to his feet.

"Will that be all, sir?" Cotton and I stepped back and came to attention.

"Yes, of course."

I followed Cotton out of the office and into the passageway. Once inside our ready room and by the coffee machine, I turned to him. "Was that true about your nickname? About Dorothy Cotton?"

Cotton stirred his coffee and then looked at me. "It could be."

Cotton's leadership never ceased to impress me, and it often involved some bit of risk. For instance, during our deployment and just after we pulled into Naples, our maintenance chief approached me on the flight deck.

"XO, are you aware the skipper directed me to remove the fuel tanks and Phoenix rails from half of our Tomcats!"

"No, he didn't speak to me about it." I was surprised because it was a significant change in our configuration. The Tomcat carried two fuel tanks, 300 gallons each, and they gave the airplane added range and endurance. That was important to a plane's mission to engage threats far from the battlegroup. The rails were a requirement to carry the phoenix missile—again, critical for the far engagement. I found Cotton in the ready room and asked if he had a moment to chat.

"Skipper, maintenance tells me you directed the removal of tanks and rails?"

"That's right." Cotton looked at me and, seeing my frown, continued. "I didn't tell you because I didn't want to be talked out of it. Sorry."

"But sir, tanks and rails are part of our mission equipment."

"What mission?" Cotton smiled.

"Well, you know, our mission of fleet defense."

"Defense against whom?"

I frowned again, and Cotton put his hand on my shoulder. "What do we always complain about when we are on cruise?"

"The dog machine," I grinned.

"Besides that?" Cotton grinned back.

I shrugged.

"We complain that we can't train on cruise."

"That's right," I nodded.

"When was the last time our aircrew maneuvered the aircraft? I mean, really maneuvered it?"

"Just before we left for cruise."

"Exactly! Those tanks and rails create a lot of drag and, as you know, limit the Tomcat's maneuverability. And I think our aircrew have forgotten that we are a fighter squadron, not an interceptor or patrol squadron."

"But, sir, the tanks give us the gas we need to complete our launch cycle. The Hornets take all the airborne tanker gas. We will never get any of that from them."

"Don't need it." Cotton smiled again. "Weenie, you remember the Phantom. We didn't have as much gas as the Tomcat, and we flew longer cycles. We did that because we had to."

"I don't get it."

"Weenie, when our guys take off, they zorch around rendezvousing with each other and then climb to an altitude where they go to maximum conserve because they don't have anything better to do. And when they finally do come down to land, they have so much extra gas they have to dump it to get to landing weight. It is an insane way to train."

"Yes, sir."

"So, starting today, we will hold training sessions in the ready room. I will lead those discussions, and we will start by teaching our aircrew to skip the low-level rendezvous and use a maximum endurance rate of climb to altitude. We will teach them how to save their gas until they have a bag of fuel that they can use to maneuver the airplane. They can use that bag of gas to fight the airplane against the Hornets. Tomcat guys are wasteful and lazy when it comes to fuel management. We are that way because we can be, and it causes us to miss opportunities to train."

"What about the phoenix rails? And maintenance is going to complain about all of this."

"Weenie, the strength of our maintenance department is its ability to respond. We just need to convince them that this is something worth responding to. I will take care of that. And as far as CAG is concerned, I told him if we needed to, we could replace the rails and tanks overnight and, besides, we would save him 200,000 pounds of gas this at-sea period. He liked that. I also reminded him that we are out here in the Med. The Russians are too broke to mount any kind of threat, but we continue to act like they will come over the horizon any minute. I also reminded him that our next at-sea period features training engagements against the US Air Force F-16s out of Aviano, Italy. I invited CAG to fly with us and told him I want our aircrew to feel like they can take our Tomcats to the edge of the tactical envelope when they fight."

"Yes, sir."

"What I didn't tell him was that I wanted our aircrew to experience kicking someone's ass again. Don't forget. We are flying the A-plus."

Cotton referred to our new airplanes with the GE-110-400 engines. The Tomcat's original engines were the Pratt and Whitney TF-30s, and they were underpowered and tended to compressor stall at slow speed and high angles-of-attack. This was especially true if the pilot tried to move the airplane abruptly. The GE engines didn't have any stall problems, plus they had about 30% more thrust in each engine! They were so powerful that pilots did not use afterburner for takeoff. An engine failure would create so much asymmetric thrust the pilot couldn't counter it with his rudders!

The first morning out of port, I walked up on the flight deck and grinned when I saw our six Tomcats sans fuel tanks and rails. They looked elegant, lethal, and menacing, and I couldn't wait for my first flight.

Our aircrew were tentative at first, but after a couple of flights, they grew confident in their ability to manage their fuel. They also felt good about how their flights went. Our aircrew dominated the skies with their low drag configured planes, powerful engines, and confident fuel management. They spanked the F-18s during all of our training flights.

"Wow! I feel like a fighter pilot again!" The comment came from my pilot, Aaron "Greasy" Burger, after he gunned Fang/MOL. It made me feel good.

Four days later, we entered the training opportunity with the F-16s, and I was very gratified not only by our performance but also by our morale. Fighter pilots need to fight, or they turn grumpy and desolate. Our pilots were on top of the world. I felt sorry for the other F-14 squadron as they kept their tanks and rails and struggled mightily against the Falcons. Although we didn't discuss it, I think part of Cotton's decision to remove the tanks and rails was for me. His point wasn't really just to train better and enhance aircrew morale. And it wasn't to save the 200,000 pounds of gas, although we did. His lesson was always to question what you were doing and if you don't like it, to do something about it.

Cotton and I had our change of command in Cannes, and I took over as skipper for the rest of the cruise.

THE RISE OF THE PHOENIX

"Dakota 201 from Dragon, bandits, bullseye zero one zero for sixty miles!"

"Greasy, did you hear that?" I turned up the volume on the second radio.

"Yes, sir." Greasy's voice crackled over the intercom. "Sounds like a hot vector to me."

"It sure does. Head for the orbit point." I keyed the UHF, "Franco and Dopey, stay with the refueling tanker. Rags come with me."

Greasy swung our Tomcat's nose north toward the fighter orbit point while my wingman, Rags, steadied his Tomcat on our right side. I left Franco and his two A-6s and Dopey and his two Hornets with the KC-10 tanker. They were loaded with bombs, and there was no reason to haul them into a dogfight. That said, intelligence had briefed that there were up to 400 MIGs within striking range of us. If they showed in force, I could always call Dopey to bring his F-18s.

Eisenhower had entered the Red Sea a week earlier in response to Saddam Hussein's invasion of Kuwait. Our airwing had developed a plan to send six-plane interdiction teams to an orbit point inside Saudi Arabia. This plan was to thwart any move by Saddam to the south and the oil fields near Dharan. I was the strike leader for my team, and we were the second group to launch. Jack Grant led the first group flying as Dakota 201, and it was he who had received the vector we just heard from Dragon. Dragon was our US Air Force AWACS command and control airplane. The air force also supplied the aerial refueling tankers that topped us off.

"Dragon, Dakota, say status."

That was Jocko Barnes' voice. He was the RIO with Jack Grant, a genuinely good pairing since Jack was the worst fighter pilot in the navy. Perhaps in the world. However, Jocko was a real star, and the thinking was that he could keep Jack from being a total bonehead.

"Dakota, from Dragon, two groups of suspected horses vectoring south towards you. Ten-mile trail. The lead group now bullseye zero one zero for fifty-five. Hail Mary. Hail Mary."

"Dragon, Dakota copies horses, and Hail Mary." Jocko's voice was calm and confident.

"Holy shit!" said Greasy. "Horses means MIG-23s!"

"Yeah," I grunted. "But Hail Mary means we need visual identification before we can shoot."

We accelerated toward the orbit point, and I heard Jocko bark into the radio, "Dakota has a contact bearing zero one five at forty-five, angels twenty-four."

The mic keyed, and Dragon responded. "Roger, Dakota, that's your lead bandit. Watch for the trailers. Hail Mary."

Roger," said Jocko. Moments later, he continued, "Dakota has a single bandit bearing zero one five for forty-three miles, Angels twenty-four, airspeed 680!"

"That is your bandit," replied Dragon.

"Combat checks complete," said Rags.

I rogered his call. We were ready to go.

"Confirm, TWO horses in the lead group!" It was Jack's voice.

"Roger, two horses," said Dragon. "Green Lantern."

"Green lantern means he has identified the bandits and is cleared to fire," said Greasy.

"Yep," I looked at my left knee. My red fire button glowed.

"Fox three!" The sound of Jocko's voice shocked me.

"Holy shit, Jocko just launched a Phoenix!" Greasy and I were up hot mic, so I could easily talk to him. "Jocko just fired a Phoenix!" I repeated. I was filled with pride and envy. I was proud that the Tomcat community had finally shot the Phoenix missile in combat but envious that I wasn't the person who did so.

"Trailers on my nose for thirty." It was Chain Sawyer's voice. He was the RIO with Headley Lamar, Jack's wingmen. His call meant his radar had found the two trailing MIGs behind the lead airplanes that Jack and Jocko had just fired upon.

I began to get radar contacts near the orbit point and locked onto one of the targets. I selected my Television Camera System, TCS, and an A-6 Intruder image popped into view. It was heading toward me and most likely to the KC-10 tanker. Evidently, Jack had sent his bombers back when he got the vector from Dragon.

"On my nose for twenty-two," said Chain.

"Splash two horses!" Jack shrieked over the radio.

"What?" I frowned into my oxygen mask. "Did they shoot down two MIGs with the Phoenix?"

"Must have," said Greasy.

"Fox one!" It was Headley.

Seconds later, we heard Headley's excited voice, "Splash one horse!"

"Splash another horse." It was Jack!

I couldn't believe what I was hearing. Jack and Jocko had shot down three MIGs, and Headley and Chain had shot down a fourth.

"Dakota, from Dragon."

"Go Dragon," said Jocko.

"We, uh, heard most of that, but can you say status?"

"Affirmative. We splashed four horses and have available ordnance for vectors. Attack group remains up for full tasking, but we need Texaco." Jocko's voice exuded confidence and pride.

"Roger, that," replied the Dragon controller. "Vector 160 for forty-five to Texaco."

I found the two Tomcats with my radar and tracked them as they flew past us toward the tanker. We orbited for the rest of our mission time but never got any vector. I felt dejected as we headed south, the adrenalin-high fading to the realization that any opportunity to bag a MIG was gone. The MIGs that Jack's section shot down were most likely only a probe. I wasn't any kind of Mideast expert but didn't believe Saddam would entertain a wide-scale aerial battle over Saudi Arabia.

We flew back to *Ike* and entered high holding, and as we circled the ship, I couldn't keep my dislike for what happened out of my mind. I was very happy for Jocko, Headley, and Chain. I imagined they were right now in their ready room, explaining their victories to their shipmates. But the idea of Jack Grant emerging as some kind of hero made me want to vomit. Somehow, Jocko had coached him, and now we would all be cursed by Jack's ascendance to superhero. I shook my head as I thought of it.

Soon we were debriefing in CVIC, the ship's intelligence spaces. I learned that Jack and Jocko had killed two MIG-23s with a single Phoenix shot and that they had then killed the third MIG with the gun! Talk about the alpha and omega of aerial warfare! Headley and Chain had gotten a fourth MIG with a Sparrow shot, so the two Tomcats had acquitted themselves quite nicely.

"Is there a tape we can see?" I smiled at the ensign debriefing me.

"No," he frowned and shook his head. "The machine malfunctioned, or the RIO forgot to turn it on."

I shook my head. "Jocko Barnes was the RIO. There is no way in the world he would forget to turn it on."

"Well, sir, that is all I know." The ensign shrugged and returned to his pile of papers.

I left CVIC, but instead of heading back to my ready room, I moved toward Jack's. I knew he and his crew would be celebrating, and it was only proper that I congratulate him. I imagined it would be a little like what you see after the Super Bowl when the winning team is in their locker room, the majesty of their work just sinking in and the heroic exploits hashed and rehashed by well-wishers and sportswriters. There wouldn't be any champagne, though. But I dreaded what I had to do, and I knew that was due to my ego. I was the skipper of the Pukin' Dogs, and Jack was the skipper of the Ghostriders, and when you got down to it, we were competitors as much as we were shipmates. Plus, I loathed him. So, offering congratulations was the last thing I wanted to do.

The sounds of excited voices echoed through the passageways, and I could see the excitement in the faces of the sailors as they stood to the side so I could pass. I felt their excitement, too, and cursed myself for my ego. This generation deserved to score in combat also.

I was one of the few Vietnam veterans, so most of the crew had no actual battle and victory memory. Most had been on peacetime cruises, and this deployment had been just that. It had been a summer's dream as we strolled the streets of southern France, climbed the hills of Naples, placed bits of paper in the Wailing Wall, and eaten ice cream in Palma de Mallorca. But, I think, in the back of our minds, we knew that such was not the reason we were there. *Ike* was a warship, and we were in the Mediterranean for a reason beyond personal enjoyment. Unfortunately, the collapse of the Soviet Union confused all of that, and Libya's occasional rowdiness was a Godsend in a way. It gave us somebody to fight. So, when we received the order to steam to the Red Sea in response to Saddam's Kuwait invasion, the crew was excited and expectant! Despite the fact we were on the verge of going home, the turn back west was a morale boost because it gave us a reason to be again. Who knows, it might even provide us with something to brag about when we got back home.

So, the Tomcats' shootdown was a bit of salve to a wound, and when I walked into the Ghostrider ready room, the joy and pride were overflowing! Jack was at the front of the room, surrounded by his officers and chief petty officers, and other well-wishers from the ship and squadrons.

"Had a great visit with the admiral," he said. "CAG and I even presented him with the ejector pin from our phoenix!"

As the cheers went up, I turned to a young officer who had Brad on his name tag. "Brad, where's Jocko?"

"Jocko went back out." The young man smiled.

"What? What do you mean?"

"The skipper had him hot switch into one of our jets launching on the next event."

"Why would he do that?"

"Beats me. Somebody said the skipper wanted Jocko out there because he had experienced the battlespace." Brad shrugged and turned back to the room.

I thought that was odd, but much of what Jack Grant did was strange, so I shrugged and edged my way forward.

"Congratulations, skipper." I held out my hand and smiled. "Can't wait to hear the story about your kills. You make all of us proud."

Jack frowned for a second, like he didn't believe me, then shook my hand. "Thanks." Then he turned away.

I stood a moment, then shrugged and went to my ready room and watched the aircrew brief for their events. Everybody was excited, especially when the duty officer issued them their sidearms. It was the first time any of them had ever flown in combat, and it reminded me of myself, fifteen years ago.

I watched for a while, then went to my stateroom. I clicked on the light and took a seat at my desk and looked at Gaby. I had a photo of her on my desk, and the first thing I did when I entered, and the last thing I did when I left was to look at her. And every time I did, I felt truly blessed and lucky. And I always remembered the words of Colonel Thomas, the intelligence officer at Stuttgart, who told me, "If you get married to or have any relationship with Gabrielle Shaffer, you can forget squadron command." He had told me that in a frantic phone call the morning of our wedding. I was standing in our living room at the farm in Militia Springs, and I thanked him and hung up, and drove to the church in dad's new Ford 150. Raoul, Jimmy, and Paul had taken the Triumph for the obligatory tying of boots and tin cans to my bumper. I read that tradition came from Old England when people threw a shoe at the wedding carriage for good luck. Wow! Got to love the Brits for goofiness. Anyway, today's litigious society leads us to tie a shoe or aluminum can to the bumper instead. But I didn't care anything about boots or cans or car bumpers. And I hadn't cared what the colonel had to say either. All I cared about was Gabrielle Shaffer. And before God, I married her for better or worse.

I also had to thank Cotton for my good fortune. Fifteen months ago, he had agreed to take me as his executive officer, his XO, even after finding that I had a problem with my clearance.

"Any idea what the problem is?"

"No," I lied. "I think it is because of my DUI."

I didn't want to tell him anything about Gaby's past. I knew that Cotton would have stood behind me. That she had gone to prison in Germany for smuggling heroin would not have swayed his loyalty to me. But I didn't want him tested, and I didn't want Gaby's history known. Regardless of how great a man Cotton was, he couldn't help but be influenced by such knowledge, and I didn't want Gaby to live under any cloud. I suppose that wasn't fair to Cotton, but that is what I did. That said, every day, I expected Cotton to call me into his office and tell me I had to move on, that he was getting a new XO. And every day, I kept all of this from Gaby. She knew that I had a problem with my clearance, but I told her it was due to the DUI. I also lied to her when I told her that wives were not a part of the clearance process.

Then one morning, I was fixing myself a cup of coffee in the back of the ready room, and Cotton grabbed his cup and whispered, "Got the word that your clearance is good to go." He clicked his cup against mine, and that was that.

THE RED BARON AND THE BLUE DOT

Excitement on the ship remained high as we continued to plan and send interdiction teams into Saudi Arabia. We received the world news via message traffic and read about President Bush and Prime Minister Thatcher and the beginnings of United Nations' deliberations on what to do about Saddam. We read about the mobilization of our forces, and each time I flew, I saw large groups of US Air Force planes heading into Saudi Arabia. Soon intelligence reports began to show that Saddam was not poising for a southward strike but preparing to defend his position. We read that diplomatic efforts were being mounted to convince Saddam to leave Kuwait, and we knew that the time of shooting MIGs was passed. Although our enviable, beautiful, naval first-on-the-scene presence continued with determination, it dwindled into boredom and became the nature of duty at sea; when it wasn't trying to kill you, it was trying to bore you to death.

Independence came over the horizon. She was joyful and new to our Red Sea business but eager to put her stamp on our plans, and soon she was thankless of our first-on-scene value. And in the moment of that passage, we went from heroes, the ones with stories to tell, to those who could only wonder at the exploits of others. And Jack Grant and his coterie became the ones whose exploits we praised and envied. On the trip back home, they received medals for their prowess during a flight deck ceremony, and it was all I could bear to see Jack so honored. How could God allow such a despicable creature to be so successful? Later that afternoon, Jocko Barnes stopped by my stateroom and answered at least part of that angst.

I was writing a letter to Gaby when I heard the knock and smiled when I saw who was there. Jocko and I had developed a friendship, and I think it was partly because I was a RIO like him and partly because I was a senior officer on the ship he could talk to, unlike his commanding officer, Jack.

I welcomed him in, but as he sat, I noticed his unease.

"What's up?"

Jocko frowned and took a deep breath. He fumbled around for a moment, then reached inside his helmet bag and pulled out a TCS tape. "Can you play this?"

"It's not porn, is it?"

"Yes, Sir. Two hookers and a donkey."

"What?" I twirled around.

"Just kidding, sir."

"Well, what is it?" I took the tape walked to my TV and slid it into the slot.

The tape whirred for a few seconds, then blinked, and I saw the clear horizon out in front of an F-14.

I looked at Jocko and shrugged.

"Just wait, sir."

Seconds later.

"Dragon, Dakota, say status."

"That's your voice," I said. Jocko nodded.

"Dakota, from Dragon, two groups of suspected horses vectoring south towards you. Ten-mile trail. The lead group now bullseye zero one zero for fifty-five. Hail Mary. Hail Mary."

I stopped the tape. "That's the AWACS giving you the vector. What is this tape?"

"It's the original tape, sir. From the engagement."

"But I thought it didn't record?"

"Just play it, sir, and I'll explain."

I frowned and hit Play.

The tape carried both inner-cockpit and broadcast communications and clearly showed how Jocko had held Jack's hand through the attack on the MIGs. Jocko not only directed the attack, but he also identified the enemy planes, fired the phoenix missile that killed two of them, and coaxed Jack into the correct switch settings for the third kill. The tape showed Jack to be an inept, confused, bumbling pilot.

"So, what gives, Jocko? If this is the real tape, and it obviously is, why didn't you play it?"

"Sir, on the way home, after we shot the MIGs, the skipper was musing over his performance. I could tell it bothered him. I could tell he knew how he would sound once someone played the tape. So, when he came up with the idea of sending me out again and doing the post-flight debrief himself, I knew he was up to something. Once we landed, the plane captain gave me the tape, and

I put it in my helmet bag. When the skipper asked for it, I gave him an empty copy. I always carry one."

"Well, how do you know he didn't play your blank tape? What if he was straightforward all along?"

"See this blue dot?" Jocko pointed to the spine of his tape. I nodded.

"I mark all my tapes that way. The blank tape I gave the skipper was marked with a blue dot."

"So," I shrugged.

"So, when the skipper told me my tape didn't record, he handed it back to me. But it didn't have my blue dot."

"That means Jack destroyed your blank tape, thinking it was the original and handed you another blank."

"Exactly." Jocko nodded.

"Whew!" I shook my head and slumped into my chair. Jocko sat down too and looked at me. "What should I do?"

I shook my head and took a breath. Christ, what a mess. I sighed as I stared at Jocko. "Well, the tape swapping is confusing and impossible to prove, so all you can do now is embarrass your skipper and make yourself look like some kind of conniving fool. I mean, if you know Jack Grant, what you did makes total sense, but if you don't, then it gets pretty bizarre."

"Yeah." Jocko nodded and sighed. "That's what I thought."

"I suggest you make a copy for yourself and give the other one to CAG."

"CAG? Why?"

"Because he is most likely going to rank Jack as the number one skipper out of this. That will set Jack up for a powerful future. Who knows, there may be a time when CAG feels he has to take ownership of the result." I hesitated to say more. I would be a poor leader to badmouth Jack to his junior.

Jocko nodded and stood, and I felt sorry for him. He was the undisputed hero of a fantastic navy story but could not take credit for it. Even in secret, he couldn't take the credit with his friends.

Jack's version of events cast him as a wizard of the air, the Red Baron of our time. The admiral even insisted Jack's callsign become Phoenix, and the mingling of the mythical bird with the famous missile by the same name further burnished his luster. The country, thirsting for a new hero, reached for him, and as *Ike* approached Bermuda, the navy flew Jack home to meet the press.

Jocko went home too.

THE MOTHER OF ALL BATTLES

An end-of-cruise fly-in is an emotional event and is profoundly tender when the typical military stoicism breaks down, and the pull of human passion trumps straight backs in green sage. Bending to pick up your child, for instance.

The rush of the children comes while you are still climbing out of the plane, engines winding down, fresh breath mint in place. They pinwheel forward, headlong and with arms out, screaming the most beautiful word in the world. You haven't heard the word in so many months, a name that you forgot how much you loved, a name that separates you from what you were before.

"DADDY!"

"DADDY!"

The little ones get there first. The kids who don't care that they look like kids, and Dad reaches to them and pulls them up into his arms, smelling Johnson and Johnson baby shampoo and cereal, and he hugs them as the older ones approach. They are the ones in their teens, the ones with the sideways eyes and the tentative steps and the awkward lurches. They are the ones who bend at the waist when they hold you until they realize it is OK to hug your dad. And you hug them back and tell them the words that are often too hard to say to children their age, and worse, maybe the words you won't say again until the next time you come home from being long gone.

"I love you."

And you wear your sunglasses. There is no crying in naval aviation.

It all works until you see her, of course.

She waits behind the children.

She released them because she couldn't hold them back, and she released them because she wanted them to break the veil of separation that had developed over the many months. You see, people in love don't separate and then just come back together. The children were the opening act because she wanted a moment, this

288

moment. The one when you walk up to her, and she has you alone. Even in the middle of all of the shouts and joy, even in the middle of the jet engines winding down their howl, and when the children's hands are now dropped to your side, there is a time when your eyes are hers, and hers are yours, and you are alone. Nothing else matters. And I think it is that moment that most husbands dream of when they think of coming home.

Gaby met me at our fly-in. We had no children. But she did have a bump. A bump that we created when she met me in Cannes back in June. And we did have that moment, the one she wanted and the one of my dreams. We had that moment as our eyes searched, then found each other. I smiled as I walked toward her, savoring my march, and walking it in the way I had imagined. I have heard that half of coming home is being there, but the other half is the anticipation of being there.

So, I walked slowly.

And then she was in my arms, and I kissed her, but it was beautiful and brief and not the thing of movies or television. It was not a kiss of passion because the passion was just for us. Love is not for onlookers. I know this might be hard to understand. Movies and television have groomed us to believe that when couples, long apart, next meet, they at once fall into some grand carnal reunion. Rich, open kisses practically dripping fill the camera, followed by the ripping of shirts, bras, and the like. Rutting on some kind of table, like the kitchen table, seems an in-vogue requirement.

But that's not the way it is.

You see, when you have been apart for so long, you don't just go at it. You build into each other. So, I hugged Gaby and drank in the perfume, and entered the warmth, feeling a renewed appreciation for all of the men who had done this before me and all of the families who had waited for them.

We drove home in the Triumph, and that drive held the wonderfully awkward feeling of a first date, and I was so thankful for that unexpected blessing. And as we drove, my too loud and overly animated voice and gestures were only my insistence on quickly rebuilding what we were, and it was like no other drive home, no other experience that I had ever had. And the wonderment of it was what Raoul would say if he were there. "Hell, Weenie, you don't even have that babe in the rack yet."

As we drove, part of Gaby's talk was to assure me that the officers' wives club had planned for a grand homecoming when the rest of our squadron, the enlisted men, came into port the following day. She knew the taking care of them was a priority for me, and I could tell she wanted me to approve of her plans. And the fact that she prioritized that over her personal feelings, hopes, and concerns made me love her even more.

As soon as I got home, I took a shower to get rid of the smell of "the ship" as Gaby called it while she made lunch and as we ate a sandwich we explored for a while, ensuring that each was the same, that we were still OK and that we were still who we had remembered. Later on, strangers no longer, we did go to bed. And that is all I will say about that.

Gaby is only twenty-seven, and I am forty-two, and many of the wives of the senior officers and enlisted men are older than she. It could have been a problem since the skipper's wife is so instrumental to morale, and I initially suspected from bits of conversation that some older wives were skeptical of her. At least in the beginning. But Gaby has a way of persuasion, and I think her accent helps. Strangely, Americans tend to respect the slight lilt of a European voice, and Gaby's delicate z or s instead of th was charming. It gave her an air of mystery that she detected…and cultivated. She was helped by a rich family heritage from Germany that prioritized the proper way to meet, greet, dine, and remember. I think her hand-written notes of thanks were… I don't know, timeless and more impactful because of their unexpected charm.

The squadron went into a stand-down period, and I took leave so Gaby and I could return to Militia Springs and see the family. Paul, Molly, and Kate met us at the airport, and it was great to see them again. Paul is my age, but Molly is now thirty-seven, and Kate is sixteen! I lingered for a moment as I hugged Kate, remembering the days before she was born and when our family had an intense conversation about abortion. I think that discussion united us more than tore us apart, and I know that even my beloved Grandpa Two Bears respected the strong opinions around the table, even if he didn't share all of the sentiment.

The nature of Kate's coming into this world, rape at the hands of now-dead Caleb Hodges, was never spoken of, and I am not even sure if she was aware of her beginnings. I do know that my great friend, Paul, doted on her as if he were her biological father, and I do know that Molly is infinitely happy. Paul had a bandage on his left arm and carried it gingerly, and as I loaded our bags into the trunk, I asked him what happened.

"Tell you later," he said.

We bundled into the Fairlane and had no sooner than started when Molly turned to Gaby and asked, "How are you doing?"

Women's eyes have a connection, and I knew Molly was asking about Gaby's pregnancy. We talked about babies all the way home, and once there, Mom told the story of how Kate had taken all her clothes off and put them in a bucket of water. It was laundry day, and Kate had seen her mom and grandma washing the clothes, so she decided to do the same.

"She ran all over the farm," said Mom. "I was glad we didn't live in town."

Mom and Dad looked good in their sixties, and the farm was as grand and wonderful as I remembered. And that same melancholy fell over me as we drove through the woods and around the square toward home. Militia Springs called to me. And as I looked out the window, I supposed it always would.

After supper, Paul summoned me for a walk, so we took a stroll towards the barn. I figured he would catch me up on what was happening to include what happened to his arm.

We stopped at the edge of the pond, and he smiled at me, then glanced at his bandaged arm. "Got shot."

"What?"

"Got shot the other day by one of the Hodges boys."

"The Sons of Galilee Hodges?"

"Yep." Paul nodded.

"But why?" I was stunned.

"I'll get to that," he said. Paul sat on the pond bank, and I followed suit. He squinted across the pasture. "I was looking for strays on the thirty acres that abuts their place. You know Daisy is the lead cow, and the rest follow her to the barn for milking, but some of the young ones get side-tracked. It's good grass over there."

I nodded and looked at Paul's arm. The bandage covered his bicep.

"So, I was looking for them, but as I came through the woods, I saw a couple of men walking through the pasture with shotguns. I thought it odd because it wasn't bird season or anything. Besides, we have it marked for no trespassing. As I came down the ridge and got closer, I saw it was Levi and Gideon Hodges. About that time, Levi raised his gun and shot a cow!"

"You're kidding? Why?"

"Well, it was a milk cow, so I doubt if he shot in self-defense."

"But why?"

"Because it was a Kleegan cow, and he was from the Sons of Galilee. Anyway, I yelled, and Gideon jerked his gun and fired at me. I was behind a tree, so he mostly missed except for a few pellets in my arm."

"Christ!"

What in hell was going on?

"So, I raised my shotgun. I always carry it anytime I am near the Sons of Galilee land and fired a couple of rounds in their direction. The two started running, so I followed them out of the trees. They were pretty far away, so I pointed the barrel up for some trajectory and fired a couple more shells. Levi stumbled; I was pretty sure I got some buckshot into him. I made sure the cow was dead and not suffering, then came home and called the sheriff."

"What did the sheriff do?"

"Came out and took a report. Asked me if I was pressing charges, and I said I was, for killing a cow and attempted murder. I went into town the next day and saw Dory Jenkins. Remember him? Skinny guy with red hair. He's a lawyer now; in fact, he is the Douglas County prosecuting attorney."

"Really?"

"No kidding. I think he is making up for all the times he got bullied in high school."

"What did he say?"

"Said, the Hodges were already in the office that morning and wanted to file an attempted manslaughter charge against me. Said I shot Levi Hodges in the back."

"Are you kidding?"

"Wish I was. Dory told me the Hodges admitted trespassing, but they were looking for a coyote that had gotten into their chickens and shot the cow by mistake."

"How can you mistake a cow for a coyote?"

"They said the cow was in the shadows. They said that when I yelled, it spooked Gideon, and he is the one that fired at me. Then they tried to run away, but I shot Levi in the back."

"I can't believe this."

"I couldn't either, but that is what Dory told me, and he suggested I not press charges. Said he thought the Hodges would drop theirs if I dropped mine."

"What's next?"

"I dropped my charges. I think the fact they know I won't hesitate to shoot might keep them away. Besides, the Sons of

Galilee are coming apart, Weenie. Hell, they had eighty folks out there at one time, but now they only have a handful of Hodges left."

"What caused all of that?"

"I hear it started when one of the wives tried to back out of the commune. Her husband had signed their property over to the Sons, but she never did. So, she wanted her money and wanted out, and that started the dominos to fall. Now they have all kinds of lawsuits being filed and charges of mistreating children with cattle prods and all kinds of crap."

I shook my head again. "I thought our problems with the Sons of Galilee were over. And what do you mean about always carrying a gun?"

"The Hodges clan never thought Caleb's death was an accident."

It had been sixteen years since Caleb Hodges had died, but Paul's story reminded me of my suspicions. My suspicions that Caleb had been shot by someone and not killed by accident. I looked at Paul, "What do you think?"

"Don't know." Paul shrugged and picked up a pebble. He examined it a moment, then tossed it down the bank. "I do know Caleb had a pint with him most of the time. Some homemade mash they made with corn and sugar. He drunk it hard, too, so I can see him slipping and shooting himself out here."

I nodded as Paul chuckled. "But, given the Kleegan's desire to protect their own, any one of you could have done it. Grandpa Two Bears killed men in the war; your dad and mom would do anything to protect Molly." Paul looked at me. "Hell, you could have done it."

"I was in California that weekend."

"Easy enough to take the red-eye to Saint Louis Friday night and drive a rental down here. Do the deed and be back home no later than Sunday."

I looked at Paul, trying to see if he was serious or not. His eyes kept their secret.

I nodded and held his gaze. "And you, what about you? You were in love with Molly. You knew what was going on. You could have shot Caleb."

Paul looked at me and grinned. "I guess I have proven I'm up to it."

I nodded again and looked down at the house. "Why do you carry the gun? When you are near Kleegan land. I mean, I can see doing it now, but what prompted you before?"

"A couple of things, I guess. Found a copperhead in the mailbox. It would have bitten me if I had put my hand in there."

"What?" I glanced at Paul and frowned.

"Yep, and there is no way that thing got in there by itself. Also found a salt block that had been poisoned. Wouldn't have known except there was a dead deer by it."

"Any of the cows get to it?"

"No, I had just put it out the week before, and they were still on the south pasture."

"But why now? Why the problem with the Hodges now? Caleb died a long time ago."

"I think it is probably frustration," said Paul. "I mean, they never really made a go of their farm. They milk a few cows, but they don't have any hayfield, so they probably break even there. Most of their place is sharp hills. Too hard to farm and impractical to log. They made most of their money by hiring out as laborers. I think Levi and Gideon resent us for some reason. I mean, our thirty-acre plot next to their place is perfect for hay. We got nearly 4000 bales off it last year. Got nearly sixty dollars a bale, too. The Hodges could have used that to feed their cows."

"So, you think your shooting them the other day will hold them off? They won't do anything to hurt the family?"

"They aren't the ruthless and evil Hodges of the past. The clan leader, Elmer, is dead, and he was the rottenest of them all. Malachi and Joshua, the two oldest boys, also passed away. Levi and Gideon aren't cut from that same cloth. I think my buckshot will help keep them away too."

"Well, let's hope so."

"Besides, I hear the Sons are auctioning off their farm next month, all one hundred eighty acres." Paul picked up a rock and chucked it down the side of the pond bank.

"That so?"

"Yep, and I aim to buy it."

"Really?"

"Talked with Molly and your dad and mom, and they like the idea. I think I can work some milk cows on it. Besides, Grandpa Two Bears left quite a bit of money to the farm, enough to cover most of the cost."

"That sounds fantastic," I said.

"Enough for you when you move back someday." Paul looked at me, but he didn't laugh.

"Someday." I didn't laugh either.

I suppose Gaby and I could have stayed forever, but I soon got the itch to get back to my squadron, and we headed back to Virginia.

In the meantime, the situation in the middle east continued to develop. We had no idea what lay in front of us, only that President Bush was building a grand coalition centered around United Nations' resolutions. And while he developed that team and staked out the moral high ground for possible combat actions, Saddam warned of the "mother of all battles" should we invade.

CNN developed a twenty-four-hour news cycle that educated its listeners on the coalition build-up. We knew that Saddam, broke from his eight-year war with Iran, had invaded Kuwait for the oil reserves. He also claimed Kuwait as a nineteenth province, based upon old assertions of ownership.

Those of us who were not yet in the theater patiently worked through our inter-deployment training cycles with the idea of joining should the war last long enough. And each day, we saw and heard the news of forces and supplies being transported into Saudi Arabia in preparation for the fight.

Jack Grant had his change-of-command in early January, and Gaby and I attended. Despite my disdain for Jack, I knew it was the right thing to do. Besides, it allowed us to see Grace again. Gaby had grown close to Grace, a fact that at first surprised me. But as I watched the two of them together, I could see the chemistry at work. It was Gaby who told me Grace's struggles with depression and anxiety had gotten more severe, and it bothered us that Jack's next assignment, commanding officer of TOPGUN, would take Grace to San Diego. She would be far from her circle of support.

On January 16, 1991, the air war began. We saw the round-the-clock bombing of Iraqi targets. It didn't take long to expose the weakness in navy strike tactics versus the air force. You see, navy strike tactics were based upon surprise attacks, often one-time events flown from a carrier working alone. When carriers entered the Med, for instance, the arriving carrier air wing received top-secret target folders from the ship it was relieving. These folders held targets of interest to national defense, and the new airwing re-planned the targets using any new weapons, tactics, and capabilities it had. Our tactics were designed to avoid the Soviet Integrated Air Defenses of our potential enemies, specifically to fly at low altitude to the target area, pop-up to the delivery altitude, find the target, then release the ordinance before escaping. This low altitude philosophy was a divergence from our higher altitude, large-package

Alpha strikes from the Vietnam days, and in part were patterned after successes the Israelis had with their small, surgical actions against their enemies. Unfortunately, such tactics do not enhance the use of precision-guided weapons.

On the other hand, the air force used high altitude delivery tactics to optimize the value of these precision weapons, and it didn't take long for us to realize they were right. It seems that every Iraqi and his dog had some kind of gun, and as the navy roared by at palm tree level, every one of them was shooting at us! So, our low-level attack profiles were met with much resistance. By the end of the first week, we were up high with the air force. The problem was, we didn't have as many precision weapons, and we had virtually no recording equipment. Our hits were not seen on television every night.

I was amazed at how the air force had taken their dismal performance during El Dorado Canyon and learned from it and were now masters at delivering precision ordnance. Not only did they have the systems to deliver the weapons, but they also had the training and the cameras to record their efforts, and night after night, we watched them. Many referred to it as "the video-game war", but to me, it was no game. It was a great event, and I was not a part of it, and it frustrated me much. The air force engaged in the air war more successfully than the navy too. Their F-15 Eagles were in a better position to intercept what MIGs Saddam sent our way, and so it was a frustrating time for the navy's Tomcat community. But as I watched the video of air force excellence, what I saw underscored my belief that we should develop the Tomcat's inherent capabilities as a bomber.

The original design for the F-14 had included air-to-ground ordnance capabilities, but budgetary constraints forced the navy to abandon that and focus on air-to-air warfare. However, the speed of the Tomcat, its long-range and stable platform made it an ideal bomber.

So, while my squadron was preparing to go to war, I introduced a modest air-to-ground training syllabus that included ground classroom instruction and some aerial training using the software we already had in the airplane.

Meanwhile, the coalition bombed and bombed Iraq, and after thirty-eight days, we pushed the ground force forward. One hundred hours later, Saddam pulled out of Kuwait. Many wanted the coalition to then invade Iraq, but that action was beyond what the UN-authorized. Besides, we had no idea how fiercely the Iraqis would defend their homeland and didn't want to find out with the loss of coalition lives.

THE MOTHER OF ALL HOOKS

TAILHOOK began in 1956 as a casual meeting of navy and marine corps aviators to tell sea stories and carouse and drink. It took place at Rosarito Beach, fifty minutes south of San Diego, in Mexico. But as the event grew and as the logistical challenges of convening across the border became more complex, the event, now the TAILHOOK Convention, moved to San Diego. In 1968, the convention moved to Las Vegas.

In 1991, we were all very excited about the prospect of this year's convention. It was headlined as The Mother of All Hooks, a play on Saddam's warning to us about his Mother of All Battles should we invade. Over 4000 aviators were attending, and the navy even supplied airlift to take East Coast squadrons to Las Vegas!

Although all of my squadron aviators were going to attend, I decided that we would not have a hospitality suite this year. Many squadrons had such suites, which were places for the men to meet and organize and, of course, to drink. TOPGUN probably had the most famous suite where they gave out rising sun-emblazoned headbands to anyone who could drink ten kamikaze shots.

The suites were found along a corridor on the third floor of the Las Vegas Hilton's east wing and had become a Saturday night focal point of one-upmanship on who could produce the most outrageous behavior. I know that my opinion on this was suspect since I didn't drink anymore, and teetotalers like me were considered people who had burned up all their candles and now didn't like cake. But I have to say that I didn't ever go for loud, violent, indecent, stupid stuff, even in my heaviest drinking days. Well, stupid stuff is OK. Funny, stupid stuff is always OK. But not the rest. Getting hooted up and watching a stripper's titties was about my limit, as long as she didn't mind and nobody pawed at her. And she got paid, of course. Well, and Gaby didn't know.

I also didn't want a suite because I didn't want to acknowledge something that I didn't dare to address with my seniors: that we were out of control. The last two times I had attended Hook, the third floor had become disgusting, and I think many of us were turned off by the behavior. But none of us was brave enough to stop it. I read a story once that proclaimed Genghis Kahn didn't really like war. He just liked to ride around on horses. But his men wanted war, and they liked fermented goat's milk, and we all know how that turned out.

The airlift got us to Las Vegas on Friday afternoon just in time for a giant cocktail party and time to get together with guys we hadn't seen since last year. I always made a point to look for Raoul, and he and Cotton and I would stay together for the weekend. But this year, he was on a cruise with his squadron. I did see Cotton, though, and we did spend the evening together. He was through with his nuclear training and on his way to command of a logistics ship. The navy gave this deep draft training to aviators in the nuclear program to have some ship handling experience should they be selected for a carrier. We had dinner in the hotel and caught up on all the things that had happened. Cotton's new ship was in San Diego, and he could only stay that one night, so I bade him farewell and hit the sack.

I awoke early with the blessing of no hangover nor struggle for recollection and took the elevator to the convention floor. It was already filling with aviators and industry representatives, many with the red-eyes and raspy late-night celebration voice. The schedule was packed with all manner of presentations, ranging from what we did in the war to what technology was coming down the road for the next one to what kind of manning problems we faced. I attended all of them but was most interested in the afternoon's agenda, especially the flag panel.

The flag panel was a group of six or seven naval aviation admirals and usually one marine corps general, and anyone in the audience could ask them anything. It was a time for young officers to vent if they had the balls and for the flags to explain if they had the patience. The senior-most admiral on the panel was the head of naval aviation, a three-star. And the three-star was none other than my old boss, Vice Admiral Bass, who had somehow duped enough people into succeeding. I love the navy. I do. But sometimes, when I see successful officers like Bass and Jack Grant, I wonder about us.

By two in the afternoon, officers began filling the auditorium chairs, and already-rowdy young aviators queued before the beer kegs that lined the walls. Animated, loud, excited with their red, plastic cups and anticipation of the possibilities of controversy as juniors questioned seniors. The modern-day version of Indians counting coup on their enemy. I saw a couple of gray-faced kamikaze head-banders, but they were mostly quiet and in line for the dog's little hair. Maybe a coat of it.

A navy captain served as the moderator, and after a quick introduction of panel members, Vice Admiral Bass took the mic. Despite my deep reservations about the man, I couldn't help but feel a surge of emotion as the 1500 or so aviators around me roared their approval. Admiral Bass beamed, and the chants echoed off the walls.

"Buzz! Buzz! Buzz!"

Admiral Bass slowly paced the dais, smiling, winking, drinking in the adulation. His electric grin and popping dark eyes conveyed an understanding of total control. These were his people, and he was their undisputed leader. And for a moment, my mind paused as uncomfortable thoughts tumbled…how can he be wrong? With all of this positive energy coming to him, how can he not be great, even heroic? Maybe I misjudged him somehow. Perhaps our problems were all my doing. But in that part of a second, when the ship of your mind rights itself and sets the proper course after doubts, I remembered who he was…is. I remembered the ego, the callousness, the adultery, the selfishness. I remembered the unbelievable smallness of him. So, I leaned back in my seat and smiled.

For the next thirty or forty minutes, junior officers popped up and asked questions. They were selfish for the most part and dealt with why they weren't getting enough flight hours, enough pay, and how the airlines were so much better than the navy. A real point of contention was why aviators had to do suck jobs like catapult officer instead of flying. I took exception at that, but my resentment was quiet, and I sulked a bit in my seat. A huge cheer went to a guy that complained that there weren't enough auto-dog ice cream machines onboard carriers. After each question, Admiral Bass picked the proper admiral to answer, and each dutifully tried to explain the reasons for the perceived shortfall of happiness. But each time, Admiral Bass interrupted and grinned at the questioner.

"Hey, good question, we can work on that for you."

Of course, the crowd shouted approval while the officer who had asked the question pumped his fist, and the now red-faced junior admiral slunk into his seat.

I was preparing to leave when Admiral Bass looked across the room and said, "Whatcha got, doll?"

Everyone looked to whose hand was up, and I did too. And there at the edge of the crowd, I saw Missy Sanders. Her cheeks reddened, and I knew that the "doll" remark from Bass had grated.

"Sir."

Hisses and hoots erupted from the crowd, but Admiral Bass interrupted them. He smiled and rolled his eyes. "Hey, gents, let the lady speak."

Missy took a deep breath and straightened. "Sir, previous speakers today have stated naval aviation is experiencing difficulty recruiting and that retention is also a challenge. Given that half of today's college graduates are women, have you given any thought to recruiting them more aggressively?"

Admiral Bass looked at her and took a deep breath. He frowned as in deep thought and slowly nodded.

"No."

The crowd went wild, and I saw Missy's hand fly to her mouth. It was a defensive move, a protection against what had happened. It reminded me of that day long ago when Jack Grant had tricked Missy into thinking Nolen Roundtree was interested in her. Missy had been humiliated and hurt and that is what I saw now. She lowered her hand and looked around the room and, I could see she was seeking support. Surely in this room full of fellow naval aviators, comrades-in-arms she had a friend. I saw her eyes fall when she realized she had none. I stood to move toward her.

"Any other questions?" Bass beamed broadly and winked at the crowd.

Others were standing and I lost sight of Missy, but I heard her clear her throat.

"Sir, have you given any more thought about letting women go to sea? I promise we women will gladly take the catapult officer jobs."

I weaved my way towards Missy. As I moved, I heard Admiral Bass.

"Well, we just won a war with only men. I suspect we can win the next one with only men."

Everybody not already standing jumped to their feet and screamed. Red cups flew.

"ONLY MEN! ONLY MEN! ONLY MEN!"

I lost sight of Missy again. I waded through the crowd, slipping in between and around my fellow aviators--Missy's fellow aviators.

But when I got to the spot where she had stood, she was gone. I hurried out into the passageway and then along the corridors, but I couldn't see her. I went to the front desk to see if they had the room number for a Commander Sanders, Melissa Sanders. They did not.

Saturday evening, I attended the banquet and saw my good friend and XO of TOPGUN, Commander Steve Collingwood, accept an award on behalf of Jack Grant. Jack had to accompany Grace to her father's funeral in Norfolk but was still recognized for his three MIG kills in Iraq. I looked for Jocko Barnes, but he wasn't there. I looked for Missy, too, but she wasn't at the banquet either and I was sad. Missy needed me.

Since most junior officers blow off the banquet, I sat at a table of fellow commanding officers, several of whom had been in the Gulf War. And as they chattered away, I fell into a funk. It was at times like this that I wished I could have been there. There in the gulf. And my desire was not so much to make war on somebody but to have been a participant in a great victory. I remembered watching the war unfold on television and how excited Gaby had been. She was so proud that somebody was doing something about "that Saddam." But she had noticed my mood and had asked me, "What's wrong, Schatz?" Schatz is the German word for sweetheart.

I shrugged her off, but she persisted, so I told her.

"The navy is timeless," I said. "It will last forever. And that is because the navy is a part of the great events in our history. There are battles, and there are people whose memory will last forever. And I think all of us want to be in some great event to be a part of that timelessness. I know that I do."

"Wasn't Vietnam a great event?"

I looked at her and smiled. "At the time, it seemed to be. In the beginning. By the time I got there, it was just something we had to do."

"And was the Gulf war this great event? This bid for timelessness?"

I sighed and looked at the television. Another bomb went off, and the screen brightened with the detonation. "For now, it is. For me, it may be the only one."

I guess what I dreaded was to be just another old guy with a grizzled beard and rheumy eyes and a head full of memories but no story to tell. Nobody was going to ask me, "What did you do in the war?" And if they did, all I could say was, "I watched."

Our Chief of Naval Operations, Admiral Kelso, was the guest speaker at the banquet. Like all four stars, he talked about things that only very senior officers are interested in. By 0930, I had eaten my dried chicken breast and cold mixed vegetables and was ready to go.

The third-floor shenanigans were in full swing when I walked into the east wing at 1000. A young officer with a kamikaze headband stood at the door with a handful of TOPGUN decals. All squadrons had them, we called them Zaps, and they were plastic with a sticky back. The idea was to mark your passage, something akin to what male dogs do, I guess, and every pilot's lounge across America is filled with them. But at TAILHOOK, they were to be affixed to females, and the third floor was referred to as "the gauntlet."

I moseyed around for a bit, wishing that I could drink like the rest of them but glad that I didn't. My sobriety gave me a particular position of advantage, an observation post over the carnage of the battlefield. I could tell this would be the Mother of All Goofiness, so I entered the passageway to leave.

At that moment, I saw Missy. It was early September, but she was wearing a summer dress, the kind that seems to make women feel free and makes you happy that they are. My eyes found hers, and I smiled just in time to see a man get on his knees and stick his hand up into Missy's crotch. She squirmed and screamed and kicked at him. Then she bit the hand of another man who was grabbing at her breast. I rushed down the passageway, and as the man she had bitten drew back to hit her, I grabbed him.

"LEAVE HER ALONE!" I pushed him away then kneed the other man away from her crotch. Missy quickly kicked him in the face, and he fell over with a howl. She kicked him again.

The man I pushed was a junior officer, and he screamed, "YOU JUST WANT HER FOR YOURSELF! YOU JUST WANT TO FUCK HER!"

He drew back his hand to swing, and the memory of Caleb Hodges flashed in my mind. The memory of the man who had raped my little sister flashed in my mind. The memory of my fist pasting his face flashed in my mind, and I threw everything I had at that junior officer's face.

My fist cracked into his nose, and he dropped like a sack of cement just as a horde of drunken officers swarmed me. It was a melee, and at one point, Missy and I were back-to-back kicking and swinging, and then I heard, "WHAT THE FUCK IS GOING ON HERE?"

WHAT THE FUCK IS GOING ON?" It was Vice Admiral Bass. He stepped through the crowd until we were practically nose-to-nose. He stared at my face but didn't seem to recognize me and glanced at Missy. He looked back at me.

"You shouldn't have brought her here. She isn't welcome."

I just looked at him, hating him with a renewed vigor.

"And you aren't either. Get out."

The crowd in the passageway cheered, and I grabbed Missy's hand, and we walked through the gauntlet together.

I held my arm around Missy's shoulder and clutched her tight as we waded through the angry faces. Nobody touched us, but they screamed a lot and threw beer. By the time we got out of the corridor, we were soaked.

I kept my arm around Missy as we crossed to the elevators. "Are you staying here? I looked for you this afternoon?"

Missy had her head down and shook it.

"OK, that's OK. Do you want to go to my room?"

"I just want to get out of here." She looked at me through the tears. "Could you get me a cab?"

"Sure. Sure, if that is what you want. But are you sure you want to be alone? At least let me accompany you to your hotel."

"I think." Missy looked at me. "I think alone is exactly what I want to be right now."

I looked at her and nodded. The elevator hit the ground floor, and we walked through the foyer to the street. I hailed a cab and watched as Missy got in. But as the door closed I hurried to the other side and jumped in too. Missy gave her address, a hotel at the other end of the strip, and we drove away.

I glanced at Missy, but she stared out the window. I didn't think I deserved to intrude on her thoughts. Besides, I was in shock. I mean, what the hell had just happened? Missy and I were physically attacked by our own colleagues! Attacked to the point we had to fight to get away from them! I shook my head in the darkness and watched the neon flash by. And the gaiety of all those lights and sounds made the inside of our cab even darker. They pushed our thoughts inward where we alone had to manage our feelings. It was beyond awkward. Awkward is a selfish term, a word for personal embarrassment. But this was beyond that, it was infinite sadness. It was perhaps as intense as the night we drove home after Grandpa Two Bears had died.

I took the cab back to the Hilton, went back to my room and slumped onto the bed and tried to put things in perspective. I knew that the third-floor corridor was an animal house on Saturday night, but it was packed, so what happened in front of one suite could be a different world than what happened in front of another. It was like a big city where crime in one neighborhood was entirely unrelated to what happened in another. But that didn't make me feel any better.

About a month later, the *San Diego Tribune* published a scathing article about Tailhook, to include the fact that women had reported being assaulted. A couple of days later, much of the mainstream media picked up on the story, and then the Senate Armed Services Committee engaged and directed the navy to investigate.

I could not believe how quickly the world turned on us--on naval aviation. We had been the darlings of the air! Our victory over Libyan MIGs might not have been the thing of legends but it was the first clear victory we had had in decades. The TOPGUN movie placed all naval aviation, the Tomcat community in particular, on a pedestal. We had just won the gulf war! Now, we were all monsters and cretins. Every newspaper article competed to see who could make us look the worst! Politicians who had feted us and stood on our backs as they proclaimed their undying patriotism now attacked us. We were evil, toxic, and worse, male. Bitterness bound us together. We felt betrayed. Betrayed and made the whipping boy for any politically correct axe that needed grinding.

Since all of my aviators attended the event, we were given a questionnaire and told to detail where we were that Tailhook weekend and particularly on Saturday night. We were to list any people we saw, where they were, and what they were doing. It is a pretty common investigative technique to ask for information and then cross-check what multiple people say. So, if you said you went to Saturday evening mass and somebody else said they saw you biting a woman's butt in the Rhino suite, you can bet that would get you the bright light treatment.

My interview was particularly alarming since they seemed to know a lot more about me than I would have guessed. It began in a usual way with questions about my answers to the questionnaire. I had admitted being on the third floor and had written a lengthy piece about what I had seen with Missy. But I had left the identification of her attackers blank because I had no idea who they were.

"You are telling us that you do not recognize the men who assaulted Commander Sanders? None of the photos we showed you are familiar?" My inquisitor was a pinch-faced army colonel aided by a young woman who looked like a charter member of the "cut-your-nuts-off" crowd of angry feminists that hung out at the student union when I was in college.

"That isn't what I said. I recognize many of the faces here," I pointed to the stack of photos. "But these faces are not the ones I saw attack Missy.

"That is just great," snorted the colonel. "You can't place any of these men in the hallway at the time of the attack. Yet, you are an eyewitness to a crime committed against not only a fellow officer but also a special friend, I believe."

"That's right; I know Missy well. She is a friend of mine."

"But not a good enough friend, it seems." The female officer leaned forward and almost smiled.

"What do you expect me to do? Just pick one of these photos, any photo?"

"Yes. In a word, yes," replied the woman.

"We need a face, a name, Commander Kleegan." The colonel stared at me. "That is what we are here for. That is what you are here for."

"Believe me, if I could put a face to the men who pawed Missy, I would."

"You see, I doubt that" said the colonel. "I think you navy flyboys have banded together to protect each other, and you wouldn't give me the name of a pal of yours if he raped your mother."

"Are you sure you are comfortable taking the interview in this direction?" I put my elbows on the table between us and leaned forward. "Are you sure you have the authority to insult me? Because I don't think that you do." It was my turn to glare.

The colonel backed against his chair and blinked. He glanced at his colleague then back to me. They were used to knuckling the junior officers, the ones who were intimidated by colonel's eagles and angry women. The colonel looked at me a moment longer, then glanced at the papers in front of him. He picked one up and took a deep breath.

"You are married to Gabrielle Shaffer?"

"Yes."

"Do you know a Captain Crosby? Charles Crosby?"

"Yes."

What did Cotton have to do with any of this?

"Do you know Mister George Benton?"

"No." I shook my head and frowned.

"Hmmm." The colonel studied the paper some more. "Seems you had an issue with your clearance a year or so ago."

"I had a DUI."

The colonel shot a glance at me, and a slight smile touched his lips. "No, this is tied to your wife. Want to talk about that?"

The female officer leaned forward and smiled. Well, she showed her teeth.

"No." I swallowed again and kept my gaze steady. I had no idea what they wanted or what information they had.

"Appears that your friend Crosby knew Mister Benton at Michigan State. Benton was an instructor, a mentor."

"So." I shrugged.

"Benton is a senior DOD CAF judge, and somehow he became the chief adjudicator of your clearance issues." The colonel glared at me. "For some reason, Benton took your previously denied top-secret clearance and approved it. Are you used to working outside the system, Commander Kleegan?"

"Are you used to the privilege of having your way regardless of the rules?" spat the young woman.

"Look, I don't know Mister Benton or any of this. I put in my request to renew my clearance, and I was told there were issues. I assumed they were due to my DUI." I wasn't going to tell them anything about Gaby. Evidently, they didn't have that information. Besides, it had nothing to do with Tailhook; none of this did.

"So, you and your friend Captain Crosby didn't cook this up? Convince Benton to overrule his staff?" The colonel threw the paper on his desk.

"And how did you get Crosby, a Black man, to allow himself to be denigrated with a callsign like Cotton? Have you no shame?"

"You need a tutorial," I said. "Cotton celebrates the famous civil rights leader, Dorothy Cotton, with his callsign. She was with Martin Luther King for much of his activism, and he took the name to honor her."

"Maybe so," said the colonel. "But there is a larger story here, a story about your wife." He held up a sheaf of papers. "This report only references an issue. It doesn't say what it is." The colonel waved the papers. "If I think you are not forthright, I will be forced to look more deeply into this."

I stood. "If either of you has any questions about Tailhook, you know how to contact me."

I turned and strode for the door and expected the colonel to order me back to my seat. But the only sound was my shoes hitting the tile, and I pulled the door open and left. I was still fuming when I got to the car for the drive back to my squadron.

I called an AOM, an All-Officers Meeting, to discuss our treatment from the investigators. They were frustrated and angry. Fortunately, none were linked to any misbehavior, and since we didn't have a suite, we were spared automatic guilt.

That night I thought about calling Cotton and asking him about Mister Benton. But the more I considered it, the more I knew it was better if I did not. There was no reason to have Cotton admit he had tinkered with the security adjudication system even if it were to help his executive officer and old friend.

What the press referred to as the Tailhook Scandal soon took on a life of its own, and as the stories of investigator ruthlessness circulated, naval aviators did band together. It became a "them" against "us" environment, and I think there were some bad actors in both of those camps. I believe that a more even-handed approach would have yielded better results, and some of the names of those guilty of assault would have been more quickly uncovered. However, that didn't happen, and eventually, the investigators developed a list of some 300 suspects, a list which legal experts promptly shortened due to lack of convincing evidence. But the list of victims, some twenty-five women, and the details of what they endured was sobering. So, my bitterness was complicated by my feelings of guilt. After all, I was a male naval aviator and I had seen what some of us had done.

The DOD Investigator General's team bogged down as facts of guilt and culpability proved elusive and soon their list boiled down to group of officers who could not prove their innocence but who were probably guilty enough. Those names were annotated, and when they appeared before the senate for promotion approval, they were not confirmed.

Vice Admiral Bass was forced to retire, which was about the only good thing from that mess. But not much else was accomplished.

The Tailhook situation tore me. A part of me resented the way women were treated, but I wondered if this was because I knew a victim, Missy. Another side of me was less sympathetic to the women because they shouldn't be there in the first place. I was torn.

Gaby and I discussed this, and I was frank about my thoughts and my reservations about women in naval aviation.

"I am afraid that we will open the door to quotas, and we will be forced to bring women in to satisfy some politically correct agenda."

"Winfred, all organizations are in motion. At least the best ones are, and I think your navy is one of the best, don't you?"

"Yes."

"You told me that officers like you who sat in the back seat couldn't even have aviation command until 1968. Now, look at you. You command squadrons, aircraft carriers. You are admirals. Do you think someone made that change to be politically correct? Do you think someone had an agenda to be nice to guys with poor eyesight?"

I smiled and hugged her. "No, probably not."

"I think you need to readjust your thinking about women. After all, we are going to have a daughter."

"What?" Suddenly my angst over women in the navy vanished. "What?"

"Yes, I found out this morning."

I hugged Gaby and buried my face in her hair. I was going to be a daddy.

And, true to her word, Gaby gave me a baby girl. We named her Christine.

RULES

Raoul took command of a West Coast F-14 squadron shortly after I did, and he was on a deployment to the Pacific when Tailhook happened. Thus, he avoided an excellent opportunity to screw up. Knowing his penchant for wildness, I was glad Raoul missed it as well as the horror show that ensued.

Raoul visited us just after Christine was born, and he hadn't changed one bit. Well, of course, he did! We all do. But Raoul is the kind of enduring friend who is a real blessing, the kind who stays mostly the same to kindle your best memories but evolves enough to intrigue. Despite our long periods of separation, we kept our close attachment. Gaby liked him too, and that said a lot for the both of them.

Eisenhower set off on cruise in the summer, and it was my second deployment as the squadron commanding officer. I was happy to go to sea with my men again. I was also glad I would be gone for only three months. My executive officer, Weezer Gallagher, was to relieve me at the half-way point so I would not be apart from Gaby and Christine for the usual six-month deployment. In addition, *Ike* was heading straight through the Med into the Red Sea and on to the Persian Gulf to support Operation Southern Watch, and since I had missed the Gulf War, I was excited about what that might entail.

Operation Southern Watch, OSW, was a coalition of US, Great Britain, Saudi Arabia, and France forged to enforce United Nations actions preventing Saddam from attacking the Shi'ite Muslims in southern Iraq. Shortly after Desert Storm ended, the Iraqi Air Force had bombed them in part because they had risen against him and also because he believed they were aligned with Iran. So, our OSW coalition flew sorties to ensure Saddam could not mount any aerial attack against the south.

We would launch from the carrier in a package that consisted of F-14s, F-18s, A-6s, and the EA6B jammer and fly up into Iraq as a

310

symbol to Saddam to keep his air force north of the 32nd parallel. If we detected airplanes or missile systems and guns, we would destroy them. While the USAF had success in shooting down some MIGs, we never saw any, and the missions quickly became routine.

A month into our deployment, the night before we were pulling into Cannes, my senior enlisted man, Command Master Chief Cameron Dozer, called to ask for a visit in my stateroom. It was near midnight, but I was awake because I had watched our airplanes come aboard during the last recovery. I thought it odd that he would want to talk so late, but I agreed. Besides, when the master chief spoke, I listened. Everyone listened. He was highly respected, almost revered throughout the airwing and ship, and I valued his opinion very much. Cotton had convinced Master Chief Dozer to come to our squadron when he had been the skipper, and it was one reason we were so successful. I was elated that he had agreed to stay as my command master chief. That he was Black also gave me a perspective that I knew I did not have. His knock came quickly, and as soon as I opened the door and saw the expression on his face, I knew we had trouble.

"What's up, master chief?" I pointed to the chair next to my desk and watched as my senior enlisted advisor took a seat. He looked at his hands for a moment, then at me.

"Sir, the ship's master-at-arms just caught four of our aircrew drinking."

"What?" I sat down. "What?"

"Yes, sir. I just got a call from the ship's master chief. He has the report in his hand ready to move it up the chain."

"Who did they catch? How?" I frowned and shook my head. I had delivered a speech the first day we were underway and had explicitly told all my officers that the old days of drinking on the ship were over. I emphasized that the stories they heard from back in the day were real, but the punishment was a slap on the wrist. I TOLD them that this was a different navy and that if they got caught, it could very well mean the end of their career. It bothered me that I had failed in delivering the message. It distressed me that they had not paid any attention.

"Sir, it was Lieutenants Wallace, Ross, Horan, and Cleary. I guess they were making a bunch of noise, and one of them went up to the wardroom to get ice. The master-at-arms followed him back to the stateroom and found a party."

"Christ!" I shook my head. They were my top junior officer leaders.

"Sir, the ship's master chief is holding the report chit out of a personal courtesy. He wanted me to alert you first. You know, give you a chance to speak to the ship's XO if you want."

I slowly nodded and looked at the master chief. "Thank you. I will go and talk to him."

"Yes, sir."

"And master chief, I want you to go with me."

"Sir?"

"I don't want you to think there are any special deals for officers. You deserve that; the men deserve that."

"Yes, sir."

"Would you have the duty officer instruct Lieutenants Wallace, Ross, Horan, and Cleary to come to my stateroom?"

"Certainly, sir."

Twenty minutes later, I answered a knock, and the four officers filed in the door.

"Sit." I pointed to chairs and the edge of my rack. The four silently took their places, and as I looked at them, one at a time, I could see they were afraid. I wished that Weezer was onboard. He was always good to consult with, but he was the senior shore patrol officer for the Cannes in-port period and had flown off on the COD earlier. I wanted the benefit of his thoughts, but since I was leaving in a couple of months, I needed his commitment to what would follow.

I studied the men. "Do you know what the biggest change is since I was a lieutenant? The biggest change in the navy?"

"Mercy?" Mikey Wallace glanced at me, but his smile withered under my glare. His eyes fell to the floor, and I watched them all shake their heads.

"Back in the day, officers could break the rules. We could break them because we were flying combat, and we were being shot down every day. We could break them because the navy let us break them." I slowly shook my head. "But now the rules are for everybody."

I sighed and took a seat. "You know, when I stand in front of the ready room and look back at you young men, I feel so grateful. I feel privileged. I feel like that partly because of the moment I am in, the moment that we are in, and partly because of the many moments to come, because I see the navy's future sitting in front of me. And I can't help but wonder what Chester Nimitz or James Stockdale's skippers must have felt as they looked at those admirals when they were lieutenants like you. I wonder if they knew the greatness that lay in front of those officers. You see, I see greatness when I look at you, and I feel blessed that the navy gave me the responsibility to ensure its future by leading men like you."

I bent my head and looked at my hands. I was talking too much. I was talking too much because I was trying to think of a way to get them off this terrible hook they were on. And I felt like a hypocrite. I had drunk on the ship, a lot. But I also heard other words in my head. A warning from my mentor, Admiral Jensen: "Hypocrisy is often the burden of leadership. Or the excuse for avoiding it." And I knew that while I felt some bit of guilt for what I had gotten away with, I could not transfer that to these men.

"Sir?"

I looked up. It was Ross. Everybody called him Roscoe. I nodded.

"Sir, we know we screwed up. We know we let you down."

"It's not about me." But while I said that I knew it must be partly about me.

"Yes, sir, but we let everybody down just the same."

"Do you realize that if you go to captain's mast, it will end your careers? The rules may be the same, but the punishment for breaking them isn't!" I fought to control my temper. I wanted to scream at them! I wanted to rage on them and tell them HOW FUCKING STUPID THEY HAD BEEN! But I took a deep breath, sighed, and looked back down at my hands.

"Sir, would it be possible for us to be placed in hack, put in the duty section for the rest of cruise?"

I frowned and looked up at them. "You do realize that we have another five months of the cruise to go."

"Yes, sir."

I looked at them, and they looked back, and I could see the pinch in their faces.

"You all agree with this?"

The four nodded.

"Well, I will see what I can do."

The next morning the master chief and I went to see Captain Gary Norris, the ship's XO. A sailor ushered us into the office, where we took seats in front of the XO's desk. I had spoken with him on the phone, so he knew why we were there. He offered coffee. We declined.

"So, it looks like some of your boys don't understand the ship's policy on drinking aboard Ike. Or, maybe, they weren't aware of it."

The XO's eyes held me in a steady gaze. Eyes that hinted I was as much on trial as my lieutenants were.

"They were aware, sir."

The XO stared at me as he nodded. "It is amazing how many of the old guys, guys like you, who don't realize what was okay during Vietnam isn't okay now."

"Yes, sir."

Some of those old guys fail to get the message out in a believable way. So, if your four were aware and drank anyway, does that mean they didn't believe you? Does it mean they don't respect the ship? Does it mean they don't give a shit? Which?"

"I think it means they were young and stupid, sir."

"Stupid means they were not intelligent enough to comprehend the rules that you supposedly laid out. That kind of ignorance is hard to believe for a naval aviator. Don't you agree?"

"Yes, sir."

"So, let's take stupid off the table."

"Yes, sir."

"So, what is it then?" The XO frowned and leaned forward. "Is it just 'Fuck you, *Ike*.' Is that what it is?"

"No, sir. No."

"Why would they drink the night before the day we pull into port? They can drink all they want tomorrow if they are not in the duty section. And if they are in the duty section, they can drink all they want the next day. I don't get it."

"Sir, those young men are risk-takers." The master chief startled me. He had promised to keep quiet and let me do all the talking.

The XO frowned and glared at him.

"What?"

"It's who they are, sir."

"I don't get it."

I gripped the sides of my chair. The master chief was going to make things worse!

"Sir, when I was growing up, we had turkeys. We had chickens, guinea hens, and turkeys, and my dad sold them to the local stores. It is how we made our living."

The XO frowned and shook his head.

I shook mine too. *Where was the master chief going with this?*

"There were coyotes around. Lots of them, and they liked turkeys and chickens and guineas too, so my dad had a dog. Long as I can remember, he was a police dog."

"Do you mean a German Shepherd," asked the XO.

"We called them police dogs."

The XO took a deep breath and gestured for the master chief to continue.

"That dog kept the coyotes away, never lost a single bird to them the whole time I was growing up. But, once in a while, the dog would get a chicken or a guinea. Not often, but once in a while."

"I don't get your point." The XO frowned, but I could see more confusion than anger in his eyes.

"Well, sir, to protect us from the coyotes, he had to be a killer. Deep down inside, he was a killer; it was part of him. He didn't even eat the few birds he killed. But despite all that, he was sure worth keeping around."

"The master chief has a good point," I interrupted. "I think he is right. These officers take risks every day; we all do. I don't think they intentionally set out to insult you or the ship. I think they just wanted to let off some steam and didn't think it through very much. It is kind of the way lieutenants are."

The XO frowned again, but he leaned back and looked at me and then the master chief. He nodded, "So. What do we do?"

"Sir, to avoid mast and the effect that would have on their careers, all four volunteer to be in the duty section for the rest of deployment."

"What? They do realize this is a six-month cruise. Unless it gets extended, of course."

"Yes, sir. But all four took the flight bonus. All four are career oriented. They will do anything not to have this on their records."

"You realize that I will need to speak to the captain about this?"

"Yes, sir. I can do that if you wish."

"No, let me." The XO stood. "He is in a good mood this morning. He is always in a good mood when we pull into port. I think if he believes the punishment will produce results, he will agree. But I expect you to ensure the rest of your officers know what is going on. If any of you are caught doing this again, you will all go to mast. You, first."

"Yes, sir."

The XO looked at Master Chief Dozer. "I liked your dog story."

We stood, and the master chief and I quickly left the room. As we headed down the passageway, he stopped and turned toward me. "Sorry about blurting out, sir."

I smiled and put my hand on his shoulder. "There is nothing to be sorry for. You saved them, master chief. You had the answer."

That night I gave the master chief's comment about risk-taking some more thought, and that led to my recollection of crazy risks I had taken. There was the time when Arlo Grundeen and I in one Phantom and Coco Brewster and his RIO, Fatal Christian, flew below the lip of the Grand Canyon and almost hit a helicopter. It all started our final night in Fallon, Nevada. Fallon sits at the edge of a vast piece of airspace the navy uses for training, and there are places on the desert floor to bomb targets, old military vehicles, and so forth. The whole airwing gathered there to practice our strike tactics. It was a great time.

Anyway, we got a little drunk at the club, and then Coco and Fatal convinced Arlo and me to go to The Mustang Ranch with them. The Mustang Ranch is a famous whorehouse, and I wanted to see it. I believe that seeing famous places is a requirement, especially if they are close by. It would be like touring Buckingham Palace if I were in London or Busch Stadium if in Saint Louis. Besides, Coco is a pretty cool guy, and Arlo and I were going to fly to Pensacola with him and Fatal the next day, so why not build the team?

Coco gets his callsign because his head looks just like a coconut. No kidding! His head is freaking tiny, he is dark-complected, and he has short, thin hair. If there was ever a perfect callsign, Coco has it. I always liked the way we got our callsigns from what the JOs in the squadron decided. You can call yourself Killer all you want, but if the JOs decide your callsign is Wussy, then that is what it will be. I remember when Ensign John Berry joined our squadron. He desperately wanted to be called Blue or even Straw because of how it went with his last name. Alas, the JOs named him Dingle.

Fatal's real name is Al, and he got his callsign because he has a pretty bad, or big, weight problem. Fatal is a likable guy, and the JOs didn't want to embarrass him by calling him fat Al, so they called him Fatal, which is pretty cool when you think about it. He believes we call him Fatal because he is big and intimidating, but, well, we like him, so we let him think that if he wants to.

We chugged our beers and hopped into a navy sedan that some Captain left out front and raced to the ranch, which was about fifty miles away. It was a Friday night, and the place was full of drunken locals, so we took a quieter spot away from the bar. No need to take the chance of offending some guy who rode herd or drove a bulldozer. Coco, who had been there before, asked for a menu. I thought that odd since we had already eaten some pizza at the club, but the menu wasn't for food; it was for girls! For instance, Salt and Pepper were two girls; one white, the other black. Chop Suey was a choice of Chinese girls, or they might have been something else like Filipino, but it is hard to tell. Fire and Ice was more of a mystery but involved a bunch of lotion and whips.

I don't think any of us intended to order from the menu because it costs so darned much, but it sure was fun to drink beers and watch the show. Some guys studied the menu and pulled at their hats while they talked to the hostess. Like buying a horse, I guess. Others just walked in and knew what they wanted. It reminded me of walking into McDonald's and saying, "I'll take a number three with large fries."

We were there about thirty minutes when Arlo punched my shoulder and pointed at the door. I followed his finger and saw the air wing commander walking in! No kidding, the CAG himself. We watched him from our dark corner and whispered as he studied the menu. After a while, he motioned to the hostess, and pretty soon, a huge girl slid over to him. I know some guys like a little padding for the pushing, but she was enormous.

"Mount Shasta in the menu," whispered Coco.

Shasta led the CAG towards the back and he no sooner than disappeared behind the beaded curtain when Arlo said, "start the car and wait for me."

"What?" I frowned.

"Start the car and wait for me. I'll only be a minute."

I shrugged and looked at Fatal and Coco. They shrugged back, and we headed for the door. Two minutes later, Arlo exploded out the door waving something in his hand. He jerked the back door open and jumped in, and Coco spit gravel as he roared away.

"What did you get?" I leaned around from my front seat perch.

"Got the CAG's pants," he grinned.

"Why did you do that?" I laughed, and so did Coco and Fatal.

"You heard him this morning, going on about how aviators these days don't know how to improvise. We don't know what to do when the plan changes. So, I figured I'd allow him to improvise."

We laughed all the way to the base and went back to the club, half expecting to see the CAG come in wearing his skivvies.

The next morning, we fired up our two Phantoms and headed to Luke Air Force Base as our first stop on the way to Pensacola, Florida. We had flown an hour or so when Arlo keyed the mic and said, "Weenie, call center and tell them we want to cancel and go VFR."

"What?" We had filed an instrument flight rules plan to Luke, and I was confused why we would cancel. VFR rules require you to visually navigate rather than using the high-altitude system.

"Have you ever seen the Grand Canyon?"

"No."

"Well, let's go down and take a look."

"Can we do that? I mean, is it legal?"

"Sure, it's legal. People fly around VFR all the time."

I did as Arlo requested, and we headed down. Coco and Fatal closed up on our right side, and we soon dipped below the canyon's rim. It was breathtaking! We were doing around 400 knots and the rock formations, and the valley whizzed by us.

"What do you think?" asked Arlo.

I instantly remembered when I was a freshman in high school and Mister Hudson, my English teacher, asked us to tell the class what we had done during the summer. Mister Hudson was a very dapper young teacher who had the energy and wonder of a child just before touching the candle flame. He got into his work, and when he read stuff like Alfred Noyes's, "The Highwayman," he seemed to enter another world. His eyes closed as he recited from memory:

"Tlot-tlot, in the frosty silence! Tlot-tlot in the echoing night!
Nearer he came and nearer! Her face was like a light!
Her eyes grew wide for a moment; she drew one last deep breath,
Then her finger moved in the moonlight,
Her musket shattered the moonlight,
Shattered her breast in the moonlight and warned him; with her death."

So, when Mister Hudson asked about our summer's adventures, he did so with passion in his voice and expectation in his eyes.

I remember Delmus Eaton shot up his hand, and when the teacher nodded to him, he scrambled to his feet and said, "I went to the Grand Canyon!"

"Oh, really," said Mister Hudson. "What was it like?"

"I bet I spit a mile."

I will never forget the look of astonished disappointment on Mister Hudson's face.

"Arlo, it is fantastic!" I responded.

Just then, I saw a blur whiz under our jet. "What the fuck was that?"

"Holy shit," said Arlo. "I think it was a helicopter."

"You mean, one of those touring things? The kind people ride on to see the canyon?"

"Yeah, maybe we had better get out of here."

We landed at Luke and went to base ops while they refueled our Phantoms. The four of us were in the planning room when a major stuck his head in the door. "You guys go anywhere near the Grand Canyon?"

"Nope," said Arlo. "Why?"

"Some outfit called and said some military airplanes nearly hit one of their copters. Said his passengers were still cleaning the shit out of their pants."

"Wasn't us," I said. "We flew in from up north."

I sat in my stateroom and shook my head as I thought of that flight and the risks we took. From stealing the military sedan to taking CAG's pants to flying below the rim of the Grand Canyon; it seems like we took risks of all sorts all of the time. The master chief was right: It's part of who we are.

The Cannes in-port period was a great break and very restful for me. Since Gaby wasn't coming, I didn't spend much time off the ship. I saw my four criminals every day, and I also had time to write letters. One was to Grace.

Cannes reminded me of Grace—and the hours I had spent with her years ago when I was a catapult officer at her cottage at Cap D 'Antibes, trying to help her face the reality that her husband was an abject jerk. Grace lived in Virginia Beach now, so Gaby and I had visited her a couple of times before I deployed. Jack was the skipper of TOPGUN, a severe snag in the fabric of naval aviation justice. He lived in San Diego. I hoped my letter would offer some comfort to Grace. Gaby had written to me about visiting her, a visit that revealed a deepening depression and near continual panic attacks. I also wrote to Mom and Dad and Molly and Paul.

After five days, we pulled out and headed for the gulf and Operation Southern Watch. It was a quick trip across the Med and through the Suez Canal. We had just exited the Red Sea when Weezer plopped next to my ready room chair.

"Morning XO." I smiled and sipped coffee.

"Morning, sir. I have bad news."

I swallowed and took another sip. "What is it?" I blew on my coffee.

"The master chief just popped positive for THC."

What?" I jumped. "Ouch, damn!" I spilled coffee on my hand.

"I." My head swirled. I looked at Weezer, "let's go to my stateroom."

I led my XO through the passageways, and soon we were sitting in my room.

"How is it possible?"

"Not sure, sir. It was our own administered screen from back home. The one we took just before we deployed."

"Does he know?"

"Not yet. Petty Officer Thomas administers the program; he gave me the message from the lab this morning. He is the only one who knows besides us."

"What options do we have?"

"Well, sir, failing a drug test is pretty much an automatic dishonorable discharge these days."

"Jesus," I shook my head. "Who takes him to mast? Who punishes him?"

"You do since the master chief took the test before our departing on the cruise. However, you can defer it to the commanding officer of the ship, I suppose."

I took a deep breath.

Jesus, master chief, what have you done?

"What would you do, Weez?"

Weezer looked at me and shook his head. "I would want just to be the executive officer at a time like this, sir."

"Give me the message, XO. Keep this between us for now. And get the custody log. Maybe there is some sort of explanation in the chain of control process. Maybe his sample got mixed with someone else's."

"Yes, sir." Weezer handed me the slip of paper and left the room.

I slumped into my chair and closed my eyes. I sat like that for a long time, hoping that some answer would appear. How could I save my great master chief? Was there an explanation? I had heard a story about an aviator who had popped positive for some hallucinogen and was all but out of the navy before they discovered his baggage had been stored next to a leaky package of horse tranquilizer in the cargo hold of an airplane. Maybe something like that happened to the master chief. Maybe there was a way to save him. I picked up the phone, dialed Master Chief Dozer's office, and asked him to drop by my stateroom.

I sat down, and within minutes the master chief knocked. He smiled as I pointed to a chair. "Have a seat, master chief."

"Yes, sir."

Once he was settled, I cleared my throat and held up the message. "We got the report from the urinalysis we conducted just before we deployed."

"Ohh." The master chief frowned. "Do we have problems?"

"We do." I looked at my senior enlisted man. I looked at my trusted advisor. "You are on it."

The master chief frowned and stared at me, and I could not read his face. I had expected him to go into some declaration of innocence. I had expected him to get angry, even. Furious that a man in his position could have been wrongly compromised by the system we so often used and had confidence in.

"Perhaps there is an explanation." I leaned forward. "It is rare, but sometimes people make mistakes. Do you have any idea how this could have happened?"

The master chief just stared at me. He was in shock.

"The XO is getting the custody log. Maybe there is a clue there."

Master Chief Dozer swallowed and looked at me. "There is no mistake."

"What?"

The master chief sighed and slumped into his chair. He looked at the floor and slowly shook his head. Then he looked up at me. There was moisture in his eyes.

"Shania is young. I am still amazed that she married an old guy like me." He leaned forward; hands knotted in front of him. "I have a tough time keeping up with her."

I nodded and leaned back. "I wish there was something I could do."

The master chief chuckled and shook his head again. "The rules are for everybody, remember?"

I took Master Chief Dozer to Captain's Mast a week later, and he left the ship that afternoon in the COD. And I have to say the experience devastated me. While I understood why the navy had a zero-tolerance for drug use, what that meant was zero-tolerance for momentary weakness, poor judgment, and even passion. And the punishment of a zero-tolerance policy wasn't mandatory rehabilitation or training—it was compulsory removal. It was the death of a career. And while the juxtaposition of my Black master chief's fate to that of my four white officers bothered me, my concern wasn't so much a lost lesson of some kind but the realization of life's unfairness.

Weezer and I had our change-of-command, and I flew from the carrier to Abu Dhabi, the United Arab Emirates' capital. I connected with a United flight and went on to London and the United States. The navy assigned me to Commander Air Forces Atlantic staff in Norfolk while I awaited a class in War College to open. Of course, I followed the events in the gulf and knew that Raoul and his squadron on *Carl Vinson* relieved *Eisenhower.* Two weeks later, he was shot down! The first reports were that he was flying with a junior pilot, and they experienced a plane malfunction while over Iraq. Their stricken Tomcat was limping home when a surface-to-air missile bagged them.

I was sick when I heard the news. Even Gaby and baby Christine could not console me. Raoul was so much a part of my life that the thought of his death took me into dark, dark despair, and I took God down the tear-stained corridors of Why? The passageways that never have an answer no matter how mad, or how sad you become or how loudly you scream, or softly you weep. God just takes us. He just does. The profound unfairness thing again.

Then, ten days later, a US special forces Delta team found Raoul wandering in the marshes and rescued him, and I had to replace my wet-eyed questioning of His goodness with gratitude for bringing back my best friend. The Delta team found his pilot the next day. She was dead, and since I didn't know her, I didn't take Him to task for it.

The bizarre thing, the unbelievable thing, is that soon after rejoining his squadron on *Vinson,* Raoul resigned. He just quit and left the ship on a COD. I tried to contact him, even flew to San Diego to find him. But he disappeared, vanished.

I was assigned a member of the Naval Air Forces aircraft mishap investigative team, and the files I accessed kept me "close" to Raoul. I learned that he had had an Environmental Control System turbine failure, and he and his pilot, Lieutenant junior grade Mandy Mandolin, had to act quickly to prevent porting hot engine gases to critical parts of the airplane. I knew that Raoul and his young pilot had to descend and slow down, and that is how the SAM got them. I also read from Raoul's statement to the intelligence debriefers that they were captured by an Iraqi Army Colonel and imprisoned for days without sleep or food. He could not remember any of the events that led to his escape. He did not remember how Mandy died.

The horrible news just kept coming, and a month later, I heard the news that Jocko Barnes had been killed in an accident with Jack Grant. I knew that the navy had assigned Jocko to TOPGUN along with Jack and had talked with Jocko about coming to my squadron when his tour was up. Jocko was very interested, and his detailer was going to make it happen. The last time I talked to Jocko, he said he thought Jack would let him go early, and I asked why.

"Well, sir, I was on a training hop which was designed to get Jack up to speed, and I was flying in the back seat of the TA-4 against Jack in an F-5. I asked my pilot, a good guy named Buck Curry if he would let me fly the engagements against Jack, and he said, 'sure.' So, we started side-by-side, and when Jack said 'Go,' I turned toward him slightly nose high."

Didn't he go up to match you?"

"No, he stayed where he was, so when I passed over him, I rolled inverted and pulled as hard as I could."

"So, you got separation in the vertical." I loved how two back-seaters were talking pilot talk.

"Exactly, and that gave me enough to really square the corner."

"How did you keep sight?"

"I didn't. I knew that if Jack went up, I would never see him again, but he did the dumbest thing possible and went into a nose-low left-hand turn. He flew out in front of me, and I gunned him!"

"No kidding!"

"No kidding. And I did the same thing on the next engagement and gunned him again."

"Wow!"

"Yes, and during the debrief, Buck threw it out that I was flying the jet, and that really got the skipper pissed off. "

I can still hear Jocko's laugh over the phone and my joy at the idea of him coming to my squadron. Jocko was a one-of-a-kind kid, and I liked him. And now he was dead. I later read the accident report, and evidently Jack spun a T-A4 Skyhawk with Jocko in the back and couldn't get out of it. Jocko got killed in the ejection.

Mumblings about Jack's poor performance at TOPGUN ran through the fighter community, and it didn't surprise me that the navy shuffled him off to a new post. After all, he was our hero. The fact that the navy sent him to the pentagon made me smile. I figured there was probably someone there who deserved him.

We did get a bit of good news as Cotton finished his nuclear propulsion training and took command of an oiler. The navy did that to give prospective carrier skippers experience handling and leading a large ship and crew. However, the navy stationed Cotton and Melody in Bremerton, Washington, so Gaby and I had little opportunity to see them.

WHY BIRDS SING AT NIGHT

In the Spring, Gaby and I rented out our house in Virginia Beach while I attended war college at Fort McNair in Washington, DC. War college, or Joint Professional Military Education, became a requirement for the services to support due to the Goldwater-Nichols Act of 1986, so my detailer sent me there. While the college at Fort McNair had existed since 1924, the navy had pretty much blown it off. It concentrated on navy-centric assignments for its officers, particularly it's front running officers. However, the US military had suffered some notable failures when it tried to act together or jointly. Operation Eagle Claw, our failed attempt to rescue our hostages from Iran, was an embarrassing disaster. Our invasion of Grenada exposed tremendous problems in joint communications and planning, and there was considerable congressional skepticism of the US military's ability to work together. So, the pressure was on to get military officers educated in joint operations and serving in joint commands. Therefore, for the next eleven months, I was to be a student again.

Gaby and I found a nice brick condominium on Fifth Street not far from the Capitol building and within walking distance to the metro stations. DC is an excellent town for exploring while pushing a baby stroller, and we did a lot of that. Just watch for the cobblestones!

Each weekend we would visit a new neighborhood or see a different museum, and I loved my feelings of awe and pride. I don't know how anyone can live in DC and not be proud to be an American. But I suppose our favorite place, the one we visited most evenings after dinner, was Folger Park. We had to negotiate Pennsylvania Avenue to get there but once done, the old trees and gentle pathways rewarded us with their peacefulness. The crunch of my baby's stroller tires on gravel, Gaby's hand on my arm, a hint of lilac in the spring and, later, rose, all conspired to make me a blessed man. I was awarded distinguished graduate credentials at the end of the course.

Not far from my classrooms at Fort McNair lay the pentagon and my nemesis, Jack Grant. Detailed from his TOPGUN misadventure, Jack somehow became even more of a hero than before when he went to Iraq and had a shootout with Saddam's men. Evidently, he was part of a pentagon and state department team checking on programs for the Kurds in northern Iraq when it happened. The details were sketchy, but Jack gunned his way out of a mob of attackers. According to his story, he lost his two Kurdish companions along the way, but it wasn't his fault. I scowled when I read that. Jocko's death wasn't his fault either. At any rate, Jack was then off to command an airwing in San Diego. Gaby and I visited Grace often, and she was hanging in there, primarily due to the little dog she doted on. It was a miniature poodle she named Harley. He was a cute dog and helped keep the demons of her panic attacks away. At least, that is what she said.

Next, the navy assigned me to a joint duty command as a further piece of Goldwater-Nichols requirement. While I wanted to go to the pentagon for that assignment, there were no open billets, so I opted to go close to home. The navy assigned me to the Joint Transportation Command at Scott Air Force Base in East Saint Louis, Illinois. The work was mundane, even mindless at times, as my job was to complete taskers. Imagine an assembly line that has manila folders with these little turds in them. Each tasker has a set of actions that require research, written summations, coordination with other government agencies, and shepherding to get it through the system for signature. Since only a handful of very senior officers supplied those signatures, we fellows in the turd trenches spend our time trying to get our folders through the choke points. Then, we reached into our in-box and got another tasker.

The good news was it took less than four hours to drive to Militia Springs so we could visit the family often. On our first trip, I took a few days of leave, and we arrived at the farm on a Sunday afternoon. I had traded my Triumph in for a new 1994 Ford Fairlane after briefly flirting with getting a Mustang. But I didn't like the headlights. For some reason, Ford changed the classic round headlights to goofy rectangular things in the eighties, and they got even worse in the nineties. Besides, there was more room in the Fairlane, and I had already learned that a married man with a kid had a lot of stuff. Besides, Mom and Dad always had a Fairlane while I was growing up. So, we hopped out of the car and met the family in the front yard, as I had always done. Mom and Dad looked great in their mid-sixties, and Molly was a beautiful thirty-eight-year-old. Kate was eighteen and seemed confident as she picked up Christine and hugged Gaby and me. My good friend, Paul, was sun-browned from his outside work, school-boy trim, and his grip was warm and firm.

We spent that evening catching up over Mom's meatloaf. After dinner, I walked outside to be alone on the porch for a moment. I sat on the concrete and took a deep breath, hungering for the smell of Grandpa Two Bears' tobacco. Longing even more for him. I heard the door shut behind me and glanced up to see Gaby. I smiled as she sat beside me. We looked over the alfalfa field, and she grabbed my hand and squeezed it.

"Is he here?"

I swallowed and nodded. "Yes."

Gaby squeezed my hand again. "I think your Grandpa Two Bears is wherever you are."

I nodded again, and she stood and left.

Kate bunked on the downstairs couch, and Gaby and I took her room, and the next morning we arose to pancakes and bacon. We gathered around the table and laughed and joked as we ate. I smiled as I panned the room. Mom flitted around the kitchen; Gaby was in a deep conversation with Kate, something about a boy who rode horses. Dad had baby Christine on his lap, feeding her a pancake. Paul stirred his coffee and grinned back at me. I was in heaven. I reveled in the joy of my family while I ate and listened and watched. Then Mom appeared at the door. I hadn't seen her leave the kitchen.

She had on her Sunday dress and purse. She frowned with a miffed look on her face. It was familiar to me, the kind she had when she wasn't mad yet, but soon.

"You all need to hurry, or we will be late for church!"

I frowned and looked at Dad, and the second I saw his face, I knew something was wrong. Very wrong. The mixture of sadness and alarm in his eyes chilled me, and I heard myself swallow.

"Honey, it's Monday." Dad handed Christine to Gaby and stood. "We went to church yesterday." He walked to Mom and gently took her arm. "You remember, we went to church yesterday. The preacher talked about resolution in the face of despair. You liked his sermon."

Mom frowned and looked up at him, then at the rest of us. Her brows bunched, and she squinted as if searching for a memory. I watched my mom, and her eyes slowly opened. They opened in realization, and realization isn't always fair. Because in her eyes, I saw something else: fear. I saw fear and then a blink of panic. Mom took a deep breath and swallowed. Her head quivered in a tiny shake, and her face reddened. She turned, and her heels clicked on the wood as she disappeared.

I looked back at Dad and then at the rest. Everyone's face registered alarm and shock.

Dad walked back to his chair and smiled as he sat down. "Everybody get enough to eat?"

"Dad?" I frowned and leaned forward. I glanced at Molly, then over to Paul. "Dad?"

Dad looked at me and sighed. He picked up his spoon and turned it in his hands.

"Mom is slowing down a bit."

"Slowing down?"

"She forgets things sometimes."

"Forgets things?" I looked around. "What do you mean?"

"Mom is changing," said Molly. "She gets, I don't know, very confused sometimes. And Mom has never been confused. About anything."

"Your mom is the smartest person I know," said Paul.

"She's okay." Dad smiled again and slapped the table. "So, who wants to go look at the new calves?"

"New calves?" Gaby grinned and grabbed my arm.

"Paul, you and Kate help me with the dishes." Molly smiled and pushed her chair back.

Christine reached up her baby arms and walked between Gaby and me, and we followed Dad to the barn. I joined into the conversation about cows and how calves were born, and all about milking. I could tell Dad liked explaining these things to Gaby, and she wanted to hear them. But above the chatter of all this, I couldn't help but worry about Mom. And I couldn't push away what I had seen in the eyes--hers and Dad's--and how much what I had seen scared me.

That afternoon, Gaby and Christine took a nap, and I found myself alone in the living room. A copy of Oswald Chambers' *My Utmost for His Highest* on the coffee table caught my eye, so I picked it up. Chambers was a famous theologian, teacher, and thinker, and I was familiar with him because Mom often referred to his book for daily inspiration. I flipped through the pages and found a prayer card, used as a bookmark, between the pages. A quote from Oswald

Chambers was underlined, and it read, "At times God puts us through the discipline of darkness to teach us to heed Him. Songbirds are taught to sing in the dark, and we are put into the shadow of God's hand until we learn to hear Him."

I frowned as I read it, unsure what it meant, and then felt a tap on my shoulder. It was Mom.

"Take a ride to town with me?"

"Sure."

I followed Mom to the car and sat beside her as she drove. I looked out the front, avoiding her eyes because I was still spooked from the morning's event with the Sunday dress. I was stunned by how I desperately wanted to talk with her. And how desperately I didn't want to at the same time. I felt her glance at me.

"I have Alzheimer's Disease," she said matter-of-factly. But I heard a hint of insecurity in the word disease.

I looked at her. She was watching the road, but I could still see the concern on the side of her face and as she worked her jaw.

"What is Alzheimer's?"

"It is a progressive disease of the brain. You lose brain cells and connecting tissue."

"Don't all people do that? As they get older?"

Mom glanced at me. "Not like this."

I suddenly felt sick. "It's okay to get forgetful, Mom."

Mom smiled and nodded, and we approached the edge of town, but instead of going up on the square, she took the turnoff to Highway 5. Mom didn't want to go to town; she wanted to talk. I felt sicker. Something terrible was going on with her.

"I began to get more and more forgetful. I thought it was just, you know, getting older. But then I forgot our phone number. Mister Askins, our preacher, asked for it so he could call me if we needed to change the Woman's Circle meetings. I couldn't remember it. We were standing in front of the church, and I just blanked."

"Mom, it's called a brain freeze." I forced a laugh. "Everybody gets one occasionally."

Mom nodded, and I saw her swallow. "Not like this." She glanced at me and then back to the road. "I lost the car keys for a couple of days. Dad found them in the freezer."

I didn't know what to say, so I just looked out the windshield.

"I went to see Doctor Gantry, and he referred me to a specialist in Springfield. He is the one who diagnosed Alzheimer's. You know me. As soon as I got home, I broke out the *Encyclopedia Britannica* and learned that it was discovered in the early 1900s by a German named Alzheimer. Or, at least, he distinguished the unique characteristics from the larger term of dementia."

"What happens when you get it?"

"You become increasingly forgetful, confused, angry maybe. You probably become depressed as all of this goes on. Weenie, you lose your mind."

Mom looked at me, and I could see the tears gathering in her eyes. "And I hope it isn't too boastful, but my mind is the thing about me that I like the best."

A tear dropped, and Mom wiped her eye with a finger. "I wouldn't mind the gray hair; wrinkles are okay. To a point," her laugh caught in a sob.

I swallowed and gripped my fingers together. "Getting old is okay, Mom." I found a little package of Kleenex in the glove box and handed her a tissue.

"Thank you." She took one hand off the wheel and dabbed her eyes. "Eventually, it will kill me."

"What?"

"But that isn't what bothers me." Mom's voice was thick with tears, and she balled the tissue against the wheel. "You and I have talked a lot about heaven." She glanced at me, then back to the road. "So, I am not afraid of dying."

I swallowed hard again and put my hand on Mom's shoulder. I felt helpless. I didn't know what to do or how to help her. I don't think I ever felt so lost. I patted her shoulder as we drove and fought to catalog what I was feeling. I was afraid. I knew that. But it wasn't the kind of fear I had when I saw the SAMs flying at my airplane or even the gun in the deranged man's hands. It was fear for someone instead of something. I was afraid for my mom.

"I'm afraid of being alone."

My heart broke when she said that, and I turned to her. "What? Mom, what are you talking about? You have all of us, Dad, Molly and Paul, and Kate. You have Gaby and little Christine and me."

Mom glanced and gave me a tiny smile, just a momentary softening of her mouth. I swallowed as she dabbed her eyes again and looked to the road.

"Yesterday was the best day of the rest of my life."

I swallowed as she slowly shook her head. It was a mark of desolation. "Yesterday will always be the best day of the rest of my life, and that thought makes me lonely."

"Oh, Mom." I gripped her shoulder a little harder.

Mom sniffed and wiped the tissue against her eyes and nose, then returned to the wheel. Mom was a strict 10 and 2 driver, with no deviations. She glanced at me.

"I noticed you reading *My Utmost for His Highest.*"

I nodded. "I just opened it when you asked me to drive with you."

"What did you read?"

"I only glanced at it." I looked at Mom. "I saw you had underlined something."

Mom nodded but kept her eyes on the road. I waited for a moment, but she didn't bring the book for no reason. "Was there something in the book you were looking for?"

"At times." Mom cleared her throat. "The quote I underlined is, at times, God puts us through the discipline of darkness to teach us to heed Him. Songbirds are taught to sing in the dark, and we are put into the shadow of God's hand until we learn to hear Him."

I had no idea what she meant, what the quote meant. But I nodded anyway.

"Oswald writes eloquently and like the Bible, what you find is up for interpretation by the reader."

"What do you think he means? By this quote?"

"What do you think he means?" Mom looked at me.

"I don't know." I shrugged as I struggled. "I guess that God tests us. You know, until we understand him. Something like that."

Mom nodded but kept her eyes forward. "And the songbirds singing at night?"

"Not sure what that means." I shrugged. "Maybe he means that we need to push against the darkness in our lives. That even birds do that by singing at night. I don't know." I looked at Mom again and squeezed her shoulder.

"Nightingales and Mockingbirds sometimes sing at night. Most birds don't."

"I didn't know that." I squeezed her shoulder again and kept my face on her. I shifted my gaze to the window, and we drove a mile or so. I glanced back at Mom. "Why do you think birds sing at night?"

"I think." Mom paused, and I could see her throat tremble as she swallowed back a sob. She glanced at me and then back to the road. "I think birds sing at night because they are lonely."

"Lonely?" The softness...no. It was the weakness. It was the weakness of her voice that shook me. "Mom?"

"In the dark, we cannot see the ones we love. In the dark, we're alone." Mom gulped, and I saw fresh tears at the edge of her eyes. "And I am headed for a terrible darkness."

Mom began to cry, to softly cry, and so did I. I imagine an onlooker would have thought it mighty strange to see the car go by with both of us crying. I suppose such an onlooker might have reasoned a great tragedy, and he would have been right.

"Christ, what can I do?"

Mom shook her head, and I squeezed her shoulder again. I patted it once more and put my hand down.

Mom glanced at me. "The only thing you can do, the only thing all of you can do..." Mom swallowed and dabbed her eyes. She swallowed again. "The only thing you can do to help me is to remember me the way I was."

I have never heard anything so lonely in my life.

THE MERCY OF IGNORANCE

Mom didn't have any other events or lapses during our visit, and we didn't speak about it. I did catch Dad in the barn and asked him if I could do anything to help. He just smiled and said, "She'll be okay. I just need to watch her." I didn't get the idea that Mom had shared with him any of the things she had talked about with me.

I told Gaby about my conversation with Mom. I did it in part to explain her bizarre behavior on that Monday morning but mostly because I knew I needed Gaby.

"I can't imagine what she is going through," I said. We were heading north on Highway 44 toward Saint Louis. "I mean, she knows what is coming. She knows, and she also knows there isn't anything she can do about it."

"Yeah." Gaby nodded. "I mean, the only way I can relate to it is when I was on drugs, using drugs, there was always a part of me that wanted to stop. Desperate to stop. I knew where my life was headed, but I also knew I was powerless to stop it. Or at least I thought I believed I was. I thought I would take them until they killed me. After a while, I didn't take the drugs to get high. I took the drugs to get over how bad I felt because I took drugs. My periods of lucidity were hell because it was at those times that I most clearly realized what condition I was in."

I nodded. "I don't think it was like that for me and booze. I drank because I liked the way it made me feel."

"So, you can't imagine what it's like to be conscious and witting of your coming demise?" Gaby sat sideways, leaning against the passenger side door. "To have those moments of clear understanding just before I slipped into the haze again. And I dreaded, I hated those moments. I hated them." I glanced at Gaby, and she was looking down at her hands. "So, I reached for another needle."

I shook my head again and focused on the road.

Militia Springs was a treasure for Mom and us. I think I had forgotten about how warm and supportive that little community was. Or maybe it wasn't so much a matter of memory but the fact I hadn't been in a position to need its arms. Every time I was home, a member of Mom's prayer group or one of the neighbors, even Grandpa Two Bear's old senior citizen buddies would drop by. And it was never awkward or tedious. They all seemed to have a definite purpose in mind, and they would drop off a cake or a casserole, or they would sit and listen if Mom wanted to try to talk. Dad was the chaperone, though. He was quick to sense Mom's frustration and graciously insisted upon the breaks she needed.

My new job was not very demanding, and the air force Colonel I worked for was a decent chap. He was an F-16 pilot, so we had an aviation connection. He did talk a lot about his experience in Iraq. He led a lot of strikes against Baghdad and other target areas. He respected the navy but did say he thought he could "kick the shit out of any Tomcat." I asked him if he had ever been stationed at Aviano in Italy. He answered, "No, why do you ask?"

"Just wondered."

I was able to get off early on Fridays, and on many weekends, Gaby, Christine, and I would drive to Militia Springs. Kate started her freshman year at Mizzou, and that freed up her room for us to use.

Mom's decline was subtle, and the first indications were how Dad and the rest treated her. Mom was the most independent person I knew, but now Dad never left her alone. When he had to be away, Molly or Paul stayed with her. And since Molly and Paul ran the farm now as well as Paul's backhoe business, that gave Dad a lot of opportunities to watch Mom. At first, he just made sure she didn't forget to turn off the stove and things like that. He would read the recipe to her while she cooked. When I visited later, Dad did the cooking while Mom sat silent, with the recipe in front of her.

During our fourth-of-July visit, I had another session alone with Mom. This time, I drove.

She looked more harried now, apparent concern on her face. And she rarely smiled. As we turned onto Highway 14, she turned toward me.

"Know what just kills me?"

I shook my head and gripped the wheel. "No."

"What kills me is that Christine will never know me."

I glanced at Mom, and she had the saddest eyes. I quickly looked out the windshield.

"I mean, she will never know me."

I glanced again. Mom had her head down. She clutched her purse and loosened her grip, then squeezed it again. She did that over and over.

"She may have a memory." Mom looked at me, and I glanced at her and let out a breath. Christ, I didn't know what to do.

"I wish that she wouldn't. I wish that she wouldn't remember me. Not like this."

"I will make sure she knows who you are, Mom. Who you were." I gasped at what I had just said and quickly looked over at Mom, but she didn't seem to take offense.

"Thank you, Weenie." Mom reached over and patted my hand, then went back to clutching her purse.

Mom threw a measuring cup during an August visit, shattering a window and sending Christine into a crying wail. She did it because she couldn't figure out how to double three fourths. Then she slumped into a kitchen chair. As I hurried Christine out of the room, I saw Dad kneel and hug her. Gaby quickly came to me, and I thanked God for her.

When we went home for Thanksgiving, I noticed a pile of mittens and gloves on the clothes dryer. Every fifteen minutes or so Mom would go to the dryer, I could see her from the living room. She counted the mittens and gloves, put a pair, gazed at them, and smiled. Then she put them back on the pile. She would tidy the pile and put all the mittens on top, then fifteen minutes later, she would go in and put all the gloves on top. Paul would follow her, and when she dropped a glove or mitten, he would pick it up for her. Mom couldn't figure out what to do when a glove or mitten fell.

"Here you go, Mom," he would say.

The most defeating thing about watching her wasn't her inability to count, the manic desire to keep the gloves and mittens tidy, or the fact she was dumbfounded when she dropped one. The worst thing was the fact that she smiled while she did it. Gaby caught me watching her and pulled me outside for a walk. Christine was asleep with Kate, and we bundled in our coats and went out.

"Do you know the meaning of the term, Lala land?"

I shrugged. "I guess some goofy place. I think they call Los Angeles Lala land."

"Close, but no." Gaby squeezed my hand. "Lala land is the mental state of not knowing where you are or what is going on."

Gaby pulled me to her and stopped walking. She looked up at me and pushed her cap away from her face. "It's not a bad place, Winfred. It may be bad for those of us who watch but not for the ones there."

"How can you be so sure?"

"She smiles, doesn't she?"

"She doesn't always smile. You heard her yell at Dad, and all he did was drop a spoon."

"She yells and cries when she leaves Lala land, not when she is in it. And soon, she won't leave."

"But she won't remember any of us. She won't be able to do anything."

"She will be able to do anything she wants to do in Lala land."

"Gaby, this doesn't make sense. None of this makes sense." I frowned and dropped her hand, but she reached out and grabbed it.

"Losing your mind is terrible, Winfred. I know because when I was on drugs, I was losing mine. But, after a hit of heroin, I wasn't losing my mind; I had lost it. And while that drug numbed me, I felt the delicious contentment of not looking for my mind anymore. Your mom gets angry and frustrated because she is still searching for her mind, looking for it, looking for what she used to be able to do, who she used to be. But, one day, God will bless her, and she won't be looking for it anymore."

"How can you call any of this God's blessing?"

"Because I know what it is like to search for something you don't want. I am one who knows the mercy of ignorance."

"God, this is just so terrible." I swallowed and hugged Gaby, thankful for her. And over the next months and into the following year, Gaby's words did comfort me. While the words were terrifying, her message was not. I knew that at some point, some crossover point, Mom would go to Lala land and stay there. And God would bless us with our understanding of her, bless us with our memory of her, bless us maybe with her occasional flickers of recognition but then finally bless her by taking her back. Take her back to the warmth of the darkness and the mercy of her ignorance.

I find it hard to understand just how much I had taken my dad for granted until Mom got sick. As far back as I could remember, it was with Grandpa Two Bears and Mom with whom I had shared my innermost thoughts, my hopes, and concerns. It was with them that I planned and dreamed. Dad was a part of my life, of course, but somewhere in the corners and out of the conversation. And it wasn't intentional. It was just so much easier to talk with Mom and

Grandpa. They asked for it. And, the truth was, I thought of Dad as someone who was there if I needed him, but I just didn't need him yet. It made me feel like when I was ten or eleven, and I had used the shovel to build a fort for my toy soldiers. It was near the fourth of July, and Dad and Mom let me play with firecrackers. This was before firecrackers were considered to be more deadly than atomic bombs. I needed the shovel to build a bank to protect my troops, and after I was through playing, I left the shovel there. A few days later, Dad found me in the kitchen and asked, "Are you going to put that shovel up?"

"I don't need it," I answered.

"It needs you," he said. "To put it back where it belongs."

So, I guess Dad had been my shovel all these years, and I was only now noticing him, and I felt some guilt about that. Grandpa Two Bears was dead, and Mom was sick, so was I that selfish? Was I noticing my chopped liver father because the steak was all gone? I mentioned all this to Gaby on the drive down to Militia Springs.

"So, what is the question, Winfred?" Gaby sat sideways to talk with me and keep an eye on Christine in the back seat. "Are you afraid that your father doesn't know you love him? Need him?"

"Yeah," I glanced at her. "I guess."

"And are you sure he even needs this assurance?"

"Doesn't everybody?"

"You didn't?"

"What are you talking about?"

"Well, according to what you say, you never told him that you loved him or needed him."

"Gee, Gaby. Men don't say that to men."

"So, you don't have anything to worry about then."

I glanced at Gaby's smile and frowned. I returned to the windscreen and the road. That wasn't much help.

Later, that evening we were sitting at the kitchen table finishing Molly's version of Mom's meatloaf when Mom started singing. Her voice was thin and broken.

"She'll be coming around the mountain when she comes, she'll be coming around the mountain when she comes, she'll be coming around the mountain, she will…she will…" Mom faltered, and her lips trembled in confusion.

"She'll be coming around the mountain." It was Dad! "She'll be coming around the mountain; she'll be coming around the mountain when she comes." I had never heard Dad sing before. Not in church, not along with the radio, not ever. And he had a great voice!

Dad was a crooner! He took Mom's hand and looked at her as he sang, and Mom smiled at him and started to sing too.

"She'll be coming around the mountain…" we all joined in, and Mom smiled and raised her voice, and for a moment, we were back the way it used to be. For a moment.

If I had to put one word to Alzheimer's, I guess that word is cruel. And its cruelty comes from its patience because it is content to let you see the destruction of your loved one in its often-glacial devastation. Like watching a favorite photo fade away, and no matter how you hold it, you can't quite make out what used to be there. And it is cruel because of its false promises; good days strung together, normalcy…hope! Only to have the eyes go blank or the anger spring. And there were days before the crossover when I would sit in the living room or the kitchen and talk with Mom, but while we were talking and laughing and I was listening, there was a voice in the back of my head that whispered, "this isn't real." And I would fight not to hear that voice, and I would smile so Mom wouldn't hear it. And one day, I walked into the kitchen, and Mom was holding her hands out, one in front of the other. When she said, "Boom," and swung her hands up, I knew she was mimicking shooting a gun. And then she said, "A man's gotta do what a man's gotta do."

Dad was in the room too, and I looked at him, then back to Mom.

"Shooting rabbits, Mom?"

Mom glared at me and slowly shook her head. She put her hands out again, "Boom." She glanced at me. "A man's gotta do what a man's gotta do."

The hair came up on my arms because I recognized that is what Dad had said, the night we discussed what we were going to do if Caleb got in the way of Molly. Before he turned up dead, killed with a shotgun. I frowned and looked at Dad, but he walked to Mom and gently "put the rifle down." Mom collapsed into his arms and sobbed. He hugged her and kissed her head, and I heard Mom's muffled voice, "A man's gotta do what a man's gotta do."

Did Mom shoot Caleb?

The average life span for people who have Alzheimer's is around five years, but some live for decades after diagnosis. Mom died the following year. And while I wept, I felt happy for her. And, more selfishly, I suppose, I felt relief for us. And for that relief, I felt guilt. The guilt of putting the pain of the watcher above the pain of the watched. But above all else, I knew Mom would go to a heaven of her creations, something she fervently believed was God's greatest promise. And there she would find all the people and dogs she knew and missed. Mom would wait for me, for all of us. She would discover Jane, too, and she would like her.

It was raining the day we buried her next to Grandma Catherine and Grandpa Two Bears and their little Molly. But it was a good rain for August, and she would be happy for the alfalfa. That afternoon I returned to *My Utmost for His Highest* to find something to help me. And after some searching, I found, "God does not give us overcoming life; He gives us life as we overcome." I read that a couple of times, and I knew that Mom's death was just a part of my journey, and as my family filtered into the living room—looking and needing to be together—I realized that we had grown so much closer over the past year. I looked at Christine sitting on Dad's lap while Gaby leaned against him, and I smiled as Paul gave Molly a quick kiss. We had become truly thoughtful and appreciative of each other, and I believe that was Mom's final gift. It was a good afternoon.

But over the next few days, I began to believe Mom was wrong about one thing. Birds don't sing at night because they are lonely. They sing to attract a mate. They sing to assure the survival of their species. No, I was convinced. Birds don't sing at night because they are lonely. They sing because of God's love for them.

A FALL FROM GRACE

When Grandpa Two Bears was dying, Mom sent word, and I flew home. And to this day, I am unsure how he spoke to me or if I imagined it. But whether fancied or real, his message to me was that I was meant to find Gaby. And I believed for the longest time that my purpose was to take care of her. My epiphany from Mark Twain's apocryphal statement: "The two most important days of a man's life are the day he is born and the day he understands why." But over time, I began to more fully realize what Grandpa Two Bears had meant. He surely meant for me to take care of Gaby, but he also meant that Gaby was to take care of me. And that she did. The loss of Grandpa hurt me deeply; he was my touchstone. But Gaby was there. Different, of course, but a soulmate with whom I could freely talk, more importantly, feel.

After Mom died, life slowly recovered to normal as it mercifully does. Baby Christine and Gaby, and I continued to visit the farm, but our time with the family became less about sorrow and more about growing children, cows, alfalfa, and the goings-on and rhythm in Militia Springs. My job plodded along, a 9 to 5 existence—new to me. It was so strange to be a staff officer with no decisional authority other than how strong to make the coffee after having command of a squadron. In fact, I thought the navy forgot me until it promoted me to captain. Of course, I was overjoyed, but I was genuinely astounded when a month later, I found I had been selected to command an airwing!

My airwing was located back in San Diego, so we moved from East Saint Louis across the west to Tierrasanta, a suburb southeast of the base at Miramar. I didn't have time to take any leave since I had to start my training track.

The CAG program is one of those no-kidding good deals in the navy. You start as the deputy commander, the DCAG, and your job is to fly all the airplanes in the airwing! No kidding. Your job is to fly! The CAG program had to have been designed by a lieutenant. A more senior officer would have goofed it up by requiring us to go to Total Quality Management school or stand deck watch until we carved FTN on our foreheads or something. The idea was for me to be the DCAG for a year and a half and then assume the CAG role. My CAG was Mark Fitzpatrick, callsign Lodestar. He was an exceptional aviator, leader, and probably the best strike tactician in the navy. Lodestar was a former A-7 pilot who had led strikes during the Gulf War. His infinite patience with me enabled me to increase my effectiveness and value to the battlegroup commander. Although we spent almost the entirety of my DCAG tour off the carrier, preparing for the next cruise, the time screamed by. We were in Fallon for our weapons training when we got the news that Jack Grant had bombed Iran because of miscommunication about a strike order. Top-secret intercepts showed that Iran might try something at the summer Olympics in Atlanta. This led to the development of plans to counter that or punish Iran, and somehow Jack's airwing received the green light to conduct the attack. The embarked flag discovered the mistake but not in time to stop Jack from going after his target. Odd that the rest of the airwing got the word to abort, but Jack did not. During his attack, he was hit by a SAM but managed to bring his strike damaged aircraft back to the ship. And to his good fortune, his action caused the Iranians to seek a dialogue with the United States, something that hadn't happened since our hostages were taken back in the eighties. So, Jack was a hero again!

The rest of my time as DCAG was fantastic, and I was blessed to learn at the feet of an officer like Lodestar Fitzpatrick. By the time he left, I was ready.

A week after taking command, I received word that Grace Grant was in hospice! She was dying of ovarian cancer. The next day, I flew to Virginia Beach and went to the Coastal Peace Hospice, where I met her caregiver, a man who introduced himself as Joe. Joe took me to see Grace, and I was shocked at how she had deteriorated since Gaby and I had last visited. She was a skeleton, and her hollow eyes and sunken cheeks made my throat tight. I sat on the edge of her bed and touched her hand. It was a claw.

"I knew you would come." Her eyes were morphine bright, and there was her smile. Ragged as it was.

"Why did you think that?" I smiled too.

"Because you love me. You always have."

The bluntness of her answer startled me into a broader smile. I squeezed her hand, and I remembered the first time I saw her, alone from her group, standing there with her fragile look. Fragile yet with substance, something to be desired, was the way she looked.

"Well, that is true." I squeezed her hand again.

"And I loved you. I think you know that."

I nodded. "I know." My voice was thick, and I had to drop my eyes.

"In fact, if it weren't for you and Harley, I'm afraid I would have gone through my life without experiencing love."

I looked back up at her and forced a smile. "That sounds incredibly sad, Grace. And it isn't true."

Grace shrugged. "Love is only sad if it's missed. It is a star on a dark night. Up there, somewhere above the clouds, who cares."

"Now, that's even sadder." I chuckled to change the mood.

"You remember that day in Cap D'Antibbes?" She glanced at me. "When we kissed."

I nodded.

"I miss that day. I will always miss that day."

I nodded again, unsure of what to say or do. Grace looked down at her hands for a moment. Then back up at me.

"Love requires trust. And trust requires a weakness. And weakness is something my family didn't tolerate."

"That's a callous way to grow up, Grace."

Grace took a breath and nodded. Her head fell to the side, and she closed her eyes.

"Is Jack coming?"

"I don't know." Grace opened her eyes. "I feel sorry for him."

"For Jack?" I frowned. How could she possibly feel sorry for him?

"Jack trusts his ability to manipulate. He always has. But that is his weakness." Grace smiled as if she had revealed a great truth.

I shrugged, unsure what she meant.

"One day, he will realize that he has just been manipulating himself. He will realize he is his own joke." Grace shut her eyes again, and I watched her for a while.

"Is there anything you want me to tell him? Tell Jack?"

Grace kept her eyes closed. "Tell him to take care of my dog."

I stayed for that day and another, but Grace never awakened. She was conscious but somewhere by herself. Someplace where she didn't have to trust anyone. I flew back home and a few days later learned that Grace had died. I sent a card of condolence to Jack at Grace's address. He never responded.

The week before I was to leave on deployment, Gaby and I attended Jack Grant's change-of-command. We sat near the front with the other CAGs and senior officers, and it was a beautiful, chilly San Diego day. The ceremony was held on the *Vinson's* flight deck, so I settled into my chair, and Jack began to speak.

"I am also blessed to have Admiral Titan Turner here today."

I frowned when Jack said that name. Vice Admiral Titan Turner was the flag officer when Jack and I were on *Eisenhower* together when he shot down the MIGs and became a hero. The word was that Titan Turner was Jack's sugar daddy.

"And there is a reason for that." Jack looked down at his speech, and I saw him take a breath. He looked up and above the eyes of the crowd for a moment.

"For my earlier changes of command, I wanted the prestige of senior and powerful guest speakers. And, because of the events surrounding me, I could have that. I have indeed been fortunate. In fact, the CNO's office informed us that he was available for this event if I wanted." Jack paused again and looked at all of us. I looked around, and everyone was smiling, glad to be a part of this special moment for a special man.

"But I declined the CNO's gracious offer," said Jack. "You see, I wanted Vice Admiral Turner to be here since he was the first flag officer to advocate for me. He convinced my CAG to give me the number one ticket. A ranking I did not deserve." Jack looked at Vice Admiral Turner and smiled, and I could see the confusion in the admiral's face. Hell, I was confused.

"He has supported me since the days when I was a skipper. I owe much of my success, my command of this air wing, and my reputation to him." Jack smiled again, saluted, and turned back to the crowd.

"But I do not merit his advocacy or his support." Jack paused, and the crowd quickly quieted. I heard a low buzz in the audience and looked around. I saw eyes narrowed and smiles sagging in confusion.

"Admiral Turner thought he saw in me, a future naval aviation leader. I dare to say, he saw in me as a person who one day could take the torch from him and carry it to the pentagon." Jack paused again, then continued. "But I misled the Admiral. I misled all of you." There was a collective gasp from the crowd.

What did he say?

Mouths gaped open and frowns found their places. People stared at each other, then glanced around to others. Had they heard him correctly? Was this some kind of stunt?

Jack turned to Vice Admiral Turner and slowly shook his head. "Sorry about the surprise, boss, but this is the best way to do this." He shifted his gaze to the chaplain. Jack nodded to him. "This is the next right thing to do, chaplain."

Jack turned to the crowd. He stared at his speech and then carefully folded it and put it in his breast pocket. He looked down for a moment, then swallowed and met our confused gazes.

"I am not the man you think I am," he said. "I am not the man, not the officer; the navy thinks I am." Jack swallowed again, and I saw his eyes grow wet. "I am a fraud." I watched him take a deep breath. "I have lived a completely self-centered life. I have conducted myself with only my self-interests in mind. I neglected the needs of my wife. I left her to more or less fend for herself. I don't know if you knew her. Grace was her name. She suffered from anxiety and the loss of our son. and I just walked away from her. She died a little while ago. She died in a hospice because I didn't take care of her."

The crowd gasped again. More confusion.

"I selected for fighters out of the training command because I manipulated the instructors and because I got access to the computers and changed my scores. I screened for squadron command due to a total fluke of luck. I did not shoot the Phoenix missile in Iraq. My RIO shot it because I was too timid, and if it were not for his direct coaching, I would not have shot the other MIG either. I was not a hero in Iraq and did not survive a shootout with Saddam's men. I ran out on two brave men who were battling for me. I left them to die."

Jack paused as his voice broke. He didn't make eye contact with the crowd anymore. He gripped the sides of the podium. It was so quiet I heard myself swallow.

Jack held onto the podium for a few moments, then straightened and turned toward Vice Admiral Turner. "Sir, I know I am now an embarrassment to you, and for that, I have no excuse. But I can fix this. I can fix it now. Sir, I resign from my position as Commander, Carrier Air Wing Fourteen, and I resign as a Captain in the United States Navy. My signature is on the documents, here at the podium."

Jack saluted. Vice Admiral Turner, unsure what to do, looked at Rear-Admiral Franklin. Both men stood in confusion. Jack turned and walked off the dais.

That night Gaby and I talked about Jack's resignation and the unbelievable and unprecedented scene.

"You know, now that the shock is gone, I am not surprised at what Jack did." I looked at Gaby and shook my head.

"Really? The crowd sure seemed to be surprised."

"Grace said something that got me to thinking. She said Jack would one day realize that it was he who he had been manipulating all this time. Maybe that is what happened. Maybe that is why he resigned in such a public way."

As Gaby and I sat on the couch that evening, television in the background, I thought of Jack and Grace, and I felt that somehow something good and right had happened. That Grace had gotten to Jack somehow. But I was conflicted a week later when I received news that Jack Grant had been killed in a little town in Missouri by the county sheriff. The announcement came from the Douglas County Herald; Dad sent it to me. Evidently, Jack had met a woman, and the jealous sheriff shot him in a spat that involved her, but it was over Jack's little dog. The only good part of the story was that the woman took the dog to live with her.

MAD AS HELL?

Admiral Phillips is an imposing presence, and when his head appeared inside my stateroom door, I quickly rose. "Come in, sir."

The admiral shook his head and stayed in the door frame. "CAG, you know we have to do something about that SA3."

"Yes, sir."

The admiral frowned and pursed his lips. It was a look that I had grown to view as unconfident concern. And I understood why. Admiral Phillips was a senior surface warfare officer responsible for a battle group with an aircraft carrier and airwing at its center. I think many surface officers who lead aviation-centric battlegroups lack confidence because they have not grown up as aviators. They don't truly understand the innards of the aviation business.

I believe that reality requires them to trust their staff more than they want. They also have to trust the carrier's skipper and the CAG more than they want. So, there was this thing between the admiral and me, this gap. You see the heartbeat of a carrier; the reason we are here is our capability to receive higher tasking, plan our response, and execute. I have intimate knowledge of making those plans, and I know how to lead the execution of them. The admiral does not. He knows the words, the concepts, but he doesn't know...the business. I am sure there are a million things Admiral Phillips knows that I do not, but whatever those things are, they don't matter. Not out here on this carrier.

That said, as a student of history, I was impressed by one of our greatest naval tacticians, and that was Ray Spruance. Admiral Spruance had no aviation experience per se; he too was a surface officer. But he understood carriers. He did know the business, and he led us during Midway's battle to a resounding success over Japanese aviators. Admiral Spruance saved our nation, by my notion. Whenever I hear the complaint that we don't need any "shoes" leading us, I think of Midway. That said, I get a bit frustrated when I continually need to explain things to the admiral and his staff.

Admiral Phillips looked at me a moment longer, then backed away and closed the door. I sat for a second, stunned by his abrupt message, and wondered what he had meant by his visit. Was he opining, bored, needing to act admiral-like, or did he want me to do something about the SA3?

The US-led coalition had sparred with Saddam since the end of the Gulf War. His mistreatment of his people caused us to create Operations Northern Watch to protect the Kurds and Southern Watch to protect the Marsh Arabs. Occasionally, Saddam would test the coalition, and that resulted in bombing campaigns against his military. Things had been quiet since we had taken our station in the Persian Gulf, and this morning's intelligence about the missile battery's probable existence caught us by surprise. We didn't have any photos or visual confirmation, but we did have a spot on a chart where intercepts of electromagnetic emissions corresponded to the SA3. So, it may or may not be there.

The more I thought about the admiral's visit, the more I felt I should act. And I must admit, my mind also wandered to my great friend, Raoul. It was an SA3 in this part of Iraq that had bagged him. It had shot him down, and now he was somewhere carrying guilt for it. He was lost, and I hadn't been able to find him.

I was flying on event five that afternoon, so I had my operations officer contact the squadron flight leads for the event and muster them in my office. Once they were settled, I told them I was changing our mission to a possible attack on the SA3. I planned to form up and fly toward the plotted point, and if the EA6-B electronically detected the SA3, or if my ES-3 spook squadron saw emissions, we would fire High-Speed Anti-Radiation Missiles, HARMs. The HARMS would be tuned to seek the SA3 acquisition and fire control radars. The EA6-B guys would also jam the radars, and, finally, we would hard kill the target with the F-14s and F-18s dropping laser-guided bombs.

Unfortunately, one of the crewmembers in the EA-6B was also on the admiral's staff. We occasionally flew such staff officers to give them some flight time and keep them up to date on airwing operations. However, this officer ran to the admiral's chief-of-staff, the COS, and told him that CAG would start a war with Iraq. The COS called and demanded, "CAG, are you trying to start a war with Iraq?"

I told him I was only responding to the admiral's morning visit.

"Maybe you should come down to the flag spaces and discuss," he said.

I was in my flight gear by this time, ready to head to my plane, but I walked through the blue tile area and entered the admiral's office. Gathered there were the admiral, the COS, the flag JAG officer, the flag operations officer, and the flag intel officer.

"Where's the chaplain?" I smiled. No one smiled back.

"CAG, I hear you modified your event." Admiral Phillips scowled as he swiveled his chair to face me.

"Yes, sir." I glanced around the room, still unsure of the problem.

"How so?"

"Sir, I intend on leading an element toward the suspected SA3 site, and if it lights us up with its radar, we will shoot HARM at it, Jam it, and then bomb it."

"Well, the JAG here believes it is a violation of the Rules of Engagement."

I frowned and looked at the admiral. "How so, sir? I don't get it."

"JAG." The admiral motioned to his legal officer.

"Sir, the ROE prevents us from launching an attack on Saddam. We can only respond if we are attacked and then only with available assets." The legal officer waved a piece of paper as if that gave him authority.

"Exactly," I glared at him. "I am not attacking. I am merely leading an element toward a suspected illegal SAM site, and if it lights me up, which is a hostile act, I will then respond to it."

"But, sir, if you launch from the ship with the intent to attack, a plan to attack, it is a violation of ROE." The JAG waved his paper again.

"Take a look outside," I said, fighting to keep my anger in check. "Go up to the flight deck and take a peep. You will notice these things hanging under the airplanes. We call them bombs, and we fly every day with them on. We fly every mission with the capability to attack; that is why we are here."

"Take it easy, CAG." The COS flashed a wide smile. "I think the JAG means that if we launch with the intent to attack, it is different than if we launch on a routine mission and then are forced to attack as a response."

"Have you ever been to one of our flight briefs, COS?" I was pissed. "If you go to one, you will see that on every mission, we brief the possibility of being attacked and the plans we have to respond to that attack. We don't just take off and figure it out when airborne."

"But do you normally change an event like this? And plan to evoke a response and then attack?" The admiral squeaked in his chair.

"No, sir. But we haven't had any specific target threatening us until now. The SA3 is the first. I thought it concerned you when you stuck your head inside my stateroom this morning. That is why I decided to act."

"I am concerned, CAG, but I am also concerned about violating the ROE that higher authority has developed."

"What do you want us to do, sir? Fly around until we are shot at and then ask Washington if we can defend ourselves?" What in the fuck did he think was going on?

"Of course not." The admiral glared at me.

I knew I had struck a nerve. Admirals get riled when you remind them that they are pussies. But his anger disgusted me. He had displayed unconfident concern about aviation and warfighting but was now very sure when it involved ROE.

"Maybe you can take a circuitous path towards the SA3." The ops officer, also a shoe, chimed in. "Instead of flying directly toward it, you know, circle in the vicinity of the suspected site, and if attacked, then respond."

"That kind of lunacy will only get us shot down," I spat. "Navy tactics do not feature dueling with a SAM site. We don't do wild weasel missions like the air force. We execute a timeline to attack a SAM using HARM, jamming, and bombs." I was so fucking tired of explaining how the naval aviation universe worked to shoes. Where in the hell was Ray Spruance?

"Well, if you can only execute this event by flying directly toward the target to elicit a response, then you have to cancel it," said the admiral.

"Fine! Should I contact the ordies and have them download all the planes? Don't want to take the chance of dropping something."

"CAG, that is enough." The admiral stood and glowered at me. That was the moment I knew that I would never be an admiral.

I whirled and stomped out of the room. I went to the flight deck, manned my jet, and once airborne and up the strike frequency, told my team that the event was off.

After my spat with the admiral, I went into a bit of a funk. I had never given making admiral much thought, but as a CAG, I knew I was at least in the running. Odds on, that was gone now as the admiral would probably take offense to what I had done. I was also frustrated because the ops in the gulf had become routine and boring. I wanted to attack the SA3 to do something that had a purpose! And now we were heading back home, soon to transit the Straits of Hormuz and exit the gulf. I was sitting in my office, writing an email to Gaby, when my DCAG, Dan "Merk" Merker, burst in.

"CAG, we've been attacked."

"What? By Saddam? If it's that SA3, I am going to kill the JAG."

"No, sir. I mean, the country has been attacked. New York City and the Pentagon. We need you in the admiral's cabin."

I jumped to my feet and followed Merk down the passageway.

Over the next hours, we learned that terrorists had hijacked four airliners and had flown two into the World Trade Center's twin towers, one into the Pentagon, and one had crashed in a field in Pennsylvania. Over 3,000 of our countrymen had died, with 7,000 injured. The attackers were primarily from Saudi Arabia, and the mastermind was Osama Bin Laden, who led an Islamist terrorist group named Al Qaeda. His lair was in Afghanistan's mountains, where the Taliban gave him and his followers refuge. The Taliban was an ultraconservative group formed to fight the Soviets and eventually drove them out of the country.

It is hard to describe our feelings, my feelings, as the information flowed to us. None of us had ever been attacked in our lifetimes. Grandpa Two Bears had talked to me about how he felt after Pearl Harbor was hit, but now I realized that I hadn't really connected with his words. I know that anger was a part of our response, anger and frustration and some sorrow. But I think my most forward feeling was thankfulness that I was in uniform. I was thankful because I could do something about it. I pitied my fellow countrymen who had only television to view and no weapons to use. I felt sorry for our losses for sure, but I pitied those Americans who now must feel an almost unbearable frustration because they couldn't do anything! And that gave me a great inspiration because I knew what we must do was for them.

The day after the attack, we transited the strait into the Indian Ocean and headed for a holding point south of Karachi, Pakistan. Central Command began to send us targeting data and other valuable information, and I set my strike planners to work. It was during these first, chaotic days that my relationship with Admiral Phillips changed. It blossomed into one of mutual admiration and our discussions into the wee hours bonded us as fellow warriors.

While he leaned on me to execute the strike mission, he demanded clarity from seniors and shielded me from an ever-growing torrent of "good idea" people who would have consumed us. I was amazed at the admiral's management of the situation and dramatically reevaluated my earlier doubts about a surface officer's viability in charge of a battlegroup.

As we received our tasking and studied the charts, we saw that our most pressing difficulty was the enormous distances we had to fly to get to the Taliban targets—on-average 600 miles one way! Our Hornets were short legged for sure, but even the Tomcats needed vast amounts of gas to execute the missions. We used a combination of our indigenous S-3 tankers and USAF KC-135 and KC-10 refuelers to support our flights, which were on average five hours long and sometimes much, much longer.

On October 7th, 2001, I led the first strike against the Taliban. And as we flew north I couldn't help but feel a tiny bit like Jimmie Doolittle. I don't mean the danger. Doolittle and his B-25 raiders had no friendly fighter support and they knew they were on a one way trip. They had to crash land in China after the attack! My strike didn't face any of that danger. But, still, we were executing the first attack on the Afghanistan stronghold. Just like Doolittle executed the first attack on the Japanese mainland. What we were doing was monumental. And I also knew that what I was doing, leading this attack, was the pinnacle of my career.

Our initial targets were airfields, communications bunkers, AAA sites, storage areas, barracks, and other military installations near Kabul, Kandahar, Herat Manzar-i-Sharif. We carried 1,000 and 2,000-pound laser-guided-bombs and the newer Joint Direct Attack Munition or JDAM. JDAMs used satellites for targeting, so we didn't have to worry about lazing them. They were a tremendous weapon, and the bunker buster version was extremely effective against caves. I also carried a hefty supply of piddle packs, plastic bags with a sponge inside and shaped to facilitate relieving yourself. It took a bit of digging and coaxing to get the "turtle" out, but the bags worked pretty well, and I used three on my first flight. I also didn't drink another cup of coffee the entire time we were in the theater.

After the first week, we destroyed much of the Taliban's infrastructure and shifted from attacking predetermined targets to targets of opportunity within a given engagement zone. We would lug our bombs to the circling tanker and await target assignment from either an airborne forward air controller (FAC-A) or the airborne command and control center (ACCC). This tactic allowed us to respond to a dynamic and ever-changing battlefield and supported our special operations forces on the ground. This was also when Admiral Phillips approached me and asked if the EA6B could jam communications equipment. He believed that since we had flushed the Taliban and Al Qaeda into hiding, they would be frantic to communicate. I had never heard of the EA6B used in a comms jamming role, but it turned out they could. And they were good at it. I had to give credit to the surface warfare officer for that new arrow in our quiver.

We stayed off the coast of Pakistan for a month and flew bombing missions into Afghanistan almost every day. One by one, more carriers joined, and by the time we left, we had five flattops on station. I was so proud of the US Navy and, particularly, of naval aviation. Throughout my twenty-six-years in the navy, I had always understood our value–protecting the sea lanes, deterring aggression, and carrying our flag.

But this was different. Unlike Vietnam or our past actions against Libya, Grenada, and Iraq, we were taking the war to a country that had attacked us. It was gratifying beyond my expectations and, in some ways, the fulfillment of my career.

On our way home, we had an opportunity to digest what had happened to our country, and it was sobering. We learned that our navy had lost thirty-three sailors at the Pentagon. When I read that my friend and former lover, Missy Sanders, was on the list, it personalized our losses even more. When I saw the video of the towers, the Pentagon, that cornfield in Pennsylvania, I saw Missy's face, and her death caused me to question myself. I believe great events can cause you to reevaluate even the fundamentals of what you believe. So, I pondered my feelings toward women in naval aviation, something I had never resolved. I had never liked the idea because I thought that women would destroy the chemistry we men had. I continue to believe that today, but I also realize that the bulk of naval aviation isn't old men like me. Most are young and raised in a different time. Do they think differently than I do? Are they okay with women in the ready room and in combat with them? Is there a Jane Wayne out there every bit as capable as John? But as I released my thoughts along that road, I wondered if I was slipping into some form of ambivalence. Since my flying career was over, what did I care who was in naval aviation? And the more I thought about that, the more it bothered me. Would I become just another one of these older people who only cared about what was in his direct interest?

Would I "not give a crap" about things that I had once had a strong opinion about because they no longer affected me?

My kids aren't in school, so I don't care about the syllabus or student achievement, even though I know the connection to a vibrant society and economy.

My wife isn't going to get an abortion, so I don't care about the issue even though I am distraught that a fetus with a beating heart is a human baby.

I'm getting older, so I don't care how much national debt we have. However, I know that eventually, such debt will have to be paid off by our children.

I think that there is a comfort in ambivalence. It gives us the ability to avoid. It provides us with the ability evade, to side-step solutions. But I also think there is a danger there. When humans have conflicting norms like this, we can cease to engage, which can be a signal of acceptance. That is why small groups, when left unchallenged, can cause significant damage. I remember reading somewhere that only around 7% of families owned slaves at the time of the Civil War, yet we went to war over it. Of course, we know that in the mid-1930s, a tiny group of what would be called Nazis overtook Germany. So, will I be an engaged citizen who stands for what he believes, or will I withdraw? Will I crawl into some shell or cave? Or, maybe worst of all, will I be like Peter Finch in the movie, *Network*? Will I raise a frustrated fist and, with my red face, shout, "I'm mad as hell, and I won't take it anymore" to a crowd I no longer feel part of?

DAD

I took leave after returning home, and Gaby, Christine, and I drove to Militia Springs for Thanksgiving. We had made the trip before and always took the 8 to I-40 east and through Phoenix and Albuquerque, then Amarillo and Oklahoma City. Since we pick up I-40 in Arizona, it is just I-40 without the California obligatory *the*.

It takes three days to drive, but I decompress, so by the time I cross into Missouri just west of Joplin, I am no longer worrying about my job and navy things. That said, as a constant "grinder," I do think about things that bother me, and my previous thoughts about ambivalence kept coming into my mind.

"Do you ever think that growing old also means growing apart?" I glanced at Gaby. Christine was asleep in the back seat, and the car was quiet.

"What do you mean?"

"I don't know. Is it possible that as society changes, as people change, we must change with it, with them?"

"Not always, I guess." Gaby tilted her head the way she does. "Depends on what you are talking about."

"I guess you are right." I glanced at her again. "It just seems like things are moving away from me. That I am, I don't know, disconnecting."

"What kinds of things?"

"The other day I was watching television, and there was a commercial by Apple, you know, the computer company. And the commercial had these images of Bob Dylan, and Albert Einstein, and Thomas Edison, and the voiceover was all about celebrating the misfits, the rebels, the ones who have no respect for rules and the status quo." I glanced at Gaby again. She shrugged.

"So."

"Well, I have been a rules guy, a status quo guy all my life. I'm not a rebel. I guess the commercial just caught me at an odd time. I don't know. It just made me feel like I wasn't in the mainstream anymore. Besides, what does all that have to do with me buying an Apple computer anyway?"

"You liked James Dean, didn't you? And that dumb motorcycle movie with Marlon Brando."

"Yes."

"Well, they were misfits or at least played them in movies. You probably like the non-status quo more than you think."

I shrugged and continued to drive.

I take Highway 60 west of Springfield, then to Highway 14, and by the time I cross Beaver Creek, I feel home again. I don't know why that home feeling gets me. I haven't officially lived in Missouri since I joined the navy over twenty years ago.

The farm was as we left it, and Dad, Molly, Paul, and Kate were there to meet us. As I stepped out of the car, I felt an emptiness without Mom and Grandpa Two Bears. But the warmth of the others nudged away the sadness, and our lawn reunion was indeed joyous. Kate had a young man in tow who she introduced as Roger Chamberlain, who, like Kate, was a high school teacher at Militia Springs. He taught Agriculture, which I related to since it had been my minor.

Gaby, Christine, and I bunked in Grandpa Two Bears' room and settled into a relaxing visit.

The next morning, I found Dad in the barn. He had twenty or so bales of hay to move, so I thought I would help him load the trailer.

I tossed a bale and caught Dad's eye and smiled. "Used to make big money doing this."

"I remember you hauling hay. What did you get?"

"Two cents a bale. Made twenty dollars one day putting in 1,000 for Mister King."

"That's a lot of hay," Dad grunted and tossed a bale onto the trailer.

"It WAS a lot of money. I could fill-up the car for a couple of dollars and go to the drive-in for seventy-five cents."

"Don't even have the drive-in anymore," said Dad.

"Yeah, I saw the empty spot when we drove through town." I threw a couple of more bales. "Makes me nostalgic."

"Oh, how so?"

"I don't know. I want some things to stay the same. Things that I was a part of or liked. I think that is why I come back here so often. So, when things change, the drive-in closing, for instance, it just makes me sad."

"Even if the owner shut it down because he was losing money?" Dad heaved the final bale onto the trailer.

"That makes me even sadder." I shook my head and glanced at Dad. "I guess it's like that book Mom paid me to read; *You can never go home again*." I frowned. "I can't remember the author."

"Thomas Wolfe," said Dad.

I looked at him and must have made a face because he laughed. "You aren't the only one who reads, you know. Who do you think spent time with Grandpa Two Bears and your mom before you came along?"

"I... I just didn't think." I frowned as I pitched a few more bales. I had spent so much time with Grandpa and Mom, shared so much of my thoughts and dreams with them. I couldn't think of a single time I had really talked with Dad. Except for when I told him about Molly being pregnant. He must have read my thoughts.

"Don't worry about it, son. The three of you were peas in a pod. I enjoyed the fact you and your mother and Grandpa got along so well. Besides, when I was with those two, I mostly listened. They were talkers, like you."

I glanced at Dad. He always had the same tone in his voice, so I was unsure if his comment about talkers was a good thing or a bad thing. He had hopped up on the tractor, so I stood on the hitch behind him, balancing as he slowly pulled out of the barn. We rumbled across the lot, past the pond, and up to the top of our pasture. Although we fed the cows grain and hay while we milked them, we also supplemented their winter grazing with alfalfa. We pulled up to a sheltered feeding area, and both hopped off.

"Is a talker good?" I glanced at Dad again.

"Depends on what's being said."

Dad always had a way of ending a conversation or beginning one depending upon your desire to engage him. I grinned and tossed a bale into the wooden feeder. "Well, I guess that makes sense."

We unloaded the trailer, and both leaned against it to catch our breath. It was around forty degrees with no wind, working in our coats. Dad wore the same old canvas jacket he always did. It was fleece-lined, and he got it from L.L. Bean. He wore long johns on real cold days, but today he just had on the bib overhauls.

"I think Kate and Roger will get married." Dad looked down the hill at the farmhouse. Smoke filtered from the chimney, straight up with no breeze.

"He seems like a pretty good guy," I nodded.

"I think so," said Dad. "And he is good on the farm too, which surprises me. Not that many young folks like farming. I get the feeling that he and Kate may eventually move out here. Like Paul and Molly did."

"Kind of like *The Waltons*? On T.V."

Dad grinned. "Kind of. I like the idea, though. Your mom and I moved out here with Grandpa and Grandma, and then Molly and Paul came to live with us. And now, Kate and Roger will be the next iteration of Kleegans living here. I like that."

I grunted and felt a twinge of envy. "Sounds ideal."

Dad glanced at me and nodded. "You know, you can always come too."

There was a time when I would have automatically said, "Thanks, Dad," and dropped the thought. But not this time. This time my mind seemed to accept the possibility. I looked out over the forest and smiled.

I felt Dad's eyes on me. "What? No talking now?"

I smiled again and spat out a bit of hay. "When I am stressed, I think about such a thing." I looked at Dad. "And it seems these days I think about it more. Coming back home. But I worry that it is some kind of– of, I don't know, retreat. I mean, I think my fondness for our farm, for Militia Springs, might be a yearning for the security of the past instead of the future."

Dad nodded, "I'm listening."

"When we drove around the square, I saw that the Nickel and Dime store had a new front. Neon lights instead of the old painted sign. And do you know how that made me feel?"

"Sadness seems to be the theme today."

I smiled. "Yes. And I think that is because my memories of that store have the old, hand-painted sign. The sign I looked at as I entered with a dollar Mom gave me to read one of her books." I shook my head and scraped the ground with the toe of my boot.

"It appears lots of things make you feel blue."

I shrugged, "I guess so."

"I never left here, so I don't fully understand what you mean." Dad looked at me. "The neon sign at the five and dime just means progress to me. You know, a better way to get customers to come in. Same for the drive-in. Closing it makes business sense. But then, I live here. You visit. I think that makes the difference."

I sighed and nodded again.

"There may be a time when living here makes sense to you. I suspect not yet. I think if you wanted to live in Militia Springs, you would have found your way home by now. So, give it some time, Son. And if the day comes when you want to be here, and not just to run back to here, then know you are welcome. You will always be welcome."

THE LONG-LEGGED DOG

The next spring, Cotton took command of *Enterprise* and I flew from San Diego to Norfolk in a Tomcat to attend his change-of-command ceremony. He and Melody were beside themselves with excitement and so was I. And as I sat in the audience and saw my old roommate take command of that grand ship, I thought about our time together. The beginning in Pensacola, then flying in Vietnam--our time as roommates and squadron mates. I also remembered when he got the squadron operations job that I wanted and how I had questioned whether it was because of some kind of reverse racism. Those thoughts troubled me and I cleared them from my mind by remembering how Cotton had taken me in as his XO and intervened into getting my security clearance fixed. It reminded me of the time I read a Readers' Digest quiz on whether your friends are better to you than you are to them. I never talked to Cotton about any of this. Some say if you are good enough friends with someone, you can talk about anything. I think that kind of thinking just loses friends.

A half year later, I turned the airwing over to Merk and the navy gave me orders to serve as the commanding officer of Tactical Training Group Pacific, TACTRAGRUPAC, in San Diego. We trained senior officers on a breadth of issues that faced tactical navy commanders.

Since this was our last navy assignment, Gaby interviewed for a job as an assistant manager at the Hotel Del Coronado. Over the years, she had managed to accumulate her associate degree in Hospitality Management and that degree plus her background in the restaurant business in Germany landed it. We never talked about her past, but I think Gaby's career selection was in part based upon choosing an industry where background checks were rare.

My school sat on a beautiful piece of land overlooking the ocean and I quickly settled into my job. There was some sea duty involved and my staff and I went to sea to train carrier battlegroup staffs during their pre-deployment exercises. Those periods away from Gaby and Christine were limited and for only a couple weeks at a time, so Gaby and I decided to get a dog for Christine. She was eleven and had been begging for one for years.

Gaby had never been around dogs and wasn't too keen on the idea and I had sworn I would never get a dog. I told myself it was because I was gone too much, but I think it really had to do with the little beagle, Toby. The dog that had been killed so many years ago. Killed because I had let him out of his kennel and under the wheels of Dad's car. But children can be terribly insistent with their big, wet eyes and tiny pleading voices. So, you can guess what happened.

An animal shelter is a heart-wrenching place if you believe in dogs. That is, if you believe they are more akin to us than any other animal and you also believe that if you don't act, some of them may not survive. Ambivalence may fit for avoiding much of life's concerns, but it doesn't work in a rescue kennel. In an animal shelter the barking you hear is for you.

The place was full of pit bulls and German Shepherd mixes, larger dogs that were no longer cute and cuddly. We walked slowly, giving the inmates an opportunity to introduce themselves and saw several that were really interesting. We had the staff take a chihuahua and a Labrador puppy out for us to pet. We did the same for a beagle and a Saint Bernard. Gaby almost fainted when that horse pranced out, but luckily Christine had here eye out for something else.

Then we saw this dog. It was a mix of terrier and who knows what and had a mottled brown coat with one ear that stood up and one that didn't. She had unusually long legs and eagerly stood on the hind ones to lick Christine's face. The vet said she weighed seven pounds and was approximately four months old. Christine hugged the dog and closed her eyes and wouldn't let go so I had the choice of leaving my daughter at the animal shelter for the rest of her life or getting the dog, so I ponied up $375 and signed a statement that I promised to get the dog spayed when she was six-months old.

As soon as the pup was in the back seat with Christine, we began the process of naming her. The shelter had the name Gertrude on the cage, but I didn't think that was a very good name for a little dog. I had to be a bit careful about that since Gaby's aunt was named Gertrude. Fortunately, Christine was adamant about a name change because the dog was now her dog and not the animal shelter's dog.

"If we don't change the dog's name, it might think it's still in the shelter," she said.

That made sense to me. That night Christine interrupted Buffy The Vampire Slayer to announce that she was naming the dog Shotzi.

Shotzi quickly became more than just a dog, a state of being that we human adopters insist upon. In fact, in some ways, she became a center point of our family, and I know how odd that might sound to a non-dog person. Christine and Shotzi became inseparable, and our ideas about what to do on the weekends became whatever can be done with a dog.

We bought a house in Pacific Beach near where Cotton, Raoul and I lived when I was a bachelor. The proceeds from my Virginia Beach house sale drove down my mortgage considerably, and we were happy and comfortable. The house sat back from the road and had a fence in the back which was good since it was at the edge of a green space. Green space is a romantic way to say a gully full of weeds, mesquite, and eucalyptus trees. Except for the coyotes, it was a pretty good place to live and my commute was easy. The only downside, again except for the coyotes, was my next-door neighbor, Royce Quigley.

Royce was a complete jerk and I grew to loathe him more than anyone I had ever met, except for Jack Grant. And I am not a big loather.

I didn't dislike Royce at the beginning. How could I? I didn't know him. In fact, I waved to him a couple of times, but he was on the way to his car and was quickly gone. I planned to meet him over the fence or in the front yard and strike up a conversation and, you know, be neighborly. A couple of weeks after we moved in, I was in the front yard, looking at my fine crop of crab grass, and Royce pulled up in his giant, ugly, gas-guzzling Hummer. Every time I see one of those things I think, "If you like that so much why don't you join the army and drive the real thing?" Anyway, Royce opened the door and his wife got out the other side and he walked around the car and slapped her. She is a mousy little thing; her head flopped back and she fell.

"HEY!" I shouted. It was pure instinct.

Royce turned toward me, all red-faced and scowling. I could see surprise in his eyes because he didn't realize anyone was watching.

"WHAT?"

"Come on man," I frowned. "You shouldn't hit a woman like that? You shouldn't hit anyone like that." I took a couple of steps toward him, hoping that the situation could still be resolved in a positive way.

"It's my woman and I can hit her all I want."

That took care of any thoughts of positivity. For a second I considered turning around and letting the whole thing slide. But as I walked across the lawn toward Royce, I watched his face, taking a measure of him. I saw his eyes flicker, and he quickly glanced toward his wife. He was a big man, three or four inches taller than me and a good 100 pounds heavier. Brawling in the front yard is never a good idea. Brawling with a bigger man is even worse. But I had already staked out my position. I couldn't very well just let it go.

"I would rather you didn't."

"Who the fuck do you think you are?" Royce bunched his fists. But he stepped back.

"I'm your neighbor, Royce." I held out my hand. "Your neighbor who asks that you not beat your wife."

"You bastard," he snarled. He bunched his fists again and glared at me, but I knew he wasn't going to do anything. He gave me a final frown, then turned toward his wife.

"Get in the fucking house!"

She scampered for the front door, and I knew she was probably in for a beating when her asshole husband came in.

Royce turned back to me. "Fuck you!" He stomped off toward the door.

I figured that would be the last time I had anything to do with Royce, but I was wrong. He cut the pepper tree that shaded my house.

Our green space is mostly mesquite and weeds, but it does have some trees. California oaks, gnarled and wizened versions of the grand Missouri variants, abound along with pepper and eucalyptus. Since the destiny of a eucalyptus is to grow tall and then fall on someone or turn into a roman candle in a wildfire, I was glad they were distant. But the pepper trees fringed our yards and were magnificent.

Royce had a big pepper tree, and one of its branches supplied great shade on the west side of my house. It kept the setting sun from heating my back deck and I often sat there enjoying its cooling gifts. Shortly after our encounter in Royce's driveway, he cut off the pepper tree limb that shaded my deck. Of course, it ruined the look of the tree, all lop-sided and all, but I know he did it to get back at me for revenge.

The next Monday, I heard shouting and dishes breaking. I ran to look out the patio door and saw Gaby walking toward Royce's house. She had a poker in her hand. I ripped open the door and sprinted across the lawn.

"Honey, I'm calling the police." I caught her by the shoulder. "Let them take care of this."

"Somebody has to do something!" Gaby glared toward Royce's house.

"Come with me, I'll call the cops."

I walked Gaby back into the house and called 911 and reported what we had seen and heard. Gaby still had her poker when the squad car rolled into Royce's driveway.

I stepped out onto the porch to watch the show. I could easily see the cops enter the living room because Royce was too cheap to buy curtains or blinds and grinned when I saw him scowl at his wife and shrug. One of the police officers was a woman and she took the wife into another room. I watched the other cop, a towering male, question Royce and hoped to see him taken out in cuffs. Unfortunately, the police officers left alone. But after they had driven off, Royce walked out in the front lawn. I grinned at him.

"Nice day," I said.

He scowled and went back into the house.

A couple of weeks later, I noticed more and more coyote activity in the green space and on our street and I heard them every night, calling each other. San Diego County is ridges and valleys and the houses are built on the ridges and the coyotes own the valleys and green spaces. I found a chicken carcass, the kind of thing that is left from buying a rotisserie chicken at COSTCO. It was on the other side of the fence behind my house. I suspected that idiot Royce put it there, believing the coyotes would just bother me. What an ass! My neighbor on the other side, Ms. Hutchinson, had a cat she named Mittens. It disappeared, and I am sure some cat-breathed coyote was a little fatter because of it. Anyway, I hated Royce and, I suspect, he hated me. But other than Royce, life went along without complaint. My navy job kept me busy and Gaby, Christine and Shotzi kept me amused, happy, and busy.

CHASING AFTER THE WIND

I shave every day, even on the weekends. It's my assurance that I am still vibrant and critical and ready for work. Besides, as an active-duty officer, I represent the navy and don't want to look like a bum, even down at the Vons. When I shave, I use a brush and a cake of soap in a mug instead of the aerosol stuff. Remember the scare back when we were afraid the freons and chlorofluorocarbons in spray cans were depleting the ozone layer? Whew, we somehow survived! Well, I don't shave with a mug of soap because of that, I use it because that's the way my dad did it. It's also the way Grandpa Two Bears did it, and it's the way I do it.

I run the hot water into the mug to warm the soap, and it runs onto the brush to warm it too. I let that sit while I wash my face and, I swear, every time I look into the mirror, I smile at the words of my Grandpa Two Bears who would say to me, "Weenie, just shave it. Fix it later." I was in such a Sunday morning reverie of soap and reflection when the phone rang. I hesitated, not wanting to wipe off my efforts with the brush.

Maybe Gaby or Christine will get it.

RINGGG!

Dang! I remembered they were walking Shotzi. I grabbed a towel, rubbed it across my jaw and hurried into the bedroom.

RINGGG!

"Kleegan residence." Soap squished into my ear.

"Weenie?"

I gripped the receiver and swallowed.

"Weenie?"

"Raoul?" I swallowed.

"Raoul?"

"Yeah, yes, sir. It's me."

"I…what…well. How are you? Where are you?"

"I guess you're a bit surprised?" His voice was defensive, no, contrite.

"Yes, you could say that." My hands shook and I sat on the side of the bed. "I, I. I'm very surprised."

"I'm sorry, Weenie."

"I had given up on ever hearing from you again."

"Yeah, I guess I was pretty elusive."

"Elusive! Hell, you disappeared. I called, emailed, wrote, no luck." Raoul didn't answer so I just held the phone to my ear. I was pissed at him and felt my anger rise. He had been my best friend all my adult life until the day he dropped out of it. And without a word of explanation! I needed to know why, and I wanted an apology. I could hear him breathing, waiting for me. I started to tell him what an ass he had been.

"Look, Weenie."

I heard a chair squeak and gripped my phone harder.

"I know I have been a jerk—a disappointment to you, and maybe a lot of others. I just wanted to get together with you and explain and, you know, talk."

I sighed and my anger flushed away with my breath. I still couldn't believe it was Raoul though. After all these years.

"There is a lot to talk about, Raoul. It's been nearly eight years."

"Yeah. I know, I know. Eight years."

He said it like he didn't realize how long it had been. Like he had been away somewhere.

"I hear they started Tailhook up again."

I frowned and shook my head. "Yes, it's in Reno now. Different, too. You can even take your wife or mother."

"Still fun, though?"

"Sure, it is always great to see old friends again."

"Do you drive that old Triumph?"

"I sold the Triumph years ago. I have a Toyota pickup truck now, besides the family car. I drove the Toyota to 'Hook last year."

"How is Gaby? And Christine?"

"Both great. Christine is eleven now."

"Eleven! Wow!"

Isn't it strange how fast the awkwardness can creep into a phone call? All it takes is a couple seconds of silence and the rhythm breaks. Of course, a phone call with your best friend who disappeared eight years ago doesn't help. But it got quiet.

"Do you ever have company?" Raoul's voice was... hopeful?

"Company? You mean on the ride to Reno? Gaby went with me last year and said that once was enough."

"What about this year?"

"I guess I will go alone. It's next weekend you know?" I grinned. "Why don't you go with me?"

"I... I was hoping you would say that?"

I smiled.

"Maybe you could pick me up on the way?"

"Well, sure. We have a lot to talk about." I chuckled.

"Great!" I could hear excitement in Raoul's voice. "Take 395 up to Red Mountain."

"Sure!" I felt excited too. "We can go together! But Red Mountain? What the hell are you doing there?" Red Mountain was a blot on the side of the Highway 395 as it shot north through the desert. It had been a mining village at some time but was now just a couple of ugly houses with junk in the front yards.

"I live there."

"You...you live there?"

"Yep. So, what do you think? Do you want to come by? We can drive up to Reno together."

I was dumbfounded! Raoul...after all these years? "Well, sure!"

"Fantastic! Thanks Weenie."

I smiled into the receiver. "Sure."

"When did you plan to leave?"

"I was thinking about Wednesday. I usually take a leisurely trip, stop the first night in Big Pine and then get into Reno Thursday night. Everybody will be glad to see you!"

"Sounds great, Weenie. Hey, do you still carry?"

"I still carry. At all times. But why do you ask?"

"Just interested, that's all. I keep a weapon on me too but that's cause I live out here with the weirdos and the rattlesnakes. It's a good practice to get into."

"Well, I have a gun on me when I travel."

"Great, I think that's smart. So, Weenie, when you get here, take the first left turn after the Red Mountain sign and wind around on the little road to my house. It is a whiteish cabin on the right. I have an old green Dodge truck. It will be out front."

My mind flashed to Austin, Texas. It was 1971 and Raoul had led me there on a hunt for the birthplace of his wrestling hero, Dusty Rhodes. Raoul was convinced there would be a shrine or maybe even a street named after him. After all, Dusty Rhodes was "the greatest wrestler of all time"! But we couldn't even find anyone who had heard of him. And I remember feeling this great sorrow for my friend. I was sorry that someone he had once considered grand, might not be. Raoul shrugged it off but I knew he was hurt.

And now as I thought of him living in some shack in the middle of nowhere, driving an old truck, and hiding from who-knows-what, I felt that same sorrow. Raoul had been the grandest friend I had ever had. And now, now I didn't know.

"I will be there around noon."

"Great. That's great. Look, Weenie, I sure appreciate this, and I look forward to catching up with you."

"Me too." I nodded. "Me too, buddy."

"It's been too long."

I nodded into the phone.

"I'll be ready." There was a bit of a plea in his voice, like he didn't want me to change my mind.

"Okay, see you then." I wiped the soap from the phone, put it in its cradle, and walked back to the bathroom to re-lather. As I brushed my face, I thought of Raoul.

Although we didn't meet until after college and in the navy, in some ways I felt I had grown up with him. Or, became a man, that is. Of course, he was in my first squadron and we were roommates until he went to Japan. He was in my wedding to Gaby and up until the time he disappeared I had talked to him at least weekly by phone. And then, he disappeared.

Raoul's question about whether or not I carried a weapon edged into my mind. As I finished shaving and put my mug and brush away, I remembered why I did. Shortly after Gaby and I had gotten married, we went to dinner near the Norfolk waterfront and got mugged. A couple of guys with guns. Didn't even see them until they were on us. I can still feel the helplessness of that night as the robbers forced Gaby and me to our knees. They took everything, even Gaby's ring, the one from my grandmother. The ring was a tiny thing, two small rubies set atop twists of gold but it was what Grandpa Two Bears could afford when he came home from the war. During a trip home, Gaby saw the ring and fell in love with it so I asked Mom if I could have it for her.

Since that night, I have carried a weapon. I alternate between a snub nosed .38 in an ankle holster or a 9 MM in my coat pocket I always carry Grandpa Two Bear's pocketknife too. I carry it in my back pocket like he used to. Some might think this extreme– and even if I would have had a gun that night, I'm not sure what would have happened. Would I have stopped them, or just prompted them to shoot us? I don't know but what I do know is we were incredibly vulnerable I feel better when I have a gun on me. Sad state of affairs, maybe. But it is the way it is. I was still thinking about that night when Gaby and Christine came home. Shotzi came bounding into the bedroom and I petted her head then followed her to the kitchen.

"Hey Dad."

"Hey you." I smiled at my daughter. Some kids are the rule-following, convention-supporting kind who make you feel content about their future. Then, there are others who are the braid-on-one-side-of-their-head and one blue shoe, one pink shoe kind who make you excited about their future and that is the kind Christine was. And she was smart. I tousled the braided side of her head.

"You have soap on your ear." Gaby kissed my cheek.

"Nice walk?" I wiped at my ear.

"Yep," said Christine. "Two bags full!"

"Wow! Better stop feeding that mutt so much."

"She's not a mutt." Christine settled to her knees, and Shotzi leaped into her arms.

"You'll never guess who called this morning."

"Who?"

"Raoul Hungus."

Gaby frowned and stepped back. "Raoul?"

"Yep. Raoul."

"Who is Raoul?" Christine looked up.

Gaby searched my face. "After all of this time? What did he want? Is anything wrong?"

"He wants to drive to Tailhook with me. Can you believe that?"

"Tailhook? I thought you were flying this year?"

"Not now. Can you believe it?"

"Who is Raoul?" Christine raised her voice.

Gaby squinted and shook her head. "Something's up. Your former best friend...OUR best friend... drops out of our lives for no reason. What's it been, eight years? Now, out of the blue, he wants to go to Tailhook with you?" She shook her head again.

"Maybe I'll find out what happened to him. What spooked him."

"That is the odd part, isn't it?" Gaby shook her head. "Raoul's not the kind to get spooked."

"WHO IS RAOUL?"

"Honey, Raoul was my best friend. He was in our wedding when Mommy and I got married."

"What happened to him?"

"Well, that is the strange part." I frowned. "He was flying an airplane over Iraq and got shot down. He and his pilot were captured. She was killed... I think he feels guilty."

"Was his pilot a girl?"

"She was a young woman named Mandy Mandolin."

Christine stood and came to me and I hugged her. "Then what happened to him?" She looked up at me.

"That's just it," said Gaby. "He disappeared. He resigned from the navy and disappeared without a word to Dad or anybody."

"Well, that's sad," said Christine. "Come on Shotzi, let's go to my room."

"Tell me the story again. I'm going to make some coffee. Want some?" Gaby reached for the pot.

"Sure."

"So, Raoul's group entered Iraq at the southern tip of the Al Faw peninsula and headed north toward Al Basrah. I think there was a package of two F-18 Hornets, Two A-6E Intruders, and an E-A6 Prowler. The hornets and intruders carried bombs and the prowler was to jam their radars."

"Raoul was in a Tomcat, right?"

"That's right." I settled on a stool. My memory was remarkably clear given the fact all this had taken place so long ago. "The reports I read indicated they were cruising along when Raoul came up on the radio and stated he had ECS turbine problem.

"What's an ECS turbine?"

"ECS means environmental control system. It provides air conditioning, cockpit pressurization, stuff like that."

"Why would that be a big problem?" Gaby had her back to me.

"Because the system takes hot gases off the engine to provide the air. The turbine makes all that work so if it fails, the hot gas can enter all kinds of systems. We had lost several tomcats to an ECS turbine failure and you have to immediately turn it off to survive catastrophe."

"So, they did have a big problem?" Gaby clicked the coffee pot on and opened the cabinet for cups.

"They reported a bleed duct light which means at least 575-degree air is porting inside the airplane so, yes, they had a big problem. Anyway, Raoul headed back to the ship and then came up on the radio and said he had a fire warning light on his right engine and was shutting it down."

"Jesus!"

"Flying low and slow over SAM country is the worst thing you can do. Raoul and Mandy were very vulnerable, so when the SAMs started flying their way, they didn't have a lot to defend themselves with. I mean, they only had one engine and they were slow. The reports I read showed they were fired upon, jinked to avoid the first one but the second detonated off their left side and tore the wing off. His wingman saw them eject with two good chutes."

"My God!" Gaby shook her head. "How do you remember all of this?"

"You remember. I was assigned to AIRPAC after I left the squadron. Before we went to war college. Remember?"

"Sure." Gaby nodded.

"So, for the time I was there I spent a lot of time studying and then synopsizing the various reports on what happened to Raoul and Mandy. I saw all the documents, testimony, analysis, and so forth. So, I have a pretty good idea of what happened."

"I remember that they found Raoul about a week after he was shot down?" Gaby glanced at me while she poured herself a cup of coffee.

"It was ten days." I shook my head and sipped at my coffee. "Central Command sent in a special operations team to get them. They found Raoul wandering around in the marsh and a couple of days later found Mandy's body."

"I never knew all of this," said Gaby. "I knew he had to jump out of his airplane but didn't know any of the rest of this. Why didn't you tell me?"

"No reason to get into it," I said. What I didn't tell Gaby was how much it irritated me when people blabbed about stuff that was supposed to be confidential. There were enough rumors about Raoul going around as it was. At least, there used to be.

"So, Raoul returns to the ship?"

"Yes, a helo brought him in. I ran down to medical to see him, but the doctors said to wait for a couple of days. I never did get to talk with him alone. He testified before our mishap board the day after he showed up on the ship. Then, he was gone."

"Why?"

"I talked to the air wing commander about it. You remember CAG Geno Thompson?"

"Sure, him and Sally."

"Yes, so, I talked with him and he said Raoul resigned. Said that Raoul told him he didn't want to "do this anymore." Geno said he told Raoul to take himself off the flight schedule for a while—go see the doctor—see the chaplain, but Raoul was adamant that he didn't want to fly anymore. Didn't want to be in the navy anymore, in fact. Geno told me that really pissed him off because Mandy didn't quit. She couldn't quit, she was dead. So, Geno ordered Raoul to get off the ship."

"I just don't get it." Gaby shook her head and took a sip of coffee.

"Nobody gets it." I shook my head too. "Geno told me that Raoul was the number one skipper in the air wing. He was on his way to admiral. Everybody knew it. Then, he just up and quits. And Mandy is dead. She's the one who paid the price. Everybody was pissed at Raoul."

"But you still tried to reach him. You still tried to contact him."

"That's right. Sure." I took a sip of coffee. "I was his best friend."

"And now, here he is," said Gaby. She took her cup to the sink, washed it, and turned around. "Like I said, something's up."

I started the Toyota a little after eight on Wednesday morning. It takes around three hours and fifteen minutes to get from my house in north San Diego to Red Mountain and I didn't want to be late. The first part of the ride is all interstate on the 15 to 215 until just south of Hesperia. In California you put a *the* in front of a highway number, and I have no idea why. But you do, it's some kind of rule. But after you say *the* once, you don't have to say it again in that conversation. Hey, it's California so it doesn't have to make any sense. Outside of Hesperia, I took the 395 north into the desert. The road is mostly straight, and my old truck handles well on such a ride.

Highways 15 and 215 are like all freeways in that they must be endured rather than enjoyed. Often when I drive, I select the back roads but there was no realistic choice for that on this trip. I had to get to Red Mountain by noon.

It was a sunny, warm day in early September, and the concrete and pavement rolled smoothly beneath my wheels. The California coast and forests may be some of the most scenic in the world, but the inland desert is definitely not. At least it isn't to me. It is the kind of territory where they make films about car commercials and the freedom of the road or movies about stranded motorists who wind up hacked to death in a cabin. You know, the bookends of the human driving experience. I know there are a lot of folks who swear by living out there with the horned toads and scorpions, but I always figured they were odd or up to something. In fact, whenever I drive through one of the small towns that dot the place, I figure there are the bones of a long-dead horse buried somewhere. Why else would anyone stop in the first place?

I continued on 395 north toward Kramer Junction, crossed the 58 and headed up the grade to Red Mountain. The town's namesake stands to the east and is the largest ugly hill among the other ugly hills. It produced gold though, enough for the town to have 3,500 people there in 1900 and its own theater! The gold, and later, tungsten, played out and the village I now approached had dwindled to a population of around 150. The original plots are still marked and held together by crumbling roads although most are populated by dilapidated structures and mounds of trash. Whenever I ride through places like Red Mountain, I get a feeling of wistfulness for some reason. Perhaps it is a longing for some happier, more content, less hectic past. Then again, perhaps I am just sorry because something evidently didn't work out.

As Raoul instructed, I turned left at the first road and wound around to the whitish house he described. He sat on the front porch and by the time I got my truck stopped, he was by my side. I had worried about what he might look like, unsure if the past years had been kind... or just honest. But he stood there as tall and straight as I remembered him. Woefully thin maybe, gaunt even, but clean shaven and clear eyed. He had the same old, wide-mouthed, toothy Raoul grin and the same easy stance. He took my hand in a firm grip, then drew me in for a hug.

"Good to see you, Weenie. Thanks for coming."

"You look good, Raoul. A little skinny maybe, but good."

"What did you expect?" Raoul slipped into his easy smile.

"I wasn't sure." I grinned back.

"Come on in. We can visit a spell."

"Lead the way." I followed Raoul across the yard and onto the porch. He pulled open a screen door and we entered a cool, dark living room. It was sparsely furnished, which surprised me. There was none of the Raoul flair. No bizarre posters or works of art that he had created out of his limitless imagination. It was so un-Raoul like that I found myself afraid of the conversations to come. Had he changed that much?

"How about a sandwich?"

"Sure."

"Horse cock and cheese okay?"

I blurted a laugh. "I haven't heard that in a while." Horse cock and cheese was what we called bologna and cheese on the ship.

"Gaby doesn't use that kind of language?"

"No," I grinned. "We eat a lot of wurst and deli meats, but she isn't big on American bologna."

"Pity. It's a staple of bachelor-desert life. Make yourself at home."

Raoul busied himself in the small kitchen as I looked at the photos on the wall. One was a scene of what must have been early Red Mountain days. The street that later became 395 had houses on both sides, shops, and a general store. I could also see a church. The other photo was of Raoul and me standing in front of an F-4. It was from our old days in our first squadron on a Vietnam deployment. I had a government issued 9MM handgun in my hand, held across my chest. Raoul had the pearl handled .38 revolver his dad had given him.

"Here you go." Raoul brought out a tray with two sandwiches a couple bags of potato chips. He had a bottle of Corona and a Pepsi. "I assume you still don't drink anymore."

I grinned and nodded.

We sat on the couch and ate in silence. I had a million things to ask Raoul but was unsure where or how to start. I figured it best to let him open up. But after a few more moments, I swallowed a sip of Pepsi and looked at my friend.

"Why Red Mountain? It's not quite like our snake ranch in San Diego."

Raoul looked around the room and grunted. "No, can't say it is." I watched him as he took a breath and looked out his window. He stayed out there for a while, swallowing, blinking. I smiled when his gaze shifted back to me.

"I have some things I don't want to remember. Things I don't want to think about. That fits here."

I nodded and Raoul continued. He stared at the wall while he talked, "Everybody lets me be, no questions, no bother. People come and go and I guess I've been here longer than most. In fact, some call me the Mayor of Red Mountain." Raoul glanced at me, gave a sheepish laugh, and took a sip of beer.

"The Mayor of Red Mountain!" I grinned but felt a rush of loss as I looked at my old friend. His once beaming personality was now reduced to an uncertain wariness and his haunted eyes both sought... and avoided me. One moment they conveyed the spark of some great understanding and the next, a vacuous nothingness. They reminded me of this bible passage from Ecclesiastes: "I have seen all the things that are done under the sun; all of them are meaningless, a chasing after the wind."

And I wondered if Raoul had seen "all the things that are done under the sun." And if he now questioned if anything had meaning anymore.

"What happened, Raoul? What happened to you?"

"What happened to me?" Raoul frowned. He took a breath and shook his head. Then he slowly looked at me. "You can live all of your life, thinking that you know who you are, what you are. You can like that, you know? Like who you are." Raoul swallowed and then looked away. "And then something happens... and you realize you're..." He turned his face toward me, forced his face toward me. "You realize you are not what you thought. You aren't anything that you thought."

I sat still and hoped my need to know, my curiosity, was worth the pain Raoul now endured.

"I think that deep down inside we all think we are heroic. Or at least, we think we can be heroic, do the right thing, do the manly thing when the time comes." Raoul looked at the floor. "Then God punishes you and grants you your hero's wish and you..." Raoul glanced at me and then returned his eyes to the floor. His chest heaved and he shook his yead again. "I didn't know me anymore, Weenie." He looked at me. "Didn't know who I was. Came up here because nobody in Red Mountain knows me either."

I nodded then leaned over and patted Raoul's shoulder.

"I'll be a while." Raoul stood and walked out the door and I watched him as he walked down the street and then up onto a weed-choked hill. He stood there for a long time, looking out across the open desert and I considered joining him. But as I swung the door open, I realized he didn't need me to help him find himself. At least, not yet.

It was three in the afternoon before we hit the road and I drove out of town and north toward Big Pine. The drive in September is usually dry and can be hot, but it was perfect today. Highway 395 edges next to the Sequoia National Forest and we could see the hills and peaks on our left. The Dead Valley National Park was to our right, but there was nothing to see there except desert.

It was strange now to sit next to Raoul. In the past, this would have been effortless, fun, no need to talk or, maybe, just jabber away at each other. But this was different. We were almost strangers, and Raoul's comments about not knowing himself were not idle drama. I do know that if he still didn't know who he was after eight years alone, he most likely never would. And that meant things would never be the same. We would never be the same. And that depressed me greatly.

THE MAYOR OF RED MOUNTAIN

We entered town around five thirty, just in time for happy hour, but I took us to the Big Pine Motel first. All the rooms are ground level so keeping an eye on my truck would be easy. It had been broken into on previous trips, so I was apprehensive in the desert places. Thirty minutes later, we walked up Main Street to Billy Bob's Grill. We got a table in the corner and Raoul ordered a Death Valley Pale Ale. I got a cup of coffee. It was a Wednesday so there weren't many tourists and since Big Pine only has around 1800 people, there weren't many locals either. Raoul said the ale was cold and good, and my coffee smelled freshly brewed and we grinned at each other as we took the first sip.

"Good to be back with you, man." Raoul burped softly and leaned back in his chair.

"I still can't believe this is happening." I shook my head and looked at my friend. "A couple of days ago, you didn't exist."

Raoul hung his head and I winced at my callousness. He had just said he didn't know who he was anymore.

I shook my head and leaned my cup forward and he tipped it with his bottle.

"I need you to come to San Diego and see Gaby and Christine."

Raoul frowned but nodded.

"You know, when you feel up to it."

"How's the navy these days? You a CAG now?"

"No, I left that job a little while ago. I'm the commanding officer at TACTRAGRUPAC."

Raoul looked at me and nodded. "Were you involved in Afghanistan? You know, after the towers."

"Yes," I nodded. "In fact, timing was great for my airwing. We were in the gulf when it happened and flew the first strikes against the Taliban."

"That had to have been satisfying." Raoul looked at me with a mixture of sadness and envy. "To defend the country."

"It was." I quickly took a sip. "But we were there for only a month. By the time we left, half the navy's carrier fleet was pounding away at them." I chuckled and so did Raoul and as I watched his eyes crinkle it gave me hope.

Was it possible to go back to the good, old days?

Raoul seemed to relax, and I ordered us another round. I told him about Cotton and the fact he was now a nuclear aircraft carrier skipper. In fact, I made it a point to talk about things from our past. Pleasant things. I decided not to tell him about Missy getting killed at the Pentagon. We chatted for an hour and then headed next door to Rossi's Place for some pizza and more beer for Raoul. By the time the pies arrived, he was fairly well lubricated.

"Did it concern you flying over Afghanistan? I mean, you are a long way from any help?" Raoul took a sip of beer.

"Sure," I shrugged. "But the Taliban didn't have anything to threaten high-flying jets. It wasn't like when you and I flew over Vietnam."

"Or, even like Iraq. I mean, you know, Saddam had enough stuff to throw up at us to make it interesting," said Raoul.

I was surprised he brought up the subject of Saddam's aerial defenses. I nodded and took a sip of water.

"One second we were flying along— fat, dumb and happy and the next second there is a loud pop and all hell broke loose." Raoul shook his head. "Damned ECS turbine."

"I remember the ECS failures we had in the tomcat and think I understand what happened." I bit into a slice of pizza.

"I tell you, Mandy was a pro. A second after I heard the pop, she said, 'Air Source Off.'"

"Hmmm," I thought it a bit odd that Raoul would rush to support his dead pilot. But I nodded and looked at him. "First step in the emergency procedure."

"Exactly," said Raoul. "And when the caution lights came on and the Bleed Duct and Engine Fire Lights illuminated, she performed her duties before I could rattle through the lists. She was cool as a cucumber."

"I heard she was an exceptional officer."

"Exceptional." Raoul looked at the tablecloth and traced the checkerboard pattern with his fork. "She was exceptional."

I nodded again. "Did you see what hit you?"

"Mandy saw the missiles first. She called them out and I got a tally and felt her pull into the first one to generate an overshoot.

That worked but we were out of poop for the second. It detonated behind us and blew the wing off."

"Yeah, I saw that in the reports."

Raoul looked up and took a breath. He nodded and cleared his throat. "I was still trying to look outside for other SAMs when my seat's rocket motor blasted me out of the plane. The wind ripped my helmet off,, and I felt myself tumble. A sharp jolt later, I was hanging in the straps, looking for a place to land. I saw Mandy off to my left and tried to maneuver my chute towards her. She had a good canopy and looked okay."

"Did you see anybody on the ground?"

"Not yet. As I descended, the marsh grew closer and closer and I was more concerned about getting tangled up in my chute and drowning. I hit the water and released my Koch fittings. By the time I surfaced, I was free of the chute and paddled toward a clump of reeds. I pulled myself out, stripped off my gear and hid it. Then I took off to find Mandy."

Raoul took a bite of pizza. Fascinated with his story, I did the same. I had read the reports while assigned to the AIRPAC staff, but it was very different listening to a survivor.

"Was it like when you were shot down over Vietnam?" I took a sip of water.

"Not exactly. We had been in Vietnam for years when you and I were there. We had POWs that had been in jail longer than we had been in the navy. Getting captured in Vietnam probably meant a lot of torture, too. Iraq was different. Saddam wasn't into torturing us so much. At least that is what I thought."

I shook my head. "They got you pretty quick?"

Raoul chewed for a moment then looked at me. "Yes, I only got a few yards when three guys jumped out of the brush and started yelling and pointing their rifles. They wore Iraqi Army uniforms. I put my hands up and the one nearest to me hit me in the stomach with his rifle butt. I dropped to my knees. Then, one of them hit me in the side of the head with his rifle and I blacked out. I woke up on the water board."

"Jesus!" I shook my head.

"Was it as bad as when they water boarded you in SERE school?"

"Worse! I didn't know how it would end. In SERE school I assumed they wouldn't kill me."

"I guess that's right."

"Mammals will do anything to avoid drowning and I held my breath as long as I could but then, you know, I had to take a breath. The water burned into my lungs and, I don't know man, my head exploded." Raoul looked at me and swallowed. "I mean I didn't know what was happening. I couldn't cough enough. I couldn't get it all out. I panicked and fought against the straps."

I didn't know what to say. So, I just watched Raoul. He was staring at the table as he talked, and I was glad he wasn't looking at me. It was painful enough to listen.

"They did that three times, I guess." Raoul picked up a saltshaker and rolled it in his fingers. "Then they took me to the camp."

"Hey," I nodded. "If you're done, let's get a six-pack and go to the motel."

"I don't need any more to drink."

I smiled, grabbed the check, and paid the bill. I wasn't sure how Raoul was fixed for money. We walked back along Main Street toward the motel and Raoul grunted at my banter but seemed subdued and lost in his thoughts. I hoped my attempt to drag conversation from him wouldn't ruin our trip. We said good night and I went into my room. I had only taken off my boots when I heard a knock at the door. It was Raoul.

"Mind chatting awhile longer?"

"Sure!" I was surprised but happy and nodded toward the chair. Raoul walked in, I shut the door behind him, and sat on the edge of my bed.

"I don't have anything but water."

"I'm good." Raoul leaned back and closed his eyes. For a moment, I thought he was going to fall asleep. I looked around for a blanket to cover him.

"The camp was well hidden." Raoul's sudden words stopped my blanket search and I focused on him. "It was under the canopy of trees and made of wood as you would imagine." Raoul opened his eyes. "It consisted of three or four low buildings. There was No flagpole or anything like that. It had a shed for vehicles. Looked like Toyota SUVs and a Hi-Lux truck. They parked the flat-bed they water boarded me on out front."

I sat back on my bed and leaned against my headboard.

"The soldiers took me into one of the buildings and chained me against a wall. I was only there a few minutes when a man wearing the uniform of an Iraqi Army Colonel came in. He ordered me unchained and he escorted me to his office where he gave me water and food. Some kind of rice. He spoke excellent English and told me he had attended the National War College at Fort McNair. He said he was sorry for all of this but that we caused it when we invaded his country. I said Saddam's invasion of Kuwait caused it all, and that is when the colonel went crazy."

"What do you mean?"

"Well, he contorted his face all up and started breathing heavy. I mean, it freaked me out because he had been so cool before. He started jabbering about how Americans always feel they have the high road, they have the moral position, they look down their nose at everybody else as inferior. That kind of stuff."

"Wow!"

"He ranted on awhile then screamed at the guards and they took me back to the cell. They chained me back up to the wall where I had to stand. I couldn't slump to rest because the manacles were so sharp. They cut into my wrists and every time I drifted off to sleep, they ripped me back awake."

"Jesus!" I shuddered.

"The floor was dirt and very damp and a socket light dangled from the ceiling. I stayed in there for three days, I think. Maybe four. I was really screwed up. Really, really screwed up."

"I can imagine."

"NO, it was worse than you think." Raoul looked at me with wild eyes.

I had seen my friend's eyes a million times when he was excited. Raoul was always excited about something. But these eyes weren't wide from excitement. They were wide from horror.

"Weenie, I think I lost my mind." Raoul looked at me with an intensity that made me gulp. I actually leaned away from him and my mind flashed to Mom and her frenetic eyes.

"It was like, like if a book or a magazine was flipping open and I could see a photo of myself but I couldn't remember anything before it or after it. Just photos and some of them were horrible and I recognized myself and they made me sick but I didn't know why. They were just images with no context." Raoul's eyes pleaded for understanding. "Weenie, it is easier to drive someone out of their mind than you might think." Raoul took a breath and looked down at his hands. He slowly shook his head and looked up at me. "Did you know that in the sixteenth century witch hunters would capture women suspected of sorcery and deprive them of sleep?"

"No, I didn't know that."

"It was called, "waking the witch" because after a period of no sleep, the women would begin to hallucinate. The gibberish was supposedly them talking to the devil."

I frowned and nodded. And I waited for my friend to continue. Raoul picked a fountain pen off the table next to him. A gift from the motel management and clicked it a couple of times.

"They gave me water but no food. But I think the lack of sleep was the big killer. I began to have a lot of trouble focusing on anything, even remembering where I was. Just the images. Of course, the water gave me diarrhea and made me sick, so I shit down my legs and threw up what food I had in my stomach. All that stuff kind of pooled at my feet."

"Christ! I don't remember reading that in any of the reports."

"I didn't see any value in describing that. So, I left it out."

"Where was Mandy?"

"Mandy?" Raoul gave me an odd look.

Had he forgotten who she was? How sick was my old friend?

I stood to get him a glass of water but the look on Raoul's face stopped me dead. I sat back down. He looked at the wall over my shoulder for a second, then his eyes blinked back to me. "Mandy was in the next room."

"Could you speak with her?"

"There was a vent." Raoul interrupted. His eyes fell to the floor. "A vent in the wall and I could hear her through the vent."

"Did she know you were…"

"I could hear her cry." Raoul looked up at me. His eyes glistened from alcohol, misery…maybe guilt? I couldn't quite tell. I swallowed and nodded.

Raoul took some deep breaths, and I wasn't sure if he wanted to talk anymore. His fingers trembled and lips quivered as if he intended, but couldn't, say any more. He looked past me again. "I could hear the voices of soldiers. I could hear her cry and scream." Raoul's eyes filled to drops on his lashes. "I could hear the bed begin to squeak. She cried louder. She screamed louder and the bed squeaked faster!" Tears rolled down Raoul's cheeks and I wanted to stand and somehow comfort him. But I didn't. I think it would have embarrassed him. I knew it would have embarrassed me.

"Christ!" Raoul wiped his eyes. "Sometimes I still hear that squeaking. I wake up to it."

I looked at the floor to avoid Raoul's eyes. I did that for him and for me. We sat like that for some time until Raoul got up and went into the bathroom. I heard him running water and when he came out, I could see he had washed his face. He sat in the chair again.

"Colonel Salim Muhammed was my captor's name."

I looked at Raoul and nodded. He leaned his head against the wall and took a deep breath. He looked at me and shook his head. "Colonel Salim Muhammed."

I nodded but remained quiet.

Raoul looked at the ceiling, searching for words, then stared at me again. "Colonel Muhammed was my chief interrogator. He was the leader. He was the one who asked the questions."

"I remember him. I mean, I remember reading his name. He was in the report from your de-briefing."

Raoul nodded and stared at the floor. I watched him, aware of my growing unease. He was so different now. A part of me wanted to hear his story, hoping that through the telling of it, my old friend would return. But I dreaded his every sentence, afraid that this stranger would further the distance between us. I think I was also afraid of what he might divulge.

"The Colonel had a hatred." Raoul pursed his lips and nodded as he took a deep breath. "I think his time as a student in war college turned him against us instead of the other way around."

"How so?"

"Well, you know the intent is to give visiting officers an opportunity to live here and sample America's greatness first-hand. But I think his time here resulted in resentment and anger."

I nodded but kept quiet as I looked at his vacant eyes.

"Funny," Raoul shook his head. "How I remember some of what happened clear as day." He looked at me, "The colonel especially resented what he termed as our ethical superiority."

Once again, I remained silent. I wanted to let Raoul talk if that is what he wanted. But when tears began to form in his eyes, I regretted that.

"Maybe it's time for bed?"

"He brought me back into his office. I have an image. Mandy was there too."

"Mandy? You saw her?"

"She was there and the Colonel told me he wanted to see me make love to her. He said in the Iraqi army women were routinely raped but he thought Mandy wouldn't mind.

"Would you, Mandy?" Raoul looked at me and swallowed. "He asked her, 'Would you, Mandy'? And I looked at him, I remember looking at him because I couldn't believe what he was asking. And I looked at Mandy and she was crying." Raoul's tears now streamed down his face. "Weenie…" Raoul's eyes implored me, begged me to understand. "Weenie, I wanted her to say, 'Why no. I don't mind.' Do you believe that?" Raoul gasped as he sobbed and pushed the pillow into his face. His voice was muffled but I could still hear him. "A part of me wanted to fuck her. A part of me had always wanted to do that from the time she first came to the squadron. And somehow the colonel knew it."

"Raoul, come on, man." I leaned forward and patted his leg. "It is natural for a man to be physically attracted to a good-looking woman."

"'You fly with her because you can, don't you?' That is what Colonel Muhammad asked me, Weenie. He said…and he said it real soft, 'You fly with her because you can. In fact, when you were shot down and falling in your parachute you had thoughts of finding her. You had thoughts of saving her, didn't you? You had thoughts of fucking her, didn't you?'"

Raoul pushed the pillow away and bent his head. He stayed like that for some time, sobbing and crying. I got him a glass of water. He took it and after a gulp, looked at me again.

"I can't stop the squeaking, Weenie. The squeaking of her bed. I hear it every night, just like I was still there. I hear it through the vent. It goes on and on and on and after a while I don't hear her screaming anymore. Just like I was still there." He looked at me and shook his head. "All I hear is the squeaking."

I looked at Raoul and shook my head. He abruptly stood and walked to the door. "Got to get some sleep. See you in the morning, Weenie."

I couldn't get Raoul's conversation out of my and rolled around my mattress all night. I finally fell asleep and didn't wake up until 0930. I was having coffee from the little machine in my room when Raoul knocked.

"There's a 7-11 across the street. I got you a doughnut." Raoul smiled and held up a bag. And for a second, it was the old Raoul with the lively eyes.

"Thanks," I grinned and took the bag. "Coffee?"

"No, I got a Coke to go with my breakfast burrito."

"You should be careful, buddy," I shook my head. "You never know how long that thing has been sitting under the heat lamp."

Raoul scowled a second, then looked at me and smiled. "I think I was their first customer this morning so it could be from yesterday."

I chuckled and shook my head again. "Well, don't say I didn't warn you."

We ate quickly, then grabbed our bags and jumped into the truck.

Since it was only four hours to Reno, we drove leisurely and took a pee stop at Mammoth Lakes. It is a bit of a sin to drive through that place without stopping to look at the mountains and smell the pines and catch a bit of wood smoke if it's been cool enough. I didn't get any gas at our overnight stop, so I was topping off when Raoul bent over the fender and coughed.

"Something wrong?"

"Don't know. It might be that damned burrito."

"Are you sick?" I put the pump handle into its carriage.

Raoul took a deep breath, then slowly shook his head.

"Want to sit for a moment?"

"Maybe for just a minute or two."

"Take it easy then," I smiled. "No rush."

We stood by the truck for a few more minutes, then Raoul nodded. "I think I'm okay, let's go."

"Sure?"

"Yeah, let's go."

I took us north, and we drove in silence. I occasionally glanced at Raoul; he had his head slumped against his hands. I could see his eyes were closed behind his sunglasses. We drove like that for a couple of hours but as we approached South McCarran Boulevard, Raoul moaned.

"Can you pull over a minute?" Raoul pointed to a small gas and grocery store. "There."

I pulled the Tacoma into the parking lot.

"I don't want to heave in your truck." Raoul opened the door and got out. "I'll just walk around for a while until I can throw up. Sorry, man."

"No problem. Next time eat the donut." Raoul offered a weak smile and waved his hand. He slowly walked to the corner of the lot and stood next to a eucalyptus tree.

I thought about joining him but when I feel sick, I want to be alone. So, I stayed in the car. After ten minutes or so, Raoul walked toward the store. "Getting some Pepto Bismol."

He came out after a few minutes and slowly eased into the car. He spun the top off the bottle and took a huge gulp. A pink rivulet ran down his chin. He burped and looked at me.

"I'm sorry, man. I should have taken your advice. I just need to sit for a while."

"Hey, Raoul." I grinned and patted his shoulder. "No big deal. If we need to stay the night down here, it's okay. Nothing going on until tomorrow anyway."

"You sure?" Raoul leaned against the seat and groaned.

"I'm positive. We can stay at the motel there on the corner." I nodded at the neon vacancy sign across the highway.

"Thanks, man."

I pulled the truck across the street and Raoul and I each got a room. Raoul said he was going to hit the rack in hopes of getting through his stomach problems, so I got some chow at McDonalds. I watched television until around ten, then fell asleep.

"Weenie!"

I jerked awake.

"Weenie!" It was Raoul. I stumbled out of bed and across the sticky carpet and pulled the door open.

"Come on, man, you got to help me."

"What...what are you talking..."

"I woke up and there was a guy in my room. He took my bag!"

"What? What?" I was instantly awake.

"Some guy took my bag. I watched him run across the street and go into that house behind the gas station. Where I got the Pepto Bismol."

"Well, did you lock your door?"

"What difference does that make now? Come on, I need your help. Get your gun and some clothes."

I was already putting on my jeans. "Why not call the cops? What do you mean, 'Get my gun'--what are you talking about?"

"Weenie, I got stuff in that bag. Stuff that helps me sleep. I don't need any cops."

"But we can't just bust into somebody's house!"

"Sure, we can. He got my bag, man. Come and help me. I have to get that bag back."

"Christ!" I slipped on my shoes and grabbed my 9MM.

Raoul pulled his pearl-handled .38 from his pocket and headed for the door. "Come on."

I followed him as we ran across the dark highway and toward the gas and grocery. I could see the house behind the store, there were no lights.

Raoul led the way. We slowed to a walk as we made our way toward the back door. I was breathing hard by this time and feeling a bit stunned. In fact, I couldn't believe that we...that I, was doing this!

It was pitch dark behind the house and I put my hand on Raoul's shoulder to keep with him. We edged forward then stopped and I heard glass breaking.

"What are you doing?" I whispered and shook his shoulder. "What the fuck?"

I kept my hand on Raoul's shoulder as he entered the house. I strained to see. As we crept forward, I heard our feet squeak on linoleum and smelled old grease and garlic.

"Stop right there."

Raoul froze and so did I.

"Put down your guns."

What's going on? Who is this?

"You in front, put down the .38. In back, lay your 9MM on the floor."

I felt Raoul hesitate, so I froze.

"I have night vision goggles, boys. I can see you. Now, put down the guns or I will shoot both of you."

I dropped my gun and a second later heard Raoul's .38 clank to the floor.

The lights clicked on and I squinted at a tall, dark man. He held an enormous pistol in his hand and a set of goggles in the other.

"Over there." He motioned to two chairs, so Raoul and I walked to them and took a seat. I didn't look at Raoul. I was afraid if I did, he would take it as some kind of sign to try to jump the guy. This craziness had gone far enough, and I just wanted to get out in one piece.

"Take the cuffs and put them on your buddy." The man looked at me and nodded to a set of handcuffs dangling from the arm of my chair. I did as I was told and then the man cuffed me.

He placed his gun on the kitchen table and smiled at Raoul. "It is good to see you again, Commander Hungus."

Stunned, I looked at Raoul.

What the fuck is going on?

"Colonel Muhammed." Raoul nodded toward the man.

I felt my mouth drop open and Colonel Muhammed must have found that funny because he looked at me and chuckled.

"And you look familiar." Colonel Muhammed frowned and looked at me intently. He cocked his head, then smiled. "CAG Kleegan, right? You brought your airwing to Fallon a couple of years ago."

"That's right," I nodded.

"I knew I remembered correctly!" Colonel Muhammed beamed. "I have a great memory. Yes, once I see a face, I never forget it."

I frowned and shook my head.

"I am a deputy manager at the Fallon Range Complex. I see all the airwings when they come through for their training. I think you had Airwing Fourteen, right? You did very well as I remember."

"Why did you steal my friend's bag? What is this all about?"

A smile crept across Colonel Muhammed's face. "You don't know what's going on here, do you?"

The colonel grinned at me. "Your friend told you someone stole his bag and that is why you had to accompany him over here. Right?"

I looked at Raoul and then at Muhammed. "What is going on?"

"Well, Commander Hungus can give you his version. But here is what I think." Colonel Muhammed leaned against the kitchen table. "A couple of months ago, I saw your friend drive through here in, let me see, a 1984 Dodge Ram. Green, with a busted left headlight. Do you still have that magnificent vehicle?" Colonel Muhammed smiled at Raoul.

Raoul's face was blank, but he nodded.

"I recognized the good commander and when he came back a week later, I recognized him again." Colonel Muhammed smiled at Raoul. "Then he came by three more times and I knew he was casing the joint, as you Americans say." The colonel laughed. "Now, I usually have my assistant with me in the store. In fact, he would be here now if his wife weren't ill." Muhammed looked at me and smiled again. "So, CAG, I imagine Commander Hungus suspected he might be here tonight. My guess is that he brought you along for firepower. I mean, why are you together?"

"We are going to Tailhook."

Colonel Muhammed laughed and sat against the kitchen table. "Is that what he told you? The truth is your friend was planning to settle some old grudges, and he brought you along. That is why you are together."

"Raoul?" I frowned and looked at my friend.

Raoul inhaled and looked at the floor.

"Well, no matter, you are here now and since Commander Hungus can identify me as Colonel Salim Muhammed instead of GS-14 Rami Holland, we have a problem. Hey, look at my badge." Colonel Muhammed bent over, and I could see his US Government identification badge for Naval Air Station Fallon. "It's a good likeness, yes? I mean, sometimes those government ID cards are just terrible." The Colonel laughed again.

"But the bad news for you CAG is you are now entwined into this mess." He picked up his pistol and looked at it.

I was beginning to feel very, very bad about the situation. In fact, I felt like I did when I was Vietnam with that AK in my face.

Colonel Muhammed took a deep breath and made himself comfortable on the kitchen table. He looked at me and leered. "What do you know about the commander's story? What did he tell you?"

I swallowed and fought a rising panic. I needed to drag this out. Maybe help would come somehow. Maybe when the sun came up, help would come. I shrugged. "He said you were his captor in Iraq. When he and his pilot were shot down."

"Mandy? Do you mean Mandy, the commander's lover?"

"You fucking asshole!" Raoul lurched against his cuffs and tried to stand, but Colonel Muhammed stood and slapped him with his pistol. Raoul howled and slumped back into his chair. The colonel watched him for a moment then turned back to me.

"What did he tell you?"

"He said that you deprived him of food and sleep. That you were a pervert and kept trying to get him to screw Mandy so you and your officers could watch. He told me that he could hear her, night after night, being raped by your men. Or by YOU!"

The colonel arched his eyebrows in false alarm. "Is that so? Hmmm. That isn't the way I remember it. That isn't the way I remember it at all." He smiled and looked at Raoul.

"Truth is you wanted to screw her didn't you, commander? You wanted to fuck your girl pilot. Didn't you?"

"Christ you are sick!" Raoul glared at the colonel.

"Am I?" The colonel smiled and took a deep breath. He looked at his pistol for a moment and then back at Raoul. "I remember the ethics classes in your war college. How you talked about how pure you all were. Of course, I read your papers and the Navy Times, now there's a rag... and it seems that every day you are firing somebody for fucking the help as you so cavalierly say." The colonel smiled again and swung his legs as he sat on the table. He seemed very much at ease. "You see, gentlemen, I am of the mind that men are driven by impulses. Impulses that are impossible to fully control. That is why we Muslims have the rules toward women that we do. We know we cannot contain our urges unless the women are taken from our eyes. But at least we are truthful. You parrot your values and parade around in your nobility while you poke the next thing that comes your way. So, I just set up a little experiment for our two lost aviators."

The colonel looked at me and laughed again. "Of course, Mandy played her part, too. But I will explain that in a minute." He looked back at Raoul. "Remember the squeaking?"

"Christ!" Raoul leaned his head back and shut his eyes. "You rotten, fucking bastard!"

"Did you hear the squeaking through your vent, commander?" Muhammed hopped off the table and knelt so that he was eye-to-eye with Raoul. "Did you hear it through the vent?" His voice was soft. He looked intently at Raoul. "Look at me, commander. Did you hear it through the vent, night after night? Night after night after night?"

"YES!" Raoul's eyes flew open. "YES, YOU MISERABLE FUCK!"

"Oh, no, dear commander." Colonel Muhammed put his hand on Raoul's knee. "The squeaking was from your bed. There was no sound of horror through some vent in the wall. The sound you heard was you raping Mandy every night. It was you, night after night..."

"NO! NO!"

"Oh, yes, Raoul. May I call you Raoul?" The colonel patted Raoul's knee. "You see it was you fucking your girl pilot, not my men or me. It was you. Just like you wanted to from the first moment you saw her. That is why you had her crewed with you isn't it? You were the skipper of the squadron and that is why you picked her to be your pilot. Because you hoped, Raoul, dear Raoul, you hoped against hope that someday, one day, the opportunity would come. Didn't you? DIDN'T YOU?"

"NOOOOOO!" Raoul screamed and pulled against his cuffs.

"And how did you repay her, Raoul?" Colonel Muhammed looked at me. "Did he tell you how he got out? How he escaped so he could be found alive and unharmed? And make no mistake, I made sure of that."

"No."

"Well, that is what I meant when I said Mandy played her part." The colonel looked at me and then his eyes opened wide. "Oh, you thought she played her part by letting Raoul fuck her, didn't you? You think that is the part women are supposed to play, don't you CAG? I can see why you are such good friends with Raoul. You think that women are here for you to empower, employ, and then…what? Impale?" Colonel Muhammed grinned. "You Americans are all the same." He stared hard into my eyes for a long moment, then straightened up and smiled again. "But, back to my question. The commander didn't tell you how he escaped did he?"

I shook my head.

"Well, that's amazing! In every story or movie that I have ever seen or heard the escapee wants to talk about how he escaped. Isn't that right? The fact that your hero is captured isn't what is important, it is how he escapes. Right?"

I numbly stared at the colonel.

"So, commander, do you want to tell, or do you want me to?"

The colonel beamed at Raoul who slumped his head.

"Okay, then, I will tell." Colonel Muhammed sat back on the kitchen table and put his pistol down.

"I had the commander and Mandy come into my office and they stood at each end of a table, a table a little bigger than this."

"Stop," whispered Raoul.

"What's that?" Colonel Muhammed grinned at Raoul. Raoul looked at him with pleading eyes.

"They were standing at each end and I gave them their service weapons. The ones they were captured with. Remember, commander?" Colonel Muhammed grinned at Raoul. He rocked his legs back and forth. He was enjoying this.

"And what did I tell you?" Colonel Muhammed looked at Raoul. "Oh, come on, commander. You remember. What did I tell you? Hmmm?" He stared at Raoul a moment then looked at me and smiled, "No matter. You see, CAG, I said that one of you can walk out of here but only one. So, when I turn off the lights you have to grab your gun and shoot. Or, let the other one shoot you. You only have one bullet. I also told them that if they shoot at me, both will die. Now, I had my men in the room with rifles aimed so there wasn't going to be any kind of coup if you know what I mean."

"Please stop," whispered Raoul.

"Oh, too late for that, commander. It was your idea to come to me, not mine to come to you. So, CAG, guess what happened?"

I bowed my head. I knew that Mandy had been found shot in the chest.

"I ducked under my desk and flipped off the lights. I heard two shots. I waited awhile, then turned the lights on. Guess what happened?"

I frowned but remained quiet.

"There was a bullet hole in my chair where Mandy fired at me and a hole in her chest where your hero, here, fired at her."

Raoul began to sob, and I couldn't bear to look at him. But I could hear him. As he screamed, the demons he had carried all of these years roared and feasted and declared victory over his soul. And all I could do was sit there and listen.

"So, what's next?" The colonel grinned. "Can't very well let you two go. And you know, I wasn't sure what I was going to do. There is a big desert out there, so I had a bit of an idea, you know. With a shovel and all. But, given you are both navy men, I think I have the perfect idea." He glanced at his watch and smiled.

"Perfect!" He grabbed a roll of duct tape and one by one removed a cuff at a time and bound our hands together. When he had both of us taped from the wrists to the elbows, he put gags in our mouths and led us to a van. Minutes later we were running down a highway.

"As luck would have it, CAG Nine is here at Fallon this week and guess what they are doing this morning out at the high explosive impact area? Anybody? No guesses? Well, I will tell you what they are doing. They are dropping a whole bunch of bombs! Big, live, bombs!" It was too dark to see the Colonel's face, but I knew he was smiling.

It takes two hours to get to Fallon from Reno, and the sun was just turning the sky light when we turned onto an unmarked dirt road. We bumped along for a while until we came to a chain link fence with the obligatory warning to stay out. The colonel got out, opened the gate with his keys and we drove on. I began to make out the shapes of old tanks and other hulks of military vehicles, the targets for the bombs. Muhammed led us to an old tank shell in the middle of the site and, using the tape, bound us securely to its side.

"They'll be here in a bit. Of course, there will be waves of them most of the day." The colonel glanced at his watch. "I'll be back tonight to see how you are doing. And, as range manager, I will find your poor remains." Colonel Muhammed laughed and disappeared behind a rock.

I began to work myself free. As I struggled, I glanced at Raoul. He had been despondent since we left the Colonel's house. Since we were gagged, we couldn't talk but I could see his head down and eyes closed.

My one glimmer of hope lay in the fact I had Grandpa Two Bear's pocketknife in my back pocket. When Colonel Muhammed captured us in his house, he ordered us to drop our guns, but he never searched us. If I could somehow get to it, I could cut Raoul and myself free. As I wriggled, I pushed my mouth against the side of the rusted tank in an effort to get the gag off my face. After a half an hour, I got it loose enough to talk.

"Raoul. I am going to turn my back to you. I have a pocketknife in my left back pocket."

Raoul remained motionless so I kicked some dirt toward him. "Hey, Raoul, come on man."

He continued to sit with his arms taped to the tank.

"Look, Raoul, if it does any good, you didn't kill Mandy." Raoul turned his head toward me but kept his eyes closed.

"I read the reports while I was stashed at AIRLANT. Mandy was killed with a 9MM, not a .38. The slug was still in her when they found her. You were carrying a .38, right? Like you always did?"

Raoul opened his eyes. He blinked and nodded.

"And Raoul, the reports also said there were traces of Sodium Pentothal in your system as well as Mandy's. When I read that I assumed your captors were trying to get information from you. You know? Because some people believe it to be a truth serum. But I now think the colonel just wanted to lower your inhibitions. That stuff and the sleep deprivation must have really whacked out your minds. Both you and Mandy."

Raoul frowned and swallowed. He stared at me, relief in his eyes.

"Man, what happened to you was terrible. But you were the victim. Now, snap out of it and try to get the knife."

Raoul began to move his hands up and down against the rusted edge of the tank.

Muhammed had left a tiny bit of slack in the tape and Raoul furiously worked at his bonds. In ten minutes, he was free of the tank and I turned my back to him so he could get to the pocketknife with his fingers. Raoul fished the knife out and I heard him click it open just before an F-18 Hornet streaked over the top of us.

"Shit, that must be the clearance pass! Hurry Raoul!" It was standard navy practice for the first airplane to make a pass over the target to see if there were any campers or sight seers, or desert burros in the way. Unfortunately, we were well hidden behind the tank. Muhammed had obviously taken that into consideration.

I faced Raoul and he frantically cut at the tape that bound my hands and arms. It took him several moments but at last I was free. I grabbed the knife to free Raoul and made my first cut when the world exploded! At least, the part Raoul and I was in. There was a tremendous BOOM followed by a shock wave of heat and sand.

Fortunately, the tank shielded us from the shrapnel. I staggered to my feet and helped Raoul up and started to cut the tape on his arms again. I wanted to free him so he could better defend himself. I made a second cut when another bomb went off! This blast was even closer, and I saw the tank lift before I rolled against a rock outcropping. I covered my head as a blast of dirt and heat went over me. I turned around to help Raoul and saw him staggering toward me. His left arm was gone. I started to stand but he screamed, "STAY DOWN!" and fell on me just as the third bomb went off. A chunk of the rock outcropping slid down on us and I was in total blackness. Then, the fourth bomb exploded and I felt the rock shake and I felt Raoul shake too.

I must have blacked out because the next thing I remember was edging out from under Raoul and the rocks. I pulled him out behind me, rolling him over, praying he was still alive. His face was calm, his eyes were shut and if I could take a frame of that I could convince myself that he was just asleep.

But he was dead, and I was in shock. I was, however, lucid enough to realize what I had lost. And despite the fact he had been missing from my life for the last eight years, Raoul had never really been gone. He hadn't been gone at all. He had always been in my thoughts, and he had always been in my heart. There wasn't a single day that I hadn't thought of him, there wasn't a single day that his big, goofy smile didn't touch me and now I cradled his head. But after a while I wiped my tears and steadied myself and opened my pocket-knife. And I prepared for Colonel Muhammed.

I didn't know if he would try to see from afar with binoculars, so I kept hidden behind the tank. I left Raoul in the open, knowing he would approve of my use of his last bits and I waited inside the cup of the rock outcropping that had saved me.

It was nearing dark when I heard the crunch of gravel. I hid closer to the rocks and clutched my pocketknife, praying the colonel was alone. God granted that wish and I watched him creep around the rocks, looking for the remains of his two victims. He didn't hear me as I stepped behind him and plunged my knife into the back of his neck. He screamed as the hilt popped home and jerked away from me. The colonel whirled and glared. He reached for me but cried and grabbed for the blade. I could see his fingers brush the knife. His eyes brightened with the hope of survival as the tips of his fingers touched the blade and he struggled to turn and pull it out. He groaned as he worked and I picked up a rock and readied myself to do what I had to do.

The colonel fell to his knees and I could see blood streaming down his neck and back. My blow had been lucky as he was mortally wounded. His eyes stayed on me as he slumped to his side. He turned to me and I saw his request for mercy in those dark holes. And as I saw the life seep from him, I admit I liked what I saw. I liked the look in his eyes when he realized his plan had failed and that he had lost. I don't think that taking a life is anything to trivialize, but our human condition is what it is. The fact is we live among wolves and some of us are sheepdogs and we pledge to protect the sheep. Sometimes we protect the sheep by going somewhere far away, far away where the wolves live and we kill gooks, and nips, and krauts and whatever we are calling Muslims these days. But sometimes the wolf follows us back home. Sometimes the wolf comes here and when that happens, we have to kill it here. So, I felt good killing him.

I dragged Raoul's body to the colonel's car, put him in the passenger's seat and drove to the base. I spent the next couple of days telling the story of how Raoul and I had stopped at the gas and grocery station and how we had been abducted by a man who had recognized Raoul. He was a former colonel in the Iraqi Army who had somehow duped the US Government and was not only allowed to emigrate to the United States he had also been given preferential hiring status! I told the investigators that the colonel feared Raoul and that I would threaten his new life in America. The officials were sympathetic and helpful...embarrassed, even. They put Raoul in a box and shipped him to me in San Diego.

And on a fine and sunny day Gaby, Christine and I drove up the 15 and over to the 215 where we picked up the 395. We veered off onto the 58 and climbed the mountain. And there on a wind-swept hilltop I buried my best friend. I buried the champion of Missy Sanders. I buried the lover of World Championship Wrestling and its Square Circle of Honor. I buried the Auburn man with the quick laugh and the helping hand and the bright mind, the man who grew up with me.

I buried Raoul, The Mayor of Red Mountain.

THE TRAIN TO THE RUBICON

Raoul's death hit me hard. He was a brother to me. Besides Grandpa Two Bears, he was the only man I felt comfortable confiding in. And I sometimes even held back with Grandpa if I thought he would be disappointed in me. But the cold matter of fact, the only comfort I had was the knowledge that I had learned to live without Raoul for eight years. I had lived without him, but I had never forgotten him. I had remembered him fondly. And I would continue to do so now.

I settled into the strangely unsatisfying status of has-been service in the military while knowing I would never go to war again. Well, you know, unless the Chicoms or Russians attacked...or Godzilla came back around for another go at us. And the graciousness of our nation to military folks made me feel even more odd. The attack on the Twin Towers had changed us and in my lifetime we had gone from open disdain for men in uniform to now boarding an airplane first! And I think we got that new respect because people once again saw us as protectors. But I still felt odd standing in that get-onboard-first line.

My job was okay, even occasionally gratifying but I felt the edge of the exit door. Gaby and I watched the 2002 Academy Awards and by the time Denzel Washington and Halle Barry won for best actor and actress I was groaning at every acceptance speech. Why couldn't they just grab the Oscar and get off the stage? In the navy an Oscar for an officer is a command and I had mine. It was time to get off the stage.

I did have one last opportunity for new relevance and that was to promote to rear admiral. Every year the navy's one-star admiral board reviews the records of approximately 1000 captains and selects twenty-one for promotion. So, odds are against being one of those chosen. Still, there is a chance. Evidently an admiral calls you if you made it and when that call didn't come after my second opportunity, I knew I would not be a rear admiral. While I was disappointed, I knew better than to be morose or sullen because my career had been spectacular. And when I heard Cotton had been selected, I felt nothing but genuine happiness for him. Gaby and I saw Cotton and Melody shortly after his promotion and the silver star on his collar looked grand. Indeed, it looked most appropriate.

The problem with a military career is that it ends just when you feel you have the most to offer. I retired at the age of fifty-three with thirty years of active service and the certainty that I was on top of my game. However, there wasn't anywhere to go except back to sea as an admiral's chief-of-staff, and I wasn't interested in that. But it is one thing to ponder retirement from afar and another when the event approaches reality. As I began to plan to leave the navy, my long-ago conversation with Arlo Grundeen came to mind.

Arlo had typified his life as a series of train rides on the various institutions of American life. He remarked on how his parents had put him on the grade school train, then the middle and high school trains. They had financed the college train, and he had hopped the navy train. When I asked him why he thought of them as trains, he replied that they had a known destination and understood requirements for ridership with expected outcomes. If you paid your money and did what was required, you would get to your destination. He had also told me of the euphoria and the concern he had at the prospect of jumping off the navy train to a freer life but one without the comfort of rails. According to Arlo, I had been on the train since I was about six years old, forty-seven years! So, the prospect of getting off the station with no train to catch did cause me to fret. Despite the dangers of a military career, there was a sense of security in terms of companionship, familiarity, and pay. In addition, I had a lot of life to live and Christine was only thirteen, certainly bound for college in about five more years. So, I had to find employment and structure. I had to find a new train. I interviewed a few times but ultimately took a job working for a contractor that was developing an updated syllabus for my present command, TACTRAGRUPAC.

I didn't give my new job much thought as I finished out my navy days and figured it would be pretty much a non-uniformed extension of what I was now doing. I had this vague image of a storied, wise, beloved former commanding officer returning with his bag of advice. I imagined being something like the modern, male version of the Oracle at Delphi.

I had my change-of-command on a Friday afternoon and then Gaby, Christine and I visited Gaby's parents in Germany for ten days. It was great to return to Europe and to Stuttgart. I even went onboard Patch Barracks just to check things out. Of course, the security guards viewed my retired ID card with great suspicion and it was only my passport that got me through the gate.

"Next time I visit I will take Osama Bin Laden with me to make it easier," I told Gaby.

We had a great time with Gaby's mom and dad and even Eric was friendly. He and Gaby spent several hours together and I hoped they had mended what fences that stood between them. By the time we returned home, I was well rested and ready for work.

I did feel a bit odd when I entered my old headquarters building on Monday morning. I had never worn a suit to work but pushed open the door with a smile. That smile dripped down my collar when the sailor on watch did not stand and come to attention or anything. Evidently, he didn't recognize me because he just sat at his desk and pointed towards the visitor's log. I mean, I didn't know what to expect but thought that somehow my former importance was transferrable. Then the sailor gave me a visitor's badge and I had to wait until someone could come to escort me. Escort me! ME! I used to own this place!

By the time I got to the conference room, I had shrugged off my disappointment and was greeted with smiles, handshakes, and coffee from my former officers. I felt good again and the new skipper, my relief, even seemed deferential. But when the meeting was called to order I was directed to a chair in the back with the rest of the contracting team. I hadn't sat in the back in twenty years!

The rest of the day was filled with more meetings, some with navy officers providing input and some with just the contractor staff. And I wasn't even in charge of them. We had a nice enough woman named Deloris Long who was the lead on our contract and she was very respectful of me but made no doubt that I was there to support her. She had a PhD in something called Instructional Design. Even when she talked about my former syllabus I didn't quite understand her. We chatted during a break and in an attempt to prove relevance I told her I thought my military background could be invaluable to the contract. She nodded but then gave me a sideways look and said, "As long as you don't cross my Rubicon."

That night I had a talk with Gaby and told her about my day.

"Well, I understand her reference to the Rubicon River," she said. "She doesn't want some Roman general, or navy admiral in your case, coming in and taking over."

"I suppose." I nodded. "I just expected something different." I looked at Gaby and frowned. "I guess I wrongly expected to have a rank of retired captain and treated as such. But there is no such rank. I am a civilian who used to be a captain."

"So, your rank is civilian?" Gaby smiled.

"Exactly." I nodded again.

"Well, tonight when you say your prayers sometime between 'I lay me down to sleep and thank you for my beautiful wife', ask for some perspective. Because that is what you are going to need."

As the days, weeks and months went by, I gradually grew accustomed to my job and accepted its limits. After all, I had been blessed with an exciting, fulfilling navy career and now I had to content myself with just making a paycheck. And then, my boat bumped against the Rubicon.

It happened during a newly instituted weekly staff meeting where we were to discuss our financial picture and contract performance. Our CEO/president, Ms. Long, and I attended along with the operations officer, information officer, and other senior staff. Our finance team gave powerpoint presentations to tee up the discussion. It was the slide that showed our reported costs to the government that caused my problem because all of our government contracts were what is termed as "cost-plus-fixed-fee." This means that we charge the government with our legitimate costs of doing business while also making a small fee. The rules are set by the Defense Federal Acquisition Regulations, or DFAR and cost-plus contracts are usually used when there is too much vagary to set a fixed-fee contract such as in research and development work. The slide that caused my concern contained costs of thousands of dollars for expenses that fell outside the DFAR. For instance, there was a charge for marketing which is explicitly disallowed because the government doesn't want to pay for marketing to the government! However, the CEO's son had recently graduated with a marketing degree and, viola, had landed a job at the company. There were also charges for entertainment, and business dinners and meals that had nothing to do with our contracts. When the slide popped onto the screen I looked at the numbers and then glanced around to see if anyone else saw the problem.

"Next," said the CEO.

"Sir," I turned in my seat to face our boss.

"Yes."

I had not been around the CEO much. We had had a perfunctory welcome aboard meeting and shared head nods at company parties but he gave me the feeling of being valued only for my role in winning the navy contract. I was like an O-ring to him, critical but limited and ultimately replaceable. He was young and eager but in love with his self-proclaimed mantle of a serial entrepreneur. He was also in love with the fact he could now call himself a millionaire, something I accidently overheard while standing in the passageway outside of his office. He was speaking to his lover, apparently at the stage in his marriage where his relationship with his wife no longer warranted discretion. He reminded me of my old boss, Admiral Buzz Bass, the sleaziest man to ever wear a uniform. The man who nearly ruined my career.

"Sir, I believe the lines containing the marketing and entertainment costs might need review."

"What's wrong with them?" A frown creased the serial entrepreneur's face, and he glared at me. The glare did catch me off guard as I thought highlighting a possible DFAR violation would garner praise.

"Well, sir, as you know marketing is not allowed by the DFAR and those entertainment costs on the spreadsheet were for parties we held to win new contracts. They had nothing to do with the work we are now doing."

"Hmmm, interesting," said the CEO. He pursed his lips and nodded and I relaxed and felt good for contributing to our first staff meeting. I still had some juice! But then the CEO's glare returned.

"It is obvious you don't know this business. I don't mean the syllabus work. I mean the business of how to execute government contracts. Perhaps your boss can mentor you later." He shifted his glare to Ms. Long.

"Next slide."

I felt my face grow red. I was embarrassed and pissed and turned to the screen to hide my eyes. One good thing about powerpoint; it gave you a place to stare.

When the meeting broke Ms. Long grabbed me and asked me to follow her. We walked to her office and I took the chair in front of her desk. She wasted no time on my tutorial.

"Did you interrupt your bosses like that in the navy?" She gave me the smile people give when they think they've scored a point.

"Absolutely!" I gave her the smile you give when they didn't.

Ms. Long's eyes bored into me. "Surely you didn't interrupt a navy briefing with an attack on the staff work of others. Especially about something that might violate a federal regulation. You were not hired to interpret the DFAR."

"In the navy we only held meetings to get things done. We explained our work and defended it when we needed to. And we were all charged with knowing the rules and ensuring everyone else did too."

"Like at Tailhook?"

I just stared at Ms. Long and her widening, cynical smile. Her glittering, triumphant eyes told me she had regained the high ground in this battle. Tailhook was the Achilles' heel of the navy, or at least, of naval aviation. It was our one indefensible action; the mere mention allowed even the clumsiest detractor to cripple us. The metal tailhook stopped airplanes. But the Tailhook topic stopped conversations. If history had a ripple in it and Tailhook had happened during World War Two, we would have lost the war in the Pacific. Imagine during the Battle of Midway--our bombers poised to roll in and destroy the Japanese fleet then some radio operator transmitting "Tailhook! Tailhook!" We would have had to surrender.

"You will not need to attend any more staff meetings," said Ms. Long. "Concentrate on your role in our contract delivery to the navy. Others will take care of the business of the company."

I slunk off to my desk, grateful for the fact I had no tail to hide. Later that night, in bed, I told Gaby about my day. As usual, she tried to put it in perspective.

"Well, maybe the word *marketing* was just a placeholder because the CEO's son had a degree in marketing. Maybe he is really doing a job that is legal but he has the marketing title for his resume."

"Maybe," I sighed.

Gaby snuggled up against me and I could smell the night crème and soap. "And maybe the entertainment expenses are to cover legitimate costs of doing business that cannot be captured in the spreadsheet. You said you are not familiar with contractor accounting and finance."

"Maybe," I nodded. But I was unconvinced and worried about it long after Gaby fell asleep. I had always feared getting into a situation where the drip by drip of newfound perception, resulted in a pool of corruption. For the second time that day, I thought of Admiral Bass.

I concentrated on my work and tried to forget about the weekly briefing and it's spreadsheets. However, then came a Friday and Delores Ball entered my office. Delores was the finance officer in the company and I had gotten to know her fairly well. Her husband was a former navy chief petty officer who had served in the F14 community and he was someone to talk with at company parties.

"What's up, Delores?" I smiled as she stood in my doorway.

"This." Delores walked in waving a piece of paper. She sat it down in front of me and I saw it was one of her spreadsheets.

"Here." Delores pointed to a line. It read, 'Business Trip to Canada--$27,000.00.'

I shrugged and frowned.

"It's for a skiing trip to Whistler in British Columbia. The CEO and his son, for a week."

"Wow! That was some business trip."

"There was no business. This was a junket. The CEO believes that everything he does with his son is business and, therefore, chargeable to the government."

"Because his son is a company employee."

"Exactly."

"Well, maybe there is an explanation. Maybe they met someone, another company to team with, perhaps?"

"We always publish the board minutes and they contain trip reports. No mention of any business development in Canada. Whatever they did, they charged it to the contract you are working on so your navy buddies are paying for this."

"What do you want me to do with this, Delores? I have nothing to do with the company business."

"Yes, but you do have something to do with the company integrity. The navy selected us for this contract because of you, you know."

Delores turned and walked out the door. I sighed and leaned back in my chair as my old oath, the one I took when I joined the navy, whispered to me. *We will not lie, cheat, or steal, nor tolerate among us who do.*

That night while doing the dishes, I sought Gaby's advice and relayed my conversation with Delores. Gaby had evolved into the person I now trusted with the things that bothered me, the things that scared me. She was my Grandpa Two Bears and Mom all rolled into one. The best thing about her was that she didn't misinterpret my concerns as weakness and later cudgel me with them. If I asked her if she thought I was gaining weight she didn't take that as a signal to nag me about being fat.

"This sounds like one of those constructive confrontation challenges." Gaby handed me a plate and smiled. "I mean, it sounds like you are bothered by what the CEO is doing. A leader confronts the things that bothers him. At least that is what you have always said."

I rubbed the towel across the plate and sighed. "I suppose."

"You have a strong compass, Winfred. You will know what to do."

"You know what happened the last time I confronted my boss."

"Admiral Bass was an ass. Bass was an ass. Bass was an ass." Gaby chuckled at her rhyme. "Besides, when he fired you it set in motion all manner of things that led you to me."

"True. But getting fired in the navy means getting a new navy job. Getting fired in the civilian world means losing your only job."

Gaby shrugged but didn't respond so we finished the dishes then took seats on the living room couch. "I guess I will have to ask the CEO for a meeting."

"Well, as you have always said, 'If it bothers you, do something.'" Gaby squeezed my hand and when Christine finished her homework we three turned on Home Improvement to watch Tim Allen.

I normally work onsite at the navy training facility but the next day I dropped by our corporate office. The CEO had an "open door" policy although every time I had been to the headquarters the door was closed. I toyed with meeting first with Ms. Long since she was in my chain-of-command but decided to avoid that drama. I didn't need any more …Tailhook.

I knocked on the door and pushed it open when I heard the muffled, "Come in". The CEO was sitting at his desk, eating something with chopsticks. He frowned and nodded.

"I need to speak with you about the contract." I considered sliding into one of the chairs but then figured I might not be in the room that long.

"Oh?" The CEO pinched a glob of something that looked shiny and brown.

"Yes, sir. The trip you and your son took to Canada was charged to our contract with the navy. But there was no mention of Canadian business development in the last board report."

"What are you doing reading board reports?" The CEO glared at me.

"They are emailed to all company officers."

The CEO frowned as he had apparently forgotten our company policy. He shook his head and glowered. "It was a business meeting anyway." He threw down his chopsticks and the shiny brown stuff fell onto his desk. "My son is an employee of this company. We were conducting company business!"

"During a skiing trip?"

"The DFAR doesn't forbid ski trips!"

"The DFAR assumes government contractors have integrity." I fought to keep calm. "Some milk farmer in Missouri is paying for your ski trip with his taxes."

"Fuck Missouri!"

I stared at the CEO, shook my head in disgust and turned to go.

"Wait, Captain Kleegan." The CEO only called me Captain Kleegan when we were with business clients or when he thought it would give the company an advantage. To him it was a tool, not a title. Nevertheless, I hesitated and turned back to his desk.

"Captain Kleegan, I started this company with my credit card and by leveraging my house. I was in debt up to my ass—almost went under--until I won my first contract. I now can finally enjoy some of the benefits of my efforts, of the risk I took all by myself. I mean, you surely understood. Didn't you get benefits, perks as you succeeded in the navy?"

"Any benefit from rank came as a part of navy policy, not by bending or ignoring the rules."

"Captain, these cost-plus contracts pay the bills but they only produce a five percent profit. Who ever heard of a five percent profit?"

"Isn't five percent enough? After ALL expenses, including your salary, are paid? And you are a private company. No shareholders to pay or worry about."

"Weenie, this company made $27 million dollars last year. And I can't take a ski trip with my son?"

"Sure, you can, sir. Just not on taxpayer money."

"Well, I disagree. The DFAR gives us quite a bit of leeway in interpretation. I own this company and I decide how we will interpret it, not you."

And there it was. The CEO was telling me to get in line and shut up. I had built this conversation and had taken us to this decision point and I think I knew that before I knocked on his door. Had I done that on purpose? Had I picked a fight with the CEO in order to play my ethics cards?

"I will send you my two-week notice." I spun on my heel and stormed out.

I considered going home but didn't. After all, I was being paid to deliver on a contract and a two-week notice meant two more weeks of honest labor. So, I went back to the office and tried not to think about what I had just done. While I did get some satisfaction from uttering, "I will send you my two-week notice" the reality of soon being out of a job rained on that party pretty quickly.

Now what was I going to do?

I expected Ms. Long to call me, and half-hoped she would, pleading for me to stay. Telling me that we could work it out. And I wrestled with how to handle that call when it came. After all, the CEO was not about to change his ways so if I stayed, the only thing I would have accomplished with my meeting was a strange desire to stop by Panda King on the way home. But when Ms. Long didn't call, I knew it was because the company had already figured a way to replace me. Ours was a five-year contract; and there was plenty of time to smooth over any kerfuffle caused by my departure.

I brought home General Tso's Chicken, beef and broccoli, and fried rice for dinner and after fumbling with chopsticks for the obligatory two minutes, Gaby, Christine and I dug in with our spoons.

It is our tradition to discuss the events of our day and Gaby had interviewed a new cleaning service for the hotel and had selected new art prints for the foyer walls. Christine hadn't learned anything. At least that is what she said when I asked. Christine was an impish child and I think her reply was gauged to get my reaction. So, when I said, "Well, some days, there just isn't anything to learn," she smiled.

I was pretty quiet until Christine left the table to do homework, then I told Gaby what I had done. I winced as I awaited her response. My job brought in a lot of family revenue. Although Gaby made a good salary and I had my navy pension, this WAS California after all.

"Did you give your two-week notice?"

"Yes."

Gaby frowned and took a deep breath. "I know you have been wrestling with the ethics of the company."

"Of the CEO," I corrected.

"Yes, the CEO," Gaby leaned forward on the table. "And this hasn't got anything to do with your not being in charge anymore?"

Gaby might not have nagged me, but she did remember my concerns and fears. I reached across the table and took her hand. "I don't think so. That said, being an old, retired guy does cause me to wonder about things."

"To seek perspective?" Gaby smiled. She had already told me that perspective is what I needed.

"Yes, exactly. But in my life I have usually known when something isn't right. And I think the way the CEO runs this company is unethical and it will only get worse. If I stayed with the company I would have had to compromise on what I knew was wrong."

"Any ideas on what you are going to do now?"

"You remember Frank Johnson from my old squadron days?"

"With a callsign of Dogbreath, how could I forget him?"

"He has a company doing contracting work at the navy's Space and Warfare center down in Old Town. He has been after me to join him so I am going to talk to him tomorrow."

"Good." Gaby walked around the table, bent, and kissed me on the cheek. "The high road can be expensive, but maybe not this time."

BUTCH AND SUNDANCE

Dogbreath was true to his word and hired me to work on his contract with the navy. It was also training oriented, so I did add quite a bit of value to him. That said, the years began to drift by, and the remarkable and exciting events of my navy career were replaced with a paycheck and the low-grade but never-ending frustration of those who used to be someone but aren't any longer. That said, I studied the various crafts of instructional process and made myself valuable as a modern adherent to Lean Six Sigma and certified as Process Management Professional. Our company won more contracts in San Diego, and I worked on them too.

Gaby rose in the management team at the hotel, and she was happy at her work. Our evening conversations featured more of what she had done than the events of my day and I liked it that way. She deserved a "Life after navy" as she put it. And before I knew it, Christine was a freshman in veterinarian school in Long Beach. Of course, she left Shotzi with us when she went off to school and somehow the responsibility for the dog shifted to me. And that is how I got blamed for the second immaculate conception. Well, I was blamed for what I consider to be a misunderstanding of the immaculate conception. You see, most people think the immaculate conception was the impregnation of Mary by God, producing the baby Jesus. Makes sense, right? But, no, the immaculate conception relates to the dogma whereby Mary was without sin since birth. It is one of those things most people get wrong and I think the Catholic church does sneaky stuff like that on purpose. You know, to keep you from asking for more wine or an extra wafer at communion. For a brief time in 1972 the world was educated on the immaculate conception due to what the press named the immaculate reception. That was when Pittsburg Steeler Franco Harris caught a pass that ricocheted off of the Oakland Raider defender's helmet and he scored a game winning touchdown. So, when I let Shotzi get out of the house, ostensibly to take a poop, she apparently went on a hot date, got pregnant and gave birth to three puppies. Right there on Christmas day on the living room couch.

"How did this happen?" Christine narrowed her eyes and frowned at me.

I shrugged. "Maybe she had a yearning to be a mother."

"We need a need a new couch," said Gaby.

"But, Dad, don't you watch her when you let her out?"

"Not the entire time. I mean, I don't stare at her."

"Christ, Shotzi is ten years old!" Christine shook her head.

"It is the second immaculate conception," said Gaby.

I didn't correct her.

We gave two of the puppies away to friends and fans of Shotzi and kept a little male for ourselves. Christine had told us the best thing to do for older dogs was to get them a young companion so at least that worked out. I named the puppy Buddy because that is what he was to me. I did much of my work at home on my computer while Gaby was off to work and Christine was in college. So, he became my best friend.

We drove to Militia Springs a couple of times a year, but each time my visits home made me feel more and more distant. It was as if my time to enter its orbit had come and gone, and I was no more a member of that community than any stranger who pulled off of Highway Five into Hutch's gas station. It reminded me of a conversation I had had with Grandpa Two Bears. We were sitting on the porch and after I had lit his cigarette for him he told me about an old dog from his childhood. He had grown up with the dog but it seemed to forget him when he went off to the Marines.

"After a while he wouldn't even come when I called," said Grandpa.

I remember nodding and watching Grandpa as he looked at me with a sad face. He took a hit on his cigarette and shook his head.

"After a while longer, I quit calling."

I kind of felt like that with Militia Springs. I feared that after a while I wouldn't feel like it was home anymore. Worse, after a while longer, I might not even care.

My dad died shortly after we visited for Christmas in 2017. He died in his sleep at the age of eighty-six. I was sixty-two but still held my head up as I cried at his funeral. Of course, we buried him with Grandma, Grandpa, Mom, and baby Molly. That was the year I bought a stone and had it erected there. It was of side-by-side design with my name on one side and Gaby's on the other. I just wanted to know where I was going to end up.

I turned sixty-five in 2019 but I wasn't about to retire yet. I didn't feel old. In fact, the only difference in my life was moving from my navy Tricare to Medicare. Heck, I had been getting my fifteen percent discount from Appleby's since I was fifty-five!

But if my career seemed like it was winding down, Gaby's was on the rise and she really enjoyed her work at the Hotel Del. She became a manager and was a "woman in full" to paraphrase Tom Wolfe. Unfortunately, all was not roses because our beloved dog, Shotzi, died. She was only eleven and being a small breed, we had hoped to have her with us for years to come. But God must have needed her so when He took her from us all I could think of was how thankful I was that we had Buddy.

Christine excelled in veterinarian school and since Santa Barbara is only 200 miles from San Diego she visited often. I don't think I realized how much a child's visit could mean. We started making plans and menus on Wednesday if she was coming for the weekend. I was glad that I had visited my mom and dad as often as I did. Even when the navy took me across the country from Militia Springs, I prioritized seeing my parents.

So, ours was a content and happy little family until tragedy struck on a Saturday afternoon. That was when my precious Gaby was taken from me; killed in a car wreck because a distracted driver ran a red light. He evidently leaned across his seat to grab a bottle of water and when he focused back onto the road it was too late. Gaby died at the hospital before I could get there. Fortunately, Christine was home for summer break and she took care of everything. She was always a details type of person and nothing too small...or large...escaped her scrutiny. She would have made a better naval aviator than I was.

Death brings a reckoning to humans and presents a sliding scale of misery, depending on your relationship to the deceased. I had heard that you are never too old to cry at your parents' funerals and, true, I had teared up at both. Same for Grandpa. But the scale hits a different set of numbers when it's your wife lying there. I hear it's worse still for a child, but I can't imagine that. I sure hope I don't ever find out. Strange, my memories of losing Jane popped into my mind, but by now they were vague romantic images of long-ago, rather than the raw freshness of putting your hand on a coffin. But it all made me remember my old friend, Reese. It made me remember the quote from Hemingway I had given him. The one about the broken places and how, after the world breaks you, you get stronger at those broken places. And I wondered if by some mystery of fates that my losing Jane had in some way made me stronger, strong enough to endure losing Gaby. I say that because some nights I was so distraught that I thought about my .38. I thought about it but never pulled it out of the drawer. So, it was all I could do to make it through the visitation, the memorial, and the funeral. I almost started drinking again at the wake but threw the bourbon down the sink just before it got to my lips. My life wasn't a country song and, besides, one dead Kleegan was enough.

Gaby and I had been married for over twenty-five years. That is a long time to be in the same cockpit with somebody and you don't just carry on at their loss. I never thought I could cry like that. But I did and I did it without reservation.

Christine was a blessing, but I do not think I could have made it without Buddy. Now, people without dogs will shake their head at such a sentiment. They cannot imagine such a thing, but dog people know what I mean. Dog people know the true value of limitless, literally, on call, companionship. And I hate the word literally. Dogs are pretty much a miracle when you think about it. I mean when you think about where they come from. It's amazing, isn't it? How we got dogs in the first place.

I know the theory; that somehow by human interaction, wolves became dogs.

Wow, what a clap on our collective human backs! Aren't we wonderful? We humans, the ones who can't even parallel park, somehow made a wolf into a dog just by being around us!

Bullshit!

I think that theory probably arose from zoologists who didn't go to church because, you see, God gave us dogs. Think about it. It's twenty thousand years ago and some hairy Cro-Magnon guys are sitting around a fire, talking about the stag they just killed. I mean, it took the entire camp, thirty guys, all with spears and the original Mad Max haircuts to take down that one deer. So, now these hairy alpha-top-of-the-food-chain heroes, tend the fire that a lightning strike gave them and look over their shoulders at the hairy gals hidden off in the cave. Of course, this is a trillion years ago but those guys already have wary eyes as they look toward the women. Even if they haven't evolved enough yet to walk out by the fire and nag, "don't dry it out! You always dry the stag out!"

A hairy guy sees a wolf peering out of the darkness. He looks over at his pal and grunts and motions which means, "Hey, Trog, throw a stag bone to the wolf."

Trog looks at the wolf and pitches a bone and the wolf yelps and runs away.

A thousand years later, the offspring of the hairy folks sit around the campfire. The descendent of the first hairy guy sees a wolf, again, peering out of the darkness. That's what wolves did before they ate kids going to grandma's house. Anyway, the hairy guy grunts and motions which means, "Hey, Trog, throw a stag bone to the wolf."

Trog starts to throw the bone but his now-evolved wife slaps his hand and grunts and motions which means, "What the hell are you doing? I'm going to make earrings out of those bones."

Another thousand years goes by and the offspring of all these people are sitting around a fire and Trog finally gets a bone to the wolf. The wolf likes the bone and comes closer to the fire. A couple of years later he is a Yorkie with a taste for filet and a ribbon in his hair.

Like I said, Bullshit! I don't buy it! Not for a second. I cannot believe the haphazard fumbling of men led to our modern dogs. I read just the other day that there are close to 340 recognized breeds, and this from the same geniuses that took seventy thousand years to convert a wooden wheel into a pneumatic tire. And wouldn't you think we would have spent at least a little of that dog imagination on themselves? We haven't changed at all over the past thousands of years. Don't you think we could have done something about receding hairlines and erectile disfunction?

No. God gave us dogs, I am sure of it. He gave them as a gift, a blessing of unconditional love, that some of us might even deserve, or at least try to deserve.

I was in shock, I think, for the first week after Gaby died.

The next week was even more of a blur of visitors, and well-wishers--decent people saying wonderful things about a beautiful person and a tragic event.

Christine held my hand that last day. The day of the funeral. We stood in a small group and watched Gaby as she was lowered into the ground. Then I went home. Well, I went to my house. It wasn't home now. A house can be a lonely place, I suspect, but a home that was conceived and put together by a woman who is now gone can be unbearably so. Every surface, every nook, even the squeak of the cabinet drawers reminded me of Gaby. And I spent many evenings sitting on the couch with Buddy, watching her favorite programs. On a T.V. that was not turned on.

Despondent and depressed, I moped around for two months. Then, one morning, I decided to sell the house and move back home to Militia Springs. My decision didn't come from some overnight inspiration. Instead, it came from the morning's reading of the *Douglas County Herald*. Molly and Paul mailed it to me every Friday so it was week-old news by the time I got it. But as I read the articles about the high school football team's conference championship, the plans for the annual Glade Top Trail festivities, and the solid prices for feeder pigs, I felt the strong tug to return home. I held the paper to my face with the crazy notion that the smell of newsprint might link me back. Maybe it did. Or, more likely, it was the photo of Donnie Curry, holding a prize-winning bass. He looked happy and content and maybe I could find that too!

I called Christine and she agreed to come and discuss the idea. In fact, she had suggested that I move back to Militia Springs shortly after Gaby's funeral.

Buddy watched me as I shaved. He watched every morning and now that it was just the two of us he never left my side. He also knew that after the shave came the walk and, of course, the poop. That is why I took the *San Diego Union-Tribune*. It was a rehash of the *Los Angeles Times* with lots of liberal idiocy and I did not read it. Certainly not the op-ed section. But it did come in a plastic wrapper that was perfect for picking up Buddy's poop.

I dressed and made coffee and took Buddy for his walk. Passing our neighbors' houses, I always made a point to wave with the bag in my hand. I wanted everyone to know that I was one of the dog owners that picked up the poop.

Buddy made his deposit right on schedule, but he sniffed at every bush, so it took an hour to walk the block. At 0900 sharp, Christine rang the doorbell. Buddy barked his welcome and I escorted my daughter into the kitchen. I poured her a cup of coffee and we talked about Molly and Paul and their daughter Kate's new baby, little Saxon. I felt good about the boy's name. Because later when he joined the navy and became an aviator his callsign would undoubtedly be "Anglo". That is critical because when Molly married Paul her last name became Smart. So, Saxon's name is Saxon Smart. You see, if you don't have a cool callsign when your last name is smart, the JOs will give you one. And that is "Notso." As in, Notso Smart. "Anglo" is pretty cool when you think about it.

Then, we moved to the subject of selling the house.

"Dad, there is no reason to wait. I mean, I do like having you close to me, but I think you need to find your bearings."

"The problem is I probably won't be able to sell the house for what we paid for it. You know that California real estate hasn't been the same since the 2006 crash."

"Maybe so, but you do have equity. Besides, how much money do you need to move to Militia Springs? Molly and Paul beg you to come back every time you visit."

"I suppose you are right."

"And, Dad, you need to leave before the new law kicks in. The one about pet-factor age."

"Surely they won't take Buddy! Not if I have the house on the market."

"You never know Dad. I wouldn't waste time."

Pet-factor age was a new buzzword in California and it was tied to the recently passed Medicare-For-All law. While well-intended, the law had consequences as the cradle-to-grave health system opened up all kinds of stressors. The COVID-19 pandemic made it even worse. Seniors with pets had become a major issue.

Pet-factor age is based upon life expectancy, which in California is 80 years old. That is the base number that the state uses. Then they factor in how much of your life you lived in the state, whether you smoke, drink, have high blood pressure, etcetera. Since I was a naval aviator all of my career, I was termed as "high-stress susceptible." The theory was that such an individual was soaked in stress and toxins and God knows what. Besides, I did have high blood pressure and elevated cholesterol and that reduced my pet-age factor to sixty-five.

"I can't believe that since I am sixty-five that means I cannot own a pet in the state of California."

"Dad, it's the law. Mom was so much younger than you. She had a pet age factor of seventy-eight. She was the reason you didn't have to worry about any of this. But now she is gone."

"But they can't just take my dog away. Can they?"

"They can, Dad. And they will. It's the law."

"Well, it's a stupid law. I still don't understand how they could have passed such a thing."

"Dad we went over this. The idea is to contain costs and manage the extended care challenges."

"What does owning a pet have anything to do with that?" I don't know why I badgered Christine with this. I had read the law. I knew what it said. I just hadn't paid any attention because I didn't think I had to.

"Dad, there is no longer any private health insurance in the state. That means all the costs for health from cradle to grave are born by the state and they can't support services to elders with pets. Besides, the COVID death rate among folks near your age is huge. Seniors pass away each day in this state and that leaves some pets in the hands of relatives but usually in the hands of the state. The law has the goal of reducing the number of pets that are abandoned by ill seniors as well as encourage the adoption of older pets by qualified seniors."

I looked at Christine and shook my head. Of course, she was right. The language in the law cited statistics that indicate huge numbers of senior-owned pets wind up having to be euthanized. The pets are often left for last minute adoptions because the owners get ill or must move into senior living spaces that don't allow animals. In other cases, the pets are simply not cared for. Seniors often do not have the energy or capability to appropriately care for pets, particularly dogs that need exercise and stimulation. The law concluded that most pets that live with seniors are not socialized around other people, children, or even other pets. That makes them extremely hard to adopt.

"Dad, the law can seem harsh, certainly for you. But it was well meant."

"Well meant! Do you have any idea what Buddy means to me?"

"Of course, I do, Dad. Of course, I do. Remember, I had his mother for my pet."

"I don't think you do." I looked at Christine but took care not to glare. None of this was her fault. "You never needed her. Not like I need Buddy." I swallowed at how weak I sounded but that just made me angrier. "He is my best friend. On most days, he is my only friend and I like it that way. Some might think I am a pathetic old man with a dog as a best friend. But think of a better one?"

"Oh, Dad." Christine hugged me and kissed my cheek.

"Let's say they don't care that I have the house on the market. Let's say that they think it is just a ruse for me to keep my dog. What would they do with Buddy if they come?"

Christine lowered her eyes. She took a breath and turned toward the window. "Most of the pets have a tough time getting adopted."

"So, they would put him down?" I clinched my fists and glared at Christine's back. She turned and frowned. "Possibly, Dad. But they would give him tests to see if he fits into any of their services' programs. He is young, it is possible he would not be euthanized."

I took a deep breath and slowly let it out. I shook my head and stepped toward Christine and hugged her.

"Why can't you take Buddy? Just until I sell the house and get out of this loony state."

Tears welled in Christine's eyes and she shook her head. "Dad, I would love to take him, but it's against the law. The dog is managed according to who the registered owners are and that is you and Mom."

That afternoon, the postman brought me the usual crap and the one letter I didn't want to ever get. The one from CAPA, the California Animal Protection Agency. As Christine predicted, the agency was sending a retrieval team to my address the following Wednesday. That afternoon, I put the house on the market. I was going to lose my shirt, but I was going to keep my dog.

I agonized over losing Buddy and as the fateful day approached with no takers for the house, I became frantic. I couldn't sleep and stayed up watching movies. I didn't really watch them, I just sat in front of them with my eyes open. However, one horror movie, *The House on the Left*, had a scene that did get my attention. It was when the girl's father stuck her hand into the garbage disposal and turned it on. As gruesome as that was, it did give me a great idea! The next morning, I scheduled an appointment for Wednesday at the groomers for Buddy and went to visit my friend from the navy who had a goat farm near Ramona.

On the Wednesday of the CAPA retrieval, I took Buddy to the groomers and told them to give him the works. I told them to take their time, make sure the nails were done, express the anal glands, the whole show. I went back home and around ten that morning the doorbell rang, and I opened it to two uniformed CAPA officers. I like Old Spice after shave and had dabbed a little of it on the edges of my eyes, so they were burning and tearing. I had also swallowed a cup of lemon juice and my throat was raw so when I said, "Good morning, officers" I looked and sounded like a man who had been crying. Of course, I had anyway but I just wanted to make sure.

I smiled to myself at their shocked looks.

"Sir, is something the matter?"

"Please come in."

We shuffled into the living room and I turned toward them. "I expect you're here for my dog?"

"Yes, sir." The older man spoke. I could see his partner frown behind him.

"I'm afraid you are too late." I pointed to the kitchen table where Buddy's collar, mauled and chewed by the garbage disposal, lay in pieces. "Coyotes got him yesterday."

"Oh, my God!" exclaimed the younger officer.

"Hmm," grunted the older man. He picked up a piece of collar and studied it a moment. "Hmm," he grunted again. "Interesting timing."

"You don't believe me?" I glared at him. "You don't fucking believe me?" I gave him my best display of indignant outrage and believe me, after a career in the navy, a second career as a contractor, and twenty-five years of marriage to a German, I could do indignant outrage.

"Well, sir..."

I could see doubt in his eyes. He still wasn't convinced.

"Here, let me show you." I flung open the patio door and stormed out. "Come here," I said over my shoulder. I stomped to the middle of the yard and turned around. The two officers followed me, so I continued, straight legged and angry, to the large pepper tree and to the mound of fresh earth beneath it.

"Here!" I shouted. "Here he is." A shovel leaned against the tree and I grabbed it. I stuck the blade in deep and took out a shovelful of earth. "Here, he is!" I stuck it in again and again and after the third time I felt the skin of the goat. I took off just enough dirt to expose the mottled brown fur.

"Do you want me to dig him up? You can take him with you!" My eyes were wide and red, and I was furious! I wasn't acting now, I was furious. The whole, fucking idea of having to give up my pet to the state of California outraged me!

"Sir, no sir. Stop!" Said the younger officer. "Sir, stop."

I hesitated a second, then dropped the shovel to the ground. I took deep breaths and started to sob. I was not surprised that my charade had turned so real.

"Sir, we will let ourselves out. We'll record the dog as killed by coyotes and that we sighted the body. We are so sorry for all of this, sir." The younger officer patted my arm and they left.

I nodded my head as I continued to cry and look at the grave. The patio door opened and closed, and I heard a car engine start. I stood there a few moments and thought of Gaby in her grave. I knew she would understand and not think my charade with the goat pelt had violated some protocol. Then, I went to the groomers to get Buddy.

I felt a new wariness once I got Buddy home and didn't take him for a walk the following morning. I feared someone would see us and report my sin of illegal dog ownership.

The next week I had three showings and hid Buddy in the trunk as I drove away from the house. Funny, how you have to leave to sell your most prized possession. I guess that is so the prospective new owners can talk about your poor choices in draperies and carpet colors. I think that viewing a house automatically gives people the power of having better taste.

But the god of snobs favored me and the next Monday I accepted an offer for the house. Although I began to relax, I did keep the window shades drawn and walked Buddy only at night. I wanted to keep him from the prying eyes of onlookers, especially that asshole, Royce.

I was doing a final walk through on my house when the doorbell rang. I thought it was the moving company so the two CAPA officers surprised me. They barged in and took Buddy. I argued and told them I was moving to Missouri but they just handed him to some guy with a van. It had San Diego County Animal Collection stenciled on the side. I had heard the state was contracting the collection of animals to civilians.

"Where are you taking him? Where are you taking my dog?" I stood in my driveway, tears flowing down my face.

"To the shelter. And he isn't your dog anymore." The van driver grinned and sped off.

I watched the van disappear around the corner and turned to go back inside. That is when I noticed Royce drinking a beer by his fence.

"Nice day," he smirked.

That fucking bastard! I knew he had heard or seen Buddy and had reported me to the CAPA goons. I also knew that if I didn't get out of there I was going to kill Royce so I hopped into my car and started to search for the van. I had no plan but I had to do something so I headed toward the animal shelter on Scripps Parkway. Once there, I parked out front and waited. I know I wasn't thinking straight, I mean, what was I going to do at the shelter? What could I accomplish there? I guess I figured the driver would eventually dump his collection of dogs and maybe I could see Buddy again.

About an hour later, the driver did show up but after a quick trip inside he returned to the van and drove off. That seemed odd, so I followed him as he headed east toward the back county. Thirty minutes later, he pulled inside a chain link fence and parked the van next to a row of buildings. The driver disappeared inside so I pulled my car under the trees and waited.

After thirty minutes I began to worry. I could hear the muffled barking of the dogs inside the van and wondered how hot it was getting. Channel 51 news had just featured a story on the temperatures cars can get to after only a few minutes in the sun. I walked to the fence and rattled the gate and yelled to get the van driver's attention. The dogs heard me and barked even louder. I tried to see them but the back was enclosed so I went back to my car. I waited another fifteen minutes then returned to the fence, wiggled under it, and trotted to the van. It was unlocked and when I opened the back a herd of dogs rushed me! They were a mass of wagging tails and slobbery tongues and I kept saying "Shh. Shh." They didn't hear me though.

I grabbed Buddy from the fray and stood to take him away when the driver popped around the corner of the van door.

"What are you doin', bub?"

"I am keeping my dog from dying of heat exhaustion."

"Ahh, it ain't that hot." He frowned and swung a baseball bat.

I jumped behind the van door as the bat clunked against it, swiveled, and planted my foot into his crotch. He howled as it popped against his jeans. I kicked him again.

As the driver moaned and dropped to his knees I clutched Buddy and turned to run. But the driver had recovered and grabbed my foot and I tripped and fell. I held Buddy as I went down, careful to take our weight on my knees and not on him. When I turned, the driver was coming toward me on his knees with the bat in his hand. He lunged and swung but I rolled and the bat smacked against the ground. I grabbed the end just as the driver pulled it and that drew me close enough to snake my fist into his face. He staggered back and dropped his end of the bat so I took it and hit him. I hit him on the shoulder and he reached for me so I hit him again.

I grabbed Buddy and ran to my car! Some people from the building came out and I could hear them shouting. I saw them through my rear-view mirror just before I sped away toward the parkway heading east. I figured I would keep to the back roads and get us across the state line to freedom. We were heading to Missouri anyway, just a little ahead of schedule.

Unfortunately, I had not planned for a dog rescue that day so when I saw the tank on empty, I whipped into a 7-11. I was topping off when the cops screamed in with sirens screaming and lights blazing.

Grabbing Buddy, I sprinted for the door. I ripped it open and ran inside but not before I heard the shots and felt the sting.

Why are they shooting at me?

I was shocked and my head whirled at how fast I had gone from being a regular guy to someone the police shot at. What had the van driver told them?

I scurried toward the back of the 7-11 with no plan but to seek a place to hide and figure it all out. The two guys on the shift ran out the back and I was glad for that. I have never seen a hostage situation on television or in the movies work out. I crept around for a moment and honestly did consider which aisles would protect us the most. I guess that was my navy training. Or, maybe, I just wanted to be next to the beef jerky because I thought of it as a survival tool.

Buddy and I rested next to a rack of Peppered and Original and I felt him pant and heard him whimper. Blood seeped into my fingers and I wasn't sure if it was from him or me. I started to get light in the head and I leaned against something that smelled like Slim Jims and sighed.

Was I wrong to take Buddy from the van?

I frowned. But then I swallowed and shook my head with new resolve. If the state of California was willing to contract the life of my dog to somebody like the van driver then he had no future with them. I was right to take him out of there. I looked into Buddy's face.

"Do you remember when we watched *Butch Cassidy and The Sundance Kid?*" I put my hand on his head, stroking the ear that stood up and feeling the warm beat of his heart. I touched his ear again. "Do you remember? We watched it with Mom." I looked at him and swallowed again. I love my dog.

Buddy's breath was shallow and fast and his sides heaved. I took a deep breath and tried to think. Despite my wooziness, I could hear the cops. Man are they a noisy lot! They were making all kinds of racket outside and the staccato of their radio bursts, sirens, and tire screeches echoed off the walls.

I grinned as a thought hit me. I could walk outside with my hands up.

My dog and I just wanted a Big Gulp cherry slurpy.

I frowned and I winced. A dull pain reached around from my back to my chest. I looked down at my dog.

"Look, we may get separated." I hugged Buddy and pulled his head up under my chin. I felt his warmth and heard a moan. I had gotten him here. I had gotten him wounded. I kissed the top of his head.

"But Heaven is different than here. In a minute there will be a light, sweetie, but it will be okay.

It will be okay" I squeezed him again. "You just have to find Mom. She will be in our pick-up truck. The door will be open..." I swallowed as a tear fell down my cheek. "The door will be open and Mom will be waiting there. Jump in and get on your pillow and wait for me. Wait for me like you always do."

I sobbed and held Buddy. "In Heaven time is different." I winced in pain and felt cold. "You won't have to wait long. It will just be a minute, a second before I am there too. I will get in, and say, "Ready to go and you will put your head down on the pillow and I will put the truck in gear and Mom will wave her hand and say "It stinks in here" just like she always does and I will have the window open so you can put your head out if you want. Just like you always do. And you can sit on my lap and put your head out the window and lean your paws against the window."

"MISTER KLEEGAN! WINFRED KLEEGAN!

THIS IS THE POLICE. COME OUT WITH YOUR HANDS UP."

I scrunched down and took a breath. The blood was wet now, seeping against my side. And I felt better about that. I felt better that they shot me too and not just my little dog.

"MISTER KLEEGAN! WINFRED KLEEGAN!

I felt so weak. I leaned back and swallowed.

It wasn't bad, it wasn't that bad.

I leaned over Buddy and rubbed his head. And kissed him.

It wasn't that bad.

"So, do you remember *Butch Cassidy and The Sundance Kid*? It was a long time ago so maybe you don't remember."

I took a breath and grimaced at the pain. I looked at my dog. "We had just adopted you and it was an old movie about these two robbers and you sat next to Christine, in between Mom and me, and the four of us watched it together."

I touched his ear. I leaned and kissed his ear. "Do you remember, at the end, when all of the federales were closing in? Remember, Butch and Sundance didn't know they were all out there."

I took a breath and thought about Grandpa Two Bears. I smiled as I thought of him sitting on the porch, me striking one of Mom's blue tip matches and lighting his Lucky.

But the light I saw wasn't the flame from the match but the lights reflecting off the far wall. I remembered when cops just had red lights. But these lights were red and blue. I frowned and leaned back against the jerky rack and swallowed.

When did that change?

I stroked Buddy's head and leaned over and kissed him and gasped at the pain in my side. I pulled my hand away and felt the wet.

I looked at Buddy. "Do you remember? When Butch and Sundance made a run for it?"

I took a deep breath and let it slowly flow past my lips. Then, I straightened up and grabbed my gun. It was only a cell phone but it was my gun today. I looked at Sundance and smiled.

"When we get outside and get to the horses." I frowned but it was a play frown. It was the frown that Butch had in the movie when he looked at Sundance and asked, "Hey, you didn't see Lefors out there did you?" I smiled at my dog. I smiled at Sundance. "Remember, Lefors is the one that chased us all across the west, the one that chased us here to South America. So, you didn't see him out there did you?"

I looked at Sundance but he just moaned.

"No." I checked my gun again, picked Sundance into my arms and took another breath. I stood to run. "Good, for a minute there, I thought we were in trouble."

I staggered to the door, closed my eyes, and ran out into the street. The spotlights blinded me and I clutched Sundance and waited for the federales' gunfire.

SINS OF THE FATHER

The van driver's co-workers called the police. That's what my lawyer told me. He told me in the hospital as I recovered from my flesh wound. And all the blood had been mine. Buddy hadn't been hit at all. My lawyer also showed me a video and, although grainy, it clearly showed my throwdown with the van driver in the parking lot.

I thought I might get off with some kind of warning since it was my first offense. But assault is a serious crime, especially when you put a person in the hospital. That the van driver was acting under a state contract also hurt my case. In the end, my lawyer convinced me that a plea deal was better than a trial and I agreed. That said, I was not prepared for the twenty-four-month incarceration edict at the hands of the California judicial system. Despite my squeaky-clean history, excepting a DUI years ago, the judge sent me to the slammer.

"Mister Kleegan you are very, very fortunate the police did not kill you. In fact, if you weren't holding your dog, they might have. Your actions endangered not only you and your pet but many of our citizens and you put the van driver, a contracted service provider, in the hospital."

The good news is that the judge didn't send me to a maximum security prison like San Quentin. He sent me to the California Men's Colony near San Luis Obispo where inmates served under minimum security.

Minimum security prisons are often derisively called country club prisons by those who believe harsh punishment is the only remedy for crime. And it is true, The Colony was a much better place to serve time than a super max. That said, it was still prison and I wasn't free.

My notion of a minimum security prison primarily came from watching the movie, *Goodfellas*. There is a scene where Henry, Pauli, and two other "Wiseguys" shave garlic, make meat sauce, and cook steaks while Bobby Darin sings *Beyond the Sea*. Now, that would be grand! I like Italian food, too. However, I was pretty sure that even a place like The Colony was going to be worse than that.

In my pre-sentencing research, I found that the thing that makes prison bad isn't the security but the *reason* for the security. The nature of the people inside. If a place is filled with hardened criminals--evil men--doing long sentences, a sense of desperation and finality sets in. An atmosphere of violence overlays everything and animal survival becomes the motivating factor.

At The Colony, most offenders were there for non-violent offenses. Some committed so-called white collar crimes like embezzlement or fraud. But the majority just did stupid stuff like bouncing checks, scams, and not paying traffic tickets. So, the security was minimum because of us; our nature. I was lucky to get the minimum security assignment since assault is considered a violent crime. I think my age, clean record, and military record helped. That, and the fact that the company the van driver worked for was indicted on animal cruelty charges.

One avenue of rehabilitation at The Colony was education and the arts. I almost spit up my coffee, which by navy standards was pretty good, when my processing agent told me that. The inmates were encouraged to get a high school diploma equivalent if they didn't have one. Courses on wood-working, small-engine repair, plumbing, and other trades electrician offered inmates opportunities to remake their lives.

When my processing agent asked if I played an instrument or liked to act, sing, dance, etc. I told him I played a trumpet, poorly, over fifty years ago. He asked me what I did for entertainment and I answered, "Read."

I know the look people give you when they think you are boring and he gave it to me right then. "Have you ever taught?" The processor mustered a smile as his pen hovered over checking some box, any box, to send me along. "We need high school teachers. So, we can give our General Education Degree."

"I have a teaching certificate and I was an instructor in the navy."

The processor's eyes opened wide and his smile changed from something to do with his lips to genuine happiness. The next thing I knew, I was a high school teacher in The Colony!

I have to say I was successful and I attribute that to the navy. And that was because I was used to dealing with smart men whose trust I had to earn. Rank-based organizations like the navy may place one person over another due to seniority or position. But that didn't grant automatic respect. You had to earn that. My position as a teacher placed me at the head of the classroom, but that was all. It was up to me to teach.

I taught four courses; American History, World History, Geography, and Citizenship. Just like in public school, I did that in 40 minute sessions five days a week over a nine month graduation cycle.

I started each course by placing a sign on the wall. It read:

High school dropouts are 8 times more likely to go to prison. Sixty-eight percent of prisoners have no high school diploma.

High school graduates annual salary is over 30% more than non-high school graduates.

You will become a high school graduate if you pay attention and take notes.

I also coordinated with the guys who taught the various trades courses in The Colony. They agreed to help make the connection between education with learning a trade.

I taught to ensure the students passed the course. By that, I don't mean I taught to the tests. But I did emphasize the thinking required to pass them.

I reserved a few minutes at the end of each class for fun. By that, I mean I offered my students an opportunity to express themselves. Or I would ask something not to be tested but to be known. An example was "why do men walk on the street side of the sidewalk when with a lady?"

Ronnie Johnson, one of my difficult students, answered, "We don't know no ladies."

I smiled and nodded at the laughter before I answered. "During Medieval times streets were running sewers and people threw their garbage out the window. Those closer to the walls were less likely to get dumped on or splattered. That is why the ladies walk on the inside today."

"Does Evans count as a lady?" It was Ronnie again. But this time the laughter was subdued, darker. Wylie Evans was a slight, quiet young man who sat alone in the back corner. He wore wire rim glasses and his blond hair hung over his face when his head was down. And it almost always was down. The other guys, Ronnie especially, taunted him with "Queer boy" and "Hey, gay dude". That made me uncomfortable because I had no experience with any of that. When I first joined the navy, there was no such thing as homosexuals in the military. A non-issue. Later, when we acknowledged they existed, we got rid of the ones we found. I remember when I was a catapult officer the ship's master-at-arms found two of our sailors in the forward water brake void. I don't know what they were doing but they left the ship that afternoon after a quick captain's mast. By the time I retired we had gone from "Don't ask, don't tell" to allowing gays to serve openly. I was surprised at how easy that happened. I guess the younger generation was more tolerant. Or, at least better at hiding their bias. But I personally had never dealt with a gay or lesbian. I never even talked to one. Not that I am aware of.

Fortunately, my timer sounded and I didn't have to answer Ronnie.

I had three different roommates in what was a condominium setting but I never had one for long. Fortune made for fluidity and people who served good time were often freed early. Bob White was with me the longest. I called him "Quail" after we got to know each other. Being from New York, he had never heard the distinctive call of a quail. But after I told him it sounded just like his name, he liked it. Bob was also in the teaching program. He taught math. His technique was to teach to the test but then emphasize only the basics. His goal was for his students to succeed as a mechanic, plumber, or anyone who worked with tools.

"Weenie, I teach them the crap so they can pass the test. But the only thing they really need to know is that a 7/16's wrench is smaller than a half-inch...and why. And throw the circuit breaker before touching the wires. Everything else is just for the test."

Christine visited me often and one day she brought a man with her. His name was Juan Santana and he was from New Mexico and Christine loved with him. He loved her too. At least he said so. The fact that he met his love's father in prison pretty much spoke to his bona fides in my mind. I think you have to love a woman to meet her dad in the slammer. I also liked the fact he was also a veterinarian.

Molly and Paul even dropped in for my birthday. I think they really came because San Luis Obispo is halfway between San Francisco and Los Angeles and it facilitated their once-in-a-lifetime vacation away from the farm. But it was great to see them, despite my setting. That said, being farm people, they were dog people, and were proud of my incarceration to save my pooch. Christine later told me that Buddy was in some sort of service animal program. That made me feel better. At least Sundance was alive!

I missed Gaby sorely. I had her picture on my dresser next to the bed and prayed to her every night. She was always with me. Always. And my prayers were a comfort because I was blessed in my understanding of how Heaven worked. I took solace in knowing I would someday see her, Grandpa, Dad, Mom--all of them. I would see Dooly. And I would also see Jane again and that would be okay with Gaby.

My student group remained largely intact for all my four classes, as none but Wylie had completed much high school. I did not post or publicize the grades but gave each student his own test after I graded it. I hated my flight training when the navy instructors had stuck a list on the wall with everyone's name and scores. It was a needless humiliation for the poor learners, like I was for a while, and an unneeded pump for the others. I also didn't post the grades because Wylie Evans always scored the highest. His essay work was remarkable! I sensed Ronnie and a few of the others would seek to get even with Wylie in some way if they knew how much he out-scored them. I was wise enough to know that showcasing his capability would do more harm than good.

As the semester progressed, I found myself drawn to Wylie. He was always last to leave class which often gave us a few teacher/student moments alone. It was during those short conversations that I realized what I liked about him: he reminded me of me at nineteen! Intelligent and with good humor, witty, but with no self-confidence. I also sought him in the library. None of the other students ever came in there so it was a safe place to discuss books. A couple of times we got looks from other inmates. It was a smirk, actually, and initially it bothered me because they probably wondered if I was gay too. I have to admit, that made me feel uneasy.

Incarceration does some remarkable things to you, even in relatively short and comfortable stays like mine. Like a chance to think. I mean to really ponder on stuff that you let go in a different time. Maybe that is because major interruptions—threats-- in your life help you realize your mortality. I also think that realization comes from counting the days. Counting the days until your real life will begin again. My life was great until prison, but most lives aren't. Not for the guys here with me. Although they weren't hardened criminals, most were young, uneducated and of color. And the amazing thing was that no matter how frustrating their lives had been, no matter how pitiful and cruel and without direction, they each still counted the days until you could reenter it. All except

Wylie. I don't think he counted the days until he got out. I think he counted the days that he could stay in. That realization came to me during one of our library sessions when he asked if I had seen *The Shawshank Redemption*. It was the prison movie starring Morgan Freedman and that guy who played the pitcher in *Bull Durham*. The one with Kevin Costner.

"Sure," I answered.

Wylie had smiled at me then dropped his head like he always did. I looked at the top of his blond mop a second then cleared my throat. "Why do you ask?"

The blond hair didn't move for a moment. The he looked up at me.

"Do you remember the character, Brooks?"

"No." I shook my head. "Not really. What's wrong, son?"

"James Whitmore played the part." Wylie's eyes were wet. He looked at me then shifted his gaze to some place over my shoulder. Some place safer than my eyes.

"Remember James Whitmore? He played the cop in that movie when these giant ants attacked a town in New Mexico."

"Sure." I chuckled and nodded. "It was *Them*. One of the first atomic bomb monster movies."

"Right," said Wylie. "So, Whitmore plays Brooks in *The Shawshank Redemption*."

I nodded. "I remember."

"And Brooks finally gets out. After spending fifty years in prison. Remember?" Wylie wiped at his face.

I frowned and glanced away. But when I looked back his eyes found me. I was uncomfortable because I didn't know where they were leading me.

I nodded. "I remember."

"And when he gets free he realizes he doesn't belong free. He realizes that the free world doesn't want him. Doesn't need him. He has no place in it. Remember?"

"I remember." I frowned again as I remembered the scene with Brooks swinging from a belt in his room--"Brooks Was Here" carved into the wooden overhang.

"When do you think he realized that?" The intensity in Wylie's eyes disturbed me. He continued before I could answer. "I mean, do you think he knew that he could never be free at the beginning? When he first went in?"

"I...don't know."

"Or do you think it came to him over time? Do you think Portia understood her plight at the beginning or was it later? After her suitors showed themselves. After she realized the plight she was in?"

We had been reading Portia's Lament as a part of Shakespeare's *The Merchant of Venice* in class. It was one of the fun topics I had selected. Although I admit, most of my students didn't find much fun in it. Except, of course, Wylie.

"I don't know, Wylie. What's wrong?"

Wylie gathered his books and got to his feet. "See you tomorrow in class, Mister Kleegan."

I didn't know why Wylie was in The Colony. Being so young, I assumed it was due to some repeat pattern of shoplifting or somethings like that. It couldn't be drugs, not here. They didn't send druggies to The Colony.

News from Militia Springs perked me up. The farm was thriving and Paul did buy the Sons of Galilee land next to our place. The moving company had taken all my possessions to Militia Springs and everything was ready for me to move back. The people of Militia Springs knew I was in jail as word like that gets out pretty fast. But, after Molly and Paul explained it was just "California" I think they were prepared not to judge me harshly. Besides, freeing my pet from lunatic bureaucrats was highly respected.

The night after my classes took their GED certification tests, Wylie Evans was beaten up. It happened outside his condominium unit and even from his hospital bed, he refused to say who did it. The warden was concerned about his safety so he convened a board to determine if Wylie should be freed early for his own protection. I was asked to come before the group since I was his teacher.

There were seven of them, and I eagerly reported on how well Wylie had done. I told them he had scored at the top of his classes and easily passed his GED certification.

"He will become a productive member of society." I smiled at the board.

"Is that so?" The question came from Mister Allen, the deputy warden. I was wary of him since he had a reputation for being an ass. His eyes bored into me. "Do you know why he is here?"

"No, sir."

"He is here for indecency with a child."

"Sir! Mister Evans is hardly on trial." The admonishment came from The Colony chaplain.

"I think our teacher needs to know what he is committing us to." Mister Allen glared at the chaplain who quickly, and disappointedly, lowered his eyes.

I frowned and shook my head. "I can't believe it."

"You can't believe that a good student can be a deviant?" Allen glared at me. "That's the problem with you academic types. You think that your books grant morality. That they make you better than everyone else. Well, they don't!"

I swallowed and frowned again. There had to be some sort of explanation. I stared at Mister Allen. I made myself look defiant and disbelieving. I did that for Wylie's sake. I also did it for mine. After all, Wylie was my prodigy, the young man who proved how great of a teacher I was.

"Well, bring him in." Mister Allen nodded to the uniformed officer at the door. "Let him explain."

Moments later, Wylie came in. He limped as he walked and I could see a scratch over one eye. He didn't look at anyone as he took a seat. He didn't look at me.

"I understand you refuse to name your attacker?" Allen leaned forward.

Evans stared at him then bent his head. I swallowed as I saw the top of the mop.

"Nobody saw what happened," Allen continued. "No witnesses, just your testimony to the doctor and to the chaplain here that you were attacked."

Wylie kept his head down.

"Identify your attackers, Mister Evans. We will punish them and protect you. Tell us."

Wylie kept his eyes on the floor.

Impatience crept into Mister Allen's voice. "Well, then explain to the board why you are here, Mister Evans. What you were charged with." Allen leaned back in his chair and smiled.

"Sir?" The chaplain leaned forward.

"He can talk, chaplain. Let him explain."

Wylie kept his head down a moment, then raised it and looked at Mister Allen. "Well, sir, I was charged with a sex crime."

"Sex crime? We aren't talking about getting caught with a prostitute down on Broadway. What, exactly, was the charge?"

Wylie's lips trembled and his thin throat contracted in a swallow. "Sex with a minor."

"What kind of minor?" Allen's voice was sharp.

Evans whispered but I couldn't hear him.

"Speak up," said Allen. "What kind of minor?"

"A boy." Evans voice was low and hoarse.

I didn't know what to think. I just stared at Wylie. At Evans. I guess I thought of him as Evans now.

"A boy!" Allen smiled. "So, you like boys." He looked to his left and right. The board members all frowned and tinkered with their pencils.

"And no witnesses of your beating? Wow! Tell me, Evans, do you really like to suck cocks or are you just trying to get out of here early?"

"Mister Allen! The chaplain jumped to his feet. "For Christ's sake!"

"Mind your outrage, priest!" Allen stood and glared at the chaplain. The two men faced each other and I saw Mister Allen's fist clench. The chaplain's shoulders slumped. He took his seat and looked down at the table. Mister Allen stared at his bowed head a moment, then turned to Evans. "Get him out of here."

The guard took Evans out and I was asked if I had any more testimony. I was too stunned to even answer. I think I mumbled that I didn't have anything to add. All I know is that I left. But all afternoon the events of the board meeting bothered me and after dinner I went to see the chaplain. I knocked on his door and he nodded as he let me in. It was like he expected me.

I took the offered chair and sat across a table. It was plain, and wood.

"What brings you here?" The chaplain smiled.

"Evans," I said.

The chaplain frowned at me so I cleared my voice.

"Wylie Evans," I said.

The chaplain nodded and leaned back into his chair. It was one of those overstuffed things and he partially disappeared behind a wing.

I continued. "I guess anyone who thinks he is a good judge of character is probably just waiting to be proven wrong."

"Maybe." The chaplain's nod was barely perceptible.

"I mean, Wylie Evans's vocabulary, his written work is brilliant. I can't believe a mind that can produce those thoughts can be deviant."

"Are you looking for absolution, Mister Kleegan?" The chaplain sat forward. "Do you want forgiveness for believing in him?"

"No. No, I...I just don't understand. I don't understand."

"Well, don't throw away your character-judging yardstick away just yet. Wylie Evans is who you think he is. He might be more than you think he is."

I frowned and turned in my chair to see the chaplain more clearly. He too leaned forward and sighed. "He isn't any kind of deviant. He isn't even gay— if that is what is bothering you."

"No, that's not it." I lied a little then.

"Evans is in here for sexting to a sixteen year old boy."

"Sexting?" I had no idea what he was talking about.

"Come on, Weenie. Sexting is sending photos of your privates to someone via email or text."

"And he did that? Sounds pretty deviant to me."

The chaplain looked at me for a long moment. Then he arose from his chair, walked to a side cabinet, and poured himself a large whiskey. He lowered his nose and softly inhaled the vapor. It was the way I used to do it. The chaplain closed his eyes and nodded his appreciation, then turned toward me. "Sorry. Can't offer any."

"No problem, sir. I don't drink."

The chaplain shuffled back to his chair and plopped into it. He took a large pull on his glass and looked at me. "I hope I am as good a judge of character as you are. You were right about Wylie. I hope I am right about you."

"Sir?"

"I am going to tell you some things that I learned in strict confidence. I trust your complete discretion."

"Sir?"

"Wylie told me things. He told me because he wanted someone to know the truth about him."

"And why are you telling me?"

"Because I think you need to know the truth about him, too."

"But he told you these things in confidence."

"Do you even know what that word means, Weenie?" The chaplain frowned at me. "Confidence means absolute trust. Wylie trusts me to first of all determine if someone like you deserves to hear his story. Then he trusts me to tell it. Confidence means trust, Weenie, not ignorant silence. 'Silence' is what lawyers want when they use the word 'confidence'. They use it to protect themselves. Now everybody thinks that is what the word means." The chaplain shook his head and took another drink.

I watched him and an old desire to have a drink tugged at me. But it was a familiar threat and easily cast off. Besides, it smelled of Scotch and not Bourbon.

The chaplain took another sip and looked at me. "I trust you as Wylie trusted me. It is important that you know the truth. If not for him, maybe for someone else."

I nodded but was unsure what he meant. The chaplain finished his whiskey and paused. He started to rise and get another. I know because as a former drinker, that is what I would have done. But in mid-rise, just as his knees stiffened to get him toward his bottle, he stopped. He glanced sideways at me and sat back down.

"Wylie plead guilty to sexting, Weenie. But he didn't do it. His father did. Wylie took the fall for his dad."

"Why on earth would he do that?"

"Because his mother is sick. She suffers from severe emotional issues and is totally dependent on Wylie's father. The sixteen year old's father found the photos and when the cops came, Wylie told them he had used his dad's computer to send them."

"And his dad let him do that? Take the fall? What a jerk!"

"Yes, apparently his old man is a selfish prick."

"Didn't somebody do a forensics type of thing?" I couldn't believe what I was hearing. "I mean, Wylie is a young, slight man. Didn't they do a dick and balls line-up of some kind?"

"Unfortunately, for Wylie they did not. The sixteen year old was the son of a federal judge. He sure as hell didn't want his son eyeballing a row of men's wedding tools and picking out the culprit."

"But didn't Wylie know what this would do to him? I mean forever! He will never get away from this. Not completely. Didn't he want his life?" I shuddered as the image of Brooks swinging from the overhang hit my mind.

"Sure, he did. He and I have spent many sessions here. Before you came, I was all he had. Wylie desperately wants his life. And he loves your classes Weenie. He loves them because in your fun time, as you call it, he gets to write, express, what he feels. How he feels."

"Then why in God's name did he give all of that up?"

"Because he felt his mom needed his life more than he did. His mom needed her husband and Wylie knew that. He knew that if he didn't take the fall, his mother would go to some institution somewhere and most likely would never come out."

"Christ." I shook my head.

"So, now you know. Use this for someone else, Weenie. My instincts tell me you will have an opportunity to affect people for a long time still."

I nodded and rose to go. But as I stood, I felt a wave of disgust. I glared down at the chaplain and saw the startled look in his eyes. I pointed my finger toward him. "Chaplain, why haven't you used this information to help Wylie? To set him free. Why haven't you come forward to help Wylie take care of his mother? If confidence means trust and not silence, then why haven't you been Wylie's champion?"

I saw defiance, and some anger in the chaplain's eyes. He set his glass on the table and stood. But by the time he was eye-to-eye his glare was gone. He took a breath and shook his head.

"Don't you think I wanted to?" His eyes now pleaded with me. "Don't you think that every time I see that young man I want to scream his innocence to the high hills?" The chaplain reached forward to take my hand.

I pulled my hand back.

"You know what the Catholic Church is going through now. What we have been going through. Championing a convict who is here on a morals charge with a child is something I just cannot do."

"Even if he is innocent?"

The chaplain took a breath and his sad eyes dropped. "I love the Church." I watched his head bob. I heard his voice break. Then he looked at me. "I love the Church," he said. "But some of us, some of the priests, the fathers, have let all of us down. They have compromised all of us in ways that we have yet to fully understand."

"Like protecting Wylie Evans?"

"Yes. Like protecting Wylie Evans."

I took a deep breath and shook my head. I just wanted to leave. I wanted to go back home and have Quail tell me about differential equations. Or, better, kill me with a butter knife.

"The sins of the fathers." The chaplain whispered.

"What?" I frowned.

"Exodus suggests sons suffer for the sins of the father. Yet, in Deuteronomy, we read otherwise."

"And what do you think, chaplain?"

"I think Wylie Evans suffers from the sins of his father. And I think he suffers from the sins of the Church's fathers."

I went back to my room. Bob was asleep and the butter knife was in the drawer. I tossed and turned all night. All of my life I had believed in the basic fairness of life. At least it had been fair to me. What had been my fault was only that, mine. But this thing with Wylie. There was no justice to it.

Wylie Evans left the next morning and I rejoiced at his freedom. Maybe some bit of rightness did remain for him. Then, I heard he wasn't freed. He transferred to max security at San Quentin. For his protection.

EPIPHANY

All my students eventually earned their GED certificates. All except Ronnie Johnson who, ironically, flunked Citizenship. He flunked because he refused to come to class when we discussed the Fourteenth Amendment. He felt it unjustly prevented the Supreme Court from overturning civil rights legislation that "hurt white people."

I was released six months early and a month before my prison term expired, the US Supreme Court overturned California's pet-factor age law. All of the seized animals were to be returned to their original owners. Owners with pets that had been euthanized were given a flat sum of $2000 for their loss.

I knew that Buddy had been trained as a service animal, but the law had prevented me from knowing anything else. Christine and Juan called me shortly after the verdict and told me that Buddy belonged to a man who lived in Escondido. They told me the man had been informed that the dog was to revert to its rightful owner and that he needed to surrender him.

I thanked them and hung up. Then I went into my room and cried my eyes out. Bob White had gone back home to New York and my new roommate was out in the garden. So, I didn't have to muffle my misery. I had prevented myself from thinking about Buddy. Well, maybe a little just as a flash in my mind. But I hadn't let myself delve into the memories of him. It was a little like my not thinking about Raoul. I had explained to Christine how I felt. That sometimes it hurts too much to recall your dead best friends: one a mangy, hairy, lovable rascal…and the other a dog. She had laughed at that. But now Buddy was back. Or was he? Or was this life's cruel version of Lucy jerking the football away from Charlie Brown? Did I dare reclaim that piece of my heart, that huge piece of my heart that had Buddy sewn to it? And bring it out again?

But how could I not?

Buddy wouldn't hold a grudge against me. He wouldn't blame me for thrusting him into a world of people he didn't know. I mean, dogs don't understand the pathetic crap of human lives, they just want to be with the ones they love.

And Buddy loved me!

The month dragged by until, finally, I walked out of The Colony to freedom. Christine and Juan drove me to her house and during the trip they told me they were getting married.

"We wanted to wait until you got out," said Christine.

"Yeah," grinned Juan. "She didn't want you to give her away with shackles on."

"We're driving south tomorrow," said Christine. "Buddy will be in Grape Day Park in Escondido on Saturday."

"You ready to get your dog back?" Juan smiled.

"Sure! You bet I am." I grinned and looked at Christine. "He'll remember me, right?"

"Dad."

"Christine, when I was in prison I saw this movie. It was about this guy in Japan who had a dog. The dog waited for him in front of a train station forever!"

"Dad, I think it might be helpful for you to observe Buddy and his new owner for a moment."

"What do you mean?" Alarm bells tinkled in my ears. I looked at Christine then Juan. "What do you mean?"

"I mean don't just rush up to them."

"Why? I don't get it." I frowned. What was she talking about?

"Dad, I mean this has been a traumatic time for you and for Buddy. If he is what you say he is, he needed a friend, too. He needed someone to bond to all this time. It's the way dogs are. They don't just *need* someone; they *have* to have someone. It's been two years and maybe Buddy has moved on."

"You mean, Buddy has forgotten me?" I struggled with my emotions. Christine pissed me off!

"Dad, he is a dog, a little dog. He is a loving creature that needs human contact. That is what we did to them. We made them the needy things they are. We did that and so Buddy hasn't forgotten you. It isn't personal. He has just found someone else to need."

Christine pulled me to the couch and I slumped and she sat and put her hand on my knee. "Dad, I love your Trog story. Juan and I also believe God created dogs. But, Dad, if God is working the way you say He does, then He has taken care of Buddy during this time just the way He has taken care of all of us. Buddy hasn't been left somewhere, wanting, and waiting. For you, or anyone else. He has been given the gift of moving on. And the young man who is now Buddy's new owner is attached to him. Dad, he is attached to him every bit as much as you were. You know how it is with dogs. It's immediate love. That young man refers to himself as "Daddy" when he talks to Buddy. You can bet on that."

"What are you saying? That Buddy won't want me anymore?" I swallowed and shook my head. I had forced myself to forget Buddy while in prison. Not forget, but not remember either. And when I found I was getting him back, I let myself remember. I did find that big old piece of my heart, and it had BUDDY sewn right on it. RIGHT ON IT. I shook my head and leaned against the back of the couch.

"Dad, just see how Buddy and the young man interact...see if you feel it is best to take him back. And if you do, if you must, then go and take him."

"Why wouldn't I want to take him?" I shook my head again.

"Dad, will you just go and watch first?"

"Sure, sure."

That Saturday we drove to Grape Day Park and as we strolled into the open space, I watched the families gather. It was fall and pleasant and the braziers celebrated their spiced meats over charcoal. Soccer balls and frisbees rolled and flitted amid the shouts that celebrated them. A radio station played happy music.

Christine and Juan pointed me toward the center of the park and I walked ahead of them, looking for my dog. I felt strange, almost like I was on a first date. It was weird but wonderfully so. It made being free from prison, free.

At first, I didn't recognize Buddy because he had grown so much.

He must weigh thirty pounds!

But it was him! It was him alright! I could tell my Buddy boy from a mile off!

I hurried toward him and felt the smile start and the tears begin. You see, it was his strength, his Buddyness, that had gotten me through the loss of Gaby. He had gotten me through prison, too. Despite my attempts to forget him, I never had. He had always been there. Sewn in tight. And I swallowed my heart back into my throat and started to call him. I lifted my hands to my face and framed a megaphone with my hands.

I had dreamed of this moment for so long! The moment when my boy and I would reunite. I had lain awake, hoping that he wouldn't forget me. I had tossed and turned with the wonderful, selfish, and embarrassing hope that my dog missed me as much as I missed him. But that dream was troubled because how could it be so? How could Buddy be free and miss me? Wouldn't that be a torment? Could I selfishly wish that on my best friend?

I opened my mouth to call, but then saw Buddy bolt toward the man. The man had his back to me so I couldn't see his age or anything. I could see by his arms and back that he was young, much younger than me.

Buddy's eyes were fixed on the man and I felt jealous. I felt some tiny rage, even. Here I had gone to prison to save him from likely death and now he had forgotten me?

I hastened my step.

The dog knows nothing of my sacrifice!

All I need is to get to him.

I started to trot!

Each second away allowed Buddy to drift farther from me.

Us.

My dog and me.

Us.

What if? What if he doesn't remember me? What if he doesn't want me to be his daddy anymore?

A flicker of Butch and Sundance darted into my mind...and the dark desire for it to have ended that way with the federales.

We would be in Heaven with Mom now.

The man swung his chair and I saw it was on wheels. He swung and I saw he had no legs.

He laughed and yelled and threw the frisbee and Buddy ran like a demon, and he leaped and he caught it! And as he returned to the man he held his tail high with pride and that dog look of "no big deal" in his eyes. And Buddy stood high. He stood way up high on his long back legs and put the frisbee on the man's lap.

He put it onto the lap of the man who could not bend down, the man who needed a long-legged dog.

"Good boy! Good boy," the man said, and he threw the frisbee again.

I felt a rage surge through me! A spark of fury filled me with anger and a righteous teeth-grinding and hate. I hated the fact that my best friend was now his best friend.

I didn't blame Buddy. Not a bit. He was just a dog. And this was the first time I ever let the thought...*just a dog*...pass my mind.

There is no such thing as *just* a dog. Buddy had chosen the man. He might not have chosen him over me, but he had chosen him.

Sometimes your heart can warm…but it can ice at the same time. Sometimes you can love and hate and it isn't balanced or equal. It doesn't make sense. But sometimes that is what happens and that is what happened to me as I watched my dog, my best friend with that man, that stranger. So, I seethed and I tormented and I watched them for some time. And it wasn't just throwing and fetching a frisbee. It was my feeling that each time Buddy brought the toy back, he gave a little of himself to the man. To the man and away from me.

I brooded behind the cedar, unsure now what to do when a fellow in a CAPA uniform interrupted the play. He came up to the man, bent over and said something and as I watched the dog thief's face I expected to see some dark sneer of ownership. I expected a look of defiance and arrogance. But all I saw was a look of total loss.

And as I watched the man's young face, too young to be in a chair like that, I felt my hate for him leave me. He wasn't my enemy. He wasn't fighting me. He didn't know me.

And Trog, in our story of ancient humans, he hadn't planned to steal the wolf from the pack with his lure of the stag bone. He hadn't thought, I will make this wolf my own. Trog threw the bone because it was a gesture of kindness, of friendship. He just wanted to give the wolf something. And this young man hadn't thrown the frisbee to lure Buddy away from me. He had just thrown it because the dog wanted to fetch it. And as infinitely sad as it was to watch the man play frisbee with Buddy, it was even sadder when he stopped. Because the man knew he could never bring this wolf to his fire regardless of how much he wanted to or how much the wolf wanted to come. I watched him put his head down and begin to cry.

The man in the CAPA uniform took Buddy away, I suppose to bring him to me. I was supposed to wait in the parking lot. Buddy barked and fought and his eyes were frantic. He was looking at the man in the wheelchair the same way he had looked at me.

He loved the man now.

The man was his daddy now.

I clutched the cedar and one thought blazed through my mind. One name hammered at me. And that name was Wylie Evans. Wylie Evans had wanted his life more than I wanted Buddy. And he had given it away because he knew his mother needed it more than he did. And I remembered the chaplain's words. When he said, "I trust you as Wylie trusted me. It is important that you know the truth. If not for him, maybe for someone else."

And the chaplain wasn't only talking about the truth of what happened to Wylie. He was talking about the bigger truth. The truth that in an unfair world we often have to give up what we want the most because someone else needs it more.

I slumped against the cedar and let the tears fall. And as they dripped down my cheeks, I remembered the words from a book I had read in prison. "One of the secrets to life, Epiphany, is to find your gifts and focus on those. Leave your liabilities in the dust of the road not taken." The book was *Dandelion Summer* by Lisa Wingate and I had read it over and over.

And was one of the gifts to find this dog?

And was one of my liabilities the desire to take him back even if he was now not mine anymore?

I wiped my new tears and separated from my cedar and walked toward the wheelchair. The man's head was down and he was crying and he didn't see or hear me until I was next to him. I put my hand on his shoulder.

He looked up, red in his eyes and tears on his cheeks.

I smiled and patted his shoulder. "I am Weenie Kleegan."

He squinted through his tears, then quickly wiped at them to remove the traces of how deeply he hurt. I wanted to say, "There is no shame in crying over a dog." But I just patted his shoulder again.

"You have come for your dog, then." His voice was choppy and hoarse.

I raised my eyes and gazed in the direction that Buddy had gone. My eyes stayed there on the trail, and I strained to see him. I longed to see him for a last memory. And I hoped not to for my breaking heart. Then I took a deep breath and reached into my pocket.

"He is your dog now. He is your dog."

The hope in the man's eyes made me forget prison. It made me forget my loneliness. It was my epiphany.

"Do me one favor," I whispered.

"Sure," the man's eyes dewed with fresh tears. "Anything."

"Give him this." I handed the man a Hershey's Kiss.

"But it's chocolate." The man frowned then laughed through his tears as he realized his good fortune. He took the candy.

"I know. But it's okay just once. Just for him to know what to expect in Heaven."

I turned and went to find Christine and Juan and my tears didn't embarrass me. Not one bit. In fact, they were tears of joy. Joy for a dog who had a master who loved him and needed him.

The next day I bought a car, a Ford Fairlane, and headed back north to San Francisco. There was something I had to do.

HOME

So, my trip home this time was different than before. I started east from San Francisco, took Highway 80 to Cheyenne, then 25 south to Denver and 70 over to Kansas City. Once in Missouri, I headed south to Springfield then took Dad's preferred route to Militia Springs. That took me through the mountains and down Dogwood Hill onto the flatland west of town. As always, I felt a thrill when I popped over the final hill and saw the outskirts of the city.

Yes, this time it was different. I didn't have the same melancholy as my eyes found their old sites. And I knew why. Before, I was a visitor to my home. I was a navy man, married to my sea mistress, and therefore never really part of my land lubber home. I now knew that my sadness at seeing the drive-in theater and five and dime store go was due to my lack of being a part of the change. Not the change itself. So now, I drove around my square with a new appreciation. Many of the old stores were gone but there was a new boutique and an antique store. My heart lurched when I saw the Dairy Queen was gone. But I felt a quickening when I saw Hartley's Shoe Store was still there and on the corner of Highway Five and JJ, Spurlock's was still in business. Still ringing the bell after 100 years!

I think part of my new joy and appreciation was explaining what I saw and felt to the passenger in my Fairlane. To Wylie Kleegan, my adopted son.

You see after I left Buddy in the hands of his new owner I called the chaplain at The Colony. He answered on the first ring. I think he recognized my voice on the first word. It was actually a name: Wylie.

I asked him where Wylie Evans was and he told me Wylie had been released from San Quentin and he gave me an address. It wasn't in The Tenderloin, the black hole of the city, but it was close. Close enough to be worried about the boy. I drove all day and into the night until I found the address he had given me— a seedy hotel.

Wylie was frailer than I remembered. He looked more like sixteen than nineteen. He worked as a busboy and called himself Wylie Thomas to get away from his last name. From the life he had given to his mother.

I told him about Buddy. I told him I needed a new best friend— more. More than that. I told him I needed a son. I know this sounds strange, unbelievable to you. But you probably haven't been in prison. You probably haven't lived my life, or Wylie's. But that is what we talked about that first night. He asked me to read the quote from Hemmingway to him. The one about the broken places. And I did.

Wylie's name is now Wylie Kleegan because I adopted him. It took me six years to clear his name from his dad's misdeeds. Wouldn't have done it if the old bastard hadn't admitted his crimes. And it took a threat of eternal damnation from the chaplain to get that done. At least two fathers cleared up a sin or two for all the others.

Wylie's mom died during the muck of all this, oblivious to the circumstances but still believing her son was a deviant. She never knew the real story and Wylie insisted she be spared it. We buried her under the Molly tree at our home.

Wylie calls me Dad.

EPILOGUE

"There was a boy called Eustace Clarence Scrubb, and he almost deserved it."

If you like C.S. Lewis, as I do, you will have read "*The Chronicles of Narnia*." Or, better still, someone like your grandpa read it to you as a child. The third novel in that series, "*The Voyage of the Dawn Treader*," introduces the reader to Eustace, and contains the sentence above.

The first time I heard that sentence, I was lying in bed with a cold, and Grandpa was reading to me. I'm not sure how old I was.

It was the age when I still chose Juicy Fruit over Doublemint when the barber gave me a haircut treat. So, maybe, I was eight. I remember asking him to reread the sentence.

"There was a boy called Eustace Clarence Scrubb, and he almost deserved it."

That struck a chord in me, and as Grandpa read the sentence a third time, I modified it and said it to myself.

"There was a boy called Winfred Kleegan, and he almost deserved it."

I remembered looking up at Grandpa and asking, "Do I deserve to be called Winfred Kleegan?"

He reached over and patted my head.

"I mean, it's your name, Grandpa. Your name is Winfred Kleegan. Is it okay for me to have your name?"

Grandpa kissed the top of my head and hugged me. "Your daddy thinks so. My son, Wylie, thinks so." He kissed me again and I felt his beard on my cheek.

"You see, Winfred Kleegan is my name. The same name as my grandpa and everybody calls me Weenie. And I love it."

CUTTING-EDGE NAVAL FICTION
BY

JEFF EDWARDS

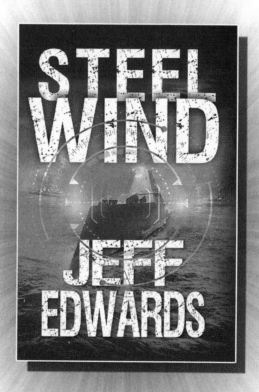

A battle we never expected to fight, against an
enemy we can barely comprehend...

www.braveshipbooks.com

IT WAS NOT JUST ANOTHER HOSTAGE RESCUE...

LARRY CARELLO

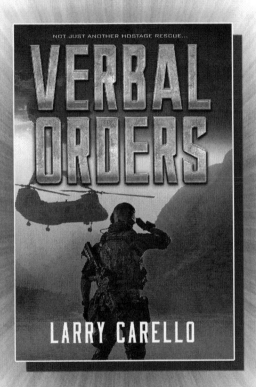

They called themselves Abu Sayyaf,
the *Bearer of the Sword.*

FROM TODAY'S MASTER
OF CARRIER AVIATION FICTION

KEVIN MILLER

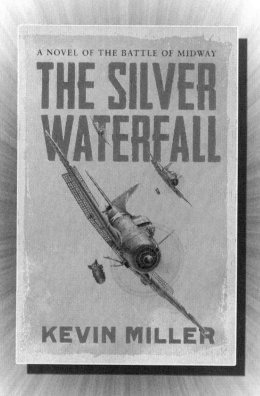

A NOVEL OF THE BATTLE OF MIDWAY

THE SILVER WATERFALL

KEVIN MILLER

Midway as never told before!

www.braveshipbooks.com

Made in the USA
Middletown, DE
16 June 2021